THE
Genius
OF
the Sea

THE
Genius
OF
the Sea

Anne Redmon

SINCLAIR~STEVENSON LTD

For Benedict, Piers
and in memory of
A.I.S.

First published in Great Britain by
Sinclair-Stevenson Limited
7/8 Kendrick Mews
London SW7 3HG England

British Library Cataloguing in Publication Data
A CIP catalogue record for this book is available from the
British Library.

ISBN: 1 85619 193 1

Typeset by CentraCet, Cambridge
Printed and bound in Great Britain

She sang beyond the genius of the sea.
The water never formed to mind or vice,
Like a body wholly body, fluttering
Its empty sleeves; and yet its mimic motion
Made constant cry, caused constantly a cry,
That was not ours although we understood,
Inhuman, of the veritable ocean.

The sea was not a mask. No more was she.
The song and water were not medleyed sound
Even if what she sang was uttered word by word.
It may be that in all her phrases stirred
The grinding water and the gasping wind;
But it was she and not the sea we heard.

For she was the maker of the song she sang.
The ever-hooded, tragic-gestured sea
Was merely a place by which she walked to sing.
Whose spirit is this? We said, because we knew
It was the spirit that we sought and knew
That we should ask this often as she sang . . .

from *The Idea of Order at Key West*
by Wallace Stevens

Acknowledgments

THE WRITING of this novel involved much research into the circumstances surrounding the death of Tsar Nicholas II and his family at Ekaterinburg on 16 July 1918. It was necessary to study the period in some detail, and I read many memoirs and histories too numerous to mention. I am conscious of using only one small detail that comes from A. A. Mosolov's *At the Court of the Last Tsar*, Methuen, London, 1935. My chief source of factual information was *Nicholas and Alexandra* by Robert K. Massie, Gollancz, London 1985. His account of the death of the Romanov family provides the basis for my own.

Above all, I would like to thank my friend the late Anna Ivanovna Schouvalova, who inspired in me a great love of Russian language, history and culture. Her acute memories as a living witness to the Bolshevik Revolution provided me with atmospheric detail which I could have gained in no other way.

As for other aspects of the novel, I am grateful to Peter and Anna France for information about life on Patmos, to the many islanders who befriended me there, to Mrs William, Dorrell and Dr Hamish McMichen for some medical information, and to Todd Olson. None of the above is responsible for errors that may have crept into this wholly imaginative work.

Thanks to the following for quotation permissions: Aleksander Pushkin, 'Eugene Onegin', translated by Charles Johnston (Penguin Classics, revised edition 1979) © *The Word and the Symbol*, Charles Johnston © 1977, 1979. Reprinted by permission of the publishers, Penguin Ltd. 'The Idea of Order at Key West', *The Collected Poems of Wallace Stevens*, Faber and Faber Ltd. 'Lullaby', *W. H. Auden Collected Poems* ed. Edward Mendelson, Faber and Faber Ltd.

THIS NOVEL has an enormous number of characters, both living and dead. A large number of them are Russian émigrés, and they use customary names with patronymics, surnames and diminutives. To avoid confusion, here is a cast of characters with basic relationships sketched in.

Marina Holt – *a widow*
Arthur Holt – *a poet and her recently dead husband*
Jane Holt – *his first wife*
Henry and Claire – *his children by his first marriage*
Jeremy – *his grandson*

Helena Taggart – *a senior lecturer in English literature and author – Lena Lenochka*
Mungo Taggart – *her former husband*
Sophia Petrovna Mirkovskaya – *Helena's Russian aunt, often called Tyotya, Sonya, and princess*
Boris Mikhailovitch Mirkovsky – *her dead husband, called Borya by her.*
Sergei Borisovitch Mirkovsky – *their son, called Serge, Seryozha*
Varvara Borisovna Mirkovskaya – *their daughter, called Varya*
Fiona Mirkovsky – *Serge's wife*
Paul Mason – *a doctor and old schoolfriend of Serge.*

Gregory Lipitsin – *a colleague of Serge*
Tanya Wood – *an English student of Russian and an au pair*
Dmitris and Evangalia – *a Greek couple – servants to the Mirkovsky household*
Sophia – *their niece*
Father Nikon – *a Russian Orthodox priest*

Throughout the story, the Russian royal family is alluded to, and their assasination at Ekaterinburg discussed. They were all Romanovs:

Tsar Nicholas I – *Nikolai, Nicky*
Tsarina Alexandra Fedorevna
    Their children were:
Olga Nikolaievna, called Olya and Olenka at times in the book
Tatiana Nikolaievna
Marie Nikolaievna
Anastasia Nikolaievna

Alexis Nikolaievitch – *the Tsareivitch, a haemophiliac and sometimes called Alyosha*.

Their summer palace at Livadia is mentioned. It is in the Crimea. Rasputin is referred to – *once as Father Gregory*.

Other information:

PATMOS is an island in the Dodacanese group. It was officially incorporated into Greece in 1948, having swapped hands between Turks, Italians and Romans throughout the ages. In ancient times, it was sacred to Leto, then Artemis, her daughter. It is most famous, however, for the role it played in the writing of The Book of Revelations or Apocalypse. In 95 AD, St John was exiled to Patmos under the authority of the Emperor Domitian. According to tradition, he was the Beloved Disciple of Christ and the Evangelist, and he lived to a very great old age. Some say, however, that the author of the Gospel and the author of The Apocalypse were two different individuals. In Orthodoxy and on the island, he is called St John the Theologian.

Where mythological figures crop up in the novel, I have used Greek names throughout. Aphrodite (Venus) is the wife of the lame smith-god Hephaestus (Vulcan). Artemis (Diana) is identified both as Apollo's virginal sister and goddess of the hunt, and as The Great Mother – the Asiatic deity Cybele.

All characters in this novel are fictional, and there is no intention on the part of the author to represent any person living or dead. This excludes, of course, the historical figures mentioned, and the two restaurateurs depicted on Patmos. Their two establishments, the Patmian House and the Patmian Hotel are highly recommended.

The action of the novel takes place in 1988

I

THE STEAMER was late. Helena Taggart had been standing on the quay for some time – quite still – in one position, her heels carefully together in neat shoes. An English couple, visitors to Patmos, remarked on her. Under an awning at a quayside taverna, they drank Metaxa while the evening promenade of Greeks and tourists began to dwindle into the night. The boat almost invariably arrived at 11 p.m. sharp, but it was nearly half past that hour now. Waiters were scouring tables and whatever crowds there had been earlier, had either dispersed towards the main pier in expectation of the ship's arrival, or had gone to bed in holiday flats; to berths in yachts docked under lights; or home to their own Greek opinion of things. In any case, this left Helena isolated on a long, dark stretch of quay watching the horizon. The English woman told her husband that Helena had stood there unmoving for so long that she had thought her a statue, until, with a gust of breeze, the shawl had moved and Helena had hunched her shoulders into it. 'It gave me a fright,' the English woman said. 'I quite literally thought she was made out of black marble or bronze or something like that. You know, just like that little mermaid at Copenhagen.'

Helena was expecting a guest to arrive on the steamer from Piraeus. She looked out with controlled annoyance towards the great bluff that shelters Patmos harbour from the sea, but she forebore to crane her neck for the first sighting of the ship's lights. She could not remember when she had last met the steamer, even though she had been coming to the island almost every summer since her girlhood, and she was now approaching sixty. She was not at all sure that she liked Patmos. She usually arrived with sunken spirits made lower by the duration of her stay. Indeed, in recent years, she had come to like the island less and less.

Whether or not she was going to find real friendship with Marina Holt, it was much too soon to say. Nonetheless, her eyes were quite fixed on the shadowed horizon, and under her breath, she found herself saying, 'Marina, oh, Marina, be on that boat!' In fact, she said it on an intake of breath so that the consonants sounded backwards. No boat, however, appeared in the harbour at her words, and so she gazed at the dark water underneath her feet. Little, rough wavelets slapped the concrete pier. Was Marina on the boat? Surely, she was. They had arranged her arrival this day only a month ago just before Helena had taken her sabbatical. It was only that there was something faintly unreliable to Helena about Marina, even though this was in no way substantiated by anything Marina had actually done during their short acquaintance. Helena bit back a nervous sigh. She imagined Marina on the boat now surrounded by pilgrims. For some reason or other, Helena herself always seemed to be thrust in with pilgrims when she arrived on Patmos where she shared her large house with her elderly aunt. Pilgrims and tourists came in droves. She wondered if Marina were sailing on the 'Kamiros'; she wondered if she were standing on the deck with black-clad, grim-lipped, Orthodox Athenians, the women wrapped away in Greek cerements of middle-age. Although Marina was in mourning, Helena doubted she would be wearing black. In contrast to the Athenian women, Helena suddenly saw Marina in her mind's eye as tall, pale, crepuscular – arising from the thronged pilgrims like Primavera in some old painting.

In Helena's experience, the lights of Patmos always emerged suddenly as the steamer rounded the bluff, and religious travellers would clasp their hands over the first sighting of the famous place, rapturous at the apparition of its jewelled holiness in the moonlight. It never failed, she thought, to stream generously over the scene as if there were some subtle conspiracy to entrance the viewer into an illusion about the place. Helena wondered if Marina would see it this way, or if she would see it at all. She really might have confirmed her time of arrival. Even a postcard would have helped. But she supposed she must make allowances for Arthur's death. Marina was Arthur's widow. Yes, Arthur was dead.

Well, what *had* happened to the boat? Helena checked her watch and saw that it was a quarter to twelve. She wondered if she should try to find out what was going on. Nikos would probably know, if she could find him, or Yiannis, perhaps. She did not, however, want to venture further down the quay in case she was observed by Patmians other than those who stood in the crowd by the dock. There, where the throng thickened and jostled with fretful impatience, the islanders would speculate about her visitor, and might even ask about Aunt Sonya. Although the dusty mansion, perched high in the lofty town of Hora on Mt St John, belonged to Helena (for, indeed, it was her mother's bequest to her), it was generally assumed to be the property of Sophia Petrovna Mirkovskaya, her mother's sister known by one and by all as 'the Princess'. The Greeks always referred to the place as 'Mirkovsky', and spoke of her Aunt Sonya in terms of reverence, owing, Helena always thought, to her fervent Orthodoxy. Of course, Aunt Sonya was a Russian, but this very slight dissidence mattered only to a few theologians in the Monastery. For thirty years now, she had made passionate prostrations in front of every icon on the island, had larded the nuns with money she did not have, and had smothered relics with kisses. As if to demonstrate that she had a special line to Heaven, she had conned one of the most powerful and austere monks, a Russian himself, to hear her confessions. She communed, in a pointed and decorous way, with slightly more frequency than others, as if, when she did take the sacrament, it was a sign of Father Nikon's – or God's – special favour. The locals loved all of this Slavic lavishness and high taste, but they frowned on Helena as an atheist. Helena was, indeed, an atheist, and found something loathsome about the piety of the Greeks themselves.

Each year, during the last week of Lent, Aunt Sonya would be ferried out to the summer house on Patmos by Helena's cousin Varya, who kept the aged lady half the year in Paris. Sometimes Varya would stay until Helena arrived to take over. Sometimes her brother Serge would come from England. They had an informal rota, but Helena could not bear Easter, and so her cousins never pressed it on her. In any case, Helena was a don at Howlett College at the University of London, and because of her job, was able to maintain her independence until June. Helena was quite fond of her cousin Varya, whom she had patiently tried to liberate in a step by step way, as one might catechize a savage. It had seemed at one point that the quietly devout Varya had been destined to take the veil after her mother's death, but to everyone's amazement, she had fallen in love with a Frenchman only last year, and had announced quite calmly this spring that she was going to marry him in the autumn, no matter what anyone thought. This was not quite what Helena had had in mind for Varya, but the engagement gave her a secret feeling of triumph nonetheless. Because of it, however, it had been Helena's task to take up Varya's cross for this year anyway, and so she had taken her sabbatical and had already been in Patmos for a month being slowly driven to a sort of compressed lunacy by her aunt. Recently, and much to her relief, her cousin Serge had arrived. He was the apple of the old lady's eye. Then a guest of Serge had come, a man

3

Helena did not particularly care for. And now, there was Marina. *If there was Marina.*

'Marina, oh, Marina, be on that boat!' she said again, and suddenly, without warning, it appeared huge and heavy laden around the bluff and into the harbour mouth. Helena's shoulders relaxed and all at once the port began to bustle. She turned and moved towards the pier, but stood a little apart. A crowd, whom she presumed were Turks, strained against the barrier where the boat was about to dock. They, some Germans and Americans, a few Greek Orthodox priests in their cylindrical hats, canonical beards and robes, were muddled together with a strange little enclave of gypsy women. They were all bound, it seemed, for the boat's continuing voyage to Rhodes. Porters with empty trolleys bumped along the quay, and out of the dark side streets of the port town, there emerged two prostitutes, one dressed in black, the other in white, their skirts well above their knees. They wore high-heeled boots bound with thongs, their hair lacquered and pompadoured, they could have been sisters from a former age. They sauntered and their glossed lips and iridescent eyelids shone in the light from under taverna awnings.

The steamer approached with immense efficiency and speed. Its engines churned and thundered in the harbour, shuddering and dwarfing the little port of Skala with sound and size. The ship seemed more vast to Helena than she had remembered. It was tiered and decked and stacked with lights ablaze in every porthole. Its funnels snorted smoke into the air and its deep, hoarse horn blasted the peace of the night. For so large a vessel, it docked with hardly a jolt. The hull opened, revealing a huge, lit cavern, and from its depths, lorries, cars, carts and passengers streamed off, frantically contending with the group on the quay wanting to get on. Spivs whistled and waved signs for rooms and taxis. Elder unmarried daughters tried wanly to impress the visitors with the convenience and cleaniness of their families' flats . . . the hotels of their brothers-in-law.

Instead of joining the mêlée, Helena stood still and extended her fingers through the knitted web of her shawl. There was an hexagonal geometry to the pattern and she studied it. She did not want to look in case Marina was not there, but it would be equally true to say that she preferred to remain concealed from Marina for a little while, that is if she had, in fact, arrived and was waiting on the quay. She waited as the crowd steamed off, and tourists went off to be gypped or pleasantly surprised. And then she raised her eyes.

4

There Marina was. There she was! She was standing in a little pool of light looking collapsed and blowsy from the journey. She was simply standing there not quite the Botticelli of Helena's imaginings. In fact, she looked curiously inactive, almost unalive, as she stood in her crumpled dress of pale blue sprigs. In the harsh light, she looked quite fully forty, attractive and very pleasant-looking, but not the wand-like girl that Helena somehow thought she remembered. In fact, Marina was far from tall, and though she was not exactly plump, her figure had no particular elegance. She was looking about herself in a daze with that same hazy expression that Helena had noticed at Arthur's funeral, and she had the same aureole of pale, blonde hair done up in combs. This gave her face a fragile look and Helena noticed again the porcelain fineness of her features.

Helena was one for moments. She liked to draw a moment out and preserve it and was afflicted with a love for a dying fall. She realized that it was time to let this instant pass and gathered herself to move. Almost in response to Helena's thoughts, Marina seemed galvanized to search her new surroundings. With that air of naive helplessness she had, she let her eye wing up and settle on the Monastery, which crowned and dominated the island. Her skin was like parchment. She was so pale. Helena noticed that she was carrying two heavy suitcases with which she seemed much encumbered, and even though she had stood there for quite a while, it had not seemed to occur to her to put them down.

Helena stepped forward, but before she fully did so, Marina spotted her. 'Oh!' she cried. 'Oh, there you are Helena! I was beginning to think I had the wrong day!' And like a gushy puppy, she was flapping, bag and baggage, down the quay. When she reached Helena, she threw her luggage down and her arms around Helena's neck. Helena was unused to such effusions, her private life was free of them. Her aunt's finest form of torture was to accuse her subtly (and sometimes not so subtly) of being unfeeling and thus unlike herself. Nevertheless, Marina's kiss quivered on her cheek for a while as if some butterfly had alighted and preened itself there, and in Helena's heart there was an imperceptible movement of response.

'Marina,' she said quite simply.

'Oh, Helena, you must be exhausted, waiting up for me so long! The boat was off late from Piraeus and no one would say why. After what seemed ages, a troop of soldiers got on and then we moved. They were going to Rhodes on military manoeuvres, you see. I *am* sorry!'

She uttered these little civilities breathlessly, as if she had swum, not sailed, to Patmos. Strands of pearly hair escaped from her hair onto her brow. Helena was stunned into self-consciousness. The full weight of Marina's strangeness to her bore down and she realized the enormity of having asked this very new friend to stay for an entire summer. Somehow after Arthur's death it had seemed very pressing, so pressing that it had affected Helena's dreams. Of course, that had been in London, but now Marina was actually standing on the dock, there was something dowdy, plain and very American about her appearance. Her accent, too, which Helena remembered as crystal BBC (or perhaps Sylvia Plath), had harsher 'r's and broader 'a's. 'Well, you've come a long way,' she said, 'so you must be the one who is tired. How is good old London?'

Marina looked aside in the anxious, guilt-stricken manner Helena remembered from the day of the funeral, the day they had met. 'Actually, I *did* mean to write to you. I went to New York first. In fact, I have come all the way from New York, and then I got so tied up there that I couldn't write, and then I couldn't find your *phone* number here. No one would give it.'

Helena was obscurely pleased at this apology. 'Oh!' she said, 'They know the house here as "Mirkovsky". My aunt, you see, is untitled queen.'

'You told me that she was a princess!' Marina cried with an innocent delight that both charmed and irritated Helena, who had first-hand knowledge, she felt, of the evils of social class. Titles were anathema to her and although she had no right to one herself, she winced when she remembered that each of her mother's ancestors had borne one.

'Russian princesses are not the same as English ones,' she said more abruptly than she meant. 'I have always thought it pretentious of Aunt Sonya to pull rank the way she does. It is meaningless in Russia now and only a courtesy title in the West. I suppose it helps to be called "Princess" if you want to sell perfume . . .'

This silenced Marina and Helena felt bound to lighten the tone. 'You really mean to say that you came all the way from New York? New York! Poor thing!' Helena had always found social remarks awkward and felt that this one sounded wrong.

Marina closed thin, blue-veined eyelids. She was pale in the arc-light of the port and her mascara had smudged. 'It was a terrible journey,' she said introspectively. She opened her eyes and looked about her. 'Patmos! How utterly lovely! To be in Patmos of all places at this time!' She looked vaguely hypnotized as she gazed up at the dark hills over the water. A large, blue neon cross stood sentinel over the harbour and Marina surveyed it dreamily.

Helena pointed in the opposite direction towards the Monastery. 'Actually, the house is all the way up there, in Hora, and we must find a taxi soon or they will all take off for the night. It would be a hell of a walk in the dark with all of those cases.'

'Oh, I've brought too much!' Marina cried, 'but then I can never think what I am going to need when I travel.'

Helena had, indeed, been surprised at the bulk of the luggage. 'Oh, well, you have been all the way to the States,' she said. She made to lift one of the old-fashioned, strapped leather valises, and noticed Arthur's initials engraved under the handle.

Marina lifted the other case, then looked around. 'Goodness!' she said, 'The boat has vanished!'

Together they looked, and indeed the ship had silently and utterly disappeared around the bluff. They were virtually alone together now on the quay.

II

MARINA PLAYED WITH HER RING, a reflexive action. As they wended their way up the snaking mountain road to Hora, she looked out of the window of the taxi and tried to catch some scent of the place. Oleander? She did not know the names of flowers, nor this part of Greece. Not really far from Turkey, she thought. Maybe jasmine. Helena was conversing tensely in fluent Greek with the driver, but her aquiline head with its serious, crisp and cropped white hair gave Marina the impression of a Roman consul on a coin, its neck urged forward. Helena was arguing about something and this relieved Marina of the necessity to talk. The simple fact of seeing Helena again swallowed her in shyness and she reddened in the dark at the thought of having embraced her so freely. An overwhelming sense of intimacy had sprung up between them after Arthur's funeral, but seeing Helena on Patmos now, especially after a harrowing time in New York, put the whole thing on another footing. She wanted not to be awkward with Helena. In fact, she had really thought for the whole three months since Arthur's death that the one thing she wanted was to be Helena's friend. Indeed, she had chosen the sprigged dress she was wearing because she thought Helena might like it. Helena had certainly said she detested black. Clothes to please others fell into Marina's instinctive hands off racks and shelves and sale trays. Helena had seemed a pure gift to Marina at the funeral, and the offer of a summer in Patmos had been kind beyond anything in her wildest imagination.

But now that she had done what she had done in New York (and she was still stunned by having done it), things seemed in different proportion to themselves. But, everything had seemed out of proportion since Arthur died. Marina could not quite credit her own motives and feelings at the moment, nor fathom them. For instance, she had been aware that she should have confirmed her arrival time with Helena, but the address had weighed in her handbag unused, and furthermore, she had secreted herself in Athens for a whole two nights before taking the arranged berth to Patmos – the sight of which, from the boat, had filled her with hushed awe. There was, of course, no reason for telling Helena where she was, but it pricked Marina's conscience that she had not been open. Apart from anything else, it had been a solecism not to write, and that sort of thing made Marina feel ashamed. In fact, she realized that she had not been entirely truthful with Helena, even though she was, on the whole, a very truthful person who disliked concealment.

The previous day in Athens, Marina had tried to be open with herself and to look at things that she thought she had hidden for perhaps too long. This had been the point of her stay. Notwithstanding the time of year, late May, the temperature had been nearly a hundred. On her arrival from New York, she had checked into the first hotel that had caught her eye on a list in the airport, The Aphrodite, not a five-star place, and she could have afforded better. Nonetheless, it was quite comfortable and close to the Plaka too. She had taken the room late in the evening and had gone up to the roof garden where she bought a bottle of mineral water. There was a view of the Acropolis from the terrace where Swedes and Germans with boiled-looking skin drank beer and where an American couple surreptitiously canoodled. Marina did not feel fixed about her own nationality. She carried an American passport, but had lived in Britain with her English husband Arthur Holt for the duration of their twenty-year marriage. She was forty, young for a widow, she thought. Arthur and her own family had left her well-provided, so much so that she really had no need to find a job. In any case, she was qualified for nothing. She was also childless. It had been Arthur who had not wanted children.

The American couple had irritated Marina on her first night at The Aphrodite, so much so that she could not really look at the stars and the Parthenon from the roof garden. The second night, the sight of them became unbearable, and rather than tell them to stop, Marina had gone down and spent a stuffy evening in her poorly air-conditioned room close to tears. She was, indeed, young *for* a widow, but not a young widow. Arthur had found it hard to tolerate the signs of her getting older even when he had been twenty years older than herself. A forkful to her mouth could bring a shudder of disgust to his face, even though he would never actually say she was getting fat. Well, she had not been fat, and was not fat now, though she had gained a little weight since his death. During his life, she had even gone to health farms for him and had spent days on end drinking lemon juice in hot water in order to slim. Deep down, she had felt that this was wrong and he should accept her as she was, but she had done it all the same. There were all sorts of things like this that she had done for Arthur.

9

He had been a poet. She supposed she ought to think that he was a poet rather than that he had been one, for poetry expressed something deathless to be sure. He had certainly been anthologized, lauded early in his life; yet, in his latter years, things had not gone so well for him, and she could not bear for him to see it even though he saw it only too plainly. For that matter, she did not really like to look at it squarely herself even now. She had dieted and worn good clothes mainly to give him courage. Yet, really, he had been quite famous enough, if the people who had come to his funeral had been anything to judge by and together, throughout their marriage, they had travelled all over the world on his many lecture and reading tours. Marina had always thought that people stared at her because of *The Hephaestus Cycle*, and this had made her feel ashamed and deeply embarrassed – both for the explicit nature of the poems and for the feeling that she was letting down their image.

Arthur's first wife had died a bitter woman, and Marina's step-children, who were nearly her contemporaries, hated her and thought she had killed their mother, at least, Claire did. So, it had seemed a guilty and an almost occult thing to do, to stay in Athens alone at this time, but Marina felt helplessly blurred about why this was. Athens had been the first place Arthur had taken her when she was only twenty, not even a graduate, and the wife did not know. There had been other places as well, of course, his rooms at Oxford where, as a summer student, she had taken her own verses to show him and had ended up entwined with him on the couch. But Athens had been the place where the affair had found the momentum of its destiny. All of this had been a long time before they had become unhappy. It had never crossed their minds that they would be unhappy with each other. Now, she realized that he had been dead for barely three months and she could still not believe the news nor understand what had happened to her.

On her visit to New York, the city where she had grown up, she had found everything distorted. She had not planned to do what she had done when she went, but she must have known deep-down, because there had really been no good reason for her to go. Arthur's solicitors in England could have easily sorted out the small confusion there had been over his American royalties and her minor problem over some American shares she had forgotten about. In Wall Street, where she had gone to consult a man of business, the vast, thrusting towers had suddenly looked unimaginably spindly and frail, like ninepins made of glass. Papa had worked on Fulton Street, but the whole area looked very odd now and she felt as if she could push it over.

On her way back uptown on the screeching subway covered in graffiti, Marina had suddenly conceived a passion to revisit Athens. Before she went to Patmos, she would climb the Acropolis and see the Parthenon again. She wanted to remember Arthur in a certain way, and thus she had felt that she did not wish to share her conception of this desire or its fulfilment with Helena. Helena had not said anything too dreadful about Arthur, but Marina felt that distinct judgments were being made, judgments she would have to come to terms with on Patmos as she entered into fuller conversations with the clever and intense Helena, whose goodness to her after the funeral was now the one thing that could bring her to tears of genuine gratitude.

Marina wanted to remember Arthur in this way because she wanted to acknowledge that she had, after all, loved him. Of course, she had loved him. It made her squeeze her eyes shut reflexively when she remembered him getting older, getting ill and then dying. She remembered her cheek laid against the coarse tweed jacket that he would insist on wearing even in his wheelchair, and a whole sort of love she had been unable to give him until that time when his hair had fallen out and his teeth had fallen out and he was powerless. After the death she had stood in their nice, safe, childless flat in Kensington and had become a different person for her realization that she had not, after all, wanted him dead. She really had not. The godless ceremony later at Putney Vale Crematorium had been awful. There had been piped Schubert and readings from his poetry and, oddly enough, readings from George Herbert and Yeats whom he had admired, all intoned to a massed intelligentsia by an actor from the Royal Shakespeare Company whom Arthur had known before their marriage. Marina had wanted to have a Mass said, but Arthur's will had prevented this and had designated the actor as psychopomp – a man whom Marina had never set eyes on.

So, the morning after her arrival in Athens, Marina, dressed in black and feeling a little foolish, had set out from The Aphrodite on foot. She still felt oddly weightless from the flight. Even at nine in the morning, the sun had hit the buildings and the Cathedral Plaza, where she had first found herself, glared back its reflected light. Marina hesitated in the Plaza and watched Greeks pause in their daily business in order to greet the day with prayer. It touched a memory of her Catholic childhood to see so many people of all ages and classes make their way up the long steps of the splendid Cathedral or cross the pavement into the little Byzantine chapel beside it. She felt not quite up to the Cathedral, so she peered into the doorway of the ancient church beside it where the faithful kissed icons and lit candles in the wholly natural way she herself had once talked to the saints, greeting them as loved and revered relatives who would be sure to give help and encouragement during the day. Marina was about to go in and bless herself before the Virgin, but an old woman, also dressed in black, shuffled in before her. She gave Marina an approving look, as if to say that there were some nice tourists after all – some decent women – and this made Marina turn away from the church door, filled with a revulsion at herself. She felt like calling after the woman, 'I'm not a true widow! It's all a pose. It's all to do with guilt. If only you knew!'

She had not told Helena a thing about her faith, nor how she had screwed up her courage and gone to confession after the funeral. Even though Helena had a house on Patmos, and might for all Marina knew be Orthodox, she felt an admission of this kind might lead Helena to think her a hypocrite. Marina herself thought she was a hypocrite. She had spoken to a priest at Farm Street Church initially, and he had been very kind. A weeping prodigal, she had slept deeply that night for the first time in years. Then, the enormity of her crime had struck her, perhaps because she had acknowledged it, and again and again, she had obeyed what she knew to be a neurotic impulse. On the pretext of forgotten sins, she had slipped at random into confessional after confessional only to admit the same and central wrong with which she was obsessed. It was as if she had never been forgiven in the first place and she wondered if the reason for this was that she was not really sorry. Although most of the priests she had spoken to had been encouraging and helpful, one of them had given her this idea and had told her that she ought to spend the rest of her life in prayer and penance. From his hard, burring voice in the pulpit, she had known she should not have spoken to him, but had done so all the same. She shrank from the ascetic path. In a peculiar way, he had seemed to concur with Arthur, who had often quoted Ivy Compton-Burnett as having defined remorse as a change of mood, and not of character.

Marina walked on towards the Flea Market. She found she kept on closing her eyes tightly. She passed ecclesiastical shops hung with icons and brass lamps and she felt better when she emerged into the street full of tourist stalls hung with gaudy souvenirs: imitation statues of Athena and Poseidon, drama masks of Comedy and Tragedy, woven woollen bags and brass figurines of the laughing Priapus. Her dress of stiff muslin was beginning to wilt and it clung to her in the heat, but she pressed on through the warren of little streets on the upward path towards the Acropolis. She kept on trying to remember Arthur's face, but she could not. A middle-aged man brushed by her, leered, and mumbled an obscenity in her ear. She looked far above her for the airy columns of the Parthenon, but as she trudged, they kept slipping from view behind the bulk of the Acropolis as she approached it. Surely, she would remember him there.

The worst of it had been that previously she had been unable to forget him. She saw the back of his head in the street or on the tube in London. She thought she had seen him in New York coming at her head-on in Columbus Circle. His voice, with its perennial cutting tone, seemed to insinuate remarks into her most quotidian conversations. Snatches of his verse would cleave to her head as she wrote perfunctory replies to notes of sympathy from complete strangers. In fact, she sometimes felt impelled to tear the letter up and start on a fresh sheet. *The Hephaestus Cycle* had been about her, and on it hung his reputation. Well, one could hardly say that it was, precisely, *about* her. In fact, although he had pressed the notion upon her that she had inspired the Aphrodite figure in the poems, Marina had often had the bewildered sense that they had little to do with her actual self. He had, however, written his *Cycle* in response to that trip to Athens way back in the sixties – and oh, how the lame smith-god, coarse with the hammering rhythms of the forge, had yearned for the lovely blonde! The poetry was self-mocking (of course) but dense and full of his pained acceptance of a time when his vision of love would fly to some Ares or Adonis. But, of course, there had been no flight, nor had that irony he had so prided himself on ever reflected a true detachment from his own voracious ego. 'Stop!' she had said to the unwelcome thoughts filling her mind. 'Stop.'

Now, she could remember nothing of the wounding monologue that seemed to generate itself from her unconscious mind as if he were actually speaking. This had come to her so often after his death that she sometimes wanted to scream to cut it out of her mind. In what she regarded as a shameful but useless attempt to get rid of him, she had removed photographs from her wallet and had put the silver-framed one away in a cupboard. It showed Arthur in a studied pose with cigarette smoke curling. But as she climbed the hill, she would have done anything to recall even this picture, which had been used in

13

obituaries. The cancerous Arthur obliterated all memory of the way he had looked when they had first climbed the Acropolis together.

Although it had never occurred to her before, it suddenly struck her now that he had then been her present age, forty, and this thought made her feel queasy and odd. Would she use some young Adonis – some boy – in the way he had used her? She put a hand over her mouth to curb the disloyalty of this. Arthur had been tall, not handsome but striking, and somewhat bent into a donnish pose, which he had dropped when they became lovers and had taken up again once they were married.

Had he spoken to her about his wife Jane then in Athens, or had these discussions come later? When had they begun, those earnest denunciations of a woman he had called 'terminally cold'? Oh, but it *had* been in Athens! He could hardly bear to touch Jane. He could no longer make love to her and had not been able to for some time. He had seen straight through it, the dead seventeen-year marriage, before he had met Marina. She could be sure of that. He had never really loved anyone but Marina, Marina, Marina!

As she climbed and puffed, it came to her that he had stood next to the Nike Temple and had called her name over the parapets of the Acropolis so that all of Athens might hear it. It had awed her to see such a cynic give tongue to such romance. She had felt an almost spiritual power over him, as if she had given sight to the blind to see all things anew. She had felt as if they were fresh, innocent, primordial beings. Marina remembered that this had happened, but the incident would not embody itself in her memory. She could not visualize it.

Rivulets of sweat from under her arms were no longer absorbed by her tight sleeves and bodice and they ran down her torso. She stopped outside a restaurant with a palm tree in its large courtyard. Tables with starched cloths stood under the shade of the tree. In front of her, the polished steps of the pavement went up and up past the restaurant. Although she was very thirsty, she did not stop to buy a drink but went on.

Her American-ness had charmed Arthur. She, as a panicked little student, had delighted him. To be fair to him, he was one of those Englishmen who have a soft spot for 'the States', and who get a dirty pleasure out of surreal chromium diners, hot dogs, cool jazz and Elvis. He had thought she bleached her hair, and was slightly crushed when he found that it was natural. She often thought he had Arthur Miller's marriage to Marilyn Monroe somewhere in the back of his mind, as he admired the playwright and they had identical first names. Marina, the busty and innocent blonde. Once, after much had been said and implied between them, but before the affair had actually started, he had brought a packet of gum to their tutorial and offered her a piece – Juicy Fruit – he had a piece himself. Perhaps it had been the intolerable sexual tension in the situation, but she had cried. It had been a *joke*, he had said, and besides he found her liberating, not common. Of course, he did not think she was common! 'You are most uncommon, Marina,' he had said. But later on, she knew that he really did think her vulgar and hated it, although in some ways he wanted her to be more so. Marina sighed. 'Common' had been her mother's favourite word of opprobrium.

With a resurgence of purpose, she straightened her back and picked up her feet as she continued to climb. Allegations of cultural lowness against them had driven her mother wild, along with the other things she had detested about Arthur, who had never, to be fair, actually said anything condescending. It had all been implied with quizzical eyebrows. Thinking of her mother, Marina's hand went automatically to her hair, then shot to her heart. What had she done? Oh God, what had she done? The truth about Marina's mother was that she had not been her actual, biological parent.

Now, walking under the battlements of the Acropolis high above her, fringed with yew trees, Marina began to reflect on what she *had* done in New York, and stopped for a moment – cold. The whole thing had come about because of Helena and because of what Helena had said to her on the night of Arthur's funeral when they had had dinner together. Marina, in a half-mad way, had blurted out her adoption story. Almost no one knew that she had been adopted and she had no idea why she had told Helena, but she had. Perhaps she had been impelled to do what she had done in New York by the look of astonishment on Helena's aquiline face when she had said that she had never attempted to discover her true parentage. Perhaps it had been Helena's story of her Russian mother and aunt, for Marina had always thought there was something Slavic in her own features. At any rate, the whole tenor of the evening had stimulated Marina into doing what she had done. Her mind was now snarled into knots of confusion over it. Whenever she thought about it, she realized that the very antithesis of thought was what she gave it. When it came into her mind, beams of emotional direction seemed to cross her heart and paralyze her conscious will. Her mind was a rabbit in headlights. Helena, with her fine Russian brow and her fine Russian eyes arched and articulated to a point of horror, had said, 'But how *could* you have let Arthur prevent you from finding out something of such immense importance? What right did Arthur have to make such a choice for you!' – or words to that effect, and Marina had not thought consciously about it (that was the odd thing), but had gone to New York on the slimmest of pretexts.

On the spur of the moment, in the manner of someone buying shoes, she had found a private detective agency in the Yellow Pages and had decided the whole thing all at once. A kind of blackness overcame her when she thought of it now and she felt faint; but, since her bereavement, such patches of giddiness came upon her maybe once or twice a day. Had she really instigated the search just like that? A mere fortnight ago? She wondered what other things she had done – if she had bought herself, for instance, a diamond tiara or had given away large sums to Mother Teresa. In a bizarre way, she thought, it might turn out very well if she knew her true parentage. Of course, at one point in her life, the idea of finding her real mother had come upon her in fits of obsession until Maddy, her adoptive mother, had virtually had a nervous breakdown. Now Maddy and Papa were dead and Arthur was dead. Why not? she thought. In truth, she had always been terrified of knowing. She had developed a way of sweeping the question from her mind as if it were an impersonal thought having to do with someone else. She now said half-aloud to the bright Greek morning, 'They'll never find her anyway,' and this cheered her.

She turned her mind again to the climb ahead and tried to rediscover her attitude of pilgrimage. At last, she reached the foot of the Acropolis itself. Well, at least Helena would be pleased when she heard of the decisive action in New York. Marina vacillated and wondered if she might, after all, tell her of this ascent. The sun now slammed down heat upon the pavement. Marina had no scarf nor hat nor sunglasses, and her throat was sticking to itself from thirst. There was a little kiosk where they sold drinks before the last approach to the site, but she forebore to buy the proffered lemonade. Her sandals slipped on the worn stones as she went higher. All she could remember from her last visit was a bas-relief she had seen, but she could not remember where. Had it been of a girl, a Nike or a Nereid or a nymph adjusting her sandal? The figure was of an absolute grace. The girl's tunic was carved almost as if it really fell translucent over her knee as she lifted her leg in order to tie the thong. She did not remember whether Arthur had been with her. She simply recalled the figure as if she were looking at it.

Marina did not notice the hordes until they engulfed her and until she realized that she was trapped in a queue at the gate near the Propylaia. In front of her was a group of Italian tourists, behind her a jam of Americans so packed in that had she wanted to turn around she would not have been able. There were people with shorts and headsets. She was squeezed between a fat woman in Bermuda shorts and a boy chewing a wad of gum. He wore a baseball cap and was listening to a transistor, which clashed out rock chords softly but insistently. She was squeezed, then thrust up the steps towards the ticket booth. The crowd surged. She felt irrational. She bought a ticket and was then borne along and forced through the ancient gates with golden columns above. A harsh-looking Greek guide was trying to call some order into the crowd in heavily accented English. Marina saw a couple above her trying to descend. They were clearly British and she had the odd idea she had met them somewhere before. They clung to one another as they were jostled downwards. Suddenly, she caught their fear and the fear in the hoarse, shouting voice of the guide. She realized that if one person were to trip, then the whole crowd would fall. She put her hand to her mouth, imagining what it would be like to be crushed and suffocated by the sweated bodies. But the moment passed and she was loose and free.

There it was, the Parthenon, standing in pure reference to itself alone. Its ruins were so perfectly proportioned that the eye supplied the lack, making the whole temple manifest in spirit. Its fluted columns caught the strong light so that they seemed to absorb it and transmute it into a softer refulgence. It was almost as if Marina had never seen it before, neither in the art history course she had once attempted nor with Arthur. The crowd jollied slipshod around her, snapping each other's photos next to the temple. There were roped-off areas where fallen stone and metopes lay numbered. Where the goddess Athena carved by Phidias had once stood, there was now a large derrick standing idle.

But Marina did not notice any of this. She slid on the hot, worn stones, and establishing a gait, walked around the Parthenon, regarding it from every angle. It came to her excited imagination that with just a little effort she might be able to see it as once it had been in all its glory. Indeed, she could almost hear the jostling and the flutes of an antique procession, complete with garlanded, sacrificial heifer lowing to the skies. It would have been no less crowded then with spectators pressing to catch a glimpse of robed priests and graceful maidens making their way to the altar of Pallas Athena . . . Suddenly, she was caught on the heavy sarcasm that Arthur would have dealt to this idealization of an ancient past. He had always tried to train her away from sentimentality and feyness. So, she retreated from her imaginings. It was enough to look at the thing as it was. There was scaffolding around the Erecthium and a caryatid was missing. The monumental figure of a man lay on the ground. It was worn and weather-beaten, its features obliterated. A cultivated looking woman of about Marina's age was taking pictures of the statue with an expensive camera. She wore an immaculate green dress.

'Mathilde, *viens donc*!' her husband called to her. Marina expected that they had nice, well-groomed children, and indeed, these appeared from around the corner. 'Papa, Papa!' they cried, two little, tow-headed boys in neat shorts, nothing that looked like Addidas about them. Marina felt a deep urge to follow them, but she restrained herself. Soon after Arthur's death – in fact, the very week after, she had found herself looking into a pram in the supermarket. In a moment when she seemed light-headed and almost a mile away from herself, she nearly picked up the baby and walked away with it. Returning to herself, she had run into Sainsbury's car park, got into her little Fiat and burst into tears.

Any goddess *but* the one he had wanted her eternally to be! She would have been willing to be anyone but that one – Aphrodite. Athena, Demeter, Artemis, Hera – any would have been preferable. If Athena or Artemis, she would not have wanted children. If Demeter, nothing he could have done would have stopped her. But as for having to be Aphrodite in perpetuity through his poems . . . Marina shook her head. She certainly had not given birth to any Eros in or for herself, nor, finally, for him. Sometimes she wondered if either of them had been capable of love.

She looked again at the Parthenon. It seemed to have resumed its place as a key monument in the history of art. Shrugging, she passed by way of the Nike Temple, with its fine, Ionic capitals, down again to the Propylaia. Someone had restored order to the crowds, and her descent became easy.

She bought herself a drink at the stall, then had lunch below in the restaurant with the palm tree in its courtyard. She ate moussaka under shady fronds and refused to think about Arthur. When she returned to her hotel, she was struck wth a certain, grim hilarity. Without having given it any thought, she had chosen to stay at a place named after the very goddess whose influence in her life she had just deplored . . .

Aphrodite, wife of Hephaestus, mother of Eros, born on the foam. Waking in sweats, sinking in dreams, her mind revolved upon it until dawn.

The taxi drew up next to a low wall. From the window, it was possible to see Patmos port and harbour spread beneath and lit up like a jewelled robe. Marina had not realized how high they had climbed. The wall guarded a steep parapet. Above them, the upper town of Hora seemed to escalate further, almost into the bright, high-risen moon. Helena was still discussing something with the taxi driver, and seemed to be urging him to take them higher, but he was surly and reluctant so she shrugged and paid him, telling Marina they must walk the rest of the way.

'He's a cousin of our cook Evangalia,' said Helena, 'and he has got it into his head that my aunt is suffering from a fatal illness and that I am behaving callously. That is what she tells everyone.'

'Oh dear!' Marina exclaimed, truly perturbed.

'Not you too!' said Helena, though pleasantly. 'I've exhausted myself enough for one evening explaining it all to him. I'd rather not do it again. It's sufficient to say that we have this little extra hike to make with these bags because he did not accept what I had to say to him. It really is none of his business, you know.'

They started with the luggage up the steep incline, which was cobbled and angled with shadows thrown by the moonlight and found themselves in a labyrinth of narrow streets so silent that Marina found herself whispering.

'It's all white! Everything is white! Or is it just the moon?'

'No,' said Helena, 'it is all white. The whole town except for the Monastery is painted white. The whiteness always strikes visitors as extraordinary, but I suppose I am used to it.'

'It seems to come from another time – another era,' said Marina. 'Like something in a dream.' They passed doorways of dark, shut houses, and under blank and silvered arcades.

'Most of it was built during the seventeenth century under a Venetian influence,' said Helena, 'but Orthodoxy has prevailed. It tends to make things stand still.'

'It's beautiful,' said Marina earnestly. They seemed to glide along. At length, they reached a façade in which there was a carved, wooden door topped by an ornate, wrought-iron fanlight. 'Well, here we are!' Helena said.

'Are you sure there is going to be room for me?' Marina blurted this, then thinking it sounded rude, added, 'I feel I shall be such an imposition.'

Helena laughed. Her hair was a silvery cap, whitened by streaming moonlight and her sharp features gave her the appearance for a moment of some night bird.

'Believe me,' she said, 'when I tell you that the house is most substantial. It is only my aunt who could possibly conceive of it as a cottage!' Impulsively, she dived for Marina's cheek and embraced her lightly. 'Oh, I am so pleased to have you here! You really have no idea!' Helena fiddled with her key and opened the front door onto a little atrium planted with tubs full of bright red flowers, which retained part of their colour even under the moon. She shut the door behind them, and through the little courtyard, they entered the house.

III

THE PRINCESS heard the big front door creak on its hinges. She froze and listened while somebody entered the courtyard just below her window. She was bedridden, and she divided her time between her room and the large, walled garden behind the house where she spent the cooler part of the day in her wheelchair. She was wholly attentive to the noise now and strained to catch what it was. Could it be Serge returning with Paul? So late? Or was it late? She felt disoriented and closed her eyes against the moonlight, which streamed in through shutter slats onto her coverlet. Why did Serge stay out so late? Where did he go? Evangalia, who had always been so helpful with her network of relatives, had really rather let her down this summer. Either she was being evasive, had become too deaf to catch the Princess's imperfect Greek, or she was too taken up with her own affairs – what with that niece of hers getting married. No one, it seemed, knew anything about her son, and the Princess was beginning to wonder if he had found a mistress. Piously, she hoped he had not. She had always had a great fear and dread for Serge, and strove to stem the ominous tide of anxiety about his moral or physical well-being with whatever little evidences she could glean that he was truly all right. She supposed that he was with Paul. Surely he would be all right if he were with Paul.

She opened her eyes and listened carefully. The bone-white eeriness of the moon disturbed her. Yes, there were, indeed, two people in the atrium below and they spoke sotto voce. No, it was not Serge's tense, staccato pitch, nor was it Paul's voice with its slower cadence. Then who was there creeping? The larger fear, which was always present just below her conscious thoughts, rose up and clenched her throat in panic. Who could it be? She had chosen this particular room overlooking the front of the house for a number of reasons. She had heard her niece call it 'the crow's nest' to Serge and to her shame, he had giggled like a child. Well, whether or not they thought she was an old crow, she had stationed herself at this front window not only because she could see the very tip of the Monastery with its ghostly crenellations, but also because it made her portress to the house. She was attuned to the softest click, creak or footfall.

Down below it was Lena! The Princess breathed out and closed her eyes again. It was Lena's urgent and sibilant hiss. Yelena Ivanovna, born hatcher of plots. Thinking of Helena with her Russian name and in Russian terms, the Princess could imagine her niece as the Regent Sophia, sister to Peter the Great, gliding through Kremlin doorways. She saw Helena as implacable and scheming and, for all of her chic modern politics, like an ancient Boyar princess in a caftan stiff with pearls. Lena was one skilled in the craft of power. Indeed, she had excercised this craft over the Princess herself at key points and in significant ways. Lena, of course, preferred to be called 'Helena' with an English stress on the first syllable, and *Helena* would repeat, whenever the lesson needed to be given, that her father had been English – not Ivan but John – and that she herself was not a Russian; that, indeed, she was a senior lecturer in English literature at London University, so English was she. Helena Taggart, a name to be reckoned with.

So, it was Lena in the courtyard, but who else? There was an unfamiliar, breathy, gasping whisper. Male? No, female. The Princess struggled to remember. What was it? A visitor. Who? Because of perilous lapses of memory, the Princess had become accustomed to relating her thoughts in a rhetorical way to an imagined interlocutor – a different process altogether from her prayers to God in Whom she believed and of Whom she was afraid. It was not as if she had formed a mental image of the shadowed listener, nor did she expect a response to the querulous questions she sometimes posed it. Still, it was something in the nature of a dialogue. Who was the visitor again? What was the name? Lena had been emphatic enough about it – this woman's visit to the island – and, in preparation, had spent all week bossing the servants. The Princess knew a lot more than anyone thought. She observed a good deal. She knew, for instance, that Lena had taken to keeping late hours in the garden at the back of the house. The Princess herself did not sleep at night and had developed radar like a bat. A movement, a rustle or a cough alerted her, and even if a fellow watcher in the night were still, she could identify that person.

Last night, a bolt eased back, a footfall on the stair, a little sigh in the room next to hers, informed her that Helena had waited out the night in expectation of this visitor, but who the woman was who now whispered in the forecourt of the house, the Princess could not say. 'It was a Russian name, though, wasn't it?' she asked half-aloud now to the patient, shadowed figure in her head. 'It was the row we had about it, though, that has blown the memory away, and Father Nikon will remonstrate with me now. He is so cross when I've been angry!' Then she remembered that Father Nikon had left the Patmian School and the Monastery of St John the Theologian in order to help out in the Russian Church in Athens for the summer. When he was absent, it subtly relieved her. He was as ferocious as she, and she swallowed his advice for the moral improvement the nastiness of it gave her. Nevertheless, they got on, and in a larger way she missed him.

There really had been a row about summer plans this year. Remembering it, she remembered too that she had indeed told Father Nikon all about it, for his minatory glance loomed up and cut her again. She was not, however, sure she had really explained herself to him, nor to Lena, nor to her daughter Varya with whom she spent her winters in Paris. The Princess had an overweening dread of strangers, and of a number of other things besides, things she could not articulate except to the icon of the Mother of God that hung over her bedside table and before which, day and night, there wavered a votive light. If she told Father Nikon the worst of it, she knew he would think her mad, and it had crossed her mind many more times than once how quickly and easily her present and unhappy situation could change. Now that Varya was planning to marry, she might even have to spend the rest of her days at St Geneviève des Bois, the shelter for aged Russian exiles in Paris. Helena, she knew, pitied Varya from the bottom of her heart (wherever that was – in the Princess's view, it was a shallow place) and she would go to some lengths to have her confined there if she could manage it. And Varya, who did have pity, pitied Serge, though for what reason the Princess could not assay, and they all pitied each other a great deal – except her.

So, it was in the Princess's mind, as a matter of some priority, to die on Patmos this summer before the thing she dreaded more than strangers really got out of hand. That was why all of these summer plans of the children upset her so. Of all summers, this was the summer that her house on Hora should be kept free of all but her usual votaries. Instead, there were six people staying, including herself, and Serge had even hinted at a seventh visitor, not Fiona his wife nor her grandchildren, but some other person in addition to Paul Mason and this newly arrived woman. She became angry again just thinking about it. There had been, as it were, a palace revolution and she had been pushed aside. Of course, she did not mind about Paul, for besides being Serge's oldest friend and something of a saint, he was also a doctor,

23

and this in itself was very reassuring. But, when she had finally come out with it and said that she was expecting to die very soon, when she had expressed the wish that her house should be kept in a quiet state of readiness for this event, there had been an outcry, fomented by Helena, she was sure. In the first place, no one believed she was dying; in the second place, it had been pointed out to her that the house actually belonged to Helena, and this forgotten fact, of course, was true. In the third place, it had been mooted but not stated that enduring the Princess all by themselves for an entire summer was something Serge and Lena felt they could not manage, no more than Varya could manage Paris winters with a mother who opposed the match with that André.

The upshot of the whole thing had been a Magna Carta. In the summers, Lena and Serge might have as many of their friends as they wished to stay with them on Patmos in what was, after all, an enormous house and in winters, she would be living in a flat occupied not only by Varya but by André as well. It was that or St Geneviève des Bois. After all, (and they had all three spelt it out) Helena's mother, most beloved sister of the Princess, had purchased the property on Patmos, and had left it outright to Helena, and Helena, who might have sold it, had maintained it almost entirely for her aunt's sake. And Varya, an old-maid of fifty-five, had every right to marry this perfectly decent Frenchman, a widowed librarian. To the chagrin of the Princess, Father Nikon had thought the solution most just and had told her, as he often did, to use the circumstance of being foiled as an opportunity for grace.

Indeed, the Princess did remember the purchase of the property so many years ago. She and her sister Masha had made a somewhat perilous pilgrimage to Patmos, just after the war and before the island had been fully annexed to Greece. It had not been a tourist place then; it had captured her with a sense of its looking East. Patmos with its unabashed Orthodox crosses, white churches, its scented groves and views of azure sea, had put her in mind of Yalta. It had produced intense nostalgia in her, the sight of this lovely island, so brave a bastion of resistance to the Germans, for somehow it had endured.

Memories she had locked away had burst her own resistance. As a young girl, she had accompanied her mother to the shores of the Black Sea and in Patmos it all came back, or much of it had. Much that exile had distorted or suppressed. There had been the vivid sense of her adored Maman, and a plethora of aunts, one of whom had been lady in waiting to the Tsarina. The court had removed to Livadia during the young Princess's stay in the vicinity, and this had been just before the

Revolution. One afternoon, she had been taken in a pony trap to a picnic spot where she had been bidden to charm the Archduchesses Olga, Maria, Tatyana and Anastasia. And charm them she had. Had there been the recitation of a Krilov fable? She could not be sure. But games and romps had ensued in the Crimean Arcadia under the benevolent eye of the Tsar. The Tsarina had been ill. Did she really remember what she remembered now, or was it a story she had so often told that she only thought she remembered it? There was an episode where she had chased the Royal Family's spaniel Jimmie with the Tsareivitch, who had worn a sailor suit. And the Archduchesses had twittered and petted her like so many gauzy birds. They had been oddly motherly to her, even though she had been a contemporary of Olga, the eldest. Oh, Olga Nikolaievna! That of all memories was the worst and saddest, for they had formed a tentative friendship on that day, and were never to meet again.

It was that sort of thing the Princess could not bear thinking about – the grave, grey eyes of Olga. Of girlish confidences given and received. Of Olga liking poetry. Her memory stood at tangent to the searing vision of these things, and could not fully enter it.

Of course, a lot of people had been shot. The Princess's own father had been shot. Her mother had died in the hovel they had been allotted. Friends had been shot – uncles. No one had been able to absorb the news that the Romanovs had been part of this general abattoir. Even now some resisted the idea. The death of Olga Nikolaievna had filled the Princess with the irrational guilt of the survivor, and had seemed the sum of all those other losses. If only she had known, she would have, that very day, abducted Olga Nikolaievna – Olya – and they could have dressed as sailors and absconded over the Crimean Sea.

Why think of this? She often thought of it. She herself had been shipped off to a labour camp in Tyumen and had spent several months there when, by some miracle, she had been released and allowed to join her sister Masha in Paris. Eventually, the Princess had found that Masha had done the trick, but she would never say how. She would never, never say. And once accustomed to that ghostly émigré habit of keeping silence over seemingly trivial matters, over any matter at all that had to do with Russia, the Princess ceased to ask.

Father Nikon said that one must forgive even the KGB – but what was he? A monk and only sixty-five. She shrank from this rebellious thought. How sad that there was so much evil in the world, she tried to think instead.

At any rate, her sister Masha had jumped at the chance to provide a summer place for them in Patmos. It had helped being Orthodox and it had helped having friends in the diplomatic corps. Oh, they had made such plans about how their children would be properly influenced by the island, and they had spent happy seasons together there. All of a sudden, Masha had died of a heart attack, leaving orphaned Lena the house on Hora. And so, the Princess had been instrumental in bringing the rest of Lena up – Yelena, Helena, Lena, who, by that time, had been on her way to university. But that was another story, involving as it did what had happened after the death of Boris and so on. Lena was hard-boiled and not at all like her mother of sainted memory. She was a real career woman and childless by choice, who from girlhood had hated and resented everything her aunt had done for her.

Suddenly, it came to her! The woman's name was Marina! Marina was the woman's name. She thanked the shadowed listener in her head, for with patience, he or she or it usually informed her with answers to the questions she asked. Now in possession of the name, she cocked her head on the pillow and gave an ear. Marina (she must not forget the name of the interloper) and Helena ascended the stairs now and the Princess caught the sound of careful whispers vanishing down the tiled corridor towards the bedroom at the end of the hall. She tried to catch the sound. They all thought she was deaf and, oddly enough, she was deaf to direct statements. At night, she could hear the sigh of a pigeon in its nest. *Marina*'s steps were tentative and light. Who was she? Was she Russian? There was an au pair girl whom Lena had imported on account of the extra company. Her name was Tanya, but she was not Russian at all, merely a student of Russian from Helena's college. The Princess did have to admit that Tanya was working out all right, although initially she had resisted the idea of having her. Her family always laughed at her and told her she thought everyone was in the KGB, and of course it was ridiculous that she had entertained the notion that Tanya might be KGB. But was Marina KGB? The ceaseless, tireless threat? Sometimes the Princess longed for death to take her beyond her fears. Who this Marina was supposed to be evaded her. Oh, an English poet's widow. That was it. Although she spoke English, the Princess preferred to speak French and Russian.

She had spent a few years in London after her husband's death, but had thought the English cold, dislikable people, *malgré* Serge, whom she had sent to Winchester and Cambridge and who had married the daughter of a baronet. She was wandering now, wandering . . . ! 'No!'

she said aloud to the pale one who held her thoughts and to the icon of the Mother of God. To God, she said, 'No, please.' For she had wandered to the brink and she knew it.

This was her wretched terror. This was what she feared, why she watched all night, prayed, patched memory together, let anger and irritation have their way. It all had to do with the returns. The return. How could she explain it to Father Nikon? Or to the sharp-eyed, quiet Russian nun in the convent of 'The Mother of God: Fountain of Life'? How to Lena? How to Varya? How, indeed, to herself? The return, the returns. These were not the same as memories, not like the memory she had of Yalta and of the Archduchess Olga, no matter how clear and pure that was. The condition had nothing to do with knowing one had had chicken for lunch on Thursday or that one's husband's name had been Boris. The difference was this, some things, such as the Bolshevik raid on her parents' house or the birth of her first grandchild she *recalled*, but to other events and circumstances, it was as if she *were* recalled, and this is what she meant by 'returns'. The returns were not focused through the mind. A 'return' meant that she was *in* the birch forest at her family home near Kiev and that the leaves quivered, not *as if* there were a breeze or *as if* the sunshine filtered through them. It was an experience altogether more profound than anything she could remember about the wood or about how old she had been when the hem of her skirt had caught in a branch and she had cried, frightened of wolves, and Matryona had come back and untangled her and had scolded her and had made her hold the basket and stand still while the others went ahead in search for more mushrooms. When she returned, she *did* howl and Matryona did untangle: the splintery basket did have heft and weight in her hand.

And there were other returns, terrible to the Princess, not for their content, but for their displacement in time. An axe fell. Someone was chopping wood. A sleigh ride took place and she was very small. There were bells of a troika and her father's hand, big and vivid in a glove. There was a fur wrap and a sense of unease. At first, she had rather enjoyed them, these episodes. It had been almost like seeing the Northern Lights or having a vision, this phenomenon of visiting childhood. They had started in her eighty-fifth year and she had thought them a gift, for so often since her memories had been unlocked in that time on Patmos just after the war she had longed to voyage back to that happy time. She would have liked to have grasped her mother's hand or to have been present once more at Easter ceremonies, or to have dashed over the grass in spring with her sister or to have teetered over new ice in the cold air, redolent with the scent of the first fires of winter. She was conscious now of what a happy family they had been. Father making jokes and roaring with cigars. There were the shaded lamps of evening, the samovar, the little treats of jam. All of this she had touched with her new-found buoyancy through time, until, like biting through to something cold, her journeys had touched future things . . . and points of past and present, which were new to her and wholly unfamiliar.

Now, she looked fearfully up past the wavering light before the icon at the rapturous bond between Mother and Child. It had nothing to do with necromancy, of that she was sure. She did not float from her body or tell fortunes, nor was there any evidence that what she saw came true or had been true, nor did she will these voyages into her dark interior.

No, it was like this: her consciousness would flatten out and she would be hurled back or forward and made present at a number of events she had nothing to do with. There was, for instance, a vivid wedding, Christian, but with an unfamiliar rite, where she witnessed the kiss of the bridegroom and the bride and their joy. There was a deathbed, too, indeed, it might have been her own, where a cry for deliverance went up. The same cry, oddly enough, went up at the wedding. Always there was pain in these excruciating visions. Often, she met a terrible blasphemer along a country road; his face was hidden from her, he cursed God, and she was filled with dread. In each instance, she was veiled from sight, but saw a wealth of unforgettable detail, the pearls on the bride's crown, the shadows on the twisted, sweaty sheets, the blades of grass beside the country road, as if she could touch them all. And there was more, more than she could possibly describe to herself that she saw, intimations garbled so deeply that it was hard to understand why she felt accused and terrified.

The house was silent now. 'Jesus!' she said aloud, for the Name held virtue and the power to dispel evil. If she promised to tell Father Nikon when he got back from Athens would it be all right? Maybe she had concealed something wilfully and sinfully from her confessor. She had cringed from telling him before about the visions and 'returns'. Maybe her seeing and her silence alike were diabolically inspired. Where would she go next? And was there a final return? A scene in which her consciousness would lodge forever? So that neither death nor God nor human aid could touch her? Could she be set the task, for

28

instance, of picking mushrooms for eternity? Or would she walk with the blasphemer until the stars died? The very thought terrified her.

The Princess had devised a few techniques to avoid these travels. Not only was she frightened by them, they also left her giddy, and she would feel unhinged for some time afterwards. In a guilty way, she thought it ought to be prayer that prevented things from slipping into that claustral area where bright imaginings loomed from the dark, but prayer only emphasized the enigmatic nature of the invisible world. In truth, she was ashamed to admit to anyone what it was that helped her the most. She had stumbled upon it quite by chance – at first with horror, but by sustaining it, she had discovered an equilibrium, a way to block all voyaging. She could not have told any of her Russian friends in Paris about it, for the few who were left might have considered it morbid and even disrespectful, but she had become as used to it now as a Catholic telling beads. Indeed, it had something in common with this practice, although she was unaware of it.

It all started one night when she had begun to think of the assasinations of the Romanovs in Ekaterinburg – or rather, the thought had clenched her in its icy grip. For a moment, she had feared herself near death or insanity, when suddenly, it occurred to her that as the Russian Church in Exile had regarded the murdered family as saints, it might be even wrong of her to put the negative construction of horror on the episode that she instinctively felt. Perhaps, as martyrs, they had died in some sense for her. Perhaps her meeting with Olga Nikolaievna, and even with the Tsar himself had been meant according to some obscure divine plan. Perhaps she had been chosen to guard their memory in some special way. So, just as she might have considered the Way of the Cross, the Princess began to go over each event: from the abdication of the Tsar to the family's incarceration at Tobolsk; from Tobolsk down the river to the finality of Ekaterinburg, she considered in depth the virtues and lessons to be extracted from each episode. From Ekaterinburg, she went down with them to the chartless depths of death's sea and beyond, where eternal glory awaited the martyrs in golden courts of heavenly love.

Almost every night, she would think of Nikolai II, not exactly as she remembered him, but iconically, being stripped of his epaulettes and honours, his face unflinching and Christlike in its gentle resignation. She would imagine the Royal Family in the sealed train, hurtling towards their doom, always correct, ever dignified and even courteous to their barbarous captors. Especially, she would think of Olga, grave, compassionate to her mother and to her siblings, no longer as a young girl to whom the promise of motherhood had been left unfulfilled, but as Virgin Martyr, elected beforehand by God to work His purpose as a sign and witness to the age. She would think of the house in Tobolsk, so mean after the palaces of Livadia and Tsarskoe Selo, where the children played bravely in the snow while guards sneered on. An image of the Tsarina came, sequestered and ceremonious in prayer, the patient victim of cruel slanders.

She could see them being moved to their final destination, bereft now of friends and all but a few faithful servants – their courage, a flame in bleak captivity. And although it was hard for her to consider the night they died, she would force herself to do so. She was sure that they must have become aware, through the purgatory of the months before their martyrdom, that they had been chosen by God for a terrible consummation in His love. Had they been prepared? At least, she hoped so – not for the hideous surprise of being dragged from bed and made to dress for the last time – but in a long-term way. She had upon their trials the perspective of Gethsemane, and though she could never follow even Olga beyond the first few steps of the fatal cellar room where they had died, the Princess always caught a glimpse of hope in the darkness of their end. One, two, three – the steps down. She could not contemplate the murder. And then a shaft of bliss. Sometimes she felt almost elevated into Heaven with them as in a dream. The very thought of this helped her drift off to sleep where sometimes Olga's face shone bathed in smiles, where sometimes she could see her mother, where sometimes she, her mother and Olga were inextricably one and the same person.

The Princess could not really think why this nightly meditation calmed her or why it prevented visionary terror of her own, but it did so all the same. This night, she would think of it again when all was still, she decided. She would keep watch with them again, she told her grey interlocutor, a vigil.

This Marina was rummaging about in her things now – unzipping and unlocking cases. The Princess heard Helena pad stealthily down the hall. When there were people about, it never seemed appropriate to think about the Romanovs. There was something private and almost hermetically sealed to her about their death, and she never let her thoughts touch them in daylight hours. There was something almost sacriligious about this pure contemplation being engaged upon in any circumstance but utter solitude. Perhaps Marina would read to her, although she doubted she would like her well enough to ask.

This was the Princess's other technique to avoid flight into those uncontrollable manifestations of the metaphysical world. Every morning and every evening, she got family or friends to read to her, sometimes until they were quite hoarse. If she heard a voice reading, her mind reached up and tangled with the words, especially if it were poetry she had learnt by heart as a child and she could whisper along. Most of all, she liked Pushkin. Prose sometimes helped, especially if she could get caught up in a story. She did not like Chekov much. As a child, she had met him in Yalta. He saw life too much in shades of grey for her taste. Pushkin, Lermontov, but not Dostoievsky, who unsettled her with his own dark mysticism and whose prose style was too complex anyhow. She liked Tolstoy. Varya had read *War and Peace* out loud to her several times, but there had been quarrels, and the Princess would forget where she was in the story and Varya would insist they had read that bit already and would not repeat it.

Sometimes, she liked a history or memoir of someone like herself. This new au pair girl Tanya, so keen to improve her Russian, had such a bad accent that the Princess could tolerate it only intermittently. It was all Soviet Russian these days, and though the girl was fluent, she read off lines of verse like a commissar ordering eggs. Lena swore she could not read Russian or speak it, out of spite, the Princess thought. But Sergei had a beautiful reading voice, particularly for Pushkin – high, light and ironic and a wonderful accent too.

She had come to like works in French or English read to her, because she had to make the effort to understand them and this concentrated her mind away from returning anywhere, from the invisible gate her mind slipped through if she let her thoughts stray. Even Paul Mason, newly arrived, had been press-ganged into the rota. Because he was so good and had such a deep voice, she liked to hear him read from the lives of the saints, from Theophan the Recluse, and The Philokalia. Of course, he had to read these works in English, but then he was English and had such a beautiful way of speaking – plainly, as she liked it. When Paul read to her from The Philokalia, the Princess would close her eyes and imagine Heaven. She would imagine fierce desert fathers who had battled with demons, who had called both anger and unchastity demons, who had shown these things up for what they really were. The Princess *knew* what they were and had a total recall of experience with them both. Paul. Pavel. Svyatoy Pavel. Saint Paul – no milksop, he! Of course, Paul Mason was not Orthodox, but as she grew older, the Princess was not sure that this mattered, though she would not have told Father Nikon so! Goodness, no. He had theories and would ram them home in sermons, pure and Byzantine.

She wondered how the congregation of Russian Athenians was getting on with Father Nikon, and she gave an involuntary shudder. He was exactly her idea of what a priest should be. How long ago had it been when first she had heard him preach at the Cave of Revelations on Patmos? Ten years ago? She could not get down there to Mass these days. She heard the liturgy intermittently in the Monastery instead. The Cave was too far and the way too steep downhill for her wheelchair. She could see Father Nikon now as she had seen him then, in her mind's eye, in the sacred of all sacred places – the Cave – preaching before the iconstasis. On it, was hung a particularly vivid icon of St Anne, holding the Virgin on her arm, and it had been against that where she had first seen Father Nikon, standing before the burning red of St Anne's robes as if he were emerging from the burning bush, his beard flowing, his fiery eye informing the little chapel with a glimpse of the Apocalyptic Vision itself. Into his face, she had thought, had been carved holiness, just as the Cave itself had been carved into the steep, Greek hillside so many centuries ago.

To the Princess, the whole complex of buildings belonging to the Cave seemed to hang in air over the port and the bay of Patmos. In the wreath of incense that day, she had imagined, but not heard, as Father Nikon had preached, the great voice, as of a trumpet, saying: 'I am the Alpha and the Omega, the first and the last.' It had made her breathless with wonder and she shivered to recall it even now. No, she was not convinced that she could tell him about these stupid travels of the mind when he returned from Athens. Deeper into the Cave, there was the most important icon of all, that of the Holy Apostle John, himself, in deepest swooning. No, troubling Father Nikon with her little junkets out of time might even be a sacrilege, she thought.

All at once, the front gate clanged again, and the Princess was instantly alert to the sound of voices. When she realized that not only Serge, but Paul too was in the courtyard, she relaxed. They must have gone on for a walk or something after dinner at Vangelis's taverna where they dined nearly every night – though sometimes they ate at Yiorgos. In order to relieve the servants of the burden of preparing two meals a day for them, 'the children' (as she called them) went out to supper. This is what they said. The Princess believed that they wanted to avoid her, but in truth, she insisted on being prepared for bed so early that it was impractical for them to eat with her, especially as her supper invariably consisted of an egg on a tray in bed. She half-knew she was being inconsistent and unreasonable, but it only made her more cross when she realized that she had no evidence to support her suspicion that she was being abandoned. She was always relieved when she heard them return to the house. 'They are back,' she said now to the silent one to whom she offered observations. She sharpened her ears.

Had Serge been drinking? Surely, not with Paul. She worried about him. She worried so very much about him that she was never really sure what she perceived. From his home in England, he rang her every week in Paris during the winter. Did she hear a slur of words, a gulp? Or was it just the line? In the dead of night on Patmos this summer, she had caught the sound of a stumbling and a lurch, the soft clink of glass, a hiss from Lena, a growl from her son, and now and then, the soft thud of a fall. It had been all very well for Serge's father to do this, he, whose obsession it had been that he had failed to protect the Tsar, even though hc had only been a very young subaltern when the Revolution had occurred, but that was another story. It was not all right for Sergei. Nonetheless, she could tell he was sober tonight. She heard the float of comforting male voices, then the latch and then a creaking stair, then, soon enough, a silence. Perhaps she would ask Paul about it, that was a good idea, he was, after all, a doctor and a family friend as well.

And so the silence deepened, and she gathered up her grey and tattered thoughts, withdrew them to herself, and launched upon her vigil. As she let her mind engage upon that time, she dwelt upon these seemingly inconsequent details: the distinctive laugh of the Archduchess Anastasia; the lavender boudoir of the Tsarina; the noble bearing of the Tsar. And she thought about these and other things until morning.

IV

HELENA, who had fallen exhausted into bed, woke in the early hours of the morning with the certain knowledge that she would be unable to get back to sleep. She lay staring. It was excessively hot. She sat, put on slippers, found her robe, and, as on many nights before, crept softly down the stairs of the big, old house and on into the back where the terraced garden lay with its formal arrangement of ancient trees and vines. It was her mother's place, the place her mother had loved. Before her early death, she had salvaged the venerable fig tree, the plane tree, trimmed back the rampant bougainvillaea, trained up new and exotic flowers so that hibiscus and amaryllis burgeoned in May out of marbled, Roman troughs and terracotta pots. From nourished beds in the lower garden grew a plethora of things Aegean, vines and gourds and shrubs, all in a dainty tangle, both disciplined and free. Her mother had hired Dmitris all those years ago, and he had stayed on to tend the garden, whether out of pride in it or a love for her mother, Helena never knew. Helena did not invite fond or conscious memories of her mother; she had always had more in common with her English father whom she had adored. Helena's mother had always seemed to her a tenuous, other-worldly woman with a sweet, remote disposition. Servants and shop-keepers had always loved her, but Helena, who had been evacuated to Canada during the war, felt as if she had hardly known her.

Her father's family in Montreal had really brought her up. More British than the British, these cousins had helped her through his death at Monte Cassino with the sort of stiff-upper-lip behaviour that Helena really admired and they had given a necessary strength to her spine. When she had returned to England at the end of the war, Helena had been obscurely mortified by her mother's Russian heart, broken by her father's death. It had been, of course, shortly after her return to Europe that her mother had bought the Patmos house with some of the large legacy that Helena still lived on. In a curious way, she had always been Aunt Sonya's protector, even though she had seemed the weaker of the two sisters and the house had very much been seen as Sonya's bolt-hole, though quite why, Helena had never known. In any case, her poor mother had survived only long enough to make the garden lovely, and

34

to embellish the fine drawing room and dining room with deep, red Turkey carpets, antique, inlaid furniture, salvaged Russian memorabilia, and icons. Even now, Helena thought the house looked as if it had been occupied by some Turkish pasha converted to Orthodoxy. Nearly forty years on from her mother's death, nothing had really been renewed, and the place had a dark and seedy, Oriental quality. Helena could never really bring herself to ship out lamps from Heal's or stuff her case with curtain material.

Helena had been an only child. If it had not been for her cousins Serge and Varya, it would have been unlikely that she should have visited the place much, she thought. While her mother was alive, Helena had disliked the Patmos visits intensely, partly because she was an adolescent, and partly because, even then, she had mixed feelings about her aunt, Tyotya Sonya. Even though England was in a shaky state after the war, Greece represented to Helena her translation back to Europe-in-a-mess, a Europe disfigured by ruins. As if it had not been enough to lose her father, Aunt Sonya seemed to belittle his sacrifice to the conflict. She had been totally caught up in the Russian agony, her mother had mildly said. Aunt Sonya had beleaguered them with tales of Stalin and starving, persecuted countrymen. And then, there had been the thin, Greek children, and Helena had felt guilty about them. She remembered, too, events of forced worship in the Cave of the Apocalypse, the island's major shrine, where St John was supposed to have written the Book of Revelations and, where too, Greek patriots had holed themselves up during the German occupation to hatch an overthrow. Even now, a whiff of candles or incense took her back to crucial times when no one not Orthodox could be taken seriously by her powerful aunt, including her dead father, who had been an unbeliever.

Quite why she came back year after year to Patmos to be with Aunt and Serge and sometimes Varya, Helena did not know. Oh, these enervating journeys, those hot, Greek times, when she had suffocated with boredom. Of course, the house was part of her inheritance, and in a way she felt if she left Aunt Sonya in charge for too long, the property that had been bought with her father's money would become 'Mirkovsky' forever. Helena had, at times, actually let the house, and so she did look after the business of the place in a way her impractical aunt would never have done even at her zenith of physical strength. Nonetheless, it was an anomaly to Helena that she, a busy woman, spared time and energy to come. In old, bad times gone by, her aunt had been abominable. She had memories of sitting of an evening in overstuffed chairs covered with antimacassars on the verandah of the old Grand Hotel in Skala (not really such a grand place, after all), watching the evening promenade with her aunt and her aunt's few select friends from Athens, ladies she judged suitable companions for her Greek mode. For all her Graeco-mania, Aunt spoke the language very badly, and she would converse with the visiting gentry in a hodge-podge of English, Greek and French. They would all have ices and coffees and the Princess would make little jabs at Helena. This malice would come, often as not, in the form of little parables about bad women – career women, childless women, divorced women – whose fate of loneliness and despair they had brought upon themselves by purely selfish motives and a lack of human feeling, a lack of femininity. This, shortly after her split-up with Mungo Taggart, had infuriated Helena, partly because she knew that the Orthodox Church, of which her aunt was such a devout member, quite tolerated divorce, and partly because she knew what her aunt was really getting at. There was an indefinable quality about Helena she had never liked, which had something to do with her ambition. Ironically, her aunt had once had quite a powerful intellect – everyone in the family said so, though it was hard to see it now. But she had a kind of aristocratic disdain for all forms of egregious self-expression, and had written herself under a pseudonym as a translator. Fundamentally, she thought women should have children and the upkeep of large houses very high on the list of their priorities, and if they were to do something clever, it should be a spare time activity. Helena had never countered her aunt directly, but had got her own back by leaving hints that she had radical politics.

Sometimes, Helena did really wonder what she had to do with Aunt, whose vaunted love of children was belied in the way Serge and Varya trembled, even in their early fifties, in front of their mother. They would not even smoke in front of her. Helena herself had quit smoking years ago for her health's sake, but had, in the past, never failed to light up in front of Aunt. And she had stuck it out about Mungo too, making no bones about leaving him. There was no moment in her life now that she held sacred to him, nor to the memory of him. As for children, she had always wanted to be free of any such nastiness and mess. She had struck out to make herself a career and indeed, she had become a formidable academic, an author of some highly acclaimed critical works on English poetry. She had, for the most part, Augustan tastes, but hoped she was open enough to be eclectic . . . Helena had lived a life of

36

sheer, conscious ability and hard work. Perhaps it was on Patmos alone that she felt the whips and scorns of an emotional life. In her fifty-eighth year, she had no family but this one – no loves, no deep familiars. And Aunt cursed blindly on the walls of Troy – a Hecuba, she thought. Serge and Varya could never have done without her insight. They could not have gone on without Helena's way of seeing beyond her aunt's railings and tempers and indictments.

She descended into the cool part of the lower garden carefully, for the moon was so high now that its light did not suffice. The scent of flowers almost overwhelmed her and she had a sense of suffering now, although she did not know why. She had anticipated Marina's arrival avidly, and had spent nights here beforehand, full of humid and odd feelings that left her restless and afraid. Deep into the lushest place near the wall, she felt fronds at her face where some ferny bush brushed her. She was almost glad now that Marina had wanted to go directly to bed, even though she had been oddly crushed at the time. Entering the house, Marina had oohed and aahhed, but had refused even the bowl of avoglomeno soup that Evangalia had offered her and had begged to be shown to her room with many protestations of sorrow at not being able to keep her eyes open and gratitude at having been given the house's interesting guest room with its traditional Greek furniture and hangings. She had been rapturous, really. That was a word Helena could generally apply to Marina – 'rapturous' – even though, on the few times she had met with her, Marina had been grief-stricken and probably still was. Could one call it grief? Perhaps. Rapture often broke in through her smiles, nonetheless.

Helena turned and felt her way back up to the higher terrace. She felt confused and excited by this visit. It offended her, obscurely, that Marina had gone to New York without telling her. She knew this was irrational. After all, they knew each other only slightly yet, Helena had almost come to think of her as her confidante. There was a white, wire chair placed near the little garden table at the top of the terrace nearest the house, and Helena sat down. She did not know whether it was 3 or 4 a.m., and a nightingale sang. She knew she was tired, but she could not rest. Thoughts of Arthur jutted at her mind.

*

37

In point of fact, Helena had nearly missed Arthur's funeral, and if she had missed it, she would never have met Marina. First of all, there had been the problem of the poetry itself, and the news of his death had come as an awful shock to her for this reason alone. For some time, she had been uncomfortable about the way she had evaluated his work in years gone by, and she had been considering a resurrection job on his reputation, had even been working herself up to seeing him again, when she had seen his obituary in *The Times*. Certainly, he was regarded by some to be an important poet, but expected honours had eluded him. It was commonly thought that he had burnt out after *The Hephestus Cycle*, written many years ago. He had gone on publishing, but critical interest had turned away from him.

In her own way, Helena had helped this state of affairs when she had omitted him from her well-received assessment of the century's poets. She, with some others, had come to see his obsession with Greek mythology as a Romantic affectation. Actually, she thought that Robert Graves was a much better poet and had overshadowed Arthur. In addition to this, Helena had felt that even the major *Cycle* had been flawed by a naive sexism somewhat offensive to her now, even though it had not been when she had first read the poems. For all of his lyrical power, he did come on as being a little old-hat and for more reasons than one, perhaps, his fixation on a modern Aphrodite made her feel uncomfortable. When Helena had left him out of her major book, thus casting a greater length on his obscuring, it had worried her slightly that he might see the omission as a form of revenge.

In later years, however, she had begun to reconsider his contribution and to reconsider also her own life in the light of his influence on it. That this had not been publicly accomplished by the time of his death (he had been only sixty after all) gave Helena terrible qualms about attending his funeral. Having thus failed to vindicate him, she wondered if his widow and children might turn and gaze sadly down crematorium pews.

In the second place, the idea of seeing a dead lover committed to the flames disjointed Helena from that point of clarity in which she generally saw life. She was not sure whether it was this dead lover or any dead lover that she would have minded so much. When she closed her eyes, she could imagine that private moment when the gas jets would catch the coffin, when Arthur's body, lurid for a moment in the fire, would ignite, a burning, fiery furnace without angel, a journey to Valhalla without gods.

At the last moment, there had been a compulsion so strong to go that it almost seemed as if she were being guided by an unseen hand. She knew she must go. She chose the shoes and the suit and put them on almost as if she were being dressed by someone else. Impelled by an intuitive force that she rarely ever had and even now mistrusted, she hailed a cab to Putney Vale and sat in the back of the chapel while *Death and the Maiden* piped him out. A vulgar choice, Helena thought, and probably his wife's. Helena closed her eyes tightly, glad that she had come, even though she could not look. As mechanical rollers started his bier's inevitable slide, Helena played for a moment with an unwelcome and Dostoievskian notion that Arthur's soul could see her and was watching her even as his own body burned. She even entertained the thought that, irony of ironies, he was on his way to face his Maker. She was annoyed by an impulse to cross herself as her mother had taught her in childhood, and, supreme rationalist that she was, stifled the urge to do this and all thoughts that would have given the gesture credence.

When the ceremony had finished, she let her eyes dart around the crematorium chapel. For a moment, she wondered if Mungo Taggart would be there. He had, after all, introduced her to Arthur. Her ex-husband had re-married, run to fat, and now had grandchildren. She was not sure she was up to facing that, but he was absent.

She had not been sure that Marina was beautiful enough to typify a goddess when after the lugubrious event she had summoned her courage and asked Helena back to her flat for drinks. Far from being antagonistic, Marina had appeared apologetic. For some reason, she had imagined her to be dark and had been surprised to see such a pale, fair creature. Her lips had quivered and she had clutched her hands in an unconscious motion of washing them. There she had stood at the door, almost like a female vicar greeting people after church. A deep uncertainty emanated from her, and it clearly cost her much effort to invite the bland crowd of literati back. Helena knew most of them, and they each other, but nobody knew quite what to say. Standing even more uncomfortably to one side of their stepmother were Arthur's children, Claire and her brother (Helena could not remember his name). They were disquietingly close in age to Marina and, but for the look of edgy alienation on their faces, they might have been her friends. It gave Helena rather a jolt to realize that she had last seen them as young children playing on the lawn one Sunday lunchtime when she had gone with Mungo to visit Jane and Arthur in Bucks, where for a

39

while they had kept up an oddly upper-middle class existence incongruous with their inner lives. Even more disconcerting to her was the presence of an adolescent boy in a dark suit, for with his bright hair and slightly pendulous features, she recognized him at once as Arthur's grandson.

Somehow, it had seemed so important to the febrile and dewy Marina that everyone should come to the wake that they had all trailed back to Kensington in the dirty traffic and drunk Scotch. The flat was as pale as Marina herself – all done out in a wash of beige carpeting and sofas. There were a few original abstracts on the wall, but Helena did not think them very good. She wondered how Arthur had afforded this with the alimony he must have had to pay, but then she remembered that he had a private income. Although she had washed her hands of Arthur completely and thus had studiously avoided any speculation on his second wife, she did remember hearing that Marina was rich. The whole aura of the flat was one of impersonal opulence.

So this was how Arthur had ended up. Helena and, indeed, the other guests all felt uneasy, or she assumed they felt uneasy. She chatted with a few people whom she had not seen for a long time and was surprised to find that most of them had been out of touch with Arthur for nearly as long as she had been. Everyone milled awkwardly about and promised each other that this time they really would have lunch. Helena found it hard to concentrate on what she was saying and she drank more whisky than she intended. What *was* Arthur's son's name? William? No. She was sure it was Henry. Henry, then, was looking prosperous. The daughter, apparently without husband, appeared to be very jumpy and close to the surface. Even so, Helena was surprised to see them leave, after a barely polite half-hour, with Arthur's grandson. She devoted her attention to the bland drawing room while Marina seemed to be urging them to stay in that gentle, hesitant manner she had observed in her at the crematorium. It was embarrassing.

Helena spotted a little terracotta figurine on the mantelpiece, a Cycladic goddess or votive figure. Other than this piece, everything else conspired to make the flat look like the reception room of some large corporation. Marina, at odds with the decor, wore a blue suit. She kept fiddling with the sleeves and pressing drink on people. Somehow Helena could not bear to watch this, and so she went into the bathroom. She sighed and spent a long time looking in the mirror. Though well-preserved, she was old, she thought. She felt a little drunk, and so she splashed her face with water and blotted it with a lush towel. She was oddly touched to see crumbs of powder on the basin, evidence of Marina's patching before the funeral. Had her stepchildren accompanied her on the dreary drive with the hearse, or had she gone alone? Had she been weeping, or was she just vain? There seemed something hasty and messy about Marina. On her way back to the drawing room, Helena did, on impulse, peek into the bedroom, and then felt ashamed of herself. It was smeared and tousled and had the faintest smell of unwashed linen. Helena looked at the rumpled bed covered with stacks of clothes. She thought of Arthur and she thought of Marina, lying there together, and then she forced the thought away.

As she rejoined the party, Helena all at once lit upon an angle of Marina's face that stopped her. As her hands clutched onto the parting guests, as she thanked them so humbly for coming, Helena caught a curve of her cheek and bosom, a frame of hair and a length of limb, and suddenly, as if she had been Arthur himself and twenty-five years younger, she saw an awful loveliness, a preternatural beauty. Before she knew it, she had been left alone with Marina, and the thought of abandoning her, this hectic and vulnerable human being, stuck at her. It was she who suggested that they go out and have dinner together. And by the end of the evening, the two women had become not friends, perhaps, but a good deal more than acquaintances.

Each time Helena remembered this first engagement, the quality of the experience seemed to intensify. Even though they had spent several hours together, she recalled it as if it had been a single moment of great purity. Lurching out into the early spring dark, they had whistled up a cab and gone to Poon's near Leicester Square. Quite why they had chosen this loud, bright, Chinese restaurant, Helena did not know. Looking back on it, the choice seemed wildly inappropriate. Some shadowed, sheltered booth in a wine bar would have been more apt. They perched on bistro chairs in the noisy restaurant with its clean white walls and white tiled floors. Never had she seen another person look so out of place as Marina did in her funeral suit. 'I just love Chinese food,' she had said as if nothing at all had happened and as if it were a day like any other day. For some reason, Helena had not taken it in that Marina was an American, perhaps because she had a clipped diction. She asked Marina if she came from Boston, but she said 'no' and then they ordered wind-dried duck and crab with black bean sauce and chillis. Marina gnawed at the crab legs, sucking the juices out. They drank green tea and were sobered. Helena observed that Marina had delicate manners. 'It's so kind of you, this,' she said. 'I'll never forget this,' she said and kept on saying.

Helena could think of little with which to reply and was grateful for the crab, the eating of which involved long periods of silence. Besides, she began to feel a strange awe. It was as if every inflection of flawless beauty was indicated in the woman sitting opposite her. Marina's pale profile was mirrored in the restaurant walls. Helena felt herself in dialogue with Arthur's shade. 'But *of course* the *Cycle*! Of course the broken marriage! You saw,' she found herself saying to Arthur, 'and I am guilty of not reading your vision right. It's all there in the text without sentiment and without exaggeration,' she thought. And yet she thought technically of prosody and metaphor, rhythm, image and design, as if Marina herself were abstract.

'Tell me about yourself,' she had said thickly, downing tea, 'as I do not know you.' Marina dipped her fingers in the fingerbowl and wiped them with a napkin. She said she had grown up in New York and that she had been a summer student of Arthur's at Oxford. When she mentioned his name, she looked as if she were about to cry. She cleared her throat and focused her attention on Helena. What about Helena? Helena stalled on the matter of her books. It crossed her mind that Marina might not know the significant omission of Arthur from her particular canon, and she was not about to let her discover it on the night of his funeral. She desperately dug around for bland subject matter, and then came up with the colourful story of her background – her Russian mother and Canadian wartime days. Suddenly, Marina bucketed forward, almost into the crab and Helena feared the worst sort of embarrassment with tears, fainting spells, getting taxis called, and Marina in a coma of grief; but Marina evened, sat straight, and started on a curious, rambling tack. She had always thought her own mother had been Russian, and wasn't that extraordinary?

At the time, Helena had been struck by the peculiar strength and oddity of Marina's expression and tone. Her voice had been controlled but husky and her brow had been fixed in a childlike bewilderment like someone who has been violently sick without warning. 'What do you mean?' Helena had inquired.

Marina leaned forward again in an almost drunken curve, though Helena noted that she was quite sober. 'Arthur did not like me to talk about it,' she said in a piercing whisper, 'and so I've never talked about it here in England. I was adopted.'

'Goodness!' Helena had said. 'From your expression, I thought you were about to admit some monstrous crime.'

Marina picked at a claw and flushed. 'I don't know why it should feel a crime, but it does.' She looked directly up at Helena. 'One comes to think that one was not wanted for a good reason.'

'But why didn't Arthur want you to mention it?' she asked, curious at this new glimpse into his character. 'Truth,' she added, 'was one of his things, as I remember him. Emotional honesty a near fetish.'

Marina gave her a sharp glance, but it was without hostility. 'Actually,' she said, 'I didn't have anyone much to mention it to. We saw virtually no one. But I guess I became a little obsessional about it at one point. I wanted to find out – you know – who my parents were. That sort of thing.'

'I thought it was quite a common obsession amongst adopted children,' Helena said firmly, 'something one could hardly call an obsession at all.' She did not know why, but she observed a tense note in Marina's voice, a certain defensiveness in the way she put her hand to her chest, that led her to believe that Arthur had turned bully to his goddess.

'Of course, Arthur was a genius,' Marina said with every show of loyalty, 'but I think it made him peculiar at times. Or is that a romantic fallacy? He got very fed up with my talking about it. He thought that psychology was absurd and misleading and that people should not think about their childhood. He rarely talked about his own. I never got a glimpse. But more than that, I always thought that he really did not want me to know who my parents were. In the end, he was so vehement about it that I let the matter drop.' In the white, sheeny restaurant with waiters weaving in and out, with shells of crab being sorted and replaced by rice and duck, Marina finally cried. Tears fell into her rice bowl. She shaded her face with her hands and kept her body rigid as she wept. 'I'm sorry,' she said, 'It's just come over me that he is dead.'

Without really meaning to do this, Helena reached out and touched Marina's arm. 'It's been a dreadfully upsetting day,' she said, then realized how upset she was herself. After a few moments, Marina composed herself, and with great sweetness, asked Helena for her forebearance. They were both silent for a moment and ate their food seriously with chopsticks. All of a sudden, Helena was seized by an irrational fury at Arthur. It seemed to well up in her as evidence of a long unsolved murder.

'He had no right!' she said, her voice tight. 'No right at all.'

Marina looked at her, her head to one side as if to say that any kind of madness was explicable on this particular evening. 'Right?'

'He had no right to prevent you from finding out who your parents were. That is information which belongs to you – it wasn't his. I mean to say that it had nothing to do with him!' She was shocked to find that she wanted to pound the table with her fists.

Marina spoke in a muffled voice. 'I always thought he knew something that I should not know.'

'Arthur was *arbitrary*!' Helena said, a certain grand lucidity overtaking her. She saw it. 'He did not say or do things for reasons.' She found herself thundering the point as if lecturing.

Marina suddenly laughed in an odd, sad way. 'You know, that's absolutely true. He was.'

Helena often wondered incredulously what women had done before feminism, for she now regarded her own experience as unintelligible to her unless viewed in its light. In this respect, she saw herself as eclectic rather than fundamentalist and had little patience with those who devalued the work of men. Nonetheless, as years had gone by, she had found herself withdrawing from their actual society, and had come to prefer a solitary life. In writing she disliked polemic, but she found herself persuaded by what was politically correct more and more. She regarded herself as sound and she elevated woman students where she could. It bore down on her now that because their affair had taken place in the sixties, she had not seen Arthur for the chauvinist he was. The insight made her feel suddenly triumphant.

'But he *was* a genius,' Marina repeated with a subtle question in her eyes.

'Well, you immortalized him,' Helena found herself saying.

'Oh!' Marina said with some distress, 'He immortalized me!'

'Think about it,' Helena said. 'Couldn't it be the other way around?' She was pleased and astonished at this wonderful reversal, but Marina's eyes looked so sad that she forebore to develop it.

'I feel bad talking about him in a critical way,' she said, giving a wounded look to Helena. 'We scatter his ashes tomorrow.'

'Oh, did he want to have his ashes scattered?' Helena felt herself huffing despite her attempts to key down her tone. But she added a more gentle rider to this remark with a smile.

'Yes,' Marina said almost absently. 'Do you know a place called Orford? We've got to get up there tomorrow. It's in Suffolk. He wanted his ashes cast into the sea.'

Helena's heart and temples and veins thudded so much that she thought she might faint. 'Orford?' she asked weakly.

'Yes, it puzzled me,' Marina said. 'We went there once together, but we did not have a particularly nice time. Yet he was quite insistent in his will. Everything to do with his funeral was laid down in his will. Each detail.'

'I know the place, yes,' Helena said, shrugging. 'A pretty village.' How many nights had she and Arthur spent at the inn there? How many weekends? Some kinetic, animal memory made a small explosion in her skull and abdomen. She shook her head.

'Would you like to come?'

Helena shook her head again.

'Probably best. The children have worked everything out,' said Marina, relieved.

'But I will ring you,' she had said. 'I will phone you afterwards. You'll need to talk. You'll need a friend,' Helena had said. And that had been the beginning.

She had sat for such a long time in the garden chair and so still that she had become positively chilly. The criss-crossed pattern of the wire mesh dug into her thighs. From that time on, from that day on which Arthur's body had been burned, Helena had been as one under a spell. It was hardly that she had conceived a passion for Marina, she thought, or as if she were afflicted by a mania, yet there had become something about her desire to see Marina that had an autonomy to it. Thoughts about Arthur and Marina cropped up in her mind against her conscious desire to think them. It was if an automatic loom relentlessly wove tapestries around them. Images of their bodily union came to haunt and disturb her, and memories of that old desire for Arthur cradled, fingered and tortured her mind. She found herself taking up the *Cycle* and looking for new and non-literary clues, and she thought of Marina in her own right often, particularly in the intense, voluptuary delight in which Arthur had seen the goddess Aphrodite. The poems now seemed to glint arrestingly of greatness, and the Greek deity stepped forth frothily from the sea as a figure for modern women – a figure with ultimate power and authority over men and over all paternalistic concepts too. This was a blood-soaked goddess with triumphs on her hands, who yet, had the delicacy of Renaissance forms.

When Marina finally rang and asked Helena, incongruously, she

45

thought, to shop and lunch with her at Peter Jones, she leapt at the chance. She had not been inside the shop for years; it had been where her mother had bought tapestry wool. Helena had no need to ask Marina questions about the marriage. Out it all came between the gloves and the make-up, between the carpets and the restaurant, with Marina clutching purchases and pouring forth in breathless little gulps the story of a married life so awful that Helena could hardly credit it. Oh, she was discreet enough, but Helena could read between the lines, loyal enough, but Helena felt the drift of misery emanating like the smell of hunger from a beggar.

For a moment, amid vases and glassware, where Marina was trying to replace some crystal tumblers from a set that had been broken, it occurred to Helena that if she were to write the biography she planned, it might be wise to say so, but something in her resisted manifesting this to the fragile being who could not find the match among all the spindly flutes for champagne and etched Waterford. Helena told herself that she would not use these confidences, but all the same, her nostrils flared with the keen scent of the poet's life, Arthur, whom she now began to see as matchless, perhaps, in his own right. It was an odd and eerie sensation that lifted her as they made their way through fabrics to the escalator, and the poetry itself moved within her mind with its dark images and bold, dynamic rhythms. It was almost as if Marina were drawing from her an idea so creative that it was too dangerous to handle, a literary biography where the sacredness of the feminine and the profanity of a vile marriage might be 'yoked together with violence'. So she listened over the quiche and beansprout salad and uttered not a word but murmurs of unqualified sympathy.

It was sympathy, indeed, she felt. After the shopping junket, she had gone home and writhed in mental fury, wrestled with the impossibility of writing anything friendly about a man who had treated his wife as a virtual prisoner and not a modern, Western prisoner at that. To her astonishment, it came to her the very next day. In a serene and visionary way, it floated to her mind that, if taken from the injured model's point of view, the artist's life could be seen with scrupulous justice. His work seen as less, somehow, than his victim's actual beauty might have a staggering effect and might rehabilitate his verse without going politically astray. She was exalted. She even wrote to her publisher, who sent back cautious encouragement and this generated excitement in Helena's mind. She brimmed with plans and notes.

And yet, when she tried to review her own relationship with Arthur as a means to getting into the story of his life, a certain, dark declivity appeared which she was at a loss to explain. Her mind simply shut down, and this was odd because she had ended the affair herself. What had he been, after all, but a transitional phase between her marriage and her freedom? Maybe it had to do with an atavistic fear of death, for he had been her lover so very long ago and in such a different phase of her life that she had always kept the memory of the episode openly on the shelf of her mind like a mere artefact without power to disturb her. When she had heard so many years before of his marriage to Marina, she had not gone into paroxysms of jealousy. Rather, she had given a little, grim smile and left it. In fact, she had thought it unneccessary and even a little unkind to mention the liaison to Marina, and she supposed she would eventually have to, just as she would eventually have to tell her about the book.

In a way she had, however, Helena put things off. Plans were not firm enough. Arthur had just died. In any case, she felt an irresistible urge to see Marina as distinct from Arthur, and this was quite in keeping with her theme. Apart from anything else, a touching warmth emanated from the younger woman, and it made Helena want to keep such awkward details out of the way. It might be that in telling Marina she would lose the gift of her spirit – a gift that had the scent of luxury to Helena like the few she allowed herself – her Florentine-bound journals, her account at Berry Bros. and Rudd. But, it was not until the annual trip to Patmos loomed upon her calendar and she had spoken to her distraught cousin Varya on the telephone from Paris, that it struck her how many birds she could kill with one single invitation. The idea of being able to give comfort to Marina gave her own heart a weird jerk of happiness. She wanted, too, to reinforce Varya's independent decision to marry into the 'petite bourgeoisie' if she liked. And above all, plans for her book could be gently raised and hashed over during the long, effortless summer months ahead.

Helena knew it made more sense to ask Marina for a short stay, but there was something of golden largesse about making the Patmos house utterly available to Arthur's widow. To this end, she had asked Marina and had found her hands trembling on the telephone with fear of refusal. Her elation at consent knew no bounds. They had spent another long evening together at Helena's flat in Bloomsbury, mostly discussing details of the trip, but leaks occurred of Arthur's little ways.

Not only had Marina lost her freedom upon her marriage to Arthur, she had also lost her mind. Well, that was an exaggeration. She had had what she described as a nervous breakdown and had ended up in a pukka clinic in Surrey. The episode seemed to have occupied the central years of their marriage. Arthur had had 'no patience' with psychotherapy and had obstructed Marina's efforts to talk with a doctor she had liked. He had put her 'instability' down to rocky genes. When she had recovered (and she assured Helena with moist eyes that she had), Arthur had made sure she was not 'exposed' to anything upsetting, like getting a job. After only a few adroitly put questions, Helena had established that Marina's life before marriage had been free of psychiatric incident, and she was left with an acute impression that Arthur had both caused and protracted the breakdown. Pitifully, she seemed to hang onto the doctor's diagnosis that she was not insane. She had simply lost all of her confidence, he had said. Helena had sharpened her thesis with a cold sense of irony. She would not let the bastard get away with it. Not now. The discreditable details about his treatment of his wife mounted up. He had mocked her into lunacy.

Helena exhaled into the night air. Now Marina was here on Patmos, she had the odd feeling that she had known her all her life. It ran through her head like an unidentifiable tune that Arthur's widow had some strange affinity with the house, the garden and her remote past. Surely, the main thing was that she had arrived and was sleeping gently above. Although Helena had a few women friends, she had always found herself keeping a distance from any intimacy with them, but she found herself imagining an unprecedented closeness with Marina. Oh, how they would talk! She only wished Marina were a little brighter – would use her mind more.

Helena sighed, shook her head and wondered if she had caught rheumatism from the dew. She rose and went upstairs, then finally slept with fitful dreams until the dawn had come and gone. Through her shutters, grey shadows turned to rose, then filtered, forming bars of light across her sleeping form.

V

MARINA WOKE with a start. The morning light pierced the slats of her shuttered windows and fell on her coverlet in bright, knife-like creases. For a moment, she did not know where she was, and thinking she was at home in London, she cringed under the covers in her habitual avoidance of getting up. Then, realizing she was in Patmos, she hurtled from the tangled sheets in a panic and stood in the middle of the room. The time! she thought desperately. What time can it be? 'Oh, no!' she said aloud when she saw by her watch that it was nearly eleven. She ran her fingers through her hair. She was very embarrassed. Why hadn't Helena woken her? In her nightdress, she padded to the door and peered out, hoping to catch a glimpse of Helena, but on seeing the cool and empty distance of the hall, she scurried across it and rapped softly on Helena's door. Without thinking, she tried the knob, and it sprang the catch, swinging the door open on an empty room. For a moment, she stood on the threshold. The room was meticulously ordered. There was a formidable array of books, all shelved, and a neat escritoire, which stood underneath an open window. The narrow bed was made in a soldierly fashion with a grey, embroidered coverlet. The arrangement was at once private and formal as if it were on view in a stately home or the birthplace of an author. Marina, who had a continuing battle with the material world, felt a little awed at this distinguished tidiness, and then a little ashamed of her own impulsiveness at having opened the door. She shut it firmly behind her, feeling she had pried into a secret. It seemed the vestal place of one who had been alone for a long time.

Marina went back across the hall into her room. She looked into the mirror. 'Oh, no,' she said again to her image. 'I can't go down alone.' She remembered that the elderly Princess was supposed to be ailing, and it seemed a dreadful thing to do, to arrive unannounced in such a household, whether the illness were imagined or not. She opened the shutters a crack. Her room overlooked the street. As far as her eye could see, there was white. All the walls and the houses and the arches and the domes were white. There were little crosses perched on top of some of the buildings, which she took for chapels. The street itself was narrow, not wide enough for a car, and there seemed no

49

evidence of people either. The sunlight glaring off the buildings was intense, yet it looked as if it ought to be intense. There seemed to be a fierce simplicity about the place and it appealed to Marina.

She thought she would shower and dress. She looked a fright. Maybe Helena would hear her from downstairs and would come to fetch her. Cluttered with towel and sponge-bag, she sought and found the bathroom that she had been shown the previous night. She stood under the water and let it stream over her hair, all over herself. Marina loved washing. She let the sweated journey and her eclipsing sleep leave her. Then suddenly she remembered she had read that St John had been exiled to the island because there was no fresh water there, that Patmos had been a kind of Roman gulag because of this, and, frightened of shortages, she hastily jumped out, turning off the taps.

Marina had never liked looking at her body and had always had a modest disposition. There was a long mirror in the bathroom, and when she caught a glimpse of herself in it, she hastily pulled her towel around her, partly against her body's latest manifestations of sagging. 'You've given nothing but trouble to everyone,' she muttered half to the image and half to herself. She had always seen the flesh and the spirit as separate entities. She often peered at her face, though, and peered at it now as if in an attempt to discover what lay behind it. Arthur had not believed that either of them had souls and had faced his own anticipated annihilation well. Sometimes on the verge of sleep, Marina imagined the soul, an archaic thing with a rapturous face and the ability to fly. But in daylight, she brought herself up short against the frivolity (and possible heresy) of this thought, the thought of her soul flying winged.

On her return to the bedroom, Marina was chagrined to find that she had not hung her clothes up the night before and had let them crease in the suitcase. Everything was a muddle and a tangle. With relief, however, she spied a white muslin dress. It was somewhat too formal, but she had folded it properly and she put it on, thanking her lucky stars that she had one decent thing to wear. She slapped on make-up, jabbed earrings in her ears, made a helpless attempt to put things straight, then froze at the door. She was seized with social terror, and did not know the right thing to do, especially around princesses. Marina at once castigated herself for taking such note of rank. Arthur had thought it vulgar of Americans to dote on royalty and the trappings of high social caste, but Marina always thought that his was a way of saying that one was superior to a system she herself found intrinsically shocking. Although she nursed a sneaking admiration for the Queen, she had a peculiar moral horror of social contempt in any form and thought the English endemically guilty of it. Still, she was nervous.

As far as Helena was concerned, Marina felt so tongue-tied in her presence that she was almost reduced to miming words with awkward gestures. She had searched New York for an appropriate house present, and had come up with scented drawer liners from Laura Ashley. They had seemed all right at the time, but when she had given them to Helena last night, they had seemed twee and silly in this stark place, even though Helena had thanked her very graciously. Marina had the confused idea that Helena liked her very much, but she did not know why. The invitation to Patmos had implied, she felt, a more intense, ulterior invitation to Helena's deepest self. Marina had always had fantasies of such intimacy. Had she not yearned for a communion with the poetic Arthur, only to find the basis for this removed once they had married? Marina was convinced that the basis for this sort of thing was spiritual not physical. With Helena, she felt an elevation to the sort of rapport she had always dreamed of, but the proximity of Helena made her afraid. Each meeting with Helena since Arthur's death had left her breathless with new difficulties. She had found herself blurting out terrible things about him – disloyal things. She had confided to Helena the story of her breakdown too, and now she shrank from knowing she had told her a thing so private. Perhaps it was Helena's detachment, perhaps her insight that made Marina feel compelled to open her heart, perhaps her sturdy defence of women's rights. Marina, who constantly belaboured herself with feelings of guilt, felt liberated to speak in the presence of one who lacked moral judgment, that judgmental attitude Marina inflicted upon herself.

Yet, after their few meetings, Marina had been seized by even greater inhibitions and had worried over each confidence given. Arthur's ashes had hardly been cold when she had burst into little betrayals. Helena's eyebrow had shot up at incriminating evidences. What had possessed her to stay for so long in such an abusive relationship? Marina hoped that Helena did not think she was a masochist. It had been more a lack of confidence, she thought. He had a murderous tongue, and she had come to believe that everything he said about her was true. So where could she have gone or what could she have done? There was no way of going home to Maddy. Papa had died and the inference had been from Maddy that she had killed him. And then Maddy had died herself and Marina had no place to go. Yet, deep down, she knew that she had an independent income and could have gone, and should have gone, for in the eyes of the Church she had branded herself as an adulteress. None of this had she told Helena, but it had simmered and pricked at her all the same that Helena had asked the obvious question to which there was no direct or obvious reply.

Timidly, Marina sometimes hoped that she had loved Arthur. The best and most honest answer she could give was that the *Cycle* had created between them a most peculiar bond. Once, she had told Helena, Arthur, while drunk, had mocked what he had called an unwholesome preoccupation with her parentage. 'Here I have given you an Olympian origin,' he had said, 'made you a perpetual metaphor for love, and you want to reduce it to a squalid clinch between a soldier and a barmaid!' This she had confided over quiche and salad in Peter Jones, and Helena had listened like a priest. Sometimes, Marina thought that Arthur had tried to eradicate every single aspect of her personality but the one he wanted to see, one that had nothing to do with her at all, but with some other woman of his imagination.

Marina rapidly changed the subject in her mind. She did not know Russians socially. She did not know what to expect from Russians or what they might expect from her. She had found the English difficult enough to construe, and had never been a success with them, partly because she really had never got to know an awful lot of them. When first they were married, she had thought Arthur would want her to give dinner parties, but he had said he was trying to get away from all that. Bit by bit it had dawned on her that he thought her a fool and not up to his friends. However, when they had gone abroad, he had polished her and trotted her out. She had met no Russians abroad. On their third meeting, she had tried to pump Helena on what would be acceptable behaviour to her Russian family. Marina had a compulsion to give pleasure. Helena would not say. Then Marina had blurted out that she had once told Arthur that she thought she might have Russian origins, and he had laughed and teased her about the Archduchess Anastasia, who seemed to pop up in the press from time to time. This had been when they had been getting on together, but he had instructed her on the lack of taste such a fantasy evinced. Royal Russians, novelettish Russians, cheap Russians. Helena had raised an eyebrow to that. 'Whatever you can say about my family,' she had retorted, 'and you can say a great deal, Aunt Sonya can and *does* trace our ancestry back to the eleventh century. Cheap, we are not!' Then, Marina had struggled to reassure her that in no way had she meant to cast aspersions on Helena's family, and Helena had seemed surprised and had said, 'No, no. I was thinking about Arthur and how Arthur might have really seen me.' Then Marina had gone into a thing about how Arthur had sometimes spoken of her, but only with admiration, and Helena had seemed pleased.

Marina suddenly wondered if she had lost her ring. She knew she was putting off the essential moment when she must descend and introduce herself to the company at large, but the vision of the ring popped into her head. For some reason, she had bought the ring for herself during the time Arthur was ill – at Harrods, even though Arthur disapproved of Harrods, and she supposed she did too, more or less. It had been an irrational thing to do, to buy a piece of jewellery for herself. The ring was a moonstone set in platinum. It was quite old, but not very, though they had called it an antique at Harrods and it had been very expensive. She had concealed it from Arthur and had worn it only on jaunts to the shops. She now rummaged through her case, found it and put it on her right ring finger. It nestled on her fair hand. The stone was round and glowing, with more mystery than a pearl to it, Marina thought. She looked at Arthur's ring on her other hand, a thick, ornate band of gold. She spread her hands, then brushed out her hair again. It was quite dry by now, and it sparkled with static – a blonde cloud. She looked out of the window again at the vista of blank, white arcades, then back at her hair in the mirror. She wondered if she was English in origin, perhaps Scandanavian with her hair, but not the bone structure. She wondered about her father. In any case, she had always been more interested in finding her mother.

Now, a clear image of the detective she had hired came to her mind. The detective was a woman, and this pleased Marina. The detective was quite smart; she wore good clothes. She was part of a firm with offices on Madison Avenue. She had a word processor and a computer and had conjured things up on these screens while Marina's stomach had turned over and over. Sometimes Marina wondered if she had missed the twentieth century, for the soft click and quiet hum of the machines were foreign to her. In confused dreams after Arthur's death, she had found herself searching among the dead, not for him, but for her mother – her real mother – as in childhood she had often done, searching in the depths of death for her, searching limitless, unlabelled filing cabinets, cold, impersonal, like morgue drawers, stretched as far as the dreaming eye could see to a vanishing point beyond vanishing point, and it had been in the anonymity of these files that her birth certificate lay. As a child, she had searched the world of the living, too, for her mother's face. She had searched crowds on subways for a resembling face. Of all people, on the occasion of Arthur's death, she had wanted her mother. The detective had forced an intimacy into the situation from the outset and had said, 'Call me Frances,' and had called Marina 'Marina'. At the end of the interview, Marina had been pitifully glad of this and thought of her as 'Frances' now. Frances searching.

Marina still felt terrible about Maddy, her adoptive mother. Madeline Horner, that sunny beauty, New York charmer and dearest friend. Until, of course, Marina had done a bunk with Arthur. Then the wheels of Maddy's Catholic piety had turned juggernaut and crushed the bond between them. That had been Arthur's view. Or had Marina herself crushed the bond? Sometimes she did wonder. At any rate, 'exactly like your mother' had not been said by Maddy, but it had hung in the air. Maddy had shrunk with age and in bitterness at Marina's sin. Now, Marina knew something about Maddy that she had not known at the time, and she sometimes wanted to go beyond the grave and hug her. She wished she could dream of that too. She wished that the soul could do that, fly down and comfort the dead. She had had Masses said, but it was not the same as a personal confrontation. Maddy's whole outlook had been 'baby, baby, baby', and she had married with a view to ten children and had never dreamt of less. She had come from an enormous French family and she had married *very* well, into the 'Four Hundred'. Marina's adoptive father had never been very close to anyone, she often thought. Oh, they had tried and tried. Marina had been taken in only after even Lourdes had been tried. Maddy had been forty when Marina was adopted. What Marina wanted to tell Maddy now was that she understood how desperate one could be for a baby. She had nagged Arthur so much about it that he had finally gone and got a vasectomy. She had wept a lot and had even thought of leaving him then, but in the last analysis she could not go. It had occurred to her more than once that he had some knowledge of her genetic make-up. Often, she thought he knew who she really was and had concealed it from her. Above all though, he had had a dense, hypnotic power of the mind, which had always seemed to paralyze her will.

After Arthur's funeral, she had put Maddy's portrait away along with his, and this was because she had strained so after some visionary dream of her real mother. It had been unspoken but clear that questions about her real mother were unforgivable blasphemies against Maddy's

54

more than adequate love. Sometimes, she wondered if Maddy and Arthur had had more in common than they had chosen to see.

Who was she? Whose baby had she been? Whoever or whatever, Marina's mother had not been barren like Maddy or like Marina herself. Instead, she had borne Marina, and bad fruit suggested a bad tree. She was probably dead, and a large part of Marina wished this to be so.

Helena, past child-bearing age, had never been anybody's mother, and this gave her a curious weightlessness in Marina's eyes – an incapacity for sin. She remembered shopping for a coat at Peck and Peck with Maddy once. Maddy had been so proud of Marina's beauty. She remembered looking at herself in the pricey coat. Maddy had murmured in that half-conscious way she sometimes had, 'It was a *felix culpa* – a happy fault – her sin that gave me you!'

Maybe Helena did have children and like her own mother had given them away. Marina sometimes imagined that apparently childless women had secret children. She knew such imaginings were foolish, but she had them anyway. Marina was sure that she did not look a thing like Helena. She did not resemble her at all. In any case, one of the lofty things about Helena was this quality of being above the process of breeding. Sometimes, Marina came across the veiled figure of a bride in her dreams and knew it to be her real mother. The veil was always so heavy that she could never see anything but the ghost of features.

As for the business of her mother being Russian, Marina herself was puzzled by why she said it to people – the few she had told. She had never really believed it. When she was at school, she had told selected girls in order to sound glamorous and romantic. 'My mother was a Russian princess, you know. At least, there is evidence,' she had said to an awed friend once, and then had gone to confession and admitted the lie and owned up to the friend, who, to her secret gratification, had still believed it anyway. They had seen Audrey Hepburn play Natasha Rostov in *War and Peace*, and Audrey Hepburn had been what Marina had wanted to look like, only she was blonde and a lot fatter. That was how it had started. It had gone on, Marina thought, because Russia had always felt illegitimate in the United States. It was on the wrong side of the blanket and had a rich, indecipherable language. There were haunting pictures, too, of the Virgin Mother, solemn, wise, inaccessible and transcendent. Marina had always had a deep devotion to the Virgin and even when she had done the worst possible thing, she trusted Her and maintained a secret place where Arthur could not find Her. Marina spoke to Her when she did not dare lift her eyes up to God.

Marina did not count herself a liar, so why had she told Helena the night of Arthur's funeral that she thought her mother was Russian? A Russian noblewoman had been implied. Deep down, Marina thought she had the soul of a peasant. Arthur had thought so. Maybe she had wanted Helena to see her as an equal, but now the whole thing was about to get out of hand, which was what happened if you deceived people. She had tried to set the record straight with Helena, but she was not sure Helena had been listening that time at Peter Jones. Marina did not look like a peasant, though. That, she knew.

Well, she had mentioned this latest untruth in one of her serial confessions of the same sin, her adulterous liaison with Arthur, but she could not remember what had been said. One of the reasons she had gone to see Frances the detective had been to set the record straight. Marina had always had the strong feeling that she should *act* truthfully. Even when she had married Arthur she had thought she had been acting truthfully, for he had persuaded her that her scruples were based on lies and hypocrisy. In the case of fooling Helena, Marina had thought that she ought to follow the path that led to truth in order to make up for her chance, compulsive remark. At one time, she really had thought this Russian thing about her mother. It was equally true that she had considered Audrey Hepburn. She had also imagined her a suburban housewife with too many children or, a young victim of incest or rape. Whoever she was, she had abandoned and rejected Marina. On good days, Marina wondered if her mother had been forced to give her up by unforgiving parents.

All her life, she had heard or read that adopted children longed to know. What about the risk? She had heard stories of terrible women who had flung their children out only to reappear when later these had prospered. She had heard of people searching for their mothers, finding mothers who had rejected them again or wanted cash. Marina's reverence for her mother was a spiritual thing. She had come to believe that carnal truth was seldom pleasant. Was her mother a prostitute? Did these not die young? Maybe her mother had died of untreated syphilis or a knife wound. And now there was AIDS. Marina knew there were such things as child prostitutes. Maybe her mother had been only eleven or twelve when Marina had been born. She could see herself being born on a table in Hell's Kitchen. Maybe her mother was only fifty-two now. Maybe she was dying of AIDS. Sometimes she had fantasies of going to comfort her mother dying of AIDS in a hot bedroom buzzing with flies. In this particular scenario an emotional rescue would follow. The best medical care provided. Nothing too much. A grateful mother with gaunt eyes, telling all and sundry how her daughter had saved her soul.

Frances had offered Marina Kleenex and genuine sympathy. She had explained a lot of things about adoption laws. Apparently, it was unlikely that a birth certificate issued in 1948 could ever be found. Marina had an affidavit showing her to be the Horners' adopted child, and with this she had obtained her passport. When Frances had told her that she might have to remain content with this, the terrible distress had hit her. The aching loneliness still bit when she thought of never having a legal validation of herself. It was the opinion of Frances, however, that Marina had been privately adopted, and this was because her parents had been so unusually old. So, lists had been dredged up between them of family friends, old doctors, parish priests. Frances considered the clue of her being a Catholic a strong one. 'They stick together, you know,' the detective had said, not meaning to offend. Still, Marina clung to this evidence hard. 'You know,' Frances had said, 'most of the time it's only teenagers, who just didn't know what they were doing.' And Marina had thought of herself, when virtually a teenager she had married Arthur.

Finally, Marina decided that she must go downstairs whatever the social embarrassment. Suppose she were to disturb the invalid Princess? She could always apologize. Before Arthur's death and her present bewilderment, she really had had some savoir-faire. It was snobby and absurd to think that the old lady was different from anyone else. Helena was probably downstairs in any case, and, after all, they were supposed to be friends. Marina hated the abysmal way she sometimes crept about. Nonetheless, she left the room on tiptoe and listened at the top of the stairs. There was silence. She descended as if she were walking on eggs, all the while formulating excuses for her bad manners at arising late and some explanation, too, which would justify the intolerability of her being there at all. In the downstairs hall, she listened for signs of movement behind closed doors, but there was not a sound. There was a tallboy in the hall, intricately covered with painted flowers. The floor was tiled, immaculate, and there was the faint smell of herbs and cleanliness about the house. At length, not knowing what to do, she ventured through a side-door she spotted. Through it she could see some trees. She soon found herself on a broad terrace. It was the upper part of a walled garden, well-kept and surprisingly lush in the heat. Marina was struck by its loveliness. It was almost cool, sequestered by a large plane tree that stood in the lower half. There were other, smaller trees as well, perhaps olive, fig or lemon trees, and there was a profusion of flowers. Bougainvillaea climbed the walls – at least, she thought it was bougainvillaea. Cicadas chirped and there was the humming sound of bees. Marina found her toiling mind arrested and soothed. A small breeze sifted through the leaves, creating dappled, darting light on the worn flagstones. It was perhaps this that moved her to say aloud, 'What a beautiful garden!'

'It is, isn't it?' a man's voice made her jump.

'Oh!' she cried, putting her hand to her mouth. She had drifted all the way down to the lower terrace without seeing him.

'Sorry. Did I frighten you?' the man asked. He was sitting under an arbour of delicate vines with budding grapes and little tendrils and he had been reading a book. He wore a tropical suit and a Panama hat. He stood formally to greet her. 'My name is Paul Mason,' he said. 'You must be Marina Holt.' He doffed his hat. Marina had not seen such a gesture in a long time, and it gave him a quaint air. He was somewhere in his middle years, but his age was hard to guess, for he was thin and very tanned, as if he had spent a long time working in the open. His hair was iron grey and his face had a thoughtful cast. Either from his dress or his manner, he struck Marina at once as being unusual. He had a direct, open expression. Marina usually avoided people's eyes, but she felt comfortable looking into his. 'Yes, I am,' she said in a definite tone. 'And you didn't frighten me. You only gave me a start.' She felt completely unclear as to who he was and why he was there. At first sight, she had taken him for Helena's cousin.

Mason raised his eyes quizzically, and this gave a touch of humour to his otherwise sombre features. He put his finger to his lips and pointed to a space behind her. On the upper terrace, sitting underneath a large fig tree, was the oldest woman Marina had ever seen. She was swathed from head to foot in a complicated arrangement of hat and veils. She was seated in an old-fashioned wheelchair with a high, wicker back, and she was fast asleep. Someone had arranged a parasol over her head, despite the shade she already had from the veils and tree, and Marina realized she had missed noticing her because she was almost camouflaged. Her very white skin was withered and shrunken into her skull, her eyes, hooded and sunken into her head. But even in sleep, her jaw was resolutely shut, as if everything but her will had abandoned her. She had a shocking look, as though she had taken an evolutionary turn backwards and had become at one with some reptilian creature for which there was no name. Marina was greatly surprised at her appearance. She realized that this must be the Princess, but she had expected someone rather different. She turned back to Mason. He nodded and gave her a thin little smile, and together they looked again at the old lady.

All at once, the Princess opened her eyelids and looked at the pair who stood watching her from under the plane tree in the lower garden. She seemed elevated above them, perched as she was on the upper terrace. She glared in a bright, angry way, as if to signify that she had known they had been there all along and as if they had no right to stare at her. Marina's heart thumped, and she began to tremble under the gaze of the Princess, but her companion appeared to take no notice of the apparent hostility in the look. 'Oh, she's awake now,' he said. 'I suppose you had better go and meet her. Did you have a tiring journey? I hope you slept well.' A large, yellow butterfly rose from a pot of scarlet geraniums near them. The pot, of terracotta, bore a Triton's head.

Marina reddened with embarrassment. 'I'm afraid I overslept,' she said woefully, 'and now I have woken this poor lady.' She really had no idea who this man was, but he seemed quite at home, and seemed, too, to be cognizant of her identity and general movements. 'Do you know where Helena is?' she added miserably. The old woman still blinked balefully at them.

'I understand she has gone down to Skala.' Mason winced slightly. 'She left word with Evangalia that I was to look after you when you woke.' He seemed to peer directly into Marina's self-consciousness at this remark and her shyness in general. 'Not that I mind at all looking after you!'

'Oh dear, she'll be upset with me.'

'I shouldn't think so,' Mason said dryly. 'My observation of her is that she does not upset very easily.' Marina began to think him a rather crabbed and waspish character. 'To be fair,' he added, as if sensing her thoughts, 'Evangalia seemed to think my friend Serge had upset her and that is why she went to Skala. Not a word, mind, to the Princess!'

'Oh, you're Serge's friend! I mean Helena's cousin's friend.' She felt less confused.

'Oh, didn't she tell you about me? I *am* sorry. No wonder you looked bewildered. I suppose Serge is my oldest friend. We knew each other at school.'

The old lady cleared her throat in a somewhat peremptory manner.

'As for Sophia Petrovna,' Mason continued, 'I shouldn't worry about her either. Certainly not about waking her. She dozes off and on the whole time.' Marina hoped the Princess could not hear this. 'She has a poor opinion of her health, but she's in pretty good nick, considering that she is in her nineties . . . I'm a doctor,' he added by way of explanation.

'It must be convenient, having you to stay,' Marina said.

Mason's lip twitched at this remark and he laughed, bewildering Marina even more. She had formed the impression, for some reason, that he took life hard, and his sudden humour seemed at odds with the somewhat dismal expression in his eyes. But she turned her attention to the Princess as he guided her up the steps to be introduced.

'Princess!' he hollered, 'I would like to present Marina Holt to you.'

The Princess looked keenly at Marina. Although awed by the very ancient woman, Marina felt a curious interest in Mason. Despite his rather abrupt manner, she sensed him as a definite and agreeable presence. There was a coolness in him. Although his manner to the Princess was very polite, Marina felt something sharp emanating from him like a cutting shadow. The Princess extended her hand to Marina and scowled at the sunlight.

'I am terribly sorry I disturbed you,' said Marina after they had greeted one another.

'It makes no difference,' the Princess replied abruptly. She had a strong Russian accent. 'Do sit down.'

Marina arranged herself tentatively on one of a group of chairs set around a table near the Princess, but this made communication somewhat difficult. They craned their necks and peered at each other.

'Paul will get you a cup of coffee,' the old lady said.

Paul paused for a moment.

'Oh, please don't,' said Marina. 'I really don't need . . .'

'I don't mind getting coffee,' he said. 'I imagine you will need it.'

'Where is Serge?' the old woman demanded. Close to, Marina saw the Princess's face in a different light. Age had had its way with her, but it was possible to see a beauty in the angle of eyes and bones.

'He's gone out, I believe. You know I go out walking early every morning. I went all the way up Mt St Elias today. There is a wonderful view.'

'He went with you up Mt St Elias?'

'No. I said I missed him as I went out walking too early for him.'

'He should have gone with you,' the Princess said darkly. Marina realized that she was quite deaf.

'I have the impression he is in Skala with Helena. Maybe they are shopping.' He enunciated these words, Marina noticed, not in the patronizing tone usually reserved for the old, nor in an overly respectful way either. She was subtly relieved to find herself with someone so straightforward.

'Shopping? What shopping is there to do? Tanya does the shopping, or Evangalia.'

'I am afraid I did not ask them,' Paul said as he retreated into the house. He left the book he was carrying on the table which lay between Marina and the Princess.

Immediately he was gone, the old woman gathered up her forces, leaned forward and jabbed her finger at the book. 'What is that? What is he reading? Is it the Bible?' she asked Marina.

Marina picked up the book an old, leather-bound volume. 'I can't tell. It is written in Greek,' she said.

'Eh?' said the Princess. 'A Greek Bible?'

'I do not know if it is a Bible. It is in Greek and I cannot read it,' Marina repeated loudly.

'Neither can I,' said the Princess. 'I do not read Greek, and I speak it very badly.' The two women looked at each other. The Princess stared at Marina and Marina looked down at her hands.

'Do you speak Russian? Do you read it?' the old lady asked.

'A little,' Marina answered. 'I learned a little at college. Not much.' There was something of a talking skull about the Princess, as if from under her fig tree she fathomed secrets. Marina was transfixed by her inquisitorial look.

'Helena said you were Russian.' She inspected Marina more closely. 'You do not *look* Russian.'

'Don't I?' Marina felt ashamed of herself almost to the point of tears.

'Say something in Russian to me!' said the Princess.

Marina's mind and lips froze. '*Kak Vi Pazhavayetsee?*' she muttered at last.

'Sophia Petrovna!' said the Princess. 'It is rude to say just "*Kak Vi Pazhevayetsee*" like that without a name – especially to an older person.'

'I'm sorry,' said Marina. 'I did not know.'

'That is all right. You have a terrible accent. They do not teach it well. Your parents are not Russian, otherwise you would speak better.

61

Or are they? Some parents will not let their children speak the language.'

'I am afraid I do not know if they were Russian or not,' said Marina. She swallowed hard to keep from crying. 'I am not sure it matters anymore.'

The Princess gave a sly smile. 'Why do you say that? Of course, it matters who you are.'

A breeze sighed and made the light shift about their heads.

'I was adopted,' Marina said. 'I do not know who my parents are,' she added distinctly.

'Helena told me you were Russian. I thought you would read to me.'

'I'm sorry,' Marina said wildly. 'I should not have come.'

The Princess ignored this remark. 'Are you married? Helena said something about your husband. An English writer. But you are not English. You sound like an American to me.'

'I am a widow,' Marina said. 'My husband died. He was a poet.' Suddenly, she felt proud of Arthur's distinction and angry at the old lady. 'His name was Arthur Holt. He was very well known.'

'Hmpf,' said the Princess. 'My husband also died. It is sad. Did he leave you any money?'

Marina flushed to the roots of her hair, really feeling now that it was hard to answer politely. 'Yes,' she said, 'he left me money.'

'My husband left me penniless,' said the old woman.

At this point, Mason emerged from the house bearing a tray. It was evident that he had overheard some of the conversation, for he said sotto voce to Marina, 'Why don't you give her a breakdown of your annual income?' He deposited the tray firmly on the table.

A manservant darted from the house, skirted the Princess's chair nervously, then vanished into the garden where, after a moment, he reappeared with a large watering can. He fussed around the flowers for a few minutes, looked in an unsettled way over his shoulder at the company assembled on the terrace, then fell to his task and ignored them.

'This young woman may be Russian,' said the Princess. 'Maybe she is Russian and maybe she is not.'

Mason narrowed his eyes and looked at the Princess. 'I have never been a Russian in my life,' he said. 'I'll admit it has been a cross, but I have borne it.'

The Princess glared silently.

'I have brought you some juice,' he said. 'It is better for you than coffee.' He handed her the glass. Her bone hands shook around it, and he gently helped her to drink.

'Mrs Holt and I were wondering if you were reading the Bible in Greek,' said the Princess, with a guarded, sly look at Marina. Marina was embarrassed at having this speculation attributed to her, especially as she was grateful to Mason for having bailed her out.

'Why should you wonder that?' he asked somewhat sharply.

'I suppose you read the Latin one,' said the Princess. 'You are a Catholic. I forgot. I always think you are Orthodox.'

Marina shrank before this revelation of a co-religionist. Her heart sank to think she would have to spend the summer proving herself on this score.

'It's not a Bible, and if I read it, I read it in English,' he said, picking up the contentious book from the table. He looked very uncomfortable for some reason. 'I simply got this from the bookcase in the house. It appears to be about Ephesus, across the water. In Turkey. I was hoping to make an excursion there soon.'

'You are very clever to read Greek,' said the old woman. Her eyes became more hooded, and she leaned back in the chair, either soothed by the juice or tired out by the conversation. Marina wondered what she was angling at. At the same time, she felt an obscure affinity between the two, and an affection.

'Not at all. I am not clever,' Paul said gruffly.

'If you know Greek, maybe you can speak to Dmitris,' said the Princess, waving her hand towards the man who was watering the flowers. 'Everything I tell him to do he does wrong. He may not understand me. Lena speaks Greek, but she does not . . . communicate . . . what I want.'

'I do not know modern Greek,' Paul said. Marina thought his patience was wearing thin. 'This is an old text.'

'Is it Pausanias?' Marina asked deferentially. She added, 'My husband was a keen classicist.'

'No, it is not Pausanias,' he said, brightening. 'I did Greek at school, and I was only trying to see how much I remembered. The sad fact is that I can only make out enough words to see that it is about Ephesus. St Paul preached there, and it was one of the seven churches in the Book of Revelations.'

Marina knew this, but was silent. She wondered if he knew the scandal surrounding her marriage. He was probably husband to a proper wife and the father of a large family. In her mind's eye, she could see him driving a large car crammed with children to Mass, his fruitful wife beside him. Suddenly, she felt as if she were wearing a scarlet dress with a slash up the thigh.

'The Temple of Artemis there is one of the seven wonders of the ancient world,' he continued, oblivious to her discomfort. 'They say, too, that the Virgin was assumed into Heaven there. A friend of mine in Africa told me I must see it when he learned I was coming here.'

'Oh, I would love to see that,' Marina said, but blushed, feeling that she had presumed upon his projected outing.

'Well, we must make an expedition of it,' he said, withdrawing.

'What is this about Africa? You are going back to Africa? You have only been here a few days,' the Princess crossly intervened.

Mason said, 'I did not say I was going back to Africa. I have no idea whether or not I am going back.' He sounded quite edgy himself. He turned to Marina again. 'I have been working for the Red Cross in Ethiopia, but I decided I must go back to England for a while. I am taking my own good advice.'

Marina felt awe for people who did conspicuous good works. The image of paterfamilias receded, and at once she saw in him the lambent ferocity that attends heroic figures. He sipped his coffee. Sitting with someone who must have seen such terrible famine made her resist drinking hers, although she wanted it and he had made it. She felt like reaching for her handbag and thrusting drachmas into his hand. 'Oh, that must have been *awful*!' she said instead, 'And you must be exhausted.'

He gave her a swift look of appreciation, surprising in its depth. 'It was awful and I am exhausted,' he said. 'Drained.'

She felt he was about to say more, but he evidently thought better of it. Images of dried resource came to Marina, of wells and streams shut off. While Arthur was dying, she had seen reports of the famine on television. It had seemed to be of a piece with her husband's unhealthy stillness, his nightmares and his groaning. She put her hand to her cheek. A glimpse of an expression in Mason's eyes made her like him in spite of his virtue. Nonetheless, it troubled Marina that good people made her feel so bad, and she accused herself of envying them.

All at once, Helena arrived. She stood in the doorway of the garden for a moment, then entered. 'Ah, Marina!' she said, almost breathing the name. Marina would have risen to embrace her, but she moved swiftly across the terrace with an acute grace in her thin, grey dress.

Her cap of silver hair shone in the sun. Marina vaguely wondered if she had ever been a dancer. Helena scooped a kiss out of the air next to Marina's cheek. 'Did you sleep well? You do look refreshed. I see you have had coffee. I left you to rest . . . you looked so tired last night . . .' But before Marina could reply to any of these questions, Helena turned to her aunt. 'Tyotya, you have *met* Marina!' she exclaimed, as if it had been all the Princess's privilege to do so. 'I brought you some chocolate from Skala,' she said to the old woman, and she undid a little gold parcel from a string bag. The Princess looked mildly astonished at this gesture, but it seemed to please her. 'There!' Helena said, placing the box on her aunt's lap. And then the whole weight and beam of herself shifted to Marina. 'I see you have met Paul, too,' she said.

Marina observed that Paul's expression had soured at Helena's entrance, but this little interchange seemed to amuse him. He gave a thin smile and drummed his fingers on the tabletop.

'Where is Sergei?' The Princess suddenly demanded of Helena.

'Tyotya, you will never guess!' said Helena turning. She always moved as if the base of her spine were a fulcrum. 'Poor Serge, he met some English friends in the harbour. They had just come off their yacht. They are in Patmos only for the day and there was no way he could prevent them giving him lunch. I left him rolling his eyes to Heaven, but there was no way out of it. I think he met them at Cowes one year with Fiona.'

'Cowes, eh?' said the old woman dryly. With a shaky hand, she removed the chocolates from her lap and placed them on the table. She and Helena stared at each other, and the air quivered for a moment with their mutual dislike.

'He is having lunch in Skala,' Helena said, enunciating every word with a tightened jaw.

'Well, he should have been here to meet Marina,' the Princess said, changing tack. 'It was very rude, my dear,' she added, and she gave the startled Marina an appraising look like a jeweller who has found a good stone.

Helena suddenly released her back, and bestowed an intense smile upon her aunt. 'Yes, it was rude,' she said. 'It was very rude indeed.'

VI

HELENA HAD ARRANGED for lunch in the garden, and the table, set with deep-glazed pottery plates and silver, had something of a festive look. Actually, Dmitris had knocked together some trestles and boards, which Evangalia had covered with a blue linen cloth; it fluttered in a little breeze that had got up, despite its starched creases. The plates, of unknown origin, were thick and yellow. Patterns of swelling fruit and leaves swirled upon them, and they seemed to nestle in the linen. Everything had been set out so that the plane tree shaded the diners from the sun, which glinted through the leaves, making the glass and silver sparkle. There were shining carafes of wine and water and loaves of dense, Greek bread. The company had already consumed a platter of special mezze that Evangalia had made, rich dolmades in fine oil, aubergines and mushrooms, little meatballs and houmous too, creamy and thick.

The Princess sat nodding and smiling in her wicker chair at the head of the table. Helena could not imagine what Marina had said to her aunt to put her in such an expansive mood. Indeed, she had insisted that Marina be seated on her right, and this was rather more than Helena had hoped for – too much, in fact. Her aunt was doing her old snake dance and had flattered and charmed Marina, who took in every word she said with a deferential pleasure. She chatted and shouted to the Princess, fielding her aunt's barmy observations as if she had been born to the task. Helena hated the way the old woman's mind jumped about, making bizarre connections, but Marina seemed to be pleased with these senile intuitions. On the other hand, it subtly gratified Helena that Marina met with her aunt's approval. Marina's carriage, her manners, her deportment suggested an affiliation with the old values of a charmed circle from which Helena herself had come. Helena had strong socialist leanings, but from time to time, the assessment of others according to class popped out unbidden. Because of her aunt, she thought, she thanked her lucky stars that Marina was a lady. All of this soothed Helena in a way she did not recognize. She even felt an appetite for the stuffed fish Evangalia was bringing to the table.

She had had a frightful morning. After a sleepless night, she had risen at nine only to find her cousin Serge sprawled upon the stairs quite drunk. She could not believe he was doing this to her. If Helena trusted anyone it was Serge. They had been allies since childhood. Although they saw each other infrequently back in England (Helena did not like his wife), and although they often bickered during their sojourns in Patmos, Helena always thought that in a fundamental way they never needed to justify themselves to each other. Normally, she was fairly indulgent of his drinking. She thought he drank because of his mother. But in the past, he had always confined his bingeing to convenient times and places. This summer there was a marked difference in him, and he had been hitting the bottle whenever the mood struck him. She had been furious at him that it had struck him that morning, and for about an hour, she had taken him apart.

For weeks, she had been plotting this moment in the garden under the plane tree down to each detail of china and of menu. Of course, she had not told him so in so many words, but Serge was no stranger to her moods, and he had observed her anxiety about Marina's arrival. The thought of his lurching into her luncheon party had been the stuff of nightmare, particularly as she had been concealing his peccadillos from his mother ever since he had come. She could not think what had possessed him. What was more, her general dislike of Paul had been sharpened by his absence from the crisis that morning. In spite of Serge's long-standing association with them both, Helena and Paul had met only at Serge's wedding and at the christenings of his various children, and now she could see the reason.

Helena had an almost chemical antipathy to men of Paul's type. 'Worthies', she called them. They gave off a scent of self-righteousness, which masked, she often thought, personal failure. What annoyed her most of all, was that Paul had asked himself to stay. She thought he preyed on Serge's weak open-handedness, and probably always had. Of course, he made himself useful as a general physician to her aunt, but for a self-invited guest, he had a fairly presumptuous store of reproachful looks, and he seemed to have little or no effect on Serge's drinking. That morning when she had needed him to take control of Serge, he was nowhere to be found, and she had been left with the unpleasant task of trying to sober him up. She realized she had panicked, but her first thought had been to get Serge out of the house before his mother saw him. She had plied him with black coffee and had marched him down to Skala in the fresh air. She rather hoped that some of his Greek drinking buddies had witnessed this edifying scene, for through the white streets of Hora and down the snaking road to the port, she had made her displeasure felt in a way that needed no translation. The Greeks liked Serge and were tolerant of his excesses, but she knew in the last analysis that they would know she was in the right and would think less of him, too, for having been henpecked.

It was unfortunate, however, that when they had got to Skala she had lost him, truly, as it happened, amongst the yachting fraternity. She had turned her back for a moment, and had last seen him disappearing into one of the boats – a Greek tub – where one of his cronies, she imagined, would set him up with another beer or brandy. She doubted he would turn up drunk for lunch, but he had to be found and sobered before nightfall. This task she intended to give to Paul as soon as she got the opportunity.

It was he whom she observed now. In Marina's presence, he had blossomed into a raconteur, and he was chatting away about the sights and sounds of the island. It seemed he had been everywhere on his hikes. He was telling Marina the legend of a wizard called Kynops, a devoté of Artemis to whom Patmos had been sacred in pagan times. A huge theological slanging match had taken place between Kynops and St John. Kynops had lost and had been turned to stone. It was said that his petrified corpse still threatened the hulls of boats in the harbour and, to the west of the island, there was a cave of this ancient shaman where locals still feared to go. Paul thought he had found it in the bleak face of a cliff, and though he had come to no harm, he had been somewhat startled by the presence of some black goats which had surrounded him, he thought, with malevolent intent.

Helena noticed that Marina was lapping up this story, and she capped it with one of her own about a visit to the Peloponnese with Arthur where they had seen the gate to Hades through which Dionysius had passed to rescue his mother Semele. As Marina made a graceful gesture in the air with her hand to articulate some point or other, Helena thought sharply of Arthur. She could see Marina and Arthur together in the shady dale of Hell Marina was describing. Arthur, she thought, if only you could see her now. If only I could have seen you then. Arthur? Yet, the moment his name occurred, the moment she summoned him to her imagination, something unwelcome came with it, a nauseated, stifling feeling that had gripped her earlier when shortly after waking, she had tiptoed to Marina's room and opened the door a crack. Helena had stood and watched Marina sleeping. Why had she done this invading thing? She simply had. She had had the overpowering urge to check something. What had it been? And she had seen Marina abandoned to dreams, her arm outflung, her mouth open. She had been wearing a white nightdress, embroidered with white roses. Thinking of Arthur, Helena had returned to her room, had dressed in her grey, linen frock, then had trudged down the hall with the dull sound of his name in her mind and the fresh memory of his widow tangled in white and death-like sleep. And at this point she had encountered Serge on the stairs.

Helena observed that her aunt had been lightly dozing during Marina's canter into myth. Suddenly, her eyes snapped open, and she fixed Marina with a piercing gaze. 'And did you come far?' the Princess boomed in a voice so abrupt that the table fell silent. It was increasingly her aunt's wont to make disjunctive remarks. Artificial social niceties would swim to her lips unbidden nowadays like pre-recorded messages on an answering machine. Having spoken, her aunt stabbed at a piece of fish and ate it greedily.

'Yes. I came from quite far away. I came all the way from New York,' said Marina pronouncing her words carefully.

To the Princess's left, and seated slightly to one side of her, the au pair, Tanya Wood perched on a chair as if to show that she was really not a member of the company. A student of Russian at Helena's college, Tanya was ensconced for the summer to mind the old lady. Helena had carefully chosen and hired her. She irritated Helena but the Princess liked her well enough. She was a plain young woman with a bad complexion and she performed numerous functions for the Princess. At mealtimes, she would cut up the old lady's food into little pieces and would pat her mouth with a starched napkin. The Princess sometimes had fits of trembling, which made her unable to feed herself adequately at times. Tanya's presence was so discreet that it seemed as if she were hardly there at all, and so the strange impression was given that the Princess had four hands – an extra pair of arms – and that they behaved in a perfectly synchronized fashion. It was as if she controlled them all, Helena thought.

'*Chto?*' the Princess asked, turning to Tanya.

'*Ona pree-yekala eez New Yorka,*' said Tanya in a piercing murmur, which apparently the Princess understood.

'Oh, you came from *New York!*' the Princess exclaimed. 'A very long way. I had some very good friends there, but they are dead now,' she said, and she looked quite sad.

69

Marina smiled at Tanya in thanks for the translation and Tanya, pleased, lowered her eyes.

Marina was dressed in white now, too, in a rich, flowing dress with sleeves. It looked like a cut-down bridal gown. It was Marina's perfectly elevated throat, her jaw just slightly slackened with age, that made Helena quiver. There she was in final bloom, surely in her last flaring of beauty before the dark descent into sagging flesh. She took a sip of cool, white, honeyed wine, and Helena observed her swallowing. Where had Marina put Arthur's portrait of her, Helena wondered, for surely it must be somewhere in her personality? This gentle Marina, who got on with Aunt and Paul and Tanya, who smiled and made thoughtful remarks, must be a blind for the other one portrayed by Arthur. Of course, she knew it was absurd to put too strong an autobiographical case for his work, but all the same it teased her. And the rank, dark, sensual goddess of Arthur's poems almost seemed to lick her lips before Helena's mind's eye. In a smile, both whorish and perverse, she seemed to undulate herself forward, as if she were the shadow that Marina's hand cast.

'Marina,' Paul said. Everyone turned to look at him. He was sitting next to Marina. He appeared to forget what he was about to say. It was as if he had mentioned her name for the sake of it. He had taken his hat off because he was at table, but the band had left a mark, and he rubbed his temple there. 'Marina, New York is a long way from London. I thought you lived in London.'

Helena was amused at his nervous smile and at the way the words came gruffly from his throat like an adolescent boy. Her aunt loved to say he was a saint. Helena had no patience with saints, but thought she had certainly not met one in Paul. On his arrival, she had found him remote and curt. From time to time, he made biting remarks which she did not associate with saintly diction. On those evenings when she had dined out with him and Serge, there had always been that sense that certain things could not be said because he might think them frivolous. Helena herself disliked frivolity, but her definition of it was different. Of course, it was a virtue to help the starving Africans, but the fact was that she had made a large contribution to the Disaster Appeal without the benefit of a label on the cheque. She suspected him of a self-regarding piety, and this was why she enjoyed the way his head lunged forward as he spoke Marina's name, the way he perked up in the presence of a pretty woman. It was irrational, she knew, to associate any sordid motive with him for this, for he was a bachelor, but she made this attribution nonetheless. Helena thought denial of the flesh went hand in hand with prayer and other forms of lying, and she liked to see the truth arise in Paul.

'I do come from London,' Marina said. She drank a sip of sparkling water, 'but I had some things to do before I got here.' All at once, she looked across the table at Helena, directly into her eyes. A sudden intensity seemed to possess her. 'I couldn't find it in myself to talk about it last night,' she said, 'but I finally did it, Helena!'

'Did what?' Helena was unnerved by this effluence of emotion. It seemed to build and threaten to spill from Marina as it had that night at Poon's.

'Why, I started to search for my parents. You told me I should know who they were, and I acted on it!' She turned to Paul conversationally. 'As I was telling the Princess earlier, I was adopted as a baby. I told no one for years, and now I find I am telling everyone. I never went to look for them, you see, and so I thought I would make a start.'

No one said anything. Helena was hotly embarrassed at Marina's poor taste in bringing up such a personal thing in front of strangers. It seemed a very American thing to do to share one's griefs at large.

'Well, what happened?' Paul blurted it out in genuine suspense. It was, of course, the obvious thing to say, and Helena was surprised she had not thought of it.

'I hired a detective,' Marina said, and suddenly shrugged as if she realized that what she had said had been out of place. 'She said it might be weeks, months or years before I found out. Maybe never. I'm sorry,' she added. 'I suppose it has been very much on my mind.'

'It's very brave of you,' he said. 'I have some experience of the problem from my general practice in London, and it is not an easy task. It can be very upsetting. Still, it probably is better, on balance, to know.'

'Did you ever give a baby away? I mean for private adoption?' Marina's voice was muffled and tense.

'I have helped mothers to make arrangements,' he said, 'but the sort of thing that you are going through should not happen to anyone. And luckily the laws are changed so it no longer does.'

Marina looked at Paul with deep feeling. 'It is as if half my life had been cut out,' she said, succinctly.

'I know,' he replied.

The Princess, who had apparently gathered the gist of this conversation, turned to Tanya with excited eyes. A long stream of Russian ensued, and the urgency of its tone stilled the table. The beauty of the language, its harsh inflections softened by the perfect utterance of the Princess, caught them all up. It was as if someone passing the garden wall had burst into song, or as if a rare bird had begun to sing from one of the trees.

Helena had always been somewhat disingenuous when she declared that she did not know Russian. Although she would not, and now could not speak it, she did understand it. The absurdity of what her aunt was saying infuriated her, but she knew it was utterly futile to stop the old lady.

Tanya cast a worried glance at Marina, cleared her throat, then spoke: 'Sophia Petrovna wishes you to know,' she said, 'and feels she cannot express it adequately in English, that you strongly resemble a member of her family whom she has not seen for a long time. She asks me to say that whereas she did not think you were Russian this morning, she thinks you are Russian now. Having sat with you for this length of time, she feels she has seen your face before. She believes that you might be related to the Kuriensky family, who are near relatives of hers.' Tanya closed her eyes and shook her head.

The Princess, having cast a piercing and caressing eye over Marina, shot a subtle look of triumph at Helena. So that's what she's up to, thought Helena, she means to annex Marina, and gain her as an ally.

Marina lurched back in her chair and put her hand to her breastbone as if someone had kicked her in the chest. 'Kuriensky?' she asked softly. Her lip trembled, and Helena thought she could bear no more emotion. She wanted to choke her aunt.

'It would seem that you have royal blood after all,' she said, giving her aunt a withering stare, 'and what a romantic coincidence it is! You mustn't pay any attention to her, Marina, she thinks everyone she likes has royal blood.'

But it was Paul who leapt into the breach. 'Oh, Sophia Petrovna,' he said. He caught the old lady's eye and shook his head sadly. 'Do you think this could possibly be true? You do know that truth is very important to the people caught up in these matters, and that it is a very emotional topic.' Helena was actually grateful to him. 'I am sure,' he continued, 'that Marina would love to be a member of your family, as anyone would, but suppose she got her hopes up and then had them dashed. That would be awful.'

'She has the Kuriensky brow and the Kuriensky smile,' said the Princess, then withdrew into a haughty silence.

Marina stared at the Princess for a long time, and then a kind of wistfulness crept into her expression. 'I should never have brought the subject up, but I thank you for the compliment it implies . . . Your Excellency.' She spoke the title hesitantly.

Helena pushed back her plate of fishbones that Evangalia should have cleared. It seemed outrageous that her aunt should have perpetrated such a thing on a total stranger. She was maddened, too, by the obsequiousness in Marina's tone, which had made the scene more awful. Here she had planned a delightful luncheon and everyone had behaved in the wrong way. A wave of anger overwhelmed her. 'Aunt Sonya, Aunt Sonya!' she said through clenched teeth, but she checked herself. She wanted no row to upset Marina, who seemed to be quite uncomfortable at the expression in her voice.

'We cannot presume on your aunt's kindness to me any further,' Marina said with surprising sharpness. She looked around the table as if she had agreeably shocked herself by her own assertiveness. 'I think we have all tired of the subject, in any case. I know I have.' And with some determination, she finished her fish.

The old lady opened her eyes and gave Marina a gnomic look, then closed them again. 'Where is Sergei?' she asked. 'I want to know where Sergei is and I want to see him.'

Helena, too, wanted to see her cousin and share with him this latest horror story. 'I told you, Tyotya, he had met with friends. I expect he will be back soon.' She raised her eyes and stabbed a look at Paul, who was meditating on a crust of bread. 'Why doesn't Paul go and find him after lunch?' Paul looked up sharply, but catching her glance, seemed to understand the import of her inference.

'I see,' he said, sighing. 'Of course, I will.'

Helena was somewhat mollified. 'I think he expected you to meet him after lunch, but I'm not sure where, if you take my meaning. He was in Skala when I saw him last, and you may have to look around. I have plans to take Marina to see the Monastery this afteroon.'

'At last!' Helena cried, as she shepherded Marina across the silent square which abutted the house. It was blazing hot. The sun battered the white buildings, which reflected the glare and cast sharp shadows. Above, the heavens were a violent blue. The Greeks themselves had retreated from this assault, and had wisely taken shelter in shaded rooms and quiet napping. 'At last, we have a chance to bc alone. I've hardly had the chance to speak with you since you arrived. I had no idea I'd leave you victim to my aunt like that. I'm terribly sorry about it. She is quite, quite senile, you know. Varya and Serge and I are at our wits' end. But she should not have gone babbling on to you like that. It was inexcusable.' Helena felt that she herself was rambling. She peeked at Marina's face. It looked pinched with sadness under the shade of her hat in the sharp sun.

'She only meant to be kind,' Marina said. 'In any case, it was stupid of me to say why I had gone to New York. It was very gauche.'

'I had no *idea* you had done such a thing,' Helena said a bit wildly, 'nor that I had inspired you to do it.'

'Oh, I'm not holding you responsible. But it impressed me deeply when you said I had a right to know. Do you remember? The night of Arthur's funeral.'

They had swaddled themselves against the implacable sun. A trickle of sweat escaped from underneath Helena's flat breast, and it oozed down her torso. She did not know why Marina had wanted to produce such a complication in her life so soon after Arthur's death. At the thought of his name, a queasiness arose in her once more. 'Oh, you do have a right,' she said. 'It only concerns me that it was a hasty decision to make at a time when you are vulnerable.'

Marina looked vulnerable indeed. She flailed a white-clad arm. 'But it's progress for me to do something with my life instead of sitting around picking my sores and wondering. And it also struck me that everyone who has ever been close to me is dead. My adoptive parents are dead, and so is Arthur. It suddenly occurred to me that there might be one person left – my "biological mother", as they say. If they find out that she is dead too, I shan't know what to do. It's simply a burning issue with me now. I thought, "Well, why not now? Why not when I really need her?" I have needed her and needed her all my life, and I also need to know who I really am.'

Helena was captivated by the sight of Marina and her wide sleeves flapping. At the same time, she disliked it that Marina exposed herself and gave vent to her feelings in the square, empty though it was. She made for a shaded tunnel of arcades. White, like wings, they arched the narrow streets leading to the Monastery. Marina seemed to catch the confusion of her mood. Helena did, for some reason, feel quite agitated. 'I thought it would please you to know that I'd shown some character and finally stood up for myself in this matter,' Marina said. 'But I feel I've upset you. I'm sorry. I do feel a bit unhinged at the moment, vulnerable, as you say. You have been so incredibly kind.'

There was something about Marina's abjectness that both maddened and fascinated Helena. Since they had met, Helena found that Marina set her off and unsettled her. She produced ill-defined and contradictory feelings, mood swings, and intuitive flights in Helena. It was as if faculties she had not known about were straining at her conscious mind to assert themselves. Now, Helena felt an odd pleasure in letting impulse have its way. 'Not kind. I can assure you,' she said, letting a ghost of a smile, deliberately equivocal, play upon her lips. Marina was peering at her in an effort to evaluate Helena's response. 'In any case, it now appears that you are my cousin,' Helena said, involuntarily.

'You don't believe that,' Marina said nervously. 'You don't, do you?'

They passed old, carved doorways, aged to a biscuit colour by time and the elements. Helena let her discreet smile deepen. 'I'll admit it's unlikely,' she said.

'It was ironic that your aunt brought up the whole Russian thing,' Marina said. 'Because it was on my mind only this morning to tell you that I had always really known it was a fantasy. I felt guilty, you see, for misleading you. I suppose I could allow myself to think I was your cousin, but I have discovered that that sort of thinking really does a lot of harm. It simply gives one grandiose ideas about oneself. In any case, the detective more or less destroyed my Russian dreams. She is a woman, you know. I didn't think there were women detectives except in P. D. James. I like thrillers. I suppose you think that stupid of me . . .' Helena did think thrillers stupid and Marina's declamatory speech somewhat boring. 'Arthur liked them, though,' Marina continued, 'so I suppose it's all right.'

Helena imagined Arthur propped up in bed with a thriller, wasting his time. An image, perhaps inevitable, followed of his turning over to caress Marina. 'But what did she *say*? The detective, I mean.' Helena asked aloud with a show of mock impatience at Marina's digressions.

'I'm sorry. Since Arthur died, I've become so witless. Maybe I was always like that. They used to call me a daydreamer at school. The detective said she thought I might be Polish. Maybe German, maybe Irish. But you see I was adopted into a Catholic family, and she said that Catholics usually kept an ethnic continuity.' She paused, then timidly asked, 'Who are these Kuriensky people? Do you know them?'

Helena drew in her breath. For all of their Russian-ness, the Kurienskys had a strong Polish connection. Although most of them were Orthodox, a few had refused to be re-baptized, and there had

75

been a history of intrigue and secret marriages. She shook her head. The whole idea was absurd, and far too much of a coincidence to be entertained. 'I don't know much about them,' she said. 'I've always switched off when my aunt has gone into genealogy.' But Helena found herself looking at Marina in a new way, nonetheless. Was the familiarity she felt one of actual kinship? She observed the delicate brow under the fine straw hat she had lent to Marina. She looked at the finely chiselled nose. Oh, her addled aunt! She put out her hand and touched Marina's shoulder lightly. She needed no blood tie to strengthen her communion with Marina. Her hand trembled slightly. Oh, Arthur, she thought.

As if echoing her thought, Marina said, 'Arthur.' She did not seem to notice Helena's touch. She seemed troubled and deeply abstracted. 'Arthur wasn't Russian or Polish. And he certainly wasn't a Catholic,' she said.

At the mention of his name, Helena again felt a thudding in her temples. 'What do you mean? Of course, he wasn't.' They were threading their way out of a maze of streets and were about to emerge again into the sun. They were verging on the approach to the Monastery.

Marina looked back down the long, narrow, white passageways, then out onto the baking street before them. She frowned. 'Arthur used to intimate to me,' she said, biting her lip, 'and it was really only a joke, that, well, he did not know how many children he had sired. It used to upset me.' The light caught her face. She was blushing deeply.

A heavy fury welled up in Helena. 'What! You mean he tried to prevent you from looking for your family by suggesting he might be your father? I can scarcely believe it!'

'As I say, it was a joke,' Marina replied, shrugging. 'But it always preoccupied me. I could never really get the thought out of my mind. Things were very bad between us, you know. And that remark just shows, doesn't it? He liked to say I had no sense of humour and that I couldn't take teasing. Half the time, I don't think he knew what he was doing or saying. He seemed to operate on his own batteries, somehow.'

'I well remember!' Helena blurted out.

They had reached a turning point where the path to the Monastery converged with the road to the port. Marina stopped and let her eye travel up to the imposing fortress above them. Her gaze rested on the crenellated top of its massive bulk. 'Oh!' she said.

'Impressive, isn't it?' Helena said. Somehow she did not feel able to face it for a moment. She looked at its grave buttresses and high portals, then looked away. She had not been inside the place in years and had a hazy recollection of its treasures of silver and of icons. Her mother had, in any case, preferred the Shrine of the Apocalypse below. The Monastery, with its riches, disgusted Helena. She never tired, however, of the view, and so she led Marina down the steep incline to the parapet that abutted the road below them. It would balance her, she thought, to look at the vista of town and harbour. She always loved the sense of being aloft in the azure sky, as if she hung above the water and she liked, too, the way the houses and fields on the steep slope down to the port appeared tiny. The boats in the harbour always looked like toys to her from this vantage point.

Marina's sleeves fluttered against her creamy skin. Why had she implied that she remembered Arthur's cruelty? He had been exacting, rather. It was beginning to trouble Helena quite a lot that she could not remember salient points about the affair. Why had she ended it and so abruptly, too? The story she had always told herself was that the involvement had limited her independence, and until the day he died, she had never questioned this. Perhaps there was no reason to, but it unnerved her when her mind now balked over actual memories. What had they said to each other? She could not even remember where they had been when they had broken off. As she thought of it now, she had the curious sensation that there was extreme pain associated with the episode, but it was as if it belonged to somebody else. As she stood overlooking the island from the parapet, an odd question formed in her mind. She knew it was intrusive to ask Marina this, especially on such a short acquaintance, but she found she really did not care. 'Did you love him?' she asked.

Marina had taken her hat off. The little breeze wandered through her curls and shook them shining to her shoulders. She seemed taken aback, but not the least offended by the question. 'I really don't know anymore,' she said. 'I'm not sure. I was faithful to him.' Helena thought this a strange thing to say. 'I felt so guilty about him, and about the divorce, that it was hard for me to love.' Marina paused, then softly continued. 'And there were deeper guilts. I feel I wronged him in ways that went quite beyond the initial harm I did to everyone.'

'How so?' asked Helena. Whenever Marina spoke about Arthur, she had a distinct, grave manner that Helena associated with their first meeting in the Chinese restaurant. For some reason, she now noticed that Marina had fine hands with long, opaline fingernails. She looked beautiful against the hot sky and the vista of faraway sea. 'I think I am talking too much – saying too much about Arthur,' she said. 'It makes me feel vile, but, you see, I never had a friend in all those years – not one – and it feels so good to talk.' She looked out at Helena with sudden openness and trust, then out again at the view. 'Arthur did not find me – well, you know. *That* sort of thing wasn't too good after we married. You see, he had such a success with the *Cycle*, and then he found it very hard to write, and I think he put the blame on me because of sex. On my side, I wanted a child very badly, and he would not let me have one. I suppose it was a vicious circle. But I'm not too sure what happened between us. In a sense, it is impossible to say that you have not loved someone you have lived with for twenty years. How could I not love him? There was something very sad about him.'

Helena listened to this with rapt attention. She focused her eyes on her hands clasped before her, and remembered with hot clarity the first time she and Arthur had made love. She certainly did not block on that, nor on the subsequent times. The inn at Orford had been one of their places. Marina had told her all about the scattering of his ashes there over the telephone back in London, the day after it had happened. Helena had sat on the floor, gnawed at her knuckles, and cried large, silent tears as the wispy voice of Marina had come into the receiver. How could Marina talk about guilt? It had been Arthur who had erased years of guilty feelings from Helena, and feelings of bodily inadequacy, too. Oh, how Mungo Taggart would have envied him if he had ever known! Her marriage had been one of appalling frigidity on both sides, and Arthur had released her. Had Arthur had his ashes scattered there in Orford because he had felt the same? Surely not. In a way she hoped not, although she could not say why. He had probably taken many women there. But to hear Marina say that the bond between Arthur and herself had not been really sexual, gave Helena cold pause. What other sort of bond had it been that had kept them together?

'Are you shocked?' Marina asked. Helena could hardly remember what they had been talking about.

'Certainly not,' she said, gathering the thread again. 'It only set me thinking about Arthur.' But it had shocked her in a way to have the assumption removed that Arthur had enjoyed this beautiful creature. She had assumed, too, that Marina had been positively climactic with Arthur, and it oddly disappointed her that this had not been the case. But another thought, perhaps as pressing, rose to her mind. 'Do you think that Arthur disliked women?' she asked.

'He disliked me,' Marina said, and she screwed up her eyes in pain.

Turning from the wall, she wandered away towards the path that led upwards to the Monastery. There was a little tourist market above them. 'I want to look at the stalls,' she said, by way of explanation. Helena let her go so that they could both collect their feelings. She turned back and gazed out at the view again. Far beneath her, the harbour and the lower island lay, golden and blue in the radiant light. Suddenly, she caught a glimpse of Paul Mason in his Panama hat. He was standing and looking up at the parapet from the road below. She retreated slightly. She very much hoped he would find Serge before evening. She still bore Serge a grudge for what had happened that morning, and she thought it would serve him right to have the virtuous doctor pounce upon him, as pounce she knew he would. It rather amused her to think of him fishing Serge out of some taverna or other, shaking him down and sobering him up. Poor Serge, she thought. He was obliged to read from *Eugene Onegin* every night, and there could be no slurred words for this evening's performance, as well he knew. Thinking Paul must be out of sight by now, she returned to the parapet, but he was still there. He caught her eye and waved. 'I'll find him. Don't worry,' he called. She thought he was searching the parapet for a sight of Marina, but he turned and was gone. She smiled and gave a short laugh. She had a strange and brutal feeling she could not identify.

Helena turned and made her way up to the Monastery approach. She spied Marina haggling at a little stall over some purchase. She and the stall-holder were having a brisk, amiable conversation. He sold brass trinkets, postcards, icons and jewellery, and Helena knew him by sight. At length, Marina turned, and flushed with success, held out a pair of earrings for Helena's approval. It was hardly accurate to say that the poems in *The Hephaestus Cycle* had shown the goddess as unequivocally lovely. In fact, the poems had depicted her as almost barbarous. Arthur had got the barbarity of goddesses, he had captured that. He had always been fascinated by the primitive, and Helena suddenly remembered that he had thought Americans primitive. Of course, it was absurd to reduce Arthur's monumental and ambiguous figure to one woman, but it was tempting nonetheless. He had certainly not captured this bright creature proffering trinkets. They might have been sapphires, the way she held them out. It was almost as if, against the casual voluptuousness that Marina expressed in her most trivial movements, there flowed a counter-drift of spirit, a spirit that seemed to move upon the void of her formless personality and speak to the beholder of some good but oddly anarchic force.

'Do you like them?' she asked Helena. Helena would never have dreamt of buying those earrings. 'They're pretty, aren't they? I can't resist earrings.' And she put the silver baubles in pierced holes in her ears. The hoops were silver snakes, each with a blue bead in its mouth.

'Oh, Marina, yes!' Helena said suddenly and laughed. As the hoops bobbed and dangled, she saw at once why they had been a good idea. 'Yes, I do like them,' she said. 'But I suppose we ought to see the Monastery now. It's quite famous.'

'Oh, I very much want to see it,' Marina said with sudden gravity.

'Are you religious?' Helena asked lightly, thinking it striking that Marina had replied in such a way.

'Oh, yes, very,' Marina said with great seriousness.

Helena felt deflated and surprised by this turn of events, but Marina clearly misread her expression.

'Well, I know I have no right to be, but I am all the same,' she said a little defensively.

'Oh, it doesn't matter to *me*,' Helena said.

'It didn't to Arthur either, and that was part of the problem,' Marina replied with a slight acerbity that gave Helena a start. 'I thought I had taken that on board when I married him, but I had not.'

Helena did not know what to say. It had never crossed her mind that Marina might hold views contrary to her own, and she did not know in what light to consider this new information. They were mounting the steep cobbled street, and at last, they arrived at the high Monastery gate, crowned with bells and battlements. It was embellished with a gold mosaic of St John the Theologian, writing in his book.

'Well, there is much to interest you on Patmos, that's for sure,' Helena said dryly, and they went in.

VII

DIRECTLY AFTER LUNCH, Paul Mason had set out in search of Serge, but he had no taste for the quest. Quite without knowing why he felt so aimless, he meandered through the streets of Hora, looking around blind white corners and into shadowed alleyways. Was there another place on earth, he wondered, where so many churches abounded? At every turning point, a new domed chapel or oratory rose to confront him. On his arrival in Patmos, he had visited many of them in a benumbed, compulsive fashion. Inside, they were dark and hung with icons lit with votive lamps, and they spoke to him of a solitary impulse towards interior considerations, things he was not yet ready to explore after Africa. Earlier in the week, he had even stumbled on a convent hidden behind a high, white wall. On entering it in early evening, he had found two nuns weaving under a lemon tree. Unable to speak with them, he had communicated in sign language that he hoped it was all right for him to be there and one of the nuns had mistaken his meaning. She had risen from her loom and had fetched him an earthenware cup full of cold water. She had invited him to see the church, and there he had discovered an icon of the Virgin rising from a fountain from which flowed living water, he supposed. At any rate, a number of grateful saints and bishops stood before Her receiving streams of the flow. The glass covering the icon was dirty with kisses. Paul lit a taper and stuffed money in a box, mostly out of courtesy to the aged nun. In the past, he would have seen much significance in her gift of water and the vivid symbol of its source, but although he said an automatic prayer to the Virgin, he felt that any interior movement towards Her might do him harm, and so he had bowed respectfully to the nuns and had left the convent with the feeling that he stood on a steep edge of inner blackness.

He did not like to think of the country he had left. He carefully avoided any thoughts at all of the dry Abyssinian trough with its cold, black nights and blazing days. He wished he had not gone at all and, having gone, wished he had not returned. The experience of the place was, however, imprinted on his inner eye like a green after-image of the sun.

Paul hardly expected to be able to shake off the burning and unquenchable memory of Ethiopia, but it was more than he had bargained for. He had always been a man of some detachment, and thus it was peculiarly horrible to him that his own mental landscape had been torched to reveal the igneous rock and cattle bones of his own self. The eyes of the Africans held not reproach but listlessness at the private business of dying. Thousands and thousands of eyes like Argus seemed to express one baleful consciousness, and he felt a failure of grace that he could not face it head on. Many of his co-workers had seemed to thrive spiritually on the disaster, but finally, it had made him ill. To begin with, it had seemed an heroic enterprise to insure that one belly should be filled, one throat slaked, one family rescued from death by fruitless conflict; that proper cerements be found for one old woman, that tetanus, typhoid, dehydration, measles and glaucoma be altered from their pestilential progress through only one camp. There was certainly no denying that it had been a worthy effort, and he had hardly expected Moses to appear with manna and sweet water. Viewed casually and at a distance from himself, he had done moderately well and had achieved much by sheer slog and the help of others. Maybe the sun had touched him or the sheer weight of numbers dead, or the political chaos, but finally he had had to accept that if it was between him and the Africans, the Africans had to go.

What upset him was that he had always reckoned himself as a close familiar with death and the dying, and patient with the inevitable. One might even have said that he had shown a particular gift as a mediator in the process of the soul's flight from the body. Cancer patients had always loved him. In the Ethiopian furnace, however, he had been no good. He regarded his African venture as a failure, and was hard put to it to say why he was on Patmos now.

Well, why not Patmos? He was not without the irony to see what a metaphor it was for the end of the world, even if he had accidentally chosen it because of Serge. He really had no idea what to do with the rest of his life now that he had found himself unfit for heroism, and although the bad taste of apocalyptic ways of seeing himself put off thinking too much about the island, he had to confess that he had been subjected to such a lurid trial by dreams in Africa that he had felt compelled to go somewhere safe in order to escape them or wrestle them down. Sometimes he wished for the purity to be able to see his nightmares as prophecies or omens, but when he woke, conscious of them, he was only aware of their confirming personal application. The Africans themselves would have understood the dreams differently, but then they saw a communal spirit in things. He wished the images that so disturbed his sleep might coalesce into some meaning or portent either for the collective will or for himself, but all he could truthfully say was that they made him realize that things had gone too far. Even last night, he had been afraid that he had woken the Mirkovsky household with a shout. He could not now recall the substance of the nightmare, but he had lain then twisted in the heavy solitude of night, weighing his motives with heavy self-reproach. Sometimes he worked on his soul like someone trying to correct a flawed spine by means of traction.

Earlier in his life, in fact, not many years ago, Paul would have sought to empty a place in himself for prayer. Before his trip to Ethiopia, it might have been said of him that his whole inner life had been a conscious struggle to eliminate desire. Consciously and unconsciously, his choices had been the fearful ones of simplification. While in medical school, he had effected a divorce from his family by becoming a Roman Catholic. He came from Ulster Protestant stock, and his family's prosperity in their subsequent remove to Surrey, had rested on this ethic. They lived in manses or houses with Georgian doorways. Their lawns were glossy and their herbaceous borders sang with bees. His parents had looked back upon a time when they had been ascendant in Ireland where they had owned land and governed souls with a mono-lithic devotion to duty. He still remembered how an aunt had implored him to resist the clutches of the Whore of Babylon and worse still, he could not forget how his fiancée Julia, a childhood sweetheart, had rejected him in favour of his brother Rufus. He was certain it had had to do with his choice of religion, but there had been other choices too.

Paul had never wanted to be anything but a doctor, and although he briefly flirted with the idea of the priesthood, he had always supposed that he would recover sufficiently from Julia to marry. He had not recovered from Julia and he had not married. He was, in fact, something of a hermit, and for years had been quite glad of a crust of bread in a peaceful house. He was never sure whether bitterness or nature had driven him to this exigency, nor did he quite know why he had chosen to be a general practitioner when his real interest had been in psychiatry. In a charge of religious self-abnegation, he had decided that general practice was more humble and socially useful. It could, too, have been that Julia's rejection of him had rendered some vital ambition in him useless.

At any rate, he had for many years maintained a surgery in a

83

dejected part of Kilburn with a sour, semi-alcoholic partner and the occasional pert locum, the last of whom had been a cerebral woman with a change-the-world attitude, served up hot and fresh from medical school. Perhaps her horrid fervour had goaded him to Ethiopia. Perhaps the next challenge he met would drive him to the Foreign Legion or to a leper colony in the Congo where he could learn to play Bach (he loved Bach), meet Mr Kurtz and slay him, or win the Nobel Prize.

Ah! he was impatient with himself. Here he was in Hora, ostensibly in search of Serge. Paul knew he was circling in a holding motion, for he did not want to meet his friend. In the past, Serge had usually avoided delinquent behaviour close to home, and in any case, this lunar landscape of white and geometric forms seemed antithetical to drunkenness.

He walked and he walked. He had been walking all morning. He climbed higher with nimble assurance to the flagged alleyway that went around the Monastery walls and looked below perfunctorily for Serge. Beyond Hora, he could see the landscape of the island where he had walked before. His earliest and most profound impression of Patmos had been the sacred white retreats hidden in the countryside, hermitages where solitary temperaments still sought a single way of being. He spotted a few from his present vantage point and thought again about the dreams. Perhaps his psyche rebelled because he had followed a false Messiah in going out to Africa. He had not thought of the very devil for a long time, but it occurred to him now that the deceiver often dressed in holy fictions, appearing to the soul as a salvific notion that had nothing to do with its true direction. Perhaps he had been gulled out into desert places to look for a Christ whose reality lay elsewhere. Or perhaps he was simply having a nervous breakdown. Paul tried to remember the writings of Freud, Adler and Jung which he had once attempted to understand, but he could not retrieve the smallest principle. He only knew that if he were his own patient, he would be alarmed and would think that the occluding misery he now felt was an outward sign of wounds sustained in conflicts long ago.

Paul smiled at himself ruefully and tried once more to change the course of his thoughts. One would tend to think eschatologically on Patmos – would tend to place weight on dreams, visions and ecstasies, not that ecstasies had occurred. The reason he had come had been quite simply practical. Sergei Mirkovsky had always turned to him in times of need and he to Serge from the time they had been eight and had shared a prep-school dormitory. If Paul had given the matter any thought, he would have said that two such disparate characters had no real, adult business with one another: Serge, the high-flyer; Paul, the plodder; Serge the dipsomaniac Russian prince; Paul, the sober defector from the English upper-middle class. And yet they had always had a brotherly sympathy, born out of childhood need, and the basis of friendship had always lain in unquestioning loyalty. Fleeing from the wrath to come in himself, Paul had holed up in the Addis Ababa Hilton and had rung Serge in England. Part of Serge's charm for Paul was that he had never had a hero's charter and had always pulled him back from really useless martyrdoms. His wry, whisky-cured voice had come across the wire as such relief. Of course, they were going to be on Patmos for the summer! Naturally, Paul could stay! Had he not often urged him to come? And this year of all years he was welcome as Maman was becoming impossible. When could he make it? Soon as possible. Of course, it was stupid to go back to London right away, probably get the bends from coming up so fast from what must have been a ghastly experience. Paul had felt such a thief for the fresh towel and decent meal and private room, but putting down the phone, his head had swum with absolution.

When Paul had arrived, however, Serge had been in an extraordinary mood and had barely welcomed him. It was odd, extremely odd, and though they had talked about the cause of it last night, this had only deepened Paul's mystification. For a week now, he had been unceremoniously dumped with the old lady and had found himself taking her pulse and reading chunks of Orthodox meditations aloud to her. Serge would vanish first in this direction, then in that. Although always a bit of a soak, his drinking had increased to an alarming degree, and now all of this business about the Tsar's family had come up. Paul felt deserted by his own ability to make any sense of it all. Right after lunch that very day, the Princess had urgently begged him to tell her what was happening to Serge and Paul, quite truthfully, had answered, 'Nothing I can understand.'

That lunch! And Helena! In fact, Paul had tried the other day to extract himself and make his way back to London, for apart from not being able to fathom Serge's mood, he had not predicted Helena. He knew he was walking off the febrile energy of anger and he was trying not to accuse Helena in his mind of having some part to play in her cousin's apparent rejection of him. She certainly had joined Serge in persuading him to stay on Patmos, but Paul knew that she disliked him. Perhaps she did so because of his usefulness with her aunt.

85

Paul swung downwards, thinking he ought really to make his way to Skala. Just the thought of Helena provoked him into placating action. Serge had often talked about his brilliant cousin and, in fact, Paul had met her once or twice but only in a superficial way. He remembered her as a willowy blonde at Serge's wedding, stilted in her snappy hat. He had met her once after her divorce at a party given by Serge's in-laws in London, and she had been at the christenings of Serge's children, always self-possessed and possessed, too, by a sense of her own distinction. Serge had often said that Helena was more like his real sister than Varya. Once, he had called her his 'familiar', and over the years, Paul had formed a mental image of a sleek cat, purring in Serge's arms and mewing intuitions in his ear. Perhaps she was jealous of their long-standing friendship, perhaps she thought it an inopportune time for him to be in Patmos, for certainly when they had met again that Monday in the wonderful garden behind the house the day he had arrived, she had seemed glazed hard with balanced manners, but hostile to him for reasons he could not fathom. She had, since he had been on the island, made a huge display of this visit by Marina Holt and had made it clear that this august personage would take up most of her time. It seemed that she was going to write a book about Marina's husband, a poet Paul had vaguely heard of. Together, it appeared, the two women were going to carve him up.

Paul had quite dreaded Marina. He shook his head now and smiled involuntarily. He had had the most extraordinary image of what she was going to be and had, indeed, sat in the garden that morning defending himself against her appearance with the Greek text that had caused so much silly conversation. He had almost expected Marina to have talons, most certainly an insolent, libidinous stare, and probably a complexion like an expensive leather handbag. He had imagined her as one of those women who cannot let youth go, a diva teetering on her last stilettos in push-up bra and every crevice filled with paint. The legendary mistress then wife of an artist might stand, Paul had thought, in a Bohemian rapture in the garden, scarves flung about her neck like Lady Ottoline Morrell, compelling men to dance her tune, compelling him to boost a fading beauty with his eyes. She was on the island, after all, with a view to being hymned by Helena's pen, as if the comparison made by her husband (hardly cold) with Aphrodite were not enough for one lifetime.

But there she had been, the humble cause of his only joy that day, teetering not on heels, but on the brink of some wholly human difficulty. So this was Helena's friend, an improbable Venus to be sure. There was an almost painful sincerity in the woman, and it had touched Paul's heart when she had blurted out the story of her adoption and her visit to New York. She had that perennially lost look of the weak and he supposed a woman of Helena's strength would appeal to her enormously. Indeed, she had gazed with admiration at Helena during lunch as if she had been taken up by some rare creature whose superior powers might resolve the mess of her life. Perhaps she had undertaken to write the book with Helena in this spirit, for it seemed unlikely, somehow, that she would have entered into the project in any other way. He wondered what Helena was doing now with this poor goddess, what she was saying. He thought that perhaps he might run into them on their way to the Monastery, but then put it out of his mind.

He must find Serge, he told himself and he scolded himself for not having taken the task more seriously. Surely, he should not resent Helena's ordering him to do what he knew he really should be doing. It was even possible that Serge had gone on this bender as a direct result of their conversation the previous night. He tried to find the path that zigzagged down Hora to meet the main road to Skala, and as he threaded his way, he wondered why he had missed the obsessional quality in what Serge had told him and why he had taken it so much on face value at the time.

It was shortly after Helena had gone to meet the boat that Paul had tackled him. He and Serge had stayed on in the taverna garden finishing the wine. Paul had had more to drink than he wanted . . . in some way, he had wanted to re-establish the bond between them, and after a few glasses sipped in an uneasy silence, he had asked Serge straight out what the matter was.

'What do you mean, what's the matter?' Serge had asked abstractedly. The garden, a velvety, dark enclosure behind the restaurant was lit by gourds carved out like jack o'lanterns. 'I've been looking at that tree. Do you see those ants?'

Paul looked up, and above them one of the branches lit by a lantern seemed to seethe with movement. A whole battalion of huge, dark red ants was mobilized in stealthy activity and with a purpose known to themselves alone. 'Serge! I asked you.'

For a long time, he had said nothing. He had deep-set eyes and they had a way of retracting into his skull when he was upset about something. His nervous fingers had become still on the glass and then, apparently coming to a successful outcome of a struggle in himself, he had said that he had a secret.

'Do you want to tell me what it is?' Paul had asked, inclining his head forward. It was the gesture and attitude he adopted towards patients in Kilburn who were about to confess some shocking sexual difficulty.

'What do you know about the last days of the Romanov family?' Serge whispered portentously, his eyes shifting from side to side.

'That they were shot,' said Paul. He felt quite mystified.

'Suppose I were to tell you in absolute confidence that one of them was not!'

Paul looked at him in disbelief for a moment, unable to speak.

'Suppose I were to tell you that new evidence is about to come into my hands, evidence that proves that one of them not only survived, but survived to have a child. Would you believe me? Would you believe that the heir to the throne was alive?' Serge's hands trembled. He looked queasy and sick. Paul realized that he must have been drinking all day.

'It would depend on the nature of the evidence,' Paul said carefully.

'It is amazing!' Serge said, extending his arms as if to demonstrate size and import. 'Or it would be, if only we can get it. A cache of letters has been found, written to a dead relative of mine, in fact, and I have it on good authority that they contain absolute proof.'

'Have you seen these letters?' Paul felt helpless against a tide of withdrawal within himself. He sat back, his arms folded, suddenly angered by the addled, boozy face of his friend.

'No, I have not read them, but Lipitsin knows all about them . . .'

'Who is Lipitsin?' he had meant to make the question mild, but it came out in a withering way, just short of disdain.

'Gregory Lipitsin,' said Serge with tipsy grandeur, 'is a dealer in rare antiquities. It is he who has been negotiating for the letters, and I have been advising him. We are on the verge of closing the deal.'

'Deal?' Paul asked. Serge was a Northumbrian farmer. His head for business was famously absent.

'We have to buy them.'

'Well, what are you going to do with them once you have them?' Was it the vision of real need on Serge's face or the addled, boozy smile that goaded him?

'There are huge changes going on in Russia! Huge, with this Gorbachev. There are organizations now afoot, there are things happening. Suppose I were to find this child – this heir . . .'

'If there were such a person,' said Paul dryly, 'surely he or she would have been made known to us before now!'

'Ah, but that's where you are mistaken! Can you not see that the KGB would have hunted down such a person before now? Now and only now is the time when the child's identity could be revealed.'

'So you've got yourself involved with some Tsarist organization?'

'No!' said Serge. 'It is with Lipitsin I am involved. And he thinks as you do. We must get proof. And you see the exciting thing is that he is coming with what is most probably the very proof we need. To this island. I am sorry I have been so distracted, but just before I left England, he rang me.' Serge's eyes were living proof of fanatical belief.

Paul turned his glass in his hand and sipped retsina. He was so tired. 'Serge!' he said, letting the weariness escape him.

Serge leaned closer in tipsy confiding. 'It is essential that you tell no one about this, Paul. You are the only one I can trust except Lipitsin. Fiona doesn't know. Maman doesn't know. Helena doesn't know. You see, it could spell terrible danger for this person.'

'I won't tell anyone.' Paul looked at his glass, trying not to let Serge see his sudden flare of inexplicable contempt. 'I am flattered that you told me. I knew that something was wrong.'

'Wrong?' Serge elevated his voice to a discreet cry. 'There's nothing *wrong*! I'm not mad, you know. I have researched the whole thing. I'm hardly stupid, am I?' This was a mute issue between them, for Serge had always been the cleverer of the two.

'I didn't say you were stupid,' Paul muttered, smothering his queer flare of temper. 'I only meant to say that you seemed agitated.'

Serge gave a sigh, his shoulders dropping in collapse. 'The thing is that I daily expect Lipitsin. I expect him to come or ring or write and I haven't heard a word. You have no idea what anxiety it causes me. No idea at all.' He put his head to one side and looked at Paul in the same odd way he had done when they were small. He would do something outrageously naughty and then in this manner he would appeal to Paul, wheedle or cajole him into collusion or forgiveness. 'I suppose,' he added, 'that I disbelieved this myself at first, but I have become almost entirely convinced. It's pure gold, Paul. The rightful heir to the throne is alive. I know he is.'

Paul knew even at the time that he should let the matter drop, dissipate the atmosphere with a joke or some fond remark, but somehow he could not. It was as if Serge had suddenly revealed to him an aspect that they had once had in common and which Paul now saw and loathed, an infantile fervour of Quixote perhaps, or a bug-eyed love for a flattering cause. Had Ethiopia bred yet more intolerance in him? Now, he rather thought it had. 'Serge,' he had said, 'I have no doubt that you believe it. The question you must ask, however, is whether it is true.'

Serge had looked away, cut to the quick, and though they had spoken amiably enough on the way back to the house, Paul had felt a widening abyss.

Well, Paul thought, as he made his way along a shaded and luminous walkway, this binge is surely my fault. I really must find him and apologize. But he found the sense of guilt that was his habit so irksome now he made a little face. 'Maybe it is his fault,' he said to the accusatory voice within his head. Then he swiftly repressed a moment of rebellion in which he wondered if it were anybody's fault at all. He looked up and realized that quite unconsciously he had been walking in the wrong direction. Citing the crenellations of the Monastery high above him, he made for that. Maybe it was true that the Tsar's grandchild was alive. Odder things had happened. But surely the whole thing had to do, rather, with Serge's attitude to it. He had never seen anybody so consumed. He had that tormented air of someone in the grip of a compulsion. What was more, Serge had never really shown much interest in the Russian royal family, and had always made light of his grand connections. So, where did it all come from?

Paul was hesitant to lay it at the door of the Princess, for he had always liked her. As a small boy, he had confidently assumed that she lived in Buckingham Palace until someone had disabused him of this. Even then, he had been only mildly disappointed, for this tall and beautiful mother of his friend would swoop in from Paris and take him and Serge out to tea. In her Garbo hat and fur stole, she seemed to partake of the unreachable ether. Exotic though she was, she was never a cold mother, and Serge had always adored her. In their first year at public school, he had been invited to Paris to spend the Easter holidays with Serge, Paul's family had thought his French would improve in consequence. He had never seen anything quite like the Mirkovskys, the whole family.

Even now in middle-age, Paul still retained some of that awe he had felt for them at thirteen. His own home was serene and dull. The Mirkovskys' flat in Paris had the raffish and untidy air of an hotel room which the residents might soon vacate, leaving things for the chamber-maid to pick up. It was full of Russian clutter. Pictures and little objects littered every table. The Mirkovskys took jam with their tea, which they drank out of glasses and which they poured from a samovar that Serge said had been smuggled out of Russia by a maid who had pretended she was pregnant and had hidden it under her dress. The flat had high ceilings and vast expanses of floor covered with tatty Persian rugs, so faded that it was impossible to find a pattern in them. And as for Serge's parents, Paul observed that they had no interest in each other and, apparently, no sense of obligation to have one. Paul's own parents had been undemonstrative to each other, but it had never crossed his mind that they did not in some way communicate. In fact, they were deeply fond of one another and everyone simply took this for granted. But the Princess and old Boris Mirkovsky acted as if they lived together only by accident, and agreeably, only because they were civilized.

Paul shuddered to remember old Prince Boris Mikhailovitch, a grim old boy by anybody's standards. He had been a real martinet of the old school and Serge had never been able to measure up, Paul thought, to some inhuman and concealed standard. Just his look had made Serge feel a fool. For some reason, Paul had associated him with an Old Testament patriarch and had been startled to learn from Serge that he had a weakness for drink. Even now, this seemed incongruous to Paul. The old Prince had come from a distinguished military family. Paul remembered him best as standing in the dim light of early evening surveying the streets of Paris from one of the vast windows of the drawing room; erect and sombre, he had looked like a general inspecting losses, looking at defeat. That had been the eve of the Russian Easter. Later, they had gone to the émigré church, and even with the glad bells and lit tapers, the gold and the incense and the chanting, Serge's father had stood apart, his dark head on stiff neck, barely bowing.

Sometimes Paul wondered how the friendship between himself and Serge had begun and, with their manifestly different personalities, how it had been sustained. As a small boy, Paul had been quiet and introverted. Never a particularly handsome child, he had, nonetheless, an angelic soprano voice. He was fond of music, and his parents had considered a choir school. He had always loved to be in the chapel and this, in the absence of prowess at games, had earned him the terrible reputation for being good. Serge, on the other hand, had had a dark, blunt, unhappy face. Boys had chanted 'Russki' and 'spy' at him, and this would always throw him into ferocious tantrums. Perhaps this had been the time when he had started calling his mother a princess. For years before he had met the old man, Paul had thought that Serge's father was dead. Perhaps it had been because both of them, being clever, had been considered oddities, and both miserable at school, had clung together, though that sort of alliance rarely matures into real friendship. Paul thought it had more to do with his admiration for Serge's peculiar, passive strength, a largeness and a generosity of spirit. At school, he had been awed by Serge's sheer, breathtaking courage to be bad. He still remembered stifling fits of giggles in their stuffy dorm at tales of Serge's exploits. It had been like knowing Denis the Menace personally.

But it was not until the death of Serge's father that he and Paul had become permanently close, and this had not happened until their final year at Cambridge. They had followed each other around from prep school to public school to university, but this had been a matter of chance, and in adolescence their development along separate lines had become evident. At Cambridge, Serge had become sumptuously involved with a whole populace of friends very much like himself. He belonged to the Pitt Club and went to London to deb parties. Everyone thought him brilliant. He did Slavic languages and debated at the Union. From having been foreign, he became as exotic as his mother, famous at Cambridge, and although he saw Paul from time to time, they were both aware that they had grown away from each other.

Paul never really knew why it was that Serge had come to him the day the old Prince died. Serge had been going out with a woman at Girton and everyone had said they were going to marry. But early in the morning the day his father died, Serge had stumbled into Paul's rooms, waking him with the news. Paul had never seen anyone so cut up about a thing. It still moved him to pity when he remembered how Serge had wept, almost unable to draw breath.

The death had terrible consequences for Serge, dreadful ones. He did manage to scrape through with a degree, but much more had been expected of him. He jettisoned his girlfriend and started drinking heavily. He made no move towards any career at all. Eventually, he went abroad, travelled a lot, but came back none the wiser, and got a stupid job translating Russian scientific journals into English. He made a few efforts to get into publishing and wrote some book reviews. His earlier ambition had been to go into politics, but he declared now that he was psychologically a stateless person and for that reason would be unable to get very far. Paul made fruitless sallies at Serge's monolithic apathy and they did see quite a lot of each other in London while Paul was an intern at Charing Cross Hospital, at least, as much time as Paul's hectic schedule would allow. Serge needed him, and when he became a Catholic, Paul found he needed Serge. Although he never directly confided in Serge the eddying depths of Julia's rejection, his family's hostility, Serge held out instinctive support. Somehow, Serge was able to accept his new-found faith without demur. Indeed, he gave Paul some respect for it. He was never sure whether or not he believed himself, he said, but he liked a ritualistic ambiance, a sense of reverence for the sacred, whether God existed or not.

At length, and to Paul's delight, Serge married an eminently sensible woman, Fiona. If Paul had given the matter any thought, he might have recognized a common thread between himself and Serge's wife. They had similar personalities in some ways and an underlying brief to care for Serge. Fiona was heiress to acres in Northumberland and Serge disappeared there and settled with surprising ease into the role of gentleman farmer.

It was in this guise that Paul supposed he had known Serge the longest if not the best. The best he had known him had been when he had accompanied Serge to Paris for his father's funeral. He had watched Serge embrace the waxy corpse and had walked him up and down the banks of the Seine afterwards, trying to work out of him the sting of the poisoned kiss. For the last twenty years, however, invitations to the country had come for the most part from Fiona, and Paul had liked to spend the odd weekend there on the borders, traipsing round Hadrian's Wall with Serge in a wordless companionship with dogs. Paul had taken an avuncular interest in Serge's children (he made a surprisingly good parent) and had had them up to London. He was, indeed, the godfather of the eldest. At times, he and Serge would sit by the fire with whisky, talking of old friends and life, while Fiona sewed and smiled. She thought Paul a good influence.

As for this business about the Romanovs surviving the Revolution, Paul supposed it must come from old Prince Boris, but in an indirect way. Paul's and Fiona's theory, never openly voiced to Serge, was that the dead man told tales through Serge's life in every action and reaction. Serge would not hear of it. To his father's memory, he had done what his father might have done to him if he had lived. He cut his sire off without a penny. He cultivated an overt zeal to be English. He wore a Barbour and green Wellington boots, drove a Range Rover and talked boringly of sheep. Certainly, he saw his mother faithfully, but Paul always thought Serge kept Fiona and his mother apart. Either his Russianness had disturbed him or his family had. Paul could never quite put his finger on it. With the Mirkovskys' egregious foreignness of habit, one could not really discern that the family had been unhappy for other reasons. The sister Varya had always seemed a trampled woman

93

to Paul, and despite Serge's apparent domestic contentment, he had always drunk a dangerous amount too much.

Paul cut these analytic ramblings short. In a sense he could not utterly describe, there had been some other quality in Serge the night before, as if he had tunnelled through and caved right into another level in his personality. It was very disturbing. Oh, he had trailed around for the better part of a half-an-hour using reasoned argument to think *about* Serge, when all along, this imperfect tool had no power to uncover what was *in* Serge. His vision, rather kept on travelling back to the eyes like hard-boiled eggs, to new and slightly inappropriate mannerisms, and to Serge's dishonest reserve with him in the garden. It was certainly not out of the bounds of Serge's character to take a rash interest in the Russian royal family; there had always been a strand of gullibility in his nature. As if the dead were talking, Paul had sensed a faint but definite odour of corruption that seemed to emanate from Serge.

Paul shook his head to rid himself of this notion. He had spent far too long with the dead. He took off his hat and mopped his brow. He had finally reached the main road of the island, which connected Hora with Skala, the upper and lower towns. Despite a week's sleep and food, he still felt wildly disoriented here in Greece. Even though in Roman times, it had been a place of banishment because of its barrenness, the island seemed lush to him after Ethiopia. And as he dined, day after day, night after night, at the house or at the taverna on Aga Levia Square, it was a shock to him to see so much food. It really did daze and puzzle him, this abundance. He kept on thinking it must be Christmas. As for the Princess, fond as he was of her, he could barely stifle his irritation with her worries about diet, her fear of dying. 'Anger, avarice and dejection are all offshoots of gluttony,' he had read to her that morning early before the rest of the household had risen. He had gone to her bedroom to check on her before his walk, and at her request, had given her a dawn dose of guidance from *The Philokalia*, an ancient text by Church Fathers. His words drifting across her snowy counterpane had met her eager ears and she had nodded like a pleased and swaddled baby listening to a nursery tune. Along with the taking of blood pressure, this spiritual reading seemed part of his duties in a house where a day's rations would feed an Ethiopian family for a week. Every day, the distended bellies of the starved came to his mind despite a forceful effort to exclude them. How amazing was the speed of corruption in the heat! He thought of it now as the Greek sun dazzled near full Heaven. How quick was the decomposition of the dead. After a while, he had not felt like a doctor at all and maybe that was it. Why heal, he had wondered, what would merely die? Instead, he had felt like a death-camp artist – the practitioner of a savage prolonging of torment, and an efficient expert on the furnace of the sun and its capacity. He knew a few things now about bones and teeth and hair. 'Stop!' he said to himself. 'Stop thinking about it!' He made an effort to think about Patmos instead. About St John. 'Think about Patmos,' he said aloud. 'Think about making a trip to Ephesus. You will have a nice trip there.' In recent years, he had taken to addressing himself in the second person singular. He would issue commands and hold conversations with himself.

He looked again at the road and tried to focus on the task ahead. He could take the paved gradation that wound down the hill to Skala, or the shorter route, an old stony mule path, used for generations by pilgrims to the Monastery and to the Shrine of the Cave of Revelations below. Paul decided that if Serge were to be found anywhere along the way to the lower town, it would be on the easier tarmac road. Before launching down it though, he used the vantage point of the hill to survey the area for any sign of his errant friend. The sea and the hills stretched beneath him, and he was seized by a sudden calm, a gratitude for the illimitable shades of blue in the water, sky and hazy hills, evaporating in the distance beyond the power of his eye to see. It *was* beautiful. He *was* going to enjoy it. He was no saint who could starve himself forever or live on a column. He had done what he could. He could do no more. He was going home. And that was that.

There was no sign of Serge, drunk or sober. Turning around, however, he suddenly spied Marina and Helena leaning together on the parapet which abutted the road on which he was standing. Instinctively, he drew back. The women were murmuring as they stood, apparently quite deep in conversation. There again, he picked up the scent from Helena that he had caught from Serge. Why this? Why should this appalling odourless creep of maggots crawl into every situation or person he disliked? He tried the bridge of reason, but it eluded him as he watched Helena talk with her distinct charm, her layers and angles. He was sure they were talking about Marina's husband. Who else? The fluttery Marina, now grave, struck him all at once as recent widow. Why had he not seen it before, that drained look of the mourner? And Helena was going on and on in a way that reminded him of a typewriter. That was it, what he had seen at luncheon. At no point had Helena behaved to Marina as if she had been newly bereaved. And then there

95

had been this apparent misrepresentation to him before of Marina, the femme fatale ... There was a human inflection missing somewhere in Helena, but he was not clear about it. She seemed, as she talked, to be someone who added up long columns of numbers in her head without really knowing the significant figures in the sum.

Then, suddenly Marina moved, pushing away from the wall. His eye caught an aspect of her face. It was like a single note struck. Her pale hair unfurled in the wind. He thought, Oh. Despite Helena's assertions, he had not been aware that Marina was beautiful or that he had felt attracted to her, but he now realized that she was and that he had actually shown off to her rather. He was a little embarrassed.

Helena said something incisive. Oh, she was formidable. Then Marina replied, speaking earnestly, and then she stopped. Paul stepped out of the shadow of the wall, but as he did so, Marina turned sharply and vanished in the direction of the Monastery. He was vaguely disappointed, especially when it was Helena who caught his eye. He was forced to wave to her and her expression gave him an uncomfortable feeling. Nevertheless, he dismissed it, and set off down the road with a more purposeful stride.

VIII

MARINA LIT a long beeswax taper and stuck it in the sand-filled candle-holder which stood in front of St John the Theologian, flat and Byzantine. He wore a sombre garment and a silver halo. An inkpot at his side, he frowned at a gilded, bound text of his vision, the last book of the Bible, inscrutable and sealed until the end of time.

Marina looked straight into the eyes of the icon, deploring herself. All the time Helena had been speaking to her about Arthur, she had been vexed by what the Princess had said about the Kuriensky family and her resemblance to it. It left her with a nauseated, inflated feeling, and she stiffened her spine against a long, swelling ache for the story to be true. She knew she was not related to these people, and yet it hung in the balance with her that she might be. Somehow, the large icon of the saint, vivid and paternal, struck her with the notion that it was better to accept evidence of real confusion rather than to leap at a false but comforting conclusion. Nonetheless, she felt the temptation of the hungry to raid the larder. She knew she was not going to, but the appetite was there all the same.

Marina had a sudden, passionate wish to be alone. She had decided from the outset to eschew anything but the most perfunctory devotion in the Monastery, for since they had entered it, she had felt Helena fidgeting within its walls. But even though she tried and succeeded to resist effusion, she found old, half-forgotten words of prayers welling in her mind, disjointed, and she found herself whispering them. She put a few drachmas in a box, then suddenly stricken by a cold shadow over her heart, she fished out another taper and kissed it. She lit it. 'For Arthur,' she said.

Out of the corner of her eye, Marina observed Helena shifting in a kind of moody suspension. Perhaps it was because when they had gone upstairs to visit the icon gallery of the Monastery, Helena had not been able to find a painting that her mother had donated, a valuable Virgin Eleussa of the Cretan School. Uncomfortable, Marina moved through a low doorway into a little chapel where another Virgin blazed in red regalia, her face in blank passivity while her Infant, with no less mildness, observed His Cross to come, borne by an angel which hovered over His shoulder. Marina resisted offering a candle to this one, and Helena seemed relieved. To the right of the icon, there was a niche in the wall, and in it, a bier encrusted with silver. A fresco of Christ in Majesty sat holding the Scriptures open to a page, and Marina wondered what it said. She drifted with Helena towards the tomb. An inscription said the relics of a saint – 'The Holy Christodoulos' – were entombed in the silver bier. A sense of black grief invaded her. Arthur had so mistrusted her that he had planned the disposal of his body down to the very last detail. Somehow, the presence of Helena and this elaborate reliquary put her in mind of his funeral – the coffin rolling towards the furnace, and then the subsequent trip to Orford, where she and his children had scattered his ashes over the stern of the boat and into the sea.

It had been a raw, vile day in March, and the sky had been filled with wind. Marina remembered the slow journey in the suffocating limousine; first, to the crematorium to fetch his urn, and then the long, slow battle with the traffic out of London with her stepdaughter Claire, and Claire's son Jeremy, and her stepson Henry and his wife, whose silver bangles clicked all the way up the A12 to Suffolk in the otherwise silent car. Henry wore a suit, but not a black tie. The limousine had been his idea, and he had paid for it. He was a stockbroker in the City and had done very well despite, or, as Marina herself often thought, because of Arthur's contemptuous attitude towards him. The divorce had hit Henry harder than it had Claire. At least, that was how it seemed at first. He had been at a crucial stage of his education and had failed exams . . . suffered. And yet of the two, he had come to accept Marina with more philosophy than his sister. He had emerged as a small-scale tycoon, and Marina had accepted his last, ironic gift to his father, the ride to the coast in a Daimler, not a Rolls, as a gesture justified through pain, and an oddly touching one. It was all he had to give. The bruise had taken longer to come out in Claire and it remained and would remain. She was possessed of an implacable bitterness. The car started and stopped. There were unexpected road-works and they were to meet the launch at Orford at three. There had been wrangles about where to put the urn and it had been decided that it should ride with the chauffeur in front. He had had to strap it in with a seat-belt.

Claire disliked her son, a nervous child of thirteen whose grades were never good at school and who had large teeth and awkward wrists which kept jutting compulsively from his clean cuffs while his mother looked angrily at his every move. Marina was five years older than Henry and seven than Claire whose hair had already started to streak with grey and whose marriage was in difficulty. Marina remembered with shame her attempts to befriend Claire when she had first come to live with Arthur and the cold refusals, the final, vehement push. Claire always wore expensive, smart clothes now and looked like a business-woman or publisher or television executive, which she was not. It was as if she were preparing herself in readiness for a call of an obscure nature to a position of power. She sat crumpled in a grey silk blouse next to the window and refused to open it because it might blow her hair.

Marina had no idea why Arthur had chosen Orford for this last, lugubrious act. His family had come from Cambridgeshire and his father had been an Anglican divine in several cathedral towns. Arthur had lived in Buckinghamshire and he had lived in London. In the early years of their marriage, Marina and Arthur had gone on long weekends frequently, and he had taken her there. He would plough into her on these occasions with more zeal than he did in their sleek new flat where they had set up married life together. Somehow these jaunts to coastal towns or country hotels had the aura of secretive pleasure, as if they were still lovers. Arthur had seemed to be setting her up first against one backdrop and then against another, as if something had gone wrong with a tryst and someone else had been substituted for the woman he loved. Marina could not quite recall what had gone wrong in Orford, but something had. Like all of their places, it had a little inn with good food and a fire and a wine-list, bedrooms with oak beams and chintz bedspreads. Seafood. They had eaten seafood, made love, slept late. Marina remembered that from an early stage in their marriage a kind of desperation had made her doze a lot. She had dozed and whenever they went away together, she had found herself thanking him for everything, a lobster or a visit to the pub, in an abject way, apologizing to him for boring him. This was a habit which increased with time and which bled into their everyday lives together.

So surely, the little fishing town had no connection with her. She had a vague idea that they had visited a medieval tower, but that was all. Like other things which emerged at a later stage of their marriage, his wish to have his ashes scattered there was quite beyond her reach. Of course, she had his journals. Fearfully, when the will had been read and his wishes had been made known as to the disposal of his body, Marina had been tempted to open his big, old desk and raid the musty diaries he had kept for hints or news of another woman. Of the many reasons she had gone to New York after the funeral, one of the most pressing had been an escape from the task she knew lay before her. Not surprisingly, he had not made her his executor, and Marina wondered if this represented a final blow to be dealt from beyond the grave. Faute de mieux, she inherited it anyway. She simply had not been able to face it – what he had said about her and what he had really thought. And so she managed to cheer herself with the idea that Arthur might as easily have taken a pin and put it blindly in a map, choosing the place for its very randomness and its freedom from all associations. That would have been like him too.

In order to execute his will, Marina and his children had hired a launch to take them from the village to the sea. They arrived, piled out of the limousine, creased and swollen with bad feeling. The wind swooped about the stone houses and whipped the water which furled and trembled. The owner of the launch had got it up with a garland and some people had assembled on the pier, cautiously and at a distance. Out of the corner of her eye, Marina observed a few gentrified faces, not peering but immobile, and she wondered if they were readers of Arthur's work who had come to see the poet's casting in the sea. Whoever they were, it seemed ghoulish of them to be there, as if, Marina thought, they were observers at the scene of a crash. The boatman advised Henry that the wind was so far up that the scattering might be difficult to achieve without embarrassment. This had not occurred to anyone and for a moment, the Holts stood on the pier united in one emotion of controlled horror at the thought of putting off the final act.

'No,' Marina had said, 'If there is no danger to anyone, we will do it now. Some cove can be found. Or you can sail into the wind and we can throw the ashes from the back of the boat.'

Suddenly, she felt the gratitude of Henry and a small movement from Claire. 'It's now or never,' Claire added, and she began to cry. Jeremy touched her sleeve.

The launch bucked and swayed as it got underway. From it Marina could see the hotel where she and Arthur had stayed, but she swerved her gaze. Claire's hair was wildly whipping in the wind. Almost idiotically, the words came over and over '. . . have crucified my loving Saviour . . . have crucified my loving Saviour . . .', but she could not think why this shred of prayer should occur to her now. The wind whirled around the party on the boat. For some reason, the garland stayed in place nailed to the mast even though the rushing air nearly deafened them. 'Have crucified . . .' Why that now at Orford? Why did these words, so recently re-hinged to the bones of a faith he had induced her to reject, come back to her at a moment when keeping faith to him should have excluded them? Where her final act of oblation should have been utter, should have been a complete emptiness and absence of thought. She had done almost everything, at first, to avoid occasions of belief. In the early years of their marriage, she had ditched it, then later controlled it, partly because it upset her to be confronted with a memory of its rigours, and partly because it drove Arthur to a kind of frenzy to see her eye lurk on a church or stray to a crucifix. But when the suffering between them had become most profound, she had, indeed, secretly and wordlessly prayed, and it had grown into a kind of infidelity to him for which she had felt guilty, and now she gripped the rails of the launch in an effort to exclude further acts of betrayal.

Claire, Jeremy, Henry and she had stood together, touching each other. They drew closer as if now they were one face of Arthur as they separated from Arthur for the last time. The four of them had to do with his body, and only Henry's silent wife stood at any distance from them at all. Her name was Sylvia. 'A very ordinary girl,' Arthur had always said. She looked as if she felt seasick, but did not want to say because of the solemnity of the occasion.

The urn was sealed. They had agreed that Henry would undo it. Marina remembered how when she had first come to England she had wanted friends but that nothing was casual any more once she had married Arthur. No more flopping on her bed in the dorm or having a coke, no more gossiping or lolling, and to her shame, after all she had done to attain it, the purdah of marriage made all the admiring glances in which she had come to bask and rely, insolence which she felt bound to repel, but did not want to. Her first instinct had been to romp up to Henry and be pals, but she was his stepmother, and no Phaedre either. Phaedre, who had stood chewing myrtle leaves behind a bush in order to slake her lust for Hippolytus. No. Henry looked like Arthur as he hunched down over the urn, trying to break its seal. Some of his friends called him Harry and his wife called him 'Boodle', this son of Arthur Holt, who had once been mentioned, tentatively, in the same breath with Shelley. Marina could avoid the urn no longer – the ashes of that body to which she had sacrificed these people and herself – a little college girl who had been made into a Venus by this man. Henry's face was pink with effort and she knelt beside him, spoiling her knees and clipping her black stockings. He broke it. Arthur had broken her virginity in this way – like an urn. Together, they gazed on the ashes and fragments of bone tied up in a plastic bag. 'My God!' said Henry. 'Fucking hell.' Against the door to the cabin, Claire leaned as if drunk on the wind. The three of them stared at the urn. 'We have to read some of his poetry, don't we?' Claire said rather than asked. 'Anyone remember to bring a book?'

Suddenly, it was as if they were all colluding in the disposal of this body as accomplices after crime, as if they had all three poured lime on his bones and were dispensing with the evidence in this way. No 'I know that my redeemer liveth,' nor 'Ashes to ashes and dust to dust.' The wind howled on and they were numb with cold, their hands too stiff to undo the knot in the bag.

'What should we recite?' Marina asked. No one had remembered a book. Why had they all come all of this way and forgotten the book? 'What can we say?' Claire asked.

'I know one,' Jeremy said, suddenly curious over his grandfather's ashes. 'I had to learn one in school. I know one. It's the one called *The Rim of the Styx*. I can say it. Except I don't think Grandpa would think I could say it very well.' Everyone suddenly looked at the child. 'Well, I don't have to,' he said. 'I won't if you don't like.' His mother looked wild, incongruous in her expression as if she had taken a trapeze and swung over all her conventions towards a new arrival at a mad place.

'Yes, you do that, Jem,' she said.

'That's good, Jem,' Marina said. 'Really good.' But thought, I'm a murderess. A murderess and I hated that poem and I hated . . . but she could not contemplate this. Through my own grievous fault . . . she thought instead, as if the wind had snatched it up from a remote place and put it into her head. Not murdered him, though . . . he is dead, that is all.

What had Claire said five years ago? 'You killed my mother, you bloody tart. You might as well have murdered her!' and Marina wondered if Claire would say the same thing about her father in the boat.

Together they lifted the ashes in the bag to the stern, and Henry shouted to the boatman to turn the prow towards the wind. The Holts all stood at the stern. Jem muttered the poem, each word snatched to the breeze as he stammered and forgot word after word, but said it.

'My father to the sea,' Henry said, and spilled the ashes and bones.

There was a lot of it and the wind whipped and lashed the fine dust of Arthur up to meet the spume, and some of it did blow back and some gulls appeared and interested themselves in the strewn body. 'My father,' Henry said. 'He was my father.'

'He was mine too,' Claire said.

'Do you want to keep this thing?' Henry asked, picking up the empty urn. 'Does anyone? Marina? Claire? Jem?' He flung it into the sea. 'A "num" question,' Henry said. 'Father would have been pleased with that. *Num*. Latin. Expecting the answer "no".' His bitterness was such that Marina indeed started to cry.

'I think we ought to throw that garland on,' she said after a moment. The gulls were circling around the place where the ashes bobbed and gusted. And she reached up and took the nailed wreath of pale, cheap flowers from the mast and flung them after the ashes.

After they had done, Henry was all for getting drunk in the inn where so many years ago Marina and Arthur had lain entangled with sheets and had had champagne sent to the room. 'No,' said Marina, 'Not there.' So they found a roadhouse on the A12 going back to London and drank, even with the child present, an inordinate amount of alcohol while the chauffeur waited in the car.

'You still look tired,' Helena said, 'And so pensive, so sad.' The two women retreated into the courtyard for a moment in order to let a party of Japanese tourists through the main body of the church. A young monk with a black beard and hat sat gloomily invigilating the influx of the quiet herd in their delicate clothing and neat, expensive cameras. He looked limp and defeated, possibly by the sight of so many people so foreign to him. In an arched portico, his head was surrounded by frescos of saints and of angels. Marina smiled at him and he managed a look of Christian resignation.

'I am sad . . . and tired,' she said. 'I keep thinking about Arthur. I don't want to be a bore about him.' The women looked demure. In the pebbled courtyard, vehemently bright, a few desultory tourists ambled. Marina and Helena moved across it towards a gold mosaic of the Holy Christodoulos, whose tomb they had just seen. He bore a model of the church in his hands.

'Oh, no, I don't think you could bore me about Arthur,' Helena said.

Marina fiddled with the guide-book. 'This is the founder of the

Monastery here, isn't it?' she asked. 'It says here that he was a peasant . . . and a hermit.'

'You *must* think about him,' said Helena. There was a sealed-off well in the courtyard and she sat down on its cover. 'You have to "work it through" as they say in your country, and then let go.'

'I wish I could take a picture of you,' Marina said on a sudden impulse of love. She thought how cool and neat Helena looked, how shining and silvery her hair. She had a clear, silver voice too. 'It goes against the grain with me to bring a camera. It is the sort of thing Arthur used to deplore, and I got used to using my eyes instead. But I would like a picture of you all the same.'

'Well, that can be arranged,' Helena said. Sometimes she had a fresh, light laugh that seemed to spring from her with an incongruous spontaneity. Marina was pleased to have elicited this and she felt that she had somehow delighted Helena.

'I wish I could see Arthur's face in my mind's eye,' Marina said. 'I can't picture it. I keep wishing he'd let me have a Mass said, even though he did not believe in anything. I craved it very badly. Just now, I was thinking about throwing his ashes on the sea. I was thinking about the relics of this saint here, how preciously they have been preserved. Arthur had no such hope. I mean he hoped in nothing. He thought there was nothing to do with death that was worth keeping.'

'Except for the taking of women and slaves with him!' Helena said sharply, and the harshness of her voice made Marina start back slightly. Sitting on the well-cover, Helena looked slightly veiled and gnomic, oddly like her elderly aunt.

'What do you mean?'

'I'm not entirely sure,' Helena said. 'It simply came out. Arthur abhorred Christianity, of course . . .' here she paused, thought, but went on. 'He made much of having had an early bad experience of it, as you yourself must know. But he never shook, I think, the idea that forces beyond his control drove him, and in that sense he was a failed humanist. He would have expected . . . sacrifices at his funeral. I'm surprised that he did not ask for goats to be slaughtered. To appease Zeus? Who knows? I always thought that business of his identifying with Hephaestus a little disingenuous of Arthur. All that forging of words in his crucible, his Byronic limp! I don't think he loved failed gods. And I don't think you should commit suttee just because things did not work out well between you.'

The well-regulated party of Japanese filed past them on their way to a refectory behind the courtyard. Arthur had indeed had a slight limp and indeed Marina had thought it Byronic when first they had met. His wounded foot. The wounded Arthur. He had told her that it had been mangled in a rabbit trap on his grandfather's land. He had been teased at school, where, because he could not play games, he had poured over the classics. He had been surprisingly sensitive about the foot. The foot had marked him and he had said that his preoccupation with it had suppressed his strong physical nature, until he had met Marina, he had said, on whom he had splurged everything pent up. She remembered his rage at the foot. It had been inexplicable to her why it had been such torment to him to be so slightly lame. She had understood it, but not in a way that made sense. Tears welled up in her eyes. 'Oh, don't, don't, Helena,' she said.

She could not think why Helena was looking at her now in such a curious way, for her face was quite dreadful. 'Did you have any idea what you were getting into with Arthur?' she asked. 'I really don't think you had.'

'Let's see the church now,' Marina said weakly.

Helena averted her gaze, then smiled a little ruefully, Marina thought. 'Sorry to get so exercised about it,' she said. 'but Arthur exerts a fascinating pull. He was a very powerful man in his way.'

'He thought himself . . . helpless, I think,' Marina replied. 'If only I had been able to sustain his gift for him, then I would not feel so wretched.'

'All these guilts — ought and should — if!' Helena wrung her hands slightly. 'Why ought you to have done anything? Why should you feel things you do not feel? Why feel wretched about things you could not help? I am very strongly persuaded that Arthur dried up because he simply burnt out. It happens.'

They walked through the portico past the guardian monk into the tiny jewel of the Monastery church. The smell of incense lay thickly on the air from an earlier ceremony, and smoky wreaths of it still hung about the ceiling from which hung heavy, silver votive lamps. There was a richly carved reredos: on it, in gold, ochre, red and blue, were old, oiled panels of Christ and the Virgin. Marina had an impulse to lay her head against one of these, to confide as to someone human, but she went back to her ravellings. Looking up, she saw a circular Christ Pantocrator in the dome. Arthur had kept her from confronting this Judge, this weighing figure in whose balance she saw herself wanting. Maybe that was why she had married him. She had often thought this and had maimed herself with thinking it. Although she knew she must take it on faith that she was forgiven, she found it hard, somehow, to credit. Now, she did not know whether the hand of the Pantocrator was raised to smite or bless her, but she thought she caught the ghost of a smile in the eyes so far above her. A sense that Helena was making an attempt to help her off some hook sprang up delicately within her and she was grateful. It struck her that Arthur had always himself judged her harshly as he did everyone and everything. She realized how afraid she had been of his acute and critical mind.

The two women moved together through a low door into another chapel. 'I can't understand,' Marina whispered. 'I don't know why it was that I could never understand him.'

They peered into the gloom behind yet another iconstasis. There, almost completely hidden in the shadows, was a fresco, tender, sombre and vivid with innocent expression, of the Virgin enthroned with Child. 'Oh, how lovely!' Marina cried. Although the figures were painted to a regulation Byzantine stiffness, they were curiously human examples of a subject endlessly repeated, gilded, adorned and encrusted. This pair, in contrast, had an almost mischievous look about the eyes, as if the two of them, Mother and Infant, could barely suppress a delightful secret commonly shared between them and could not wait to tell the beholder what it was.

'I understood him very well indeed!' Helena said abruptly. 'Perhaps enough for the two of us.'

Marina looked at her sharply for the urgency in her tone. In the cool, hushed, intimate chapel, they were alone. Marina felt again a kind of awe at Helena, who stood taut as a dancer before her. It looked as if she were posed in readiness to making a daring leap. Glints of light from the doorway caught at her hair and crisp dress. Her neat ankles were together and her hands poised beside her.

'Marina,' she said, somewhat breathlessly. 'Marina, I have something to tell you.'

'What is it?' A rush of feeling seemed to open a space between them where they were able to look directly at each other. Marina had the curious impression that Helena was about to make some terrible declaration of love, and she found herself withdrawing slightly towards the choir stalls.

'I feel bound to talk to you about my own relationship with Arthur before we go any further,' Helena said, and for some reason this relieved Marina slightly. 'You see, I have come to care for you in this very short time, and because of that, I think you should know that Arthur and I were lovers, not at the time that you were married, and I ended it.'

Marina felt queerly still. She clenched and unclenched her hands and found her eyes fixed on the doorway to the cobbled passage outside the chapel. The light seemed very bright, framed by the dark lintels. She looked again at Helena and blinked.

'I understood him,' Helena said again, 'in a way I don't think you could. You were so much younger than he was, and an American. What is more, you have a kind of innocence that could not see Arthur credibly. He belonged to a whole different culture and generation. And because I am a part of that, I know it is unfair of you to accuse yourself of things you had nothing to do with. I knew his first wife Jane, and I knew his friends . . . so you see?'

Marina was still silent. Whatever else she had believed about Arthur, she had thought herself the only other woman, the only woman besides Jane, for he had told her so. She put her head to one side and opened her mouth to speak, but nothing occurred to her to say.

Helena seemed pricked by her silence. 'Suppose you had found out? Suppose someone else had told you? Now he is dead, there may well be books. In fact, I am considering writing one myself. And so it has to come out.' She reached a hand out, then retracted it. 'I had to tell you myself if we are to be the friends I am so sure we will be. I am so very sure.'

Marina looked quizzically at Helena, who stood before her on the worn stone floor as if on an exact point of honour. There had been a fineness in her speech and manner and Marina could not quite grasp why it gave her such pain to be told by Helena that she had been Arthur's lover. Surely, it was noble of her to have been honest. The sharp crease of the hem of Helena's dress moved in a breeze from the doorway. She had a slender waist still, like a girl's, and full grey eyes. She waited for Marina to speak. For some reason, Marina saw in her mind's eye the dusk gathering, rose and gold, towards darkness from the vantage point of the Acropolis, the sun going down over the Agora where St Paul had preached and where the Temple of Hephaestus still stood. Why this occurred to her, she did not know – the dreadful heat cooling and the sheen of light through the polluted air.

'I had no idea,' she said at last. 'He never told me. But it can't matter now, can it?' she said, although it did.

Helena slanted her eyes downwards. 'What you did not see before, but must see now is that I *know* how oppressive he was.' She looked up, engaging Marina's eyes with her own. 'We share it, you see.'

Marina felt the heft of a weight descend, but smiled brightly in order to conceal it. She moved through the doorway, and together she and Helena went to the refectory where there were yet more frescos. 'The Raising of Lazarus', 'The Visit of the Magi'. A group of Germans were now inspecting the paintings.

Marina did not wish to discuss Arthur's oppressiveness. 'He always admired you,' she said, after some thought. 'Is that because you ended the affair?'

'Did he admire me?' Helena asked, and her veiled eagerness to know made Marina flinch. 'I don't know if that is why he admired me. It's not beyond the bounds of possibility that Arthur was a puritan at heart and that could be why I felt crushed by him. But to tell you the truth, I never really knew why I did end the affair . . .' She looked at Marina with genuine puzzlement on her face.

'Were you jealous of me?' Marina asked, then regretted the question.

'No!' Helena cried. A few Germans turned their heads. 'No, I wasn't jealous. I don't believe that is a very constructive emotion.'

Marina wondered at someone who was able to help being jealous. She accused herself of feeling jealous now. 'I suppose he was upset when you ended it,' she said, yet somehow she could not imagine that he had been. He would have been angry.

Helena sighed and Marina felt an odd dart of pity for her. 'Oh, he took it well. In fact, after it was all over, he would ring me, sometimes late at night. He used to ask me my advice. He treated me as if I were a sort of colleague, which I suppose I was.' There was something infinitely sad about Helena's voice.

Marina absently trailed her fingers along an ancient stone table where in early times the monks of the place had had their meals. It was sunk low with age and there were cruciform indentations in the stone. She wondered where they had put their knees.

'Why aren't you angry with him?' Helena cried suddenly. 'If I were you, I would be angry with him. Look what he put you through! You were just a young girl!'

'I'm in no position to be angry,' Marina said. Her voice wobbled treacherously. 'I was insane to marry him, you know. He didn't force me! I had great ambitions to be the mother of his children. I don't know why. But even when he told me he didn't want any more children, I still needed him and wanted him. I knew all about Jane and Henry and Claire and I don't know what I would have done if he had not left them. I simply ceased to care about anybody but myself. It wasn't even sex. I can't explain it.'

'That was the Arthur effect,' Helena said. 'There was no resistance in one.'

'You resisted him. And I'm sure, yes, I'm very sure that is why he looked up to you. He despised me!' The Germans had left the refectory and Marina's voice welled into a crescendo. Her eye caught the tempera figure of the shrouded Christ entombed by wailing women. She covered her mouth with her hand. Wretchedly, she thought, Please no, why did I say that? For the minute her words were out of her mouth, she thought she saw Helena catch them and take them in with a curious avidity. And yet she was sure that Helena quite loathed Arthur.

'A loveless marriage has an oddly damaging effect,' Helena said. 'I know. I was in one myself. Apart from anything else, the sex disgusts one.'

Marina felt winded, as if she had been punched in the thorax. 'It was not without love, our marriage,' Marina said slowly. 'It was not.'

The women found their way back out into the courtyard where yet another party from the boats, which visited Patmos daily from nearby islands, had assembled. Some of the men were wrapped in towels, and one sheepishly wore a skirt. There was a lot of laughing from the sunburnt, pink-face crowd. It appeared that the Monastery supplied clothing to those whom they considered to be immodestly dressed and the whole conception of this seemed so foreign to the visitors that they chuckled and shook their heads like schoolchildren. It seemed an inconceivable thing for the monks to make them do.

Marina felt a great heaviness and found it hard to look at Helena. She went to the little shop where they sold postcards, copies of icons and tapes of liturgical music. She thought she would get something for Henry and Claire and Jem to whom she always sent greetings which were never returned. Out of the corner of her eye, she sensed Helena as a close, shadowing presence. She chose a picture of The Wise Virgins in procession with tapers, and one of Christ preaching to the Samaritan woman. There was another one of St Peter and St Paul embracing, which she decided to send to Jem. The dull pain she had felt throughout her conversation with Helena thickened and in place of the shock it had been to have heard that she and Helena had shared the same man, there welled up a physical disgust.

Helena, on the other hand, stood aloof with the expression of one who has found a possible clue to an interesting enigma. Marina, on paying the moustachioed man at the counter, noticed a tremor in her hands. She folded the envelope of cards into her handbag. 'Helena?' she asked.

'What is it, my dear?' Helena blinked and moved closer to Marina.

'Helena, you said Arthur had often asked your advice. Did he ever ask your advice about me?' she asked, keeping up the mood of quiet inquisition she had tried to adopt in the refectory. 'You said he had called you in the night. Did he ever call you about me?'

'No, no. He never did that,' Helena said. 'I did not even know about you until I saw the poems, and then I did not realize it was actually you until I read something about it in the papers. There was a piece in the *Observer*, you'll recall. Then I heard you were married. No, he never consulted me on matters of real importance, just little things, that's all.'

Marina looked around, then down. She felt her face about to contort. She drew breath. Helena was looking at her intently. Her face was slightly flushed. She stood still on the cobblestones and when she saw Marina's expression, she closed her eyes and swayed slightly.

IX

'MILK?' Helena inquired. 'Actually, I don't recommend it.' She was poised over the tea things under the shady leaves on the terrace, and she proffered a cup to Marina. 'Sugar? Lemon?'

'I like it just as it comes,' said Marina. 'Thank you.'

It must have been a trick of the light, Paul thought, that had earlier made Marina seem beautiful. The sun had deserted the garden, and in the afternoon slant of rays, she looked creased and wan. She accepted the cup from Helena. Her hand shook and the spoon clicked on the saucer.

'Paul? I forget. Lemon?'

'As Marina.' Helena seemed wand-like over the bone china and poured tea with a ceremonious air. She handed him the delicate brew in the delicate cup.

'And I'm glad to see you're on the mend,' she said to her cousin Serge. Like Marina, he sat in a tense slump, his handsome jaw jowly and somewhat in need of a shave. 'Strong?' Helena piped.

'Cut it out, Helena,' Serge said. 'You know I like it strong.'

Helena popped two sugar cubes into the cup with tongs. 'I bring this,' she said to Marina, 'every year from London. Once I was stopped by customs. Earl Grey! I don't know what they thought it was. Only not so long ago, I learned that Evangalia thought we were all invalids or hypochondriacs. No one drinks tea in Greece except as a restorative and here we have it every afternoon. The local tisane, though, is rather nice and you must try it. I think it is made from camomile and something else.

Marina sipped the tea, her eyelashes fluttering in the steam. Paul noticed she had been crying, for her lids were puffy, and she had applied heavier make-up.

No one could think of anything to say. Marina shouldered her way up the back of the chair in order to sit straighter and bestowed a ghastly bright smile on the company. 'It is quite lovely to have a cup of tea,' she said.

Serge similarly regenerated himself, leaned forward and said, 'So nice to have met you at last. We have heard so much about you.'

Marina smiled nervously. 'It's very kind of you to have me to stay.'

Helena arched her brow at her cousin. 'Do have lemon, Marina. It comes from our tree.' She waved a ringed hand at a lemon tree voluptuous with fruit in the lower terrace. Marina dutifully proffered her cup. She look so imperilled to Paul, like a child at the birthday party of an older and fancier friend. 'And we seem to have the Madeira cake today of Evangalia's adaptation – more lemon, same tree. I think it's rather good.' She plunged a knife into the sticky cake, thick with sugar.

'Oh yummy,' said Serge. They all solemnly ate cake. Serge scoffed it with the voracious bad manners of a grandee and asked for more. Helena nibbled hers and Paul had no appetite. Serge refused to look at him and the large muscle of his jaw worked angrily.

'So Maman is tucked up, is she?' he asked Helena.

'Indeed, *Eugene Onegin* for you. Very soon we will hear the thump of her stick.' She seemed to be displaying all these glossed actions and words to Marina. 'He must read it every night in a penitential way you would understand, my love,' she said. 'Ah, for the clear cosmology of Dante and a purgatory!' Marina squirmed a little and mouthed at the crumby, yellow cake. 'Serge,' Helena continued, 'you'll be interested to hear that Aunt Sonya thinks Marina is our relation. She made a great thing of it at lunch.'

'Oh, but I'm not!' Marina said miserably, blushing to the roots of her hair.

'You're quite right not to want to claim it,' Serge said. 'Genetically speaking we are a disaster. Remember Uncle Pasha? And, of course, there is always Maman herself.' He gave Marina a winning smile. The two seemed to transmit an evil horridness to Paul, but he felt powerless against it, having only winged and wounded Serge earlier. He had meant to strike a direct hit, score a point and make him see the need for reform. Some frisson between Helena and Marina made him feel that their afternoon had been similiarly unsatisfactory. He wished that Serge would not take it out on this fragile guest, though, for she seemed on the verge of tears. Perhaps sensing this, Serge checked himself, for he was not a cruel man. His voice lowered and he changed tack. 'You know, I was very sorry to read of the death of your husband. I hope you don't mind my mentioning it. I admired his poetry. He was a bit like Lawrence Durrell in a way, I always thought and I like Durrell . . . in some ways like Hardy.'

Marina breathed out and smiled with sudden, warm gratitude. 'Thank you,' she said. 'He did admire Durrell. I always thought he should write a novel, but he could never settle to one as he disliked plotting.'

'His work was very schematic, nonetheless,' said Serge.

A shade of her beauty returned to Marina's cheek and Paul noticed that Helena withdrew and seemed to perch her back in the depths of her chair. Under the fig tree with its new fist-buds, she looked lost in some alien thought.

'I never pretended to understand it,' said Marina smiling gently. But she cast a sidelong glance at Helena that Paul wanted to describe as fearful. 'What I can't get over is how beautiful this island is!' she said, changing the subject.

'It is,' Serge replied. 'I have always loved it.' Helena's eyes seemed to shoot a contradictory bolt. At this point, Tanya appeared in the doorway. 'Ah, Pushkin,' he said, sighing. 'Is that right, Tanya?'

The au pair awkwardly surveyed the scene.

'You will have some tea, won't you, Tanya?' Serge asked. 'And there is all of this delicious cake to finish.' It was clear he was saying this to annoy Helena, for she made a little face at him. The poor girl looked embarrassed.

'No. No thank you,' she said. 'Your mother is asking for you.'

'I'll come,' Serge said, rising, and he left with a parting glance at Paul, which Paul understood as meaning he was not yet forgiven.

'So, now you have met my cousin,' Helena said. 'Interesting what he said about Durrell. I wouldn't have made that connection precisely.'

Marina put down the bone china cup, clattering it. She cast a sudden, hidden glance at Paul that contained a wildness of social desperation, or perhaps of a deeper kind which he could not assess, then smothered the look with eyelids. 'He liked Homer better,' she said.

Helena laughed as if at a sophisticated joke. 'Don't we all!'

Marina blushed, exposing the true naivité of the remark. 'He was mad about Homer,' she said hoarsely.

Paul decided enough was enough and sailed in. 'Now, that I do remember. I do remember reading Homer, and I expect there are bits of him I could still translate. Homer and Euripides. They made us read *Medea* as children, well, adolescents. Can you imagine? Still, it was stirring stuff.'

Marina looked at him gratefully; Helena as if she had been distracted in a library.

'Yes, and Serge was particularly good at classics, you know. At school, everyone thought him quite literary. He used to write poetry himself. So did I, but I never showed it to anyone.'

'Do you still write it?' Marina asked with interest.

He shook his head. 'No, they ironed all of that out of me.'

'Me too,' she said, barely audible. But Helena clearly heard it and widened her eyes attentively.

'Really!' she said. 'You never told me that. Have some more tea.'

Marina looked up and straight at Helena, and there was a moment's curious pause as their eyes connected. 'I . . . I . . .' she was faltering horribly. Paul did not know why, but he thought there was going to be some kind of scene. 'I am *so* tired, Helena,' she said at last, accomplishing her sentence with clear effort. 'I'm afraid I'm still awfully jet-lagged. I'd be much more on top of things this evening if I took a little snooze. Would you mind?'

'Go ahead,' said Helena, but with a strained smile. 'Do.'

Marina rose in an oddly swift and blurring movement, hand on her heart, and in a flurry seemed to vanish into the dark hallway of the house. Helena sat, her hands tightly folded on her lap and her eyes screwed shut briefly as if she were in pain. Suddenly aware of Paul's continued presence in the garden, she opened them and looked at him with an almost insolent expression. 'So you found Serge after all,' she said. 'In what state of inebriation was he?'

'He was awfully drunk.'

'So you sobered him up. Well done.'

'I found him in the cemetery,' Paul said, hoping for effect.

'The cemetery?' she was somewhat surprised. 'How macabre.'

'He has it in his head that your aunt really is going to die.'

'She is?' Helena said this with a shocking blandness as if to parade a callous attitude she knew he would not like.

'I suppose she could.'

'This is medical opinion?'

He shrugged. 'She's very old. More important is Serge, I think. Something radical has happened, I feel sure.' He was not about to tell Helena about the Tsar's grandchild. 'His mother notices it. She feels it. She asked me about him.'

'You hardly need me to tell you what to say!' she replied so sharply that he coloured.

'I was simply voicing a concern I thought you shared,' he said evenly.

Her eyes became wondrously large and bright, and her silver hair almost bristled. She seemed tense to the point of snapping. 'Do we share concerns, Paul?'

'I would have thought so.'

'Well, my "concern" at the moment is Mrs Holt. We have much to do this summer . . .'

For the second time that day, he found his whole mind inflamed. 'That poor woman!'

Suddenly, she seemed to snatch herself away from her anger like someone removing a pot from a burner. 'I think you can leave her to me,' she said coolly. 'In fact, I think her idea of a rest is a very good one and I shall take one myself.' She looked at him with a shade of triumph, as if she had managed to keep her temper against the unfavourable odds caused by a barbarian. She administered a condescending smile, rose and sailed towards the house, pausing to tweak off the dead trumpet of an Easter lily that stood at the door in a pot.

Paul thought he would melt with rage. 'I must get a grip on myself!' he thought, but the harder he tried, the more angry he became. He got up and started to fume among the leaves in the lower terrace, among the lemons and the streaked and striped amaryllis.

He had, indeed, found Serge amid the tombs, and perhaps the scene had affected him more than he was willing to admit. It had been so startling, so shocking, somehow, and, as Helena had said, macabre. He had arrived in Skala late, having dawdled as he went down the winding road, having found a sudden pleasure in the savour of a small breeze that sighed through the pine trees with their long, feathery needles and having been buoyed up by the infusion of Marina's loveliness as she had stood by the parapet. It had been a private moment, a simple thing, like nature revealing itself in a rare bird or dolphin or a constellation of stars hitherto unrecognized. He had not found a woman attractive in that long. How long? So long. And yet, he made nothing of it. The moment had had a genius of its own as if it spoke of itself and not her, of itself and not him. It had simply seemed a sign or good omen for himself that he had been given vision for a brief space that had nothing to do with death or dying or human sacrifice. He had walked past the dry, piney woods, past the Shrine of the Apocalypse sequested in its crowd of bristling evergreens, not thinking of his visit there on Sunday when he had found the service so alien and oppressive he had fled. He had paused to notice bushes and blue butterflies and, far beyond the rough stone wall, the swell of cultivated fields and olive groves that sloped down to the sea. Descending lower, he caught the sight of lizards darting and then, as he neared the port, ample Greek houses, their gardens thronged with bougainvillaea, the trees humming and chattering with cicadas.

At last, he reached Skala and the harbour, feeling free, for some reason, from the clamp of intense thought that often afflicted him. By this hour, the blue of the sea was dulled by the haze of heat and the tavernas along the front were virtually empty now. A few motorbikes skirled sleepily down the wide quay and the green bus was resting at its stop. 'Where is he?' Paul wondered aloud. 'Where has he got to?' He walked along past souvenir shops and poked his head into bars where old men with worry beads sat outside watching with grizzled disdain the parade of sunburnt tourists in shorts. Serge had drinking buddies in the local community where he was considered a hail-fellow-well-met. Prince Hal. Paul had neither the Greek nor the inclination to ask after his friend's whereabouts, but he assumed that he would find Serge somewhere there among them. He was nowhere to be seen.

Paul returned to the baking quay. A woman in a bikini licked an ice-cream cone, some Australians reclined on the deck of a fast yacht brave with flags and immaculate varnish. They played cards and drank beer. Paul felt sweat trickle from his hatband, and he wiped his forehead with his handkerchief. He never noticed the stare of some Americans at his tropical suit. His figure looked inconsistent with the general atmosphere of holiday-making. Suddenly, it goaded him that he could not find Serge and launching on his quest, he walked now with directional stride, peering into the boats and under awnings. Helena had soothed her aunt with the lie that Serge had met yachting friends, but there might be some truth to it. Suddenly, he felt as if he were looking for a lost child, who might allow himself to be picked up by anyone. At last, reaching the end of the front, Paul stopped, not knowing what to do. Ahead of him, was a tree-lined beach where oiled, bare-breasted women sprawled, tanning themselves in the annealing sun, this despite a notice saying 'No Nude Bathing'. Had Serge gone off with one of these? Had he sailed off in a boat with a complete stranger? Despite his efforts to resist it, Paul began to worry. Suppose Serge had gone for a drunken swim and had drowned. That was absurd.

He shook his head and looked around again, the naked women embarrassed him as they lay still with their round domes of curved breasts.

There was a road going out of town and Paul took it, laughing a little at the incongruity of an ancient stone monument to the left of the road, which proclaimed itself to be the original baptistry of St John. A few evenings ago, Paul had followed this route all the way out to Kampos Beach and had returned as dusk fell. Passing by the walled cemetery, he had stopped and looked as a sexton had performed the evening task of lighting watch-lights on the graves. On each tomb there was a lantern and on most there were glass cases containing little icons and photographs of the dead. Paul's hands had wreathed around the iron rungs of the gate as the sexton seemed to float among the shadows and something about the warm flames, bursting up and wavering amid dark yews and cypresses, had moved him. As a child, Paul had been afraid of the dark and of death in consequence.

Now, as he passed the cemetery he glanced in. At 3 p.m. it seemed cool and hushed, a ceremonious place to be. All of a sudden, he spotted a dark shape heaving and moving at the very end of the enclosure. It seemed to sprawl on a tomb in the shade of a wall and for a moment, the hair stood up at the back of Paul's neck in an atavistic horror until it dawned on him that it was Serge. There was something strange and thrillingly awful about his movements. Paul felt that he had caught him out in some bizarre, unsavoury habit. He wrung his hands like a gibbering ghost.

Paul moved swiftly through the gates and threaded his way through the tombs, marbled and ghastly with little troughs of green coloured gravel. 'Serge!' he cried, and Serge looked up. He was sitting at the foot of what appeared to be a new grave, for there were fresh flowers on it and the surroundings of it looked disturbed. He seemed not at all surprised to see Paul.

'Look!' he cried with indignation. 'Look! It's only a child!' The portrait on the tomb was that of a little girl around twelve years old, a fading coloured photograph in an oval frame. Serge was very drunk. 'She's the daughter of some people I know here on the island. See? I brought flowers.' He waved his hand at a plucked bunch of lilies. 'She died of leukemia. Her parents believe she will rise from the dead. They really think that is true. "Maid arise!"' he continued, pointing his finger accusingly at the slab under which the child was buried. 'See? It doesn't work. Why should it work?' he asked. 'I'm smashed,' he said. 'But I am stating the obvious. Sorry 'bout that. You are my keeper, aren't you? Minder. Baby minder. Knew you were coming. You always come. Can't do anything about that. Wish you were here. I mean I'm glad. You keep me. Don't you?'

Pauls's flesh crawled. 'How did you get this way?' he asked abruptly.

'I bought a bottle of whisky and drank it,' Serge replied with a meaningful stare. Even in this state, he had a raddled handsomeness. He looked like an ageing actor, full of potential for melodrama.

'Why?' Paul asked. Against his will, he found himself freezing into a cold rage. It banked up like the clouds of an ice storm.

'Why? . . . Why not? You're so damned perfect! I am killing my mother, that is why. She will be dead soon. Like this little girl. I know.'

'What do you mean, you are killing her! I never heard such a ridiculous thing!'

'You don't know a bloody thing about it,' said Serge.

'Look! I do know something about it. She is very old. She could die, and indeed, she will die, but she is in fairly good health on the whole for her age.'

'She is dying,' Serge said, and he looked with mournful eyes at the photograph again. 'Where's Varya? When's Varya coming if Mummy's dying. Don't you think that little girl looks like my sister? Her name is Vassiliki. They all look the same to me, women. She looks like my mother and my sister and my wife and my daughter.' He pointed to the picture next to the photograph, an icon of the Virgin Orans, stepping out, hands raised.

'Why don't you go back to England?' Paul asked, his voice tight with fury. The conspicuous, consummate waste of this binge infuriated and offended him. 'Your mother is no more dying than I am! Why don't you go back to England and be with Fiona who needs you and loves you? She's your wife. She does look after you, you know!'

'Fiona does not love me and I do not love Fiona. Shocks you, doesn't it? Mind you, I rather like Fiona, but I always want to give her the slip. I gave Helena the slip this morning. Now, she is a woman to be reckoned with!'

'You are not going to give *me* the slip!' said Paul.

Serge pushed his hand through his curly grey hair. He gestured eloquently at the graveyard, the yews and the tombs, then shrugged as if he could not possibly find understanding in the world of the living. 'I told you. She *is* dying. If she thinks she is, then she is. You don't know my mother.'

'Yes, I do. And if she does die, well then she does, and you will have to learn to cope with it.'

'You don't know her. You don't know about the Tsar. I am her *son*. I know a thing or two. I know things.' And he broke into some incomprehensible Russian proverb.

It was too late to prevent the explosion. 'You may be her son, but sometimes I doubt if you really are a grown man at all!' he shouted, making rooks caw in the trees, hooded crows that circled the island. With a sudden ferocity, he found himself grabbing Serge violently by the arm and pulling him off the grave. Together, they stumbled over the tombs to the gate. 'What a disgrace! What a disgrace to get drunk in a cemetery!' he hissed. 'You pull yourself together! You pull yourself together!' he kept on saying. They wove down the road, Paul supporting Serge on his arm.

'Oh, Paul, please,' Serge said, whining and wheedling.

'Why don't you concentrate on staying sober for your mother if you care so much about her?' Paul yanked his friend towards the harbour, praying for a taxi. A few locals and tourists stared at them.

'But my drinking has nothing to do with it! Everything. Literally everything has to do with Lipitsin!'

All at once, Paul spied a cab, making its way back empty from the far side of the island. He hailed it, shovelled Serge in, refusing to say another word to him. They had made the ascent back up to Hora in cold silence, and Paul had kept his eye grimly on the fortress of the Monastery way above them. As Serge snored, it had inflicted itself on his mind, weighing against him with its heavy crenellations and battlements. Why had he not been patient? Why could he not be kind? And why was he so often filled with these remorseless waves of cold disgust.

He shook his head now as he sat on the little bench at the bottom of the garden, the bench he had occupied earlier that morning when he had met Marina. First an outburst at Serge, then one at Helena . . . he ought to go, he thought. He really ought to leave Patmos. He looked up. For a moment, in the very late afternoon light, he thought he saw time repeating itself and he started up, for there was Marina, descending the terrace steps as she had done in the same dress and in the same hazardous way that morning. It was like a split-second hallucination or a waking dream. But then she spoke and he realized that she had, in fact, risen from her nap and was there in the flesh. Her eyes, brilliant with anxiety, hunted at his through the shadow. 'I . . . uh . . .' she said, floundering and not knowing what to do with her hands. 'Hello,' she said, looking very perplexed. They looked at one another for a moment and then away. 'Have you seen Helena?' she asked, but he suspected this was a manufactured question; that she had wished to speak to him and was now at a loss for what to say.

'She went inside to have a rest, like you.'

'Oh, uh, well,' said Marina. 'I suppose I'd better change for dinner then. Do they change? After this heat I think I will anyway.'

He could not help smiling up at her as she stood there and she smiled back at him.

X

THE GREEK EVENING descended. The sun, which at its zenith, had turned the earth brazen and had warmed the lucid waves of the sea, seemed to withdraw itself, leaving shadows first of gold, then of rose and then of blue. When the sun at last took its final glint and last frail glow from the water, the moon ascended and cast another light. It arose, and the whole, white island of Patmos became lustrous. Its silvered walls and domes seemed spiritually enamoured, luminous with chaste ardour, awaiting ghostly love. The secret groves and gardens, hidden from casual eyes, released their scent into the dark and cooling air.

> The night has many stars that glitter,
> Moscow has beauties and to spare;
> but brighter than the heavenly litter
> the moon in its azure of air.
> And yet that goddess whom I'd never
> importune with my lyre, whenever
> like a majestic moon she drives
> among the maidens and the wives,
> how proudly, how divinely gleaming,
> she treads our earth, and how her breast
> is in voluptuous langour dressed,
> how sensuously her eyes are dreaming!
> Enough, I tell you, that will do –
> You've paid insanity its due.

Serge read these verses from *Eugene Onegin* to his mother and then let the book drop. She liked the following stanza, with Tatyana at the ball, condemning the 'le monde', but even so, she had fallen asleep. Her mouth was open and she was snoring. Serge ploughed his fingers through his hair. His head was cracking open with a dreadful hangover, and despite the aspirins, the coffee, Paul's lecture, the nap and the tea, he was still fairly drunk. He was sure it had not affected his reading, but he was not altogether sure that his mother had not noticed.

'Where have you been?' and 'What is the matter?' had not been said but implied in a fearful gaze from her hooded eyes. He had volunteered to tell her that he had visited Vassiliki's grave and taken flowers, for he knew she approved of acts of 'noblesse oblige'. The child's mother had once made a lace tablecloth for the Princess and was in receipt of eggs at Easter. Serge had not gone out of noblesse oblige, however, nor could he remember ever having met the dead child. He had purloined the lilies from a garden in Skala after a maudlin encounter on a caique with the child's uncle, and with a boozy, portly solemnity had made his way to the grave. Sobered now, he could not think of what had possessed him to do this thing. How like Paul it was to have found him there exposed! How like him to deliver moral judgments when he had no idea what was really going through Serge's mind. Serge had been entertaining the drunken hope that his cirrhotic liver might do him the ultimate favour of killing him then and there. Did Paul know how often he thought of suicide? Serge was squeamish about taking his own life, but if Lipitsin did not come and did not bring the letters, he thought he might. Indeed, he really might.

He looked at his mother now, so fragile on her pillows. Most of her hair had fallen out and in the light of the bedside lamp he could see large liver spots on her skull. She was not altogether continent and the room always smelt faintly of urine despite Tanya's and Evangalia's rigorous arms that scrubbed, aired and changed. On the dressing table in a little silver frame there was an old photograph of his mother and himself as a small child. She had been tall with dark good looks and lively eyes. In the picture, he, an adoring, winsome boy, gazed up at her. He looked back at the delicate cage of bones upon the bed and listened to her stentorian snores. It occurred to him, not for the first time, that he might so easily end her misery and his own, so easily snuff out her guttering life with the snowy, plump, embroidered pillow, and then put out his own with some stronger measure. He had read in English newspapers that devoted sons had done this. Her eyes, even when closed, seemed to follow him everywhere with their expression of barely veiled anxiety. Did that hunting, questing look hold within it the seed of inner knowledge? It was as if she knew what was coming and what he would ask of her when Lipitsin arrived.

But there was no help for it. There was no way of getting the letters without her help. In the present political climate, it was essential that the Tsar's grandchild be found, protected, groomed and restored for the final and inevitable return. Surely she would see that. Surely she would rejoice to have proof that Olga Romanov had survived to have a child. This, of course, was what Lipitsin continually said, and in

Lipitsin's presence, the abstract of it always made sense. It was simply a question of making her verify a few facts. How could that betray her, especially when the stakes were so high? But looking at her now in her linen cocoon, he knew the terrible risk. He was glad Varya had decided to stay in Paris, no matter how he had longed for her presence that afternoon, his moral, sensible sister with her indigenous sweetness of character. He could almost hear her voice in his head, 'Seryozha, no. You know she cannot take it.'

And, of course, so much depended on Varya, Varya's charity, Varya's endurance. On a visit to Paris not a year ago, Serge, in that chilly, high-ceilinged flat, had had colloquy with his sister on their mother's present state and future prospects. He hated visiting the home of his childhood and mightily preferred the Patmos house. His parents had assembled Biedermeyer furniture. His mother spent her days propped against a heavy headboard in the bed in which he assumed he had been conceived. Here, she received nuns and exiles and bitterly complained of draughts and food.

Varya had taken medical and even psychiatric advice. He could see the intolerable strain in his sister's eyes. Behind the armature of thick glasses, she had peered at her brother and broken the news of her impending marriage. Chiefly, she had tried to work out with the best help available what the problem was. The Princess, it seemed, was partly senile, but the doctor thought that the difficulties she presented had more to do with the horrors of the past. He said he had treated victims of torture, survivors of the Holocaust, and that their mother's behaviour, both now and in the past, suggested an inability to absorb the evil she had witnessed. Varya said it had been an immense release to talk to the doctor about their own childhood. There had been the sudden, blistering rages of their mother that seemed to come from nowhere, there had been and still were her night terrors, there had been and still was her overweening and inappropriate sense of guilt, there had been the spiritual divorce from their father, the locks, the bolts, the KGB. She was, in fact, a woman with a shattered nervous system that would never heal. That was what the doctor had said and he had added, too, that senescence removed those buffers between present time and history, exposing the raw nerve of memory, nailing her to the past like a living butterfly upon a pin.

'So you see,' Varya had said, 'her swings of mood, her temperament, her mutterings make no sense to us. But they may very well do to her. Apparently, she compensates for things like seeing Grandfather shot, the camp – by building an imaginary Russia – one that she can control to set against the actuality of her having been so helpless. That is why there were so many things we could never mention. It's why she is so obsessed with Olga, Pushkin, things like that – the eternal Romanovs. Oh, Serge, I found it all very helpful, don't you?'

Serge did not know why but he found it disturbing instead. 'What amazes me is how you got her to talk to someone about it. Where did you find this paragon?' he asked, deflecting the question.

'Thank God, the Metropolitan found him for me! He works for Amnesty and is something of a specialist in politically induced neurosis. Of course, the Church comes across a lot of it, and so they knew him.'

'Well, with enough incense, Maman . . .'

'Exactly!' Varya had said.

'What I want to know is what we are to do with this information.' He put down a crystal paperweight he had been fiddling with and lit a Gauloise.

'I wish you wouldn't smoke.'

'Oh Varya, don't be so righteous!' It gave him an excuse to explode.

She shrugged, used to his outbursts. They had wrangled in this way since childhood. 'He's given her medication which helps when she will take it. He thinks she should be kept very calm, secure.'

'And you're marrying.' He knew this was a selfish pressure to put on the unselfish Varya, but he could not help resenting her news.

'I thought you'd react that way, Seryozha,' she said coolly, 'but I have everyone's blessing from the Metropolitan on down. It is because of this new circumstance that I have taken such great care to take advice and to consult you.'

'Helena thinks she should be in St Geneviève des Bois.'

'Helena would.'

'I thought you had threatened it.' His mother had quavered out this tale earlier.

'I did. And that is why I got in the doctor. Serge, I cannot cope without your help,' and she had burst into floods of tears. 'And I certainly cannot cope without André. I love him, Serge.' She had looked at him in the most terrible way through her misted spectacles. The memory of it remained with him now.

Serge wondered if a drink would help him see the situation in a new perspective. Hung-over, he always got the gloomy sense of worst-case scenario. Surely, this vision of his mother as a stick of psychological gelignite was simply an exaggeration on the part of a medic who was keen to make facts fit his theories. Even now, she was probably being written up in some journal, filling some file, gracing some book. His own sense of his mother had always been her almost superhuman strength. This was certainly how Helena saw her. Even Paul said she was sound of wind and limb. Of course, Paul knew nothing of how obsessed she was with the Romanovs, nor what Serge actually planned to do about the letters in order to obtain them. He squeezed his eyes shut and clutched his jaw. What had possessed him to tell Paul about Lipitsin? Why had he risked so much on that? Why, indeed, had he not taken Paul at his own word and let him go back to England when he had volunteered to do so? Was it a reflex? Had it been a regression to childhood? He somehow had not been able to keep it from Paul.

Serge picked up the book he had been reading from where it had fallen on the floor. In an acute desperation of nerves he riffled through the pages. Before this crisis, before Lipitsin, he had even identified with Onegin, that 'superfluous man'. He had been Paul's friend in that mode, that guise. Paul had always loved and needed his irony, his bold self-mockery, and now he was incapable of it.

Serge rose quietly so as not to wake his mother and looked in her mirror on the dressing table. His own face gave him a shock. His grey hair was wild, his eyes bloodshot, his jowls heavy and bristled as a Greek sailor. His breath must have a remarkable stench. If Lipitsin did not come he would go mad.

Why had he not rung or at least written? Maybe 'they' had found out. Maybe something had 'happened' to Lipitsin. Maybe the papers had fallen into the wrong hands. For, of course, it had been Lipitsin's contention all along that this could occur and this was why he had excrcised the most extreme caution so far. Had the senior Romanov, who had already seen and rejected the authenticity of the letters, annihilated Lipitsin and taken matters into his own hands? Or had the right wing of the KGB got hold of them? Serge decided that he really had better have another drink.

He put the book on the dressing table. He supposed he had better call Tanya as he had better join the others fairly soon or Paul would come searching for him so that they could all go and eat. Tatyana, Tanya! He laughed at the misnomer of the little English au pair girl with her deathly left-wing politics and greasy hair. He was sure of the left-wing politics from the earnest set of her shoulders. Tanya was, however, devoted to his mother and it surprised him the way she tackled tasks that filled him with repugnance and dismay. She disliked him, that was clear. But everybody did now, even Paul. Even and especially Paul. Had Paul been friends only with his English self? That struck him suddenly with the ring of truth.

Serge looked again in the mirror. That was it! He was no longer English but was Russian to the core and had become so finally through Lipitsin. That was it. His face no longer hardened into the bland, impassive mould he had so carefully constructed for it. Oh, the Wedgewood and Labradors. Fiona and decency! Oh, the smothered feelings, the embarrassments, the inability to cry! That was Paul all over and always had been. Indeed, it had struck him on meeting Paul at the quay a week ago how like an old colonial buffer he had looked. His hat pulled down over his gaunt and burnished features, he might have been returning from a tea plantation in Ceylon, a farm in Kenya. How like him to go and be kind to the natives! Perhaps Serge had been sympathetic to Paul's conversion to Catholicism because he had sensed it as an attempt to escape this karma of a fatal correctness, a mortal pride. But one could not so easily transcend one's very being. That very afternoon, he had descended on Serge like a head boy, bound to stiffen his spine at any cost. What a dry, crusty, inward-looking man he had become, incapable of risk or love!

He looked again at his sleeping mother. By what perversity had she elected to send him away from her into the English public school system when they lived in France and when her native land was the only thing of real importance to her? Serge had learned the English language more painfully than anyone could have supposed, even Paul who had helped teach it to him. His silences and outbursts of temper as a child had been the result of frustration at not being able to express himself. For a while he had been left in a linguistic limbo, unable to communicate in English, unable to comprehend his parents' fractured French, their mobile Russian. And then he remembered – or saw it, she had done it *to get him out*. That was it. Her best solution. Always he had trusted her and that was why. It was what naturally occurred to her in any danger and the danger to him had been the heavy, punishing fist of his father. Get out of Russia, get out of France. Escape. A swell of love for her welled up. His instinct was to kiss her, but then she might wake and there would be quarrels and he would have to take up the damned book again and shunt Tatyana through the rest of the scene, that is, if his mother did not compel him to read the whole chapter again. He tiptoed out of the room and down the hall into his own.

Patmos, ah Patmos of a thousand days! There was still a little cannon in his room kept over from his childhood. It was made of brass and really fired. With Helena, not Varya, he had set it off in the garden, though really he had been far too old to play with it. They had ranged the white streets, the three of them – had known all the alleyways and passages by heart. He had been entranced to learn that the town had been built in such tortuous complexity in order to foil pirates. Well, things never stayed the same.

Serge did not drink vodka because he was Russian but because it did not smell. He eased the cork out of the bottle so that it would not creak or pop, poured the vodka into his toothglass and felt much better downing it. Just one more, he thought and he had two more. He started to work on his face and shaved at the basin. He poured another shot. It always alarmed him if he took a swig from the bottle. Fiona had been earnestly trying to get him to join Alcoholics Anonymous and Paul had said something to that effect only a few hours earlier as he had spooned Serge into bed. Of course, he knew he was a heavy drinker, but as he argued to Fiona, he could cut it out any time he wanted. He simply did not want to. In any case during the good times in the past year with Lipitsin, things had improved and he had gone sometimes for days without a drink, knowing that he must keep sober and watchful in this enterprise.

Suddenly, he overheard voices floating up from the garden and remembering that his room overlooked it, he turned out the light and opening the shutters a crack, looked down at the three assembled below, Paul, Helena and Marina. Helena's face gave him a jolt. There was an angle of light on it from a garden lantern. 'Jesus!' he thought. 'She looks rough!'

Although in some ways he felt more at home with women than with men, his sister, his mother, his wife and his cousin could fill him with dread when it came to their marked capacity for feeling. They always seemed to be boiling with vexing griefs or rages, and would adopt an accusatory tone just when he thought all was calm and delightful. Mostly, however, he had observed that they took it out on each other. Even his daughter clashed with cosy Fiona; Fiona clashed with Maman; Maman and Helena clashed; Maman and Varya clashed; but not Helena with Varya for some reason. Of all of them, he supposed he understood Helena the best and though he and she were first cousins, he had sometimes wondered what would have happened if they had married each other. There was no physical attraction between them, but they got on and communicated in an elliptical way, better than he and Fiona

127

did. If he had not been utterly at home with Helena's dilemma, he might have been jealous of her success in the literary field where he himself had tried the lists with a few desultory jabs, but his sense that she was a monster filled him with a kind of pity.

Although he had not seen her much in childhood, he remembered her as a horridly bright little girl with spectacles, thin and gawky, possessed of a peculiar malice and disdain towards the whole adult world. Together, he and she had been very clever and had made good games, excluding poor old Varya, who was an obedient sort and not so quick. He had always admired Helena's calculated insubordinations, the way she got round people. In later years, tall and blonde, she had blossomed into a handsome woman and was still. On her return from Canada after the war and when she was an orphan, Serge's mother had attempted to bring Helena out in London society, even going to the lengths of settling in England for a few years so that Helena could be presented at court. This, she had regarded as an absolute duty to her dead sister, who had left Helena a house in Kensington which later she sold for a fortune. They all moved in behind Barkers with poor Helena and Serge had been pressed into squiring Helena to balls while his mother held court as chaperone in her home. It was at this time that he had become intimate with his cousin. He had always thought she hated men. He remembered her aloof little face framed with set hair and pearls, her grim jaw. Somehow, he had felt sorry for her. He had danced with her, sometimes for a whole evening, and had got her home early, giving his mother the lie that she had had a good time and had been partner to this or that scion of some good family.

Her 'First' at Cambridge had never surprised him, but her marriage to Mungo Taggart had. To this day, he could never understand what had possessed Helena, for they had been anti-types. He supposed that in its way it had been an ambitious marriage and he knew that his mother had wanted her to make one, but not of that kind. Helena's husband had been well-connected in a certain way, his mother had been painted by Duncan Grant, and his family knew scores of people from what Serge's mother would call 'café society'. Helena wished to move in upper Bohemia: and so she had. Still, the marriage to Mungo had been idiotic.

Serge weakened, though, about going downstairs when he saw the general posture of his cousin through the window. It always dismayed him to see Helena in the grip of passion and it was clear that it possessed her now, even though her expression seemed outwardly calm.

For all her clarity of mind, he sensed in her a pool of hideous depth where curious instincts lurked and he could read them in her face or in the clench of her hand. This Marina woman, pleasant though she was, had been making Helena jumpy and brusque. Tea had been a ghastly experience with moods and hidden angles. He wished she would drink, Helena, always so groomed and finicky. Her back was bad and no wonder. She clenched herself into a tireless, straight rod. She was now crafting a shape in the air as she spoke, and her voice had that tinkling quality to it he associated with some of her assaults on Maman. Of course, she never screamed or raged as poor old Varya did. It was more that she would poise herself on the edge of her chair, on the edge of her voice, like a balanced spider ready to descend. She would get a voluptuous look on her face as if readying herself to dine and would lower onto his mother and have her wrapped in words before she knew what had hit her. In many ways, Serge welcomed these interventions from Helena, but from time to time, she expressed a cold hatred that made him shudder. His mother's power over him terrified him, but at the same time, he hated to see it reduced.

'Poor old Serge,' he said to himself, and took another half an inch of drink. He closed the bottle and returned it to the nest in his drawer and covered it with socks. He felt better; he braced himself in front of the looking-glass. 'What is going to become of you if he doesn't turn up?' He put a brush through his hair and sprinkled eau de cologne on his handkerchief. 'He must turn up! He cannot *not* turn up. Gregory, where are you?' All day he had been at the port watching and had been asking Greek cronies to look out for Lipitsin. Had checked the post and poste-restante every day. But, braced by vodka and by a determination not to rehearse his worries yet again about Lipitsin, he squared his shoulders, firmed his jacket, and made to set off down the stairs. Before doing so, however, he opened the little drawer in his night-table and, turning on a shaded, rosy lamp, found out the miniature and stood for a moment, looking at it.

In the centre of a jewel-encrusted oval, with fine beard and lustrous eyes, with collared neck and epaulettes, with arched, imperial eyebrows, was the portrait of the last Tsar. In a certain light, it almost seemed to speak to him. 'Poor Serge,' the kind, sad eyes appeared to say. 'Poor old Serge,' said the Emperor.

Serge shut his eyes tight with guilt to think how he had once so casually undervalued this prize. Misery came like a shooting pain and then he returned the portrait to the drawer. It had started everything almost as if by magic. He wondered if he would have to forfeit this picture to Lipitsin if things went wrong. He shuddered and tried to avoid thinking about it. The miniature was of immense, yes, immense value. No, he was sure it would not come to that.

Serge turned off the light and tiptoed from the room, almost as if the portrait were alive and could be disturbed. Then almost jauntily he descended the stairs to join the party in the garden below.

XI

GREGORY LIPITSIN ARRIVED in Patmos harbour just as the moon was rising, but he was indifferent to its clear beams on the deep. He had come from Turkish waters privately in a launch he had hired at Kusadasi and he now gave the boatmen the agreed sum. Thus having facilitated his smooth entry into Greece, he mounted the quay without a backward look or thanks. He had a way of appearing indigenous to any soil on which he stood. Without question, he could have been a Greek, perhaps a well-heeled pilgrim from a shipping family; perhaps a dealer in gold, which was sold in discreet shops in Skala at favourable prices. In any case, he attracted no notice. He evinced no curiosity at his surroundings and he made his way down the waterfront through the evening promenade with the confident stealth of a Middle Eastern businessman on the way to an important, slow haggle with a friend. In fact, he was looking for a room, for he had no intention of staying with Serge Mirkovsky. He was quite aware of how long and how ardently Serge had been expecting him and for reasons of his own, had not advised him of his imminent arrival. He half-expected Serge to be waiting for him, crouched under one of the taverna awnings, cradling a large Metaxa, demented with the tension of it all, but his sixth sense told him that he was unobserved. With a swift glance, Lipitsin spied an hotel along the quay and vanished through its door.

Lipitsin was, in fact, a dealer but not in gold. He sold what he came by and he did very well. Chiefly, his interest was in objects of historical importance and value. His many contacts in the East often took him to archaeological sites or to the seats of broken-down potentates who might have the head of a god to sell – or a Mesopotamian figurine. He liked archaic things, and could place coins or kouroi discreetly in good homes; but other things fell into his hands as well – manuscripts, maps, paintings, jewellery. He had an unerring eye. Lipitsin had seen no reason why he should not combine his trip to Patmos with some business in Istanbul. He had been to Ephesus too. He had got a very good price from a Turk for some eighteenth-century erotica, but had passed over a votive statue of Hermes as too much of a risk.

Lipitsin cast his eyes around the gloom of the hotel lobby. It seemed a sedate and even respectable place with its polished tiled floors and clean, stuffed armchairs. There was nobody about. The light in the reception area was dismal, and in it hung the copy of an icon. Lipitsin regarded the image with faint distaste, for his upbringing had soured him. He knew who the saint was, however, the patron of the island and poet of Doomsday. Lipitsin banged the bell to summon the receptionist, then stepped back into the shadow where he remained unmoving. Lipitsin never expended energy unless he had to. He had little use for possessions and carried only a light case with the bare essentials in it. He was even conservative of air, and breathed in shallow breaths, consuming much from little. He kept himself fit and had no bad habits, which accounted, perhaps, for his elegant appearance. He always impressed people at first sight as a man of taste and refinement and he looked a good deal younger than he was.

Lipitsin in the shadows thought now of Serge's weakness for alcohol and of other weaknesses more profound that he had observed. The handsome prince! He had a well-developed contempt for such people. In the darkness, he thought of Serge's lurid emotional fits, his deep confidences, and he wondered what his mother would say if she knew half of what he did. He shrugged for he never took a risk he could not cover and was most sure-footed on the highest rocks. Tomorrow, presumably, he would meet the old lady whom he was most curious to see. In the Russia of his grandparents, her name alone would have unfurled flags. Not that Lipitsin made much of his personal history. First he had been here, then he had been there. He did not reflect upon his life. He was accustomed to long periods of solitude, but he never felt lonely nor did he need people to care for him. But Serge was always trying to get Lipitsin to drink with him or come to stay with him as if there actually existed some relationship between them apart from the bond they had through the Romanov papers, some of which, photo-copied, lay in Lipitsin's case.

Lipitsin banged the bell again and at length a young woman emerged out of the darkness of the lounge and came to the desk. She peered at him giving him a good look. Lipitsin had a striking appearance. He had Tartar ancestry and it gave him the look of a feral cat. Women were generally attracted to him, but he had little use for them. He presented the receptionist with a request for a single room and gave her his passport in which the visit to Turkey was not recorded.

He took the key from the woman and ascended the stairs. Upon finding his room, he opened the door. The air inside was stuffy, but he did not open the window and refresh himself on the balcony. Instead, he lay in the dark, deep in thought. Much depended on his meeting with the Princess, and he had only Serge's assessment of her to go on. Although Lipitsin virtually lacked emotion, a key to his success was the ability to recognize it in others, and he was able to see that Serge's complex feelings about his mother might well obscure her reality. She was senile! She was a bully! She used her fanatical religious beliefs to control others! Swimming through that shoal of jellyfish, Lipitsin was able to see the immensity of Serge's dependence on his mother. Like a dowser or a bat, Lipitsin knew by force-fields or radar where oceans lay hidden in souls.

In the dark, he tried to imagine the old woman, a threadbare, elderly autocrat, her only link to Russia a tenuous cobweb of fictions revised over seventy years' exile. He tried to visualize her breathing, her eyelids quivering in dreams. Lipitsin liked to let his mind drift this way. He would not have claimed unusual powers for himself, but he found himself at home in the psyche and like a medium he sensed emanations. What did her slumber braid together from lost times? He was counting on the strength of that rope that linked her to the past – a woven cord of half-truths with which to lead or hang her. Lipitsin was acutely aware of what, in her circumstances, she might choose to remember or forget and this in a way that Serge himself could never appreciate, having been gently bred under Western eyes. In some ways, Lipitsin probably had more in common with the Princess than her son; he understood the fist and the boot quite well himself. There were no sheltering illusions in Lipitsin's mind, but had he wanted to abrogate memory, he would have known where to look for such oblivion in the pockets of his own mind. He laughed, and the sound of it was like a muffled shot in the airless room.

Of course, it would never be easy to convince her, but that was Lipitsin's point of departure and always had been since the whole idea began. Her precious Tsar! Her precious Olga! Although no Marxist himself, Lipitsin knew he would have given roubles to see the whole lot of them stretched out dead in the stench of their anointed superiority. And so many of his parents' generation in Russia had felt the same about Nikolai II. A weak despot was a contradiction in terms, and in a way, Lipitsin preferred the clarity of Stalin.

No, he was aware that his wooing of her needed more than chocolates and flowers before the final ravishment. Before the surrender of her signature on the document he had prepared, the document which claimed that the letters from Olga were authentic, there would have to be some strenuous assaults. Lipitsin smiled. By now, he was quite confident that he need not lift a finger. All he had to do was to let Serge loose on the fragments and snippets he had brought and let him explode into her with his own momentum.

It would not be entirely accurate to say that a lot rode on this for Lipitsin. True, he had spent a lot of time delicately constructing the scam; true, there was a small fortune to be made from his mark, that batty Russian-American zillionaire in Chicago whose conviction it already was that the Romanovs had survived Ekaterinburg. With the endorsement of the Princess Mirkovsky, there would be no stopping Medyedev, who considered himself the Armand Hammer of the new era and who had already formed strong links with Pamyat and other more recondite Tsarist organizations in the Soviet Union ... But that was another story. No, it was sufficient to Lipitsin to watch his fiction activate itself – to ride upon its swell, to veer before its crash. To provide the drug of inconclusive evidence adequate to the human craving for belief supplied Lipitsin with something like an artist's pleasure in pure construction. He was at a stage now where he wanted to sit back and watch the various ironies proceed from his creation and he was getting bored with Serge.

He supposed he had better go and present himself at the Mirkovsky villa. So, rising, he vacated the room, locked the door behind him and went to find a telephone. The receptionist was listening to the radio and a woman's voice wailed softly out, '*Agape mou, agape mou* ...' My love, my love.

The Princess thought she heard a heavy thump, as if someone had fallen off the wall that extended beyond her room into the garden: it woke her from her doze. Afflicted with sudden terror, she cast her eyes around the room. She dreaded this feeling more than she did an actual threat. Normally a dark pool at the base of her consciousness, the fear lay concentrated and passive, but when agitated by certain sounds or symbols, it became alive with chimerical visions, which threatened to engulf her. Sometimes the terror simply gathered in her unpersonified. Sometimes it took on features.

For a moment, she was too frightened to move. She had no idea what time it was. The risen moon cast a dull sheen on her coverlet and sharpened shadows on the wall. She expected an emanation from the corner of the room or from the window. Out of the pale refractions on the wall, she could almost see a dark hand move towards the shutters, and then she imagined it on the sill and then around her throat. Why had she fallen asleep? Why had she failed to watch and pray? She did not know which was worse, the 'returns' or these episodes of unconstructed dread, when her will was sucked out of her and her body lay rigid and numb. For a brief hiatus, the Princess could not breathe and actually felt her soul to be leaving her body like a hand slipped from a glove. Then, with a painful jerk, her being clenched itself inwards, her lungs filled with air, and she cried aloud, 'Help!' first in Russian, then in English. Her voice was too thin to carry. She grappled for her stick and thumped mightily on the floor. After a little while, Tanya arrived, turned on the light, and stood in all her beaky earnestness at the foot of the bed. At the sight of the plain young woman with her oily hair and bad skin, her sexless selflessness, the Princess sighed with relief. There was something vastly reassuring about the girl.

'Sophia Petrovna, what is wrong?' Tanya asked. She approached and took the old woman's hand in her warm, moist grasp.

'Tanya, there is someone in the garden!' she whispered, barely able to struggle out the words.

The young woman had an habitually sympathetic look which annoyed the Princess. 'Oh, *dear*!' Tanya said in English. Then in Russian, she offered to look. She went to the window and scanned the walls. 'Oh dear.'

'Don't just say "Oh dear" like that! What do you mean "Oh, dear"? I tell you, I heard a noise!'

Tanya was oblivious to the Princess's moods, impervious to them. She puckered up her eyebrows with even greater concern. She wore a cheap, lank Greek dress, purchased, the Princess was sure, at one of the tourist shops along the quay in Skala. It had gold thread in it and it seemed incongruous on Tanya, who reminded the Princess of her German governess. Tanya should be wearing a starched white blouse and lorgnettes. It vexed the Princess too that the girl's name was not Tanya at all but Antonia. Presumably, she had re-christened herself after Tatyana, the quintessential Russian heroine, a role she did not fill. The girl fussed around her night table and offered her a pill, rather with the air of someone offering a lion a piece of meat on a stick. 'Now you know what the doctor said about over-exciting yourself, Sophia Petrovna . . .'

'I am not over-exciting myself! Go down and check the garden, you silly girl! Get Dmitris! Get a torch!' the Princess shouted, for she really was still frightened and an eddy of terror seized her once more. Then she repented. 'I'm sorry, Tanya,' she said. 'Forgive me.'

She had this way with her of feeling a sudden and genuine sorrow when she knew she had gone too far. Tanya flushed and looked down, pleased with the apology.

'All right, I'll go,' she said, 'but you *will* take your medicine if you are still agitated when I come back, won't you?' The Princess's doctor in Paris had prescribed the pills. She disliked them intensely and could rarely be persuaded to take them.

Soon, there were bumping noises below her window. Lights were thrown on, and she could hear the murmuring of voices as the front wall and, presumably, the garden at the back of the house were being searched. A large moth flew in through the open window and made its way towards the light. It bumped and flung itself against the shade.

'Mother of God,' she said aloud to the icon. 'Oh, Mother, help me!' and her heart's terrible pounding started to cease. Sometimes she wondered if it were the end of the world she feared, and if her sudden wakings came as islands in the great sea of eternity on which she voyaged darkly in her sleep. Perhaps it was one of the culling angels she had apprehended at the window rather than an agent of the KGB, or a burglar or a psychopathic killer of old women. In the past few years, the Princess had begun to develop the strong suspicion that reality was not at all what it seemed. She often had the sensation that it was, in fact, turned inside out like a knitted garment in which one has always perceived the pattern of reverse instead of the intended picture. In other words, she wondered if the absolutes of the clock, the rising and the setting of the sun and moon, the evidence of her own flesh withered from beauty, the march and tide of history she had seen were as substantial as they looked. Sometimes she thought the oceanic swell of unremembered dreams described the essence of existence and that the figures in them were like astronomical numbers in an unintelligible sum. It was as if the arithmetic of daily life had only a glancing bearing on infinitude. When she woke in this way, it was never far from her that she reeled from the sound of the echo of one of the seven thunders uttered.

Or one of the seven trumpets. Or the squeak of the cork at the opening of a vial.

Perhaps she had come to Patmos in the first place as an unwitting cog in the wheel of the doom of things or a witness to it. It was as if in her early youth she had received one of those fat, creamy envelopes and

136

on opening it had found the invitation to a beheading and not the expected ball. Now, in old age, she had the sense that subdued fires and plagues and rumours of war surrounded her and that even her snowy counterpane could not protect her from the wild, uncertain apprehension of these things. Patmos, of course, had always buzzed with gossip that details of the last prophecies were falling into place. In fact, the nuns in the convent saw the Common Market as a tell-tale sign, particularly if Turkey were to join it and make up the ten nations predicted in the Bible. And there were other things. Some said that the Orthodox Church, by forgiving the Pope in Rome, had left itself wide open (though the Princess herself, who had spent most of her life in a Catholic country, thought that this could not be true, especially when the present incumbent on the throne of St Peter was as conservative as she). Others said that computers had something to do with it, and that the number six was always left out of the price codes on ordinary goods in shops, showing that the Beast had secret control of his mystical digits. And then there was this Gorbachev, who appeared to be moving towards the West and a free society. Did he not have a mark on his forehead? Was he not still a believer in the principles of Lenin? At the time, many had thought Lenin himself the Anti-Christ, that is until Stalin came to fill his shoes. The Greeks, she understood, had looked to Hitler as that figure. Perhaps all of these had been mere forerunners to the real and ultimate demon.

She looked again at the icon of the Virgin – the archetypal Bride – and again was somewhat reassured, not only by the sense that it might even be wrong to doubt God's certain rescue of believing Christians, but also by a connecting thread the icon sometimes gave her to her own mother. Once, on one of her 'returns', she had caught a glimpse of her mother's white, muslin frock in the late, lingering light of summer evenings, and it was as if the whole of Paradise had been portrayed. It had given her a certainty for weeks that her mother, an angel, watched over her. She had witnessed her mother's martyrdom with her very own eyes. And was there not a promise to those who had endured the persecution? The Princess had little difficulty with angels, for her mother, apart from appearing to be one in the flesh, had been tirelessly devoted to good deeds and had died in pure, clear, theological hope. She tried now to catch some sense of this absenting presence, but the glimmer of feeling evaded her. Were these fears of hers demons? She knew that demons prowled the world for the ruin of unwatchful souls.

Why had she gone to sleep? What sin had been on her conscience that could have left her prey to them?

She tried to recount them. She had been impatient with Evangalia this morning and had complained about her breakfast when all along she should have welcomed the privation as a blessing. Suddenly, she heard Tanya's voice below. Something drifted up but it was unclear. They said that if you were buried on Patmos you would go straight to Heaven. She must remind Evangalia. She was sure that she had given her the shroud she had secreted in her luggage brought from Paris, but she had better check. Where was she? Oh, yes, sins. Everyone had been cross at her today, even Paul. Helena was always in a rage at her, but there was something special. What had it been? She asked her constant companion, the grey interlocutor in her head, and without warning, her nose pinched in and her brain filled with its eddying, gluey fog, and she was back. She had returned.

Where was she? She was standing by a fence made of rough wood and she was about ten years old. She was slightly out of breath. She had run to the fence. Why? Who was with her? No one. Had she been chased? No matter. She was a little giddy. It was summer and the air was clear and pure. From her vantage point she could see the fields of rye and the country road winding gently up. She climbed the fence and sat on the split log, never minding the residue of resinous sap warmly coming from the wood, which must have been newly cut. She must have been there an eternity. On her returns, waiting seemed to take place out of time. Weeds and wildflowers at her feet, she hovered in the stock-still air above the rushing, invisible chasm of birth and dying, bees, whole chains of existence and history. It was as if even the simplest creatures darted in and out of the pattern leaving a single stitch or thread in a whole seamless garment too complex in its essence ever to be understood.

After what must have been an aeon, she saw a speck in the distance and as it approached along the dusty road, she made out the figure of a peasant woman carrying a small child. By an intuition given to her, she knew that the woman and her infant were hungry and that their movement through the landscape had been as endless and eternal as her sitting on the fence, that they had always been walking and always would walk and were walking still, pulling their dark thread of hunger behind them, moving the everlasting shuttle of their existence up the road. As they drew closer, it was possible to see that the woman was no more than a girl of about sixteen, only she looked much older. The horror of the situation was this, she had nothing to give the hungry woman. She searched the pockets of her smock frantically as the woman moved closer and closer in her queer, trundling movement with the child. She had not a crust nor a kopeck. She knew she should jump down and detain the woman, run back to the house for help, or take the ragged pair back with her to be fed by the kitchen door, but she was fixed to the spot and could not move. At last, the woman drew level with her, then stopped. She extended her hand, which was covered in jewels. 'Don't you know by now,' she asked, 'That you belong to me?' The infant at her dry breast struggled slightly, and the Princess could see that it was, indeed, herself.

As suddenly as she had left, she was back on her bed in Patmos. Tanya had not returned and the moth still bumped against the overhead light – bang, thump, thump. Again, she cried out, this time very much in earnest. 'Tanya! Tanya, where are you?' She could not get it straight. There had been a thump, a noise. Who was the woman? Whose was the face? That terrible poverty and then the jewelled hand wearing rings of sumptuous pearl, clacking together on the thin finger bones! And the expression in the eyes, so tender, so compassionate – a soft, grey ectoplasmic countenance like an angel or ghost. Was it a curse or a blessing? That hand had seen no drawing room, had touched no china knob, nor lace. She was sure it had not stolen the gems. The palm was more significant, open and outstretched in terrifying invitation, pathetic, beseeching, commanding and oddly welcome.

'Tanya!' she cried out again and this time, she vigorously thumped with her stick. At length, the doughty girl appeared, grinning at the doorway.

'I'm so sorry,' she said in English. She was given to apologies, but she never seemed able to find the appropriate Russian for them. There was something very English in the way Tanya said 'sorry', and it did not appear to translate well. 'Sorry!' she said again brightly. 'I was searching the street. I even went around the back beyond the wall. Dmitris and I have looked up and down the whole house, but there is no one there. Does that make you feel better? Are you calmer now?'

The Princess was relieved to see her and secretly touched that she had gone to such lengths to check the facts and study the situation, but she felt the breathless oppression of panic which attended the vortices of her 'returns'. As she went into them or came out of them she reeled. So she said nothing.

'I really did look,' said the earnest Tanya. 'Maybe it was a dream.'

'You know I do not sleep,' the Princess replied stiffly, then added more truthfully, 'Well, maybe I dozed. But it was a thump – a heavy thump – like something falling out of the sky, and it woke me. Tell me. Where is my son?' Suddenly, she became very agitated again and began to tremble. They were all in danger. She knew it. What was it? She must consult her son. He was in danger. That was it. He must be warned. Perhaps they were after him.

'Sophia Petrovna, please take your medicine!' Tanya hovered around the night table and pleaded. She made a little gesture towards the pills, as if, helpless as she was, she might with enough effort make one of them to levitate into the old lady's mouth. The Princess squeezed her eyes shut and clamped her lips together. She knew she was being impossible, but she could not stop it. Her mind was blank now save for chaos. The doctor they had made her see in Paris, the one who had given her these pills, had told her that the horrors she had witnessed in her youth explained her present state of mind, but she did not dwell on these. She refused to think of them, in fact. How could one think of such things? Instead, the terror of murder invaded her. It invaded her now like a thief who had broached the gates of her conscious mind by stealth in order to rummage and despoil.

'Shall I go and get your son?' Tanya asked gently, and the Princess opened her eyes in simple gratitude.

The girl shooed the moth out of the window and closed the shutters. She turned off the overhead light and left the room bathed in the soft glow of the bedside lamp.

'I know what it was,' the Princess said clearly as if she had not voyaged a thousand miles and eighty years in time to an encounter with a woman whom she did not know, nor hoped ever to see again. 'I know. I should not have told Marina that she was a relative. It was upsetting to her and I must apologize.' And comforted that she had found the fault along the line of her behaviour, she sank into a peaceful little doze.

Helena knew her way around Hora by touch or second sight, she thought, but not around Marina. When all along she had nurtured the illusion of closeness to Marina, and had even closed the distance with her confession that afternoon, Marina was travelling farther and farther away. Like water vaporized, she had become unfocused and vague, answering questions with sweet but monosyllabic mildness, looking dreamily into the middle distance, pleading tiredness, changing subjects, making observations about Greece and about weather, and diffusing all efforts on Helena's part to establish a plane of intimacy. She had trickled into conversation at dinner a mild condensation of remarks about art history. It seemed that she had done a course at the City Lit. with some view to finishing her education in this subject. If it had startled Helena to find she was a Catholic, it surprised her even further to discover that Marina hadn't a degree. Marina claimed enchantment with the icons she had seen in the Monastery. In a way that was flattering to him, she sought information from Serge about distinctions between the various schools of icon painting. There was the school of Crete, the school of Salonika. There were Russian icons from Novgorod and Pskov. What was the influence on the lovely frescos in the Monastery church? Had El Greco really been influenced by the Cretan school? How far? How interesting! She had a passion for El Greco. Serge, it appeared, had once visited Mt Athos, and this astonished Helena. She could tell, moreover, that he liked Marina, as everyone did, it seemed.

They had eaten aubergines stewed in oil, lamb and beans and tomatoes, and Helena had watched Marina talking against a bank of red geraniums in the taverna garden, against the backdrop of the bone-white dome of a neighbouring church, which seemed to frame her pale hair, her face somehow livid in contrast to the geraniums and the white fretwork windows of the domed church. Her hands had gestured upwards as she spoke, her wan, crepuscular nails, her slim fingers giving the impression of El Greco, a saint twisted in surprise or alarm, throwing up its hands at some sudden theophany. Helena had watched all this with widening eyes, with a fuller attention than she had thought it possible to give one person. It had been the lover's glimpse of the beloved veiled or the hunter's of the fleeing hind. Arthur's wife.

They were making their way slowly back to the house along the blanched, silent streets of Hora. Helena noticed Marina almost on tiptoe as if in a library or museum. Perhaps the scene demanded a kind of awe. The spectacle before them was of pallor. The long perspective of white walls and white domes of occasional chapels held them speechless. Each doorstep, porch and portal reflected or refracted moonbeams or shadow. Looking down the angled ends of sidestreets, it seemed that moon, stars and whitewashed houses all partook of the same essence, pale and insubstantial as a spirit.

For this reason, Tanya's flapping form as it lunged into view seemed, at a distance, almost portentous. Her cheap, Greek cheesecloth dress clung and billowed, giving her the aspect of a ghost or a minor mythic being. Helena, Serge, Paul and Marina stopped short as she ran towards them, alarmed for a moment.

'Oh, no!' Marina cried, breaking the silence, 'What has happened?'

'Sergei Borisovitch!' Tanya called out as she drew nearer.

'What is it, Tanya?' Serge asked a little wearily.

'Sergei Borisovitch . . . your mother . . . she's all *right* but . . .'

'Tanya, calm down!' Helena said. 'What's the matter this time?'

Tanya was panting. 'Oh dear!' she said. She laid her hand across her heart. 'Sorry to alarm you. She simply won't settle. She heard a noise, and she thinks . . .'

'I know,' said Serge glumly, 'she thinks it's the KGB.'

Despite her mood, Helena emitted a high cackle, which released a pressure in her chest. She, Serge and Varya always laughed at these spy monsters from childhood. 'Fiends from Hell' her aunt had called them, and somehow Helena had linked them with agents of evil who abducted bad children. When she had been evacuated to Canada she had been watchful on the boat for spies. In adult life, the KGB had become a shibboleth to Helena and her cousins to be mocked as an atavistic fear of goblins.

'She's really *terrified*,' Tanya said. 'She really is. She's convinced someone has broken in and gone over the garden wall.'

'Well, have they?' Helena asked.

'Not that I can see. Not in the dark anyway. Dmitris and I looked up and down with a torch. But I confess it has given me a turn. I heard something myself. I know it sounds stupid,' and she gave them a fleeting look of chagrin at her own, evident panic, 'but it is as if someone really did break in. I mean that's how I feel. I was actually quite frightened. Sorry,' she added.

'My mother is like that,' Serge said. 'She makes one feel what she is feeling.'

'You don't think we should call the police,' Tanya suggested. 'I mean, that would really set her mind at rest.'

Serge waved his hand in an indecisive manner. 'The force on Patmos is not exactly the CID,' he said.

'In any case, it would just be giving into her!' Helena said, more emphatically than she had intended. Although she did not know quite why, Tanya rubbed her the wrong way. She could almost hear her aunt's pathetic quaverings seducing Tanya.

Tanya looked askance at the sharp words. 'As you say, Dr Taggart. But she wants to see you, Sergei Borisovitch, right away. Maybe you could calm her down or at least make her take her medicine. Maybe she would listen to you.'

Helena caught Serge's eye, and together they sighed. Over many years, they had evolved this way of handling the old lady's fits of nerves, and like brother and sister, would become united in one common expression of humorous exasperation. Yet for all that he rolled his eyes, Helena felt him distant from her, the joke perfunctory. He must still be sulking, she thought, from the wigging she had given him that morning. It was only small consolation that he seemed annoyed with Paul too. Helena shrugged irritably. She had enough on her own plate, enough tense, uneasy thoughts in her own mind. And it was so like her aunt to create a drama like this when she felt herself to be slipping from the limelight.

'Oh, I'll go, I'll go!' Serge groaned. Helena noticed that his lip quivered oddly like a child.

'Do you want me to come too?' Paul asked. 'I'll come with you if you like,' he said gently. He and Marina had been standing apart as if to avoid intruding, two guests and strangers to the island. They were linked by this and coupled by the shadow. Together, they stepped forward on the silvered cobblestones as if they shared one mind. Helena could not avoid this impression and it made her uncomfortable.

Serge darted a look at Paul and Helena observed a surprising hostility in it, but his expression softened into gratitude. 'I'll never get her to take her pills,' he said, 'and if you don't come, I expect I shall be with Tatyana and Onegin until dawn.'

'Well, I'm sorry to have caused so much trouble,' Tanya said bleakly. 'It was just that this episode seemed different, that's all.'

'You did the right thing,' Paul said, patting the young woman's arm. The three of them set off towards the house, leaving Helena and Marina to catch up with them.

'My wretched aunt!' Helena exclaimed, giving way to spleen when she knew she should not.

Marina did not look at her directly. Her arms, face and hair were all whitened in the moonlight so that she looked like a wraith. 'Poor old lady,' she said at last, almost in a whisper.

'It's all very well for you to feel sorry for her,' Helena said energetically, 'but you don't have to live with it. She's old, all right, but I imagine she is far from poor, although she gives it out that she is. She's a tyrant. I've always thought she had the blood of the khans in her veins and she terrorizes my poor cousins. You have no idea what it

143

is like, living with her past. History since 1918 hasn't happened for her. She thinks poor Gorbachev is an agent of Satan. It's a kind of slavery to the past!' She felt that getting embroiled with Marina in an argument was quite the opposite of what she wanted to do, but she was churned up inside and could not help herself.

'I was only thinking that she was probably frightened of dying. Of death. Death knocks, you know,' Marina said mildly. 'It made a noise to her.' She looked around at Helena. She seemed more at home in the dark and less self-conscious. 'That happened to Arthur. Arthur heard noises. Before he died things would wake him and he often thought we had burglars. It is a kind of calling. I know.'

It horrified Helena to hear this. Somehow she had managed to think of him travelling boldly over the rim. She shuddered. Still, she was grateful that Marina was discussing him and no longer avoiding her eyes.

'Oh, he died bravely, Helena,' Marina continued tiredly. 'He died quite well, considering. Stoically.'

'What do you mean . . . considering?' Helena could not help asking.

'Considering that he thought it was final – that he would be snuffed out. It's funny. I wasn't there when he died. I was out. I went on aimless shopping trips all the time. Towards the end, I lost the stamina. You know who was there? Henry was there. Henry was visiting and was there. Isn't that wonderful? It is the way it should have been. Arthur's death was not a moment that belonged to me.'

Helena was silent. For some reason, she had not thought of Arthur's last moments. It was like biting on something cold to think about his actual transition from life to death. Why had Arthur vanished? Where had he gone? She found herself actually casting her eyes around, as if looking for him.

All that she could see was white, blank Patmos. In a quirk of cynical fury, it occurred to her that the white crosses of the island had won a kind of victory. Suddenly, she felt overwhelmed by them. In her mind's eye, they thrust themselves on her, the bleached domes topped with crosses. Everywhere one looked, there was an oratory or church or chapel with these cruciform signifiers aloft. You could almost tell the time by the crosses in the hot sun as they cast their shadows on white domes. In fact, you could tell the time by them. They negated life to Helena, told her it would end. She had kissed her white, stiff mother goodbye under one of these. The dead woman had believed, but Helena had not, not even as a child. There had been black vestments and incense and weaving prayers like spells and Aunt Sonya had told her, 'Your mother was a saint. She will go to Heaven.' She had said this complacently, as if she had known the judgment of God in whom Helena did not believe. Her father's military funeral had been so much clearer a thing, clean from exposed emotion, Anglican and grey.

No, it had been Arthur who had won the victory for courage in the face of his wife's eager plans to make the whole thing sacred with organ tones and rituals and bells. Helena was, if anything, more aghast at what she had learned earlier from Marina about her wish to have a Mass said. She had assumed (and not without evidence, she thought) that Marina had the same views upon religion as herself. Helena was used to the patter of faith from her family, her aunt's rigour, Varya's real devotion, Serge's equivocal reverence for ritual, but amongst equals, she did not expect it. Lately, she had given some thought to the evils of patriarchy and this had only stressed her feeling that essential freedoms were at stake when a positive attitude towards any religious system was mooted by anyone she considered to be a serious person. Thus, her heart had sunk when she caught Marina really praying at the Monastery that afternoon and as she spoke of Arthur's godless death in those muted, half-regretful tones, Helena began to get a glimpse of why he and Marina had been unhappy together. Had he fallen in love with simplicity only to find it stemmed from primitive ignorance? Was her beauty, in fact, a product of puritanism? Lovely to behold as Chartres Cathedral, but damaging to live with? She brought herself up short with these thoughts. Surely nothing could justify the way Arthur had treated Marina. He had hurt and humiliated her. Even as a self appointed martyr, Marina had not merited that degradation. In a sense, her religious beliefs made her more and not less a pitiable creature, for not only had she spectacularly failed to observe them, she was also the victim of an ideal of redemptive suffering and this led to the poisoned chalice from which she had freely imbibed. Marina was fixed in the notion, Helena was sure, that woman's abasement should be utter, more utter that that of men and less utterly rewarded. Helena could not help the sharp little laugh that escaped her: poor Marina, damned on all counts, a whore in the eyes of her church and a ridiculous virgin in the eyes of the world.

Marina looked at her with some astonishment and Helena realized that she had lost the thread of the conversation and had appeared to laugh at the story of Arthur's last moments with his son. 'Oh dear, I'm sorry,' she said. 'I have so many recollections of Arthur, you know. Everything you say about him sends my mind wandering.'

'I know,' said Marina, her voice muffled. She made a broad gesture with her arms, a mannerism Helena had come to recognize, it always seemed to presage something large. This time, she spoke in a rather blurting way. 'I have to confess that it threw me rather to hear that you and Arthur had had an affair, but when we were in the taverna, I began to see it was hypocritical of me to mind. The thing is that you must mourn him too.'

Helena did not know why the remark made her feel uncomfortable, but it did. She was glad that they had reached the door, that the lights were on, and that the house appeared to bustle with surprising activity.

She put the key into the lock and as she did so, it occurred to her with a queer thrill of horror she could not control that perhaps her aunt actually was ill, but she shook it off. In any case, the explanation for the unaccustomed signs of life soon became quite clear. In the hallway, standing with Serge and Paul, there was a stranger. His appearance made an immediate impact on Helena, for he was one of the most attractive men that she had ever seen. As soon as she entered, he raised his eyes and took her in with one compelling stare. Helena was not to be thrown by such blandishments as these, but she could not help but connect to such a presence. He looked newly arrived from some business of immense importance and had the general air of gracing the house with his distinction. Serge seemed to acknowledge this too, for he was quite beside himself, bowing and scraping and tittering like an inept butler.

'Ah, Helena,' her cousin cried. 'I'd like you to meet my mother's thump in the night!' Helena squirmed at this archness. 'My friend from London, Gregory Lipitsin.' Lipitsin extended his hand to Helena and took hers in his dry grasp. 'It's all been explained to Maman. Evangalia knocked over the telephone when Gregory rang. The whole thing, as you said, was a storm in a teacup.'

Lipitsin only faintly raised an eyebrow, perhaps in embarrassment at Serge.

'Nonetheless,' Paul said, 'I think she still needs calming down. Don't worry, I'll go.' And to Helena's satisfaction, he took flight up the stairs, looking mistrustfully at the visitor over his shoulder as he ascended to the gloom above.

XII

THE DRAWING ROOM had been opened up on Lipitsin's account and preferring not to sit, he stood next to the fine, stone mantelpiece while Serge sat slumped in a threadbare old sofa, willing, Lipitsin supposed, Helena and Marina to go away. Lipitsin rarely smoked, but he always carried a silver case of hand-rolled cigarettes, which now he offered round. At the merest pucker of Helena's eyebrow, however, he put the case away, as if forebearing to smoke in his presence. It had taken him a swift minute to assess the advantage it would be to have such a formidable woman as his ally, and though he had originally planned to confer with Serge in secret, he had quickly seen that Helena was someone to be reckoned with. He had not anticipated a house party on his arrival and had certainly not expected to find a smart, nervy don to be holding sway. He began to wonder if laying his cards on the table in an open spirit of enquiry might not be the best way of concealing them, and so he had made it difficult for Serge not to include Helena, who in turn had included this other guest in the general hospitality.

Lipitsin was quite sure of Serge's anguish. His disintegration since their last meeting was evinced in a whole cluster of signs: his face was bloated, his hands trembled over the bottle of seven star Metaxa which he sloshed into brandy balloons, his clothes were slightly dishevelled. He was quite without the means to offer any critical opinion of the sample letters Lipitsin had brought. But Lipitsin had not banked on his hostess. From the moment she had walked in at the front door, he had had her down for an arrogant bluestocking and after the smallest conversation, he had established that she was, indeed, an academic. Well, there were academics and academics, but most had some knowledge of techniques to authenticate texts, and though this did not throw him, it put him on his guard. In Lipitsin's line of work, he had met a number of women like Helena, and though he disliked women, he never underestimated them. Gawky archaeologists, shabby art historians could be wooed and got round up to a point, but Lipitsin was careful never to attempt a genuine virginity of soul, for busting integrity was far more difficult than it looked.

He wondered whether Helena possessed that quality. Her cousin

Serge had not been easy to seduce, but Lipitsin saw him now as a mere jelly, quivering for the slightest word or look. Of course, he could always exclude Helena from the dialogue about the letters, but the intelligence might leak, and she would be sure to find it preposterous that the Romanovs had survived if she had it second-hand. As the airy chatter between them continued, he watched her closely. She had self-consciously draped herself over a faded, florid chair with high wings and back and accepted a brandy. With her articulated back, her fine ankles crossed, her feet in slim kid shoes, she generated the very picture of languid elegance. Her interest in him was extreme, though, and hidden behind her hooded eyes, Lipitsin thought he saw a degree of ruthlessness that made him see the pitch of disdain she might climb to if she were asked to evaluate the letters through any other agency but his own. She was certainly not a royalist. Of that he could be sure. No more, of course, was he. She adopted, rather, the whole high-handed and high-minded manner of someone on the road to an Oxbridge appointment. Would her next book translate her to Balliol? She mentioned no book, but Lipitsin was sure she was writing one. She had that quality of ambition, he observed, that would drive her to calculate her moves quite precisely. He could not imagine her failing to acknowledge a source, for instance, if it were in print, but he could see her making a decision with politically advantageous ends in mind, no matter what the consequences. If in terms of the family – the great Mirkovskys – she had nothing to gain or lose, then well or good, but if she stood as protector to the old Princess, then things might be more difficult.

Lipitsin warmed the brandy in his hands, inhaled the fumes through his nose, and took a sip of the pure spirit. It occurred to him that even though this woman might see through the forgeries in a way that Serge could not, as long as she trusted him, this could be turned to a definite advantage. He was quite certain that she had no means with which to explode his credibility, and he had a strong hunch that she would judge him by her own standards, seeing in his immaculate appearance her own idea of truth.

'It really is a shame, but I cannot possibly stay,' Lipitsin was saying now in response to Serge's beseeching. This dissolute individual was trembling on the brink of tears and Lipitsin was beginning to find him intolerable. 'I told you, I already have a room in Skala. Besides, I have business in Athens tomorrow. I shall catch the boat to Samos and fly from there.' He noticed with satisfaction a curl of irritation on Helena's lip. She seemed thoroughly fed up with her cousin's bumblings and mouthings.

'Oh, but Gregory . . .!' Serge exclaimed. His hands shook over the instruments of hospitality on a nice inlaid table. He reminded Lipitsin of a failed priest fumbling over the Mass. Lipitsin had once been an altar boy and was privy to the privileged secrets of the sanctuary.

'Don't worry! You worry too much . . . Serge. I shall return. I only wanted to leave you with a few small things I could not send through the post (here, he looked at Serge meaningfully) so that you will have time to think about them . . . time to discuss them with your mother. It has been my week for Asia Minor and the Balkan peninsula,' he added with a little smile to the ladies. 'I was really only passing through, you know.'

Serge looked as if he were about to burst. He hunted Lipitsin's face for a sign. Lipitsin raised his eyebrows in the way an efficient parent controls a child. 'I . . . we could . . .' Serge spoke weakly and hoarsely.

Lipitsin changed the subject. 'You don't happen to know Geoffrey Banes?' he asked Helena in a relaxed way. 'It suddenly occurred to me that you might, for I believe he is associated with your college.'

'The archivist?' Helena asked, now all ears at the lofty name. 'Only by nodding acquaintance.'

Lipitsin, who had had entirely legitimate business to do with the man, chuckled warmly into his brandy. He threw Serge a look of 'not yet, not now'. 'An admirable fellow. I was speaking to him not long ago about a manuscript I just sold in Turkey. I suppose you heard about the Rabelais scandal . . .'

'I can't think that Geoffrey would have anything to do with a scandal,' Helena said primly, and Lipitsin noted how she had used this acquaintance's first name.

'Oh, Geoff had nothing to do with that,' said Lipitsin, going one better. 'In fact, he became the instrument of downfall to the poor vendor, who was trying to flog the manuscript at Sotheby's. It was quite a clever forgery, but old Geoff saw through it. Mind you, I don't think the poor Viscount was wittingly trying to deceive, but there were lots of questions. They even had the fraud squad in. Awful business. I have to watch myself like a hawk. I was absolutely on the edge of purchasing the most beautiful head of Hermes the other day. Maybe it's genuine; maybe it is not. To tell you the truth, I almost acquired it for myself, I liked it so, but instinct warned me off at the last moment. I go very much by my intuition in these things.'

Helena had all the appearance of one fascinated in the exploits of a high-powered antiquarian dealer. Lipitsin was surprised, therefore, when a small cough from the other guest, Marina whatsits, swerved her attention from him. He had barely noticed her, but turned and looked at her now. She was seated in a large chair, eighteenth century and rather good, Lipitsin noticed, brocaded, with separated wings held together with swags of silken rope with heavy tassels. The chair had the appearance of a throne and it gave the stiffly sitting woman the appearance of an ennobled child, an infanta, perhaps. The chair seemed to swallow her. Serge was staring at the carved trapezium above the fireplace with an absurd and almost mad intensity and the Marina woman seemed to be addressing this with some sympathy and subdued alarm. She was an attractive creature. Lipitsin had some idea that he had met her before and made a mental search out of his perfect recall. No. He did not know her. But it was clear that her slightest movement engrossed Helena, and Lipitsin thought this a potentially useful bit of information. When she realized they were looking at her, she flushed. 'Sorry,' she said.

He judged it the right moment in this Italianate room with its heavy carved ceiling, its ottomans and threadbare fineries. 'And it's my intuition in another matter that I feel prepared to discuss. As Serge is undoubtedly anxious to hear me say, I have uncovered the most extraordinary cache of correspondence. And for what it's worth, my instincts tell me that the letters may well be genuine.'

'You have the papers? You've seen them?' The questions came from Serge as an uncontrollable cry that hung like a chill on the warm air.

Lipitsin, in command, held up a hand. 'What papers? What letters are you talking about?' Lipitsin let Helena cut in, and gave her a swift glance of approval as if to say that he had found a kindred spirit of sanity in a place he had not looked for it.

'I would have thought your cousin might bring some light to bear on this, wouldn't you, Serge? I can't think there would be any harm in telling her. In fact, I wouldn't mind a completely disinterested reaction.'

'But I thought you ...' Serge was too far gone to mount any objection. Lipitsin was sure that his obsession was now complete.

'Oh, I think we can safely assume we are among friends. He gave Helena a veiled glance of sexual appreciation and noted a slight but definite quiver of response. 'No, the whole thing seems quite absurd,' he said, addressing her. In fact, it is so implausible that I can hardly credit it myself. About a year ago, I got wind of a rumour that a very old

Russian lady, an indigent Russian lady, who has throughout preferred to remain strictly anonymous, had some correspondence to sell. At first, they appeared to be letters from the last Tsar to his family. Of course, there is always a market for things like that, and I told the middle-man that I was interested. But as time went by, another story started to emerge. The lady was very reluctant to sell and seemed to need all sorts of guarantees. In short, she claims to be in possession of correspondence from the Archduchess Olga, the Tsar's eldest child, correspondence that is dated from 1919. The letters come from Canada and they were written over a period of years to a relative of yours, Dr Taggart, who had briefly been lady-in-waiting at the Romanov court. It is claimed that when she died, this relative of yours entrusted the letters to the present vendor, who has kept them in a bank vault for over forty years. The decision to sell was based on the present political situation and, I believe, on the extreme poverty of the woman. If you can call these documents evidence, then evidence there is here that not only Olga, but her entire family survived Ekaterinburg, – the Tsar, the Tsarina and all five children, even the Tsareivitch.'

The room fell completely silent. Not a breath stirred and all eyes were fixed upon Lipitsin.

'All? All were saved?' Serge spoke weakly at last. He could barely enunciate the words.

Lipitsin shrugged an assent. He looked pointedly at Serge. His whole attention, however, was on Helena. It was a favourable sign, he thought, that she sat very still as though stunned. 'That is the story,' he said, 'extraordinary as it may seem.'

'But surely you don't believe it?' Helena said at last, an edge on her voice of disappointment in him.

'You should never have told my cousin this thing!' Serge cried. 'Helena would not believe the Second Coming if she saw it with her very own eyes.'

'On the contrary,' Lipitsin replied coolly. 'The sceptic is often the dealer's best friend.' To Helena, he said, 'I neither believe nor disbelieve, but there the papers are. I have seen them . . .'

'You have seen them?' Serge seemed to gasp in trickles of information like one in need of air.

'Not only have I seen them, I have spoken to the vendor. If they are forgeries, they are certainly not her doing. It is more than possible that someone else falsified them, but my hunches rarely let me down. They look genuine.'

'Well, presumably you have a handwriting expert on tap,' said Helena crisply.

'Alas, I have only photocopies of a few,' Lipitsin replied, 'but so far those do look authentic.' As the author of the letters was, in fact, the expert herself, Lipitsin had little to fear on that score. 'What persuades me most are the psychological factors which have emerged from a cursory analysis. There are some aspects of the writing that would suggest someone who had suffered some breakdown or trauma. It would seem to me that the task is now to establish the contents of the letters. Whether they are consistent with historical fact. We need, of course, someone who knew the Archduchess.'

'Which is where my aunt comes in?' Helena leaned back in her chair and laughed.

'Precisely so.'

Lipitsin was struck by a shift in Serge's attention. Throughout the conversation, his eyes had been preternaturally fixed like a doll's or like those of a patient expecting crucial news from a doctor on Lipitsin himself. At the mention of his mother, however, his gaze swerved to Helena, who, in turn, moved restlessly in her seat, fidgeting. So, the two were complicit about the old lady, he thought. They exchanged a curious glance, its meaning quite indecipherable.

'She would not be my first choice,' said Helena at last. 'There are a few odd Romanovs still hanging about. Why don't you ask them?'

'They refuse to have anything to do with survival stories,' Lipitsin said, casting up a hand. 'They got rather badly burnt in the Anastasia nonsense.'

'So, you do agree that was nonsense!' Helena said.

'Of course it was! Arrant nonsense.'

'Well, I doubt if you will get any sense out of my aunt, especially if it has to do with the divine Olga. She does quite literally think she is a saint. What is more, she is immensely emotional about the whole thing. It is quite the forbidden topic here, you see.'

'Suppose,' Lipitsin said, lowering his voice to a conspiratorial hush, 'she were told that there was a possible heir. What then?'

'Gregory, have you gone mad?' Serge cried in an appalled voice. Suddenly, all eyes were on Marina. In fact, Lipitsin had completely forgotten she was there. She flushed with dreadful embarrassment.

'What do you think, eh? Do you think the Tsar of all the Russias is alive?' Helena asked her in a gentle tone thick with emotion. With a swift look, Lipitsin communicated to Serge that he would have as soon expected Helena's pet dog to betray their cause.

'I have no opinion on the matter whatever,' Marina said with surprising acerbity.

'Well, it's an unlikely scenario,' Helena said dryly.

'Likely or unlikely, I shall keep your confidence,' Marina replied a little stiffly. Then, touching Serge on the shoulder as she rose, she said, 'I think it would be very nice to find . . . a lost king. Even to look might be a good thing.'

Serge started at this unexpected gesture. Marina's eyes were filled with kindness and he looked into them. 'Even to look means something,' she repeated. 'So you mustn't worry about me. I won't tell.' This was very simply said, Lipitsin noted, like one child addressing another. 'And now, if you will all excuse me I think I shall go to bed. I am still quite tired from my journey.'

'Thank you,' Serge said. 'Thank you, Marina.' And they all looked after her as she left the room.

Marina and Paul collided in the dark hall. 'Sorry!' she said.

'Sorry!' said he. 'I was coming to get you, in fact. The Princess wants a word with you.'

Marina felt unaccountably confused and upset by all that had transpired in the drawing room. Quite without meaning to, she grasped at Paul's hand in the dark, thankful for him.

He extricated his hand and she felt embarrassed. 'What is going on in there?' he asked. 'Are you all right?'

'Oh, fine, fine. It's some business thing of Serge's, I believe. Why does the Princess want to see me?'

'I have no idea. She likes you, I think,' he said, and she perceived the shadow of a smile on his face, which made her feel a little less awkward.

'Maybe she has remembered who my grandmother is,' Marina laughed, surprised at the strain in her own tone of mild hysteria.

'Marina!' he said in a chiding, gentle voice, which gave him a reassuring presence in the dark.

'I know,' she said. 'I do know.'

'As long as you do . . . Look,' he continued, 'I wonder if it would be a good idea to steer the conversation away from Lipitsin. She seems abnormally curious about him and is dreadfully upset that Serge abandoned her the moment he arrived. She'll pump you, I think.'

'It's . . . he's . . .'

'What?'

'Nothing,' said Marina firmly. The smoothness of Lipitsin put her in mind of some cruel resemblance that she could not quite find. A perpetual smile seemed to hang about his jaws, and for some reason she had regarded him with horror. She remembered her promise, however. 'Don't worry,' she said.

'Come along then,' he said. They felt their way along the dark corridor. 'Marina,' he said.

'What?'

'No . . . I just . . . nothing. It's . . . don't stumble. It's dark.' He grappled for her hand and led her by the forearm to the bedroom of the Princess.

On opening the door, she looked up at him. His face looked harsh in contrast to the expression that had been in his voice and he looked away. 'Well, here she is,' he said to the Princess.

The old lady was propped on large pillows covered with snowy linen. There was an icon lamp lit and a bedside lamp, too, with a rosy shade. The room was neat and snug, suffused with a pink glow. Again, Marina was struck with a fragile beauty in the old woman's appearance. Some frail grace seemed to extend itself through what had collapsed or withered.

The Princess extended a hand. 'I am so glad to see you, my dear,' she said. 'I wanted to apologize to you before I went to sleep. Not that I do sleep!' Marina sucked in her breath, suddenly aware of a curious power the old lady had over her.

'I was not aware that you had offended me,' she said, but she felt rocky, tricky and vulnerable.

'But I spoke rashly to you earlier today, and what I said was untrue . . . not that I intended to lie. I believe I upset you.'

'You did not upset me!' Marina longed to be a part of this old woman. A wish to be related to her besieged Marina so that she almost stopped her ears before she could hear the unvarnished truth.

'You are upset! Look at you!' The Princess said sharply. She glared over the coverlet. 'You are very, very upset. It does no good to tell lies.'

Marina looked wildly at Paul, who still stood by the door, but he only rolled his eyes and smiled. 'Please believe me,' she said, 'I know you were only trying to be kind, and it is not your fault if I am upset. My husband's death, you know, and many other things . . .'

'You are a poor orphan under my roof and I . . . excited you!' The Princess herself was very excited.

'A widow, perhaps, but not necessarily an orphan,' Marina said, beginning to see the absurdity of the conversation.

'Your parents, poor things, may they be alive!' the old woman said piously. 'whoever they are, they must miss you. And if they do not, they should. You see, you do remind me of my Cousin Nina, and maybe of someone else, I do not know. It is as my niece said. I want you to be a relative, but I do not think you are. Perhaps Paul is a relative, eh? It is not a thing I know, whether you are a relative, but my heart goes out to you, even though there may be no connection between us.'

Marina was at her mercy. She sat down on the chair by the bed and tears welled up in her eyes. 'Thank you,' she said. She held the Princess's dry hand. It was a little chilled at the fingertips.

For some reason, perhaps because of the rosy light, this conversation had achieved a deep intimacy of tone. Marina and the Princess gazed at one another, and for a long while said nothing.

'I must say good-night,' Paul said from the door, and Marina started to hear his voice. She looked up and caught an expression of great tenderness on his face, as if he too had been moved by the old lady's sincerity, but he looked away and quickly slipped from the room.

'Each night I wonder if it will be my last night,' said the Princess, subtly withdrawing. 'I become afraid when I think I have offended people.'

Marina, too, sat back, increasing the distance between them. 'Oh,' she said, 'I really do think you will live a long time.'

'I do not think so,' said the Princess. 'Have you seen my son this evening?' she asked. 'Don't you think he should have said good-night to me?'

'He is busy, that's all,' Marina said, squeezing her hand.

'Who is this man? This man who has come?'

'Oh, he is just a man,' said Marina, stroking the old lady's fingers. For a moment, the memory of his presence eclipsed her thought. She supposed he was still in the drawing room, plying his wares to Serge and Helena. It gave her a blank, numb feeling as though there were something dead in the house.

'Why are you a friend of my niece?' the Princess asked abruptly. Oddly, she seemed to be satisfied with Marina's explanation of Lipitsin.

'You are not at all like Lena. You are a bit like my sister Masha. But there! I said to myself I would not tell you if you resembled people.'

'I do not know Helena very well,' Marina replied. 'She was a friend of my husband before we were married.'

'Why do you make a face? What is the English for it?' The Princess peered sharply at Marina, who had, indeed, winced.

'My husband died recently,' Marina said guiltily, feeling she betrayed the old lady's high standards of truthfulness.

'You already told me that several times! At first one misses one's husband, and then one does not miss him at all.' She was so patently trying to give comfort that it made Marina smile.

'Do you have children? That is the important thing.'

Marina sadly shook her head.

'Men are very selfish,' the Princess said. 'Don't you think they are selfish? But maybe your husband was not selfish. Maybe you could not have children. I wanted more, but my husband did not want to pay for them.'

Marina said nothing in the face of this inquisition, but was grateful for the bluntness and frankness of the Princess.

'Did you want them? Maybe you did not want them. My niece did not. She hates children.'

Marina smiled. As complicated as Helena was, she did not think she hated children. 'I wanted them very much,' she said.

'Helena is unnatural. She has always been unnatural. She hates children and she does not believe in God. Do you believe in God?'

'Yes . . .'

'Then,' said the Princess, 'you must not be afraid.' Her hooded eyes were sibylline. 'You will marry again,' she said. 'You are young and you will marry again. You will marry Paul. He has no family, and you will marry him.'

Marina was very embarrassed and felt deeply uncomfortable. 'Well, he would have to ask me and I would have to accept,' she said. 'Now, you must get some sleep.'

'Hmpf!' said the Princess.

'I will sit with you for a moment, but it is probably best not to talk,' Marina said.

'You loved your husband and I have offended you.'

'Sophia Petrovna,' said Marina, trying her luck with this form of address, 'I am not offended. He was a difficult man, but of course, I loved him just as you must have loved your husband.'

156

'Yes. I did love him,' said the old woman, surprised at herself. 'One does. Do you believe in Heaven? Maybe he is there.'

'Only God knows that,' said Marina. 'But you must rest and I must go to bed.'

The Princess said nothing, and Marina sat still holding her hand. The thought of Arthur's voyage of soul troubled her deeply. Often she tried to imagine some flowered Elysian field for him, where he could have discourse with Plato, Homer, Virgil, Sophocles, a pagan place, flowing with rich wine, high talk and sex free of remorse, an empery for Arthur, a limbo free from pain and short of joy where he could wander effortless amongst his peers. But her heart was not in the fantasy. She looked at the Princess and saw she was asleep. Marina had a deep urge to kiss the old lady, but she resisted it. She untangled her fingers and stood. As she made to turn off the light, she noticed a faded photograph in a dull silver frame hanging on the wall. It was a picture of the Russian royal family, the Tsar, the Tsarina, surrounded by daughters diaphanous in flounces. They and the sober little Prince looked out, almost in accusation. There they were, with their blank, strained, Edwardian faces, victims of what anybody chose to make of them. Arthur, who had maintained an apolitical personality in a vague cloak of socialism, would have disapproved, she knew, but she felt a twinge of pity for the Romanovs. She switched off the light. A terrible exhaustion hit her, so that for a moment she was almost unable to move, but at last she crept from the room and went to bed.

XIII

PAUL TOSSED in a web of sweaty sheets, then woke abruptly. He sat, attentive to some inner moment of alarm, then reached for the clock. It was 3 a.m. What had he been dreaming? Why wake? Why sit? Someone had been sitting behind a large pierced grille or screen. Why was it a woman? What woman? She was holding a spherical object, perhaps a gem. A pearl? There was an ambiguity in the dream suggesting that her face, once revealed, might be hideous or beautiful and that the object she held might be pure treasure or an all-seeing, yet revolting eye, trained forever on his inmost thoughts. He had woken in an unbearable distress of longing. He sat bolt upright, panicked. But in the few moments it took him to find out where he was, the dream slid from him, and despite his efforts to catch at its meaning, it was gone.

In the last few nights, his sleep had been interrupted by other strange, drifting figures which would wake him, then vanish. There was a pock-marked Arab who kept trying to sell him poisoned couscous from a cauldron set up in a bazaar; and then, sometimes, there was Julia, his sister-in-law, who would appear on his brother's lawn, her dress unbuttoned, her lips mouthing some covert message, possibly obscene and he would wake burning with shame and with intense feelings of rejection, too, feelings he thought he had rid himself of many years ago. Oddly he never seemed to dream of Ethiopia, even though that was where the dreams had started – grotesque, visionary nightmares of large earth-movements, bulldozers rumbling sightless over plains, gouging vast chunks out of the land at random.

Paul untwisted the sheets and slung them to the bottom of the bed. He had a sense of mortal combat going on somewhere inside himself, but he did not know the battlefield nor the engagement. Before Africa, his psyche had been blind, unworked, blank. He sat shivering in the heat, in want of some charm or mantra against himself. The only words that occurred to him were 'Jesus wept', Paul could not weep, but imagined the weeping of Jesus over Lazarus, a friend. Mostly, he saw God as a picture of iron resolve, a deity contained. He tried to formulate a thought of Deity unbounded, but he could not. Why was he no longer on speaking terms with God? He knew he cowered on the edge of an abyss of atheism. One small step and he would be plunged into the dire certainty that he had predicated his life on a figment of his imagination. The former eloquence of God, God's looks and smiles in secret moments would reverse into a mere memory of his having been fool enough to believe that God had actually communicated with him. It was for this reason that he stifled prayer lest he should find God to be nothing more than the utterance from radios that schizophrenics heard. Psychobabble. It hurt him so much that he thought it best to let God pass in darkness. Paul made the sign of the cross as if to mark his threshold for the notice of the destroying Presence. Absent.

It occurred to him that this was why he disliked Helena. He thought of her as a degraded human being past repair. Whenever she could, she got in a dig about religion. She saw him as a goody-goody, a hypocrite, fasting on bread and feasting on self-regard. And she was all too right and it was all too true. The quarrel they had had that afternoon had simmered during dinner into petty jibes aimed at his deepest feelings, all under the tyranny of humour by which Serge the Fool also betrayed him. He disliked Helena, in short, for the mirror she was of his true self-image, and worse because her disbelief reflected the chasm of doubt into which he looked ... this dry, damned up, unspeaking-to-God self. God. Self. He tried to change the subject.

But he could not. There He was. In crosses and in trials. In all things close. Since he was three years old in a dusty pew, engrossed. There He was, almost without attribute. Neither a good nor evil God. Not envisioned, simply there. It was a whole instinct that travelled of its own accord towards anything to do with Him and he had kept quiet until he had had to do something about it. There was no more virtue in it than in a salmon's struggle and the instinct still struggled in him beyond his conscious wish for it to leave him for a little while in peace. Upwards, onward, a truly shining path. Paul hated his cringe to God, his slavery to God, his guilt towards God, his fear of God, his awe of God, his anger at God, his love of God, his obsession with God, his inadequacy before God. His former joy in God he now mistrusted. But if the mountain was not there, why did he, Paul, climb it? What was the point when at the top you saw nothing but where you had been or were lurched into the bottomless pit of your own being at one foot fault or stumble? It had not top, there was no pit, and so why were you doing this all the same. Just for the hell of it? Certainly not because it was there like Anapurna, and especially when half the world thought the graded slopes to be illusion. So, for whom had the climb, the slavery, the love, the self-abasement been? For some parent figure? 'Nobo-daddy'? Some sexual, climactic substitue? A UFO. A way to pass the time of the day. An imageless, formless demi-urge? An archetype with other nicknames, Zeus, Odin? No, there was no getting round it. God there was, God there had been and God there would be, drawing the death out of him in silence, in cold snubs and shut, stifled urges until he gave up. Gave up what? Simply gave up.

This reflection suddenly made Paul feel better. There was no doubting the strength of his adversary. If he could extinguish Him, he might. Perhaps that had been the hopeless cause of Judas, to try to blot the whole thing out, do away with it, sell it as if it were an object or could be objectified, but it had only risen against him, empowered even more by the very tomb, no longer local, but global. No use. What could you, after all, do with a God who wanted so much from you? Who resolutely chucked everything out of your heart but Himself? Who scorned whatever substitutes you offered Him and who took such a very dim view of holy bribes? Whose friends were the sort your mother never wanted you to play with and whose best friends stank of hunger and disease? Who detested flattery and lies and insisted that you tell the worst about yourself? Who gave you no rest, no peace, but woke you up in the middle of the night like this and asked you hard questions like a secret policeman in a banana republic . . . ?

Paul cut himself off here abruptly, not so much alarmed at the turn this inner rhetoric was taking, but impatient with it. He had not had so much of a childhood, more an early training with captaincies, consultan-cies in view. One was not introspective. One took decisive action. If one went out into the desert, one stood by the consequences. One should not sink to self-absorption. In the dark, he poured some water from a carafe the thoughtful Evangalia had put beside his bed, and, trying to dissolve his mood, drank it. He lay down again, making an effort to sleep, but in place of dreams and reflections came a horrid crowd of the day's business. Perhaps it was his own toxic inner atmosphere, or perhaps the atmosphere of the house that made him wakeful. Certainly, the arrival of Lipitsin was disruptive.

Paul tried not to thrash, but his skin itched and prickled. Lipitsin had a Bond Street look, a Savile Row look, a Sotheby's look, but not quite. Perhaps he had a stereotypical demon in mind when he con-demned Lipitsin's elegant appearance as sinister because Paul disliked shabbiness and rather primly thought he owed it to others to look smart. No, it was more the sense that Lipitsin had a narcotic personality. Paul sat up again, pleased with the cleverness of this perception. A narcotic personality, what would that be? Perhaps it disturbed him to think that Serge was a little in love with Lipitsin, whom he had met in the geranium-filled atrium with slavish devotion. There were such people as Lipitsin. At one point, Paul had tried to set up a drug-dependence unit in his area, squashed for lack of funding, and in the course of his researches had stumbled upon the supplier of the needs of addicted teenagers. If such a thing as an addictive personality, then why not a narcotic personality – the symbiotic other half of a Platonic whole? He lay down again. This was glib and silly. Yet, surely Rasputin had been one of these, supplier to very complex needs. And, in a sense, there was that about Paul's memory of his stay in Paris with the Mirkovskys that gave him an instinct for the indefinable gap that Lipitsin had to fill. What was it? What had it been? Whatever it was, it was so obscure to Paul that he dismissed it as trivial. He lay first on his right and then on his left-hand side. He tried to imagine some place he would like to be and something he would like to do as a cure for insomnia.

He tried to imagine mountain streams, concerts at the Festival Hall and seascapes, but his imagination would not lodge in any of them. Had he not imagined Patmos? And here he was. Suddenly, the image of Marina crossed his mind, Marina as she had held the hand of the Princess in the rosy half-light of the old lady's room and like a tight fist opening out, his chest expanded to a kind of secret sweetness. At once, he marshalled his thoughts against this invasion – against romantic bursts from such clay as his.

He made a strictly clinical assessment of the woman. She reminded him of a patient. Whom? What patient did she resemble? He had done a mini-course in bereavement counselling once and there were some classic pathological signs here. . . The absurdity of what Paul was thinking hit him and he sat up again on the verge of crying out with irritable exhaustion. 'Bereavement counselling!' 'Mini-course!' Inexorable memories of fly-blown, starved children finally attacked and he was gripped by them. He breathed slowly in panic, hoping to escape them by some Houdini trick. Little eggy heads lolling. An absurd supply of peanut butter had arrived. Those dry-breasted women, some of them as eerily beautiful as fashion models, maintaining a stick-like grace, maintaining a studied hauteur at the helpless, pink-faced, Western rescue teams. With an extreme, sweated effort, he replaced the lid over the heat-blast smell of death, and it was gone. He would read up on shell shock when he got back home.

Perhaps he attached her grief – Marina's – to his own and made it into a mourning for her that did not really exist. That afternoon in the garden, she had wanted to talk with him, but guiltily he had resisted her. Why? She simply needed a friend and Helena was anything but that. He gloated a little at this. Had she found collaboration over this book a strain already? Ridiculously, he saw her over her husband's corpse, beating her breast, tearing her hair, her voice raised in a wild lament of keening, as if she were free from all Western reserve – honest, uninhibited, primal in her response to life. In touch with herself and feeling. The thought gave him pleasure, then frightened him.

Something within him closed like a silent door on Marina and he lay in a blank sort of pain.

Apart from the dreams, he never thought of Julia, and he did not think of her now. He had been dreadfully shy with women until Julia had found him and taken him up. A saucy, dimpled, vivid girl, who had flagged him down at a dance. She had been a nurse. She had claimed boredom with the beer-swilling extroverts she knew. Perhaps not a femme fatale, she had, nonetheless, been earthy and broad-minded and had transformed him. She had claimed his spirituality drew her, though why, it would have been hard for anyone who had known them then to say. It had never crossed Paul's mind that she would deceive him and the most charitable construction he could put on things had been that she deceived herself. She had seemed terribly caught up in his process of becoming a Catholic until he had actually made the leap and done it. Then there had been the letter, saying that she was terribly sorry but she was marrying Rufus and a visit from Rufus saying he was awfully sorry, and a Christmas dinner at their mother's house from which he had fled rather than sob at the table, and then there had been the cataclysmic, silent nervous breakdown no one had ever guessed at, and this had involved a great deal of pain until he had stopped with it, and had gone on without it.

Such an inhibited man.

He was exactly as he hoped he was, faithful.

Faithful to God, faithful to Serge, faithful to Julia who had been his only youth.

Such an unhappy, lonely, ageing man, not really self-deceived, just sad.

And yet his life had had the oddest punctuations of joy and these were times he was not prepared to discuss with himself in case they unmanned him or left him forever. He considered the absurdity of falling in love with Marina, a woman widely advertised by her own husband as a siren.

This time, he actually got out of bed. He looked at the clock. He had been an hour cozening these thoughts to himself. He yanked the sheets into place crossly, then thinking how stuffy it was, he went to the window and parted the shutters.

Helena was sitting in the dark garden below. It gave him a start, seeing her there in that almost audible silence of the night before streaks of light would appear in the east and bleed over a greying sky. She sat so still she might not have been breathing, and, for some reason, this immobility reinforced in him the unpleasant sensation he had had of her earlier as she had watched Marina at dinner. What was she doing out there so late? He supposed she had been unable to sleep in the hot night like himself and had gone into the garden for some air. It was hard to say what the stiff, unmoving form of the woman told him except that he got the idea she was willing something. The whole tension in her neck and back implied concentrated thought, as if she were gazing into a crystal ball. That thought would have entertained him – its being so incongruous with such a set rationalist as Helena, but the sheer, controlled intensity of her whole form gave her the aspect of one in touch with the occult. He almost wished he had not seen it. What was the object of her concentration? Lipitsin? Somehow he doubted that. No, it had to do with this book, with Arthur Holt or with Marina herself.

He swung the shutters to again silently, not wanting, for some reason, the air between them to be unguarded. All of a sudden, he remembered what Marina reminded him of, not a patient, after all. She reminded him of a white rabbit he had had to kill as a student. He had had to pick it up quivering and inject it with a noxious substance and it had stiffened and died. He wished he had not remembered this. Tiredly, he lay down again and soon was fast asleep.

XIV

SOMETIMES AFTER DAWN, Marina, who had slept fitfully, gave up the night as lost. Filled suddenly with a restless energy, she washed and dressed. Perhaps an early morning walk would clear her head, or a visit to the harbour. Her mind had declared one of those senseless states of emergency where the body is alert to unspecific dangers and will not rest or reason with itself. Since Arthur's death, she had had many such nights, almost as if she expected his return, and they left her staring thoughtless into mid-air, barely conscious of the fact that she was frightened at all. This morning, she found she had a great need to get out of the house, for she timidly admitted to herself that it oppressed her. It might be an idea to find this Cave of the Apocalypse that everyone spoke of. Surely it would be open early, but in any case, she could stand outside and look. It was then that she thought about Helena and the possible rudeness to Helena her escape might imply. Of course, she was not trying to avoid Helena, she told herself. Many people made a habit of a morning constitutional. Nonetheless, she felt guilty as she scribbled a little note to Helena and pushed it under her door. It was too late to retrieve it now: Marina hoped it would not offend her.

On reaching the downstairs hall, however, Marina noticed that the garden door was open. Perhaps Helena herself was up. Marina's first impulse was to gain the front door before she was seen, but sternly she reminded herself that she was Helena's guest. One had to look at people's intentions really and by Helena's lights, she had intended to be kind, to forge a deeper friendship, she had said . . . And so, Marina, made her way onto the terrace and was at once relieved to see Paul Mason, standing with his arms akimbo in the early morning sunlight. Marina slipped out into the cool air of the morning. The light was still tinted with the gold of dawn. Mason was startled to see her. 'Oh, Marina, it's you,' he said, but he did not seem particularly pleased to see her.

'I couldn't sleep,' she said awkwardly, looking for a way to retreat. All night she had been tossed on the horns of strange dreams that she could not now remember. Edgily, she wondered if he had been part of them. She recalled the Princess's prediction that they would marry and blushed.

'Nor could I,' he replied, 'but then I often wake early. Living in hot countries, one learns to make use of the best part of the day.' There was a silence.

'I . . . well . . . I thought I would take a walk . . . see if I could find this shrine.' She made a helpless gesture and started to back away. He said nothing, so she turned away, then turned back again. 'You couldn't tell me how to get there, could you?'

For some reason, his face lost its rigid expression and he smiled. 'Look,' he said, 'let's go down to Skala and get some breakfast and then I will take you to the Cave if you like. It ought to be open by then.'

'Oh, I couldn't impose,' she said, but at the same time she felt a strong desire for him to accompany her. It was a nervous and uncomfortable feeling. 'But it would be nice if you'd like to.'

He gave a brief nod as if to indicate that it was already settled and together they left.

Once outside, Marina felt a sense of freedom, as if she really were on holiday abroad with a day before her to explore a new place. She glanced at Paul warily out of the corner of her eye. He had set his hat at an angle so that the sun struck his face sharply at his cheek and neck. She did not know whether he was being kind or whether he genuinely wanted to be with her. They threaded their way through the streets; the white houses were a tinge of eggshell in the dawn. At length, they emerged at the brow of the mountainous highland on which Hora was situated and found themselves at the path used for many centuries by pilgrims.

'This is the short-cut,' Paul said. 'It's very stony and we can walk down the road if you like. I'm afraid it is better for mules than for people.'

Marina drew her breath in at the view. She glanced at Paul and then again at the promontories, islets and the harbour far below them. The water had taken on the colour of profoundest blue, edged on little waves with tones of pink and gold as the sun broke through the morning haze.

'It's lovely, isn't it?' he said, as if pleased to share it with her.

Marina had not talked to a man alone for twenty years except on a professional basis, and she felt a void of panic as if she needed to explain to Arthur why she was doing this, where she was going and when she intended to return. He was neither dead nor living in her mind, only absent.

They started on their way down the track, slippery with worn and dusty stones. Marina, who wore sandals, slithered a bit and waved her arms to achieve balance. 'We can go the other way,' he said. She flushed, realizing that he must think the shoes a sign of vanity (which they were) and shook her head.

'I'll get the hang of it,' she said. She darted covert looks at him as they descended the arduous path. He wove nimbly round the stones, giving the matter of walking some concentrated effort. She wondered what Arthur would have made of him, then in a moment's liberal thought, when her eye took in the scope of sea and landscape brightening in the sun, she wondered what she made of him herself. As she wavered over a gravelly slide, he held out his hand and she felt his grip firm and pleasing. 'Be careful!' he said. 'We should have taken the longer way. It would have been shorter, if you see what I mean ...' then added, somewhat grudgingly, she thought, 'I can set a broken ankle, but I'd rather not.'

'Just a minute,' she said. She put her foot up on a low-lying wall beside the path and adjusted her sandal. The thin blue muslin of her dress fell translucent over her knee. 'They're too tight,' she said. He glanced sharply at her and then looked out to sea.

They descended now in silence, but seemed oddly unified in a pained self-consciousness. They passed houses, glorious with bougain-villaea, perched on the path's declivity. An old woman dressed in black tended to the plants on her porch. '*Kahleemerah*,' Paul said, raising his hat to her. She exchanged the greeting with a broad smile showing gold teeth. She nodded in what seemed to be a vigorous approval of the passing couple.

'*Kahleemerah*,' Marina repeated slowly. 'That's "good morning" is it?' She felt stuck for what to say and he nodded. They reached a smoother path, properly paved and stopped for a moment.

'Look at that!' Paul said energetically. He pointed up to the Monastery, clearly visible from where they stood. 'It looms so!'

Marina did not see it as looming. It seemed, rather, to nestle in the hilltop town. 'It is big,' she said, 'but surprisingly small inside. The walls must be very thick. Helena and I went there ... but then we talked about that at dinner.' She felt so lame.

He put his head to one side and like a bird looked at her with a bright eye. In all of her diffidence, she caught the tune of some quality in him other than his fortified appearance. 'I like monasteries and places like that,' she murmured. 'They make me feel safe.'

He shot an eyebrow up and laughed and she was mortified. 'Well, I shouldn't . . . feel safe, that is,' she added in confusion. All at once, the coils of memory came round her of what Helena had told her there the day before and she winced.

The Greek population was moving now into the routine of morning. Through doorways, they heard coughs and in gardens saw women hanging out clothes. Men started to work from gates. There was the welcome smell of coffee and shaggy Easter lilies past their prime bloomed in cans in doorways.

'Maybe it shows you are in a state of grace,' he said lightly.

She felt suddenly moved to trembling. Even as she spoke, she knew what she said was wildly inappropriate. 'You know I am a notorious woman, don't you?'

He was quite taken aback, but said nothing.

'I don't know what Helena told you about me. I was the cause of a very nasty divorce. Children involved – everything. You see, I am a Catholic too. It has been on my mind that you were one and I thought it best to be straightforward.' She was aghast at having said this to a virtual stranger. Marina realized that she had gone around telling everyone everything about herself since Arthur died.

'Is that bougainvillaea?' he asked, pointing to a dull green plant with exuberant pink flowers. Marina might have been offended, but oddly she was not. He smiled at her as if to say that he acknowledged what she had said but did not wish to discuss it.

'I don't know. I don't think so,' she said. 'I don't know anything about flowers.' She felt overwhelmed with embarrassment at having mentioned the divorce. He most certainly would despise her now, but at least things were clear. She felt her eyes tear up and she struggled not to cry. All at once, she felt the light brush of his hand on her shoulder, just above the blade.

'Let's find breakfast,' he said, for they had arrived in Skala. She was grateful for the touch. She looked at him through a thin veil of hair to see what he had meant to convey by it and although she could not read his expression, she sensed a release of human warmth which puzzled her.

They made their way to the quay and found the little tavernas open. They chose a place fronting the harbour, and they sat under a tree in a slight breeze in which a blue awning flapped and Marina's blue dress belled out slightly. A waiter brought them coffee, strange, watery juice and underdone toast which tasted fine to Marina. They watched the water and the activity of the waking port quietly for a while.

'How did you happen to meet Helena?' Paul asked, launching into a plastic pack of marmalade.

Marina held her hands together on her blue frock. 'Actually, I met her at my husband's funeral,' she said, 'only a few months ago.'

'I got the impression you had met through him.'

'It *was* through Arthur in a way. That is how it feels to me.' She gave a queer laugh. 'It feels as if Arthur arranged everything. He always did.' It struck her that this explained to some extent why Helena had upset her so the previous afternoon: she had become, now, a kind of extension of Arthur in Marina'a mind.

'You are utterly unlike her,' Paul said.

Marina said nothing. She was slightly perturbed that his remark had disappointed her. Perhaps, despite the Princess's denials, she still clung to some faint evidence of kinship to Helena.

'Have you known her long, Helena, that is?' Marina asked after a pause.

'For years in a very superficial way, but properly for only a week. I know her best by reptuation.'

'And what would that be?' Marina asked. 'I am very curious to know.'

He paused and took a sip of coffee. She could see him measuring what to say. 'I only meant that Serge used to talk about her a lot. His clever cousin. He was always a little in awe of her achievements. But he used to laugh at her, too. I don't know why.'

Marina ducked her head. She felt she had been caught out in an attempt to elicit gossip from him. She knew she would have welcomed an uncharitable remark. The nuns at her school had particularly disliked this kind of activity. Marina felt suddenly afraid of Paul's goodness. The idea of his philanthropy constellated in her mind as a monolithic image, rather like the Pantocrator she had seen the day before, high in the ceiling of the Monastery church.

She was dimly aware, however, that he was trying to elicit something from her. 'I suppose this whole set-up is very strange to you, then. These Mirkovskys!'

'I am a bit in over my head,' she said, 'but then I'm feeling a little unhinged at the moment.'

He moved forward as if to emphasize his words. 'Your husband has just died!'

'I feel numb,' she said. 'It's very strange.'

'But that is normal! It's completely normal. It's a psychological defence against pain.'

She shrugged. 'I'm a great evader.'

He snapped back into his chair, sighed and fiddled with his toast. 'It's very traumatic, the death of a spouse. Then you go all the way to New York to look for your biological parents, and that is very, very disturbing to most people. It would be to me. Did Helena really put you up to that?'

'Oh, it would be quite wrong of me to suggest that! She simply told me how unfair it was of Arthur to prevent me looking for them . . .'

'Did she, just?'

Marina was surprised at the edge on his voice. 'But it *was* unfair. Arthur could be very dominating, you see . . . but there I go, putting the blame on others again. I am sure I married him in the first place because he told me what to do. It made life easier. In fact, I often think that I really did not want to know who my parents were . . .'

'If you did not want to know, then why, as soon as he was dead, did you go directly to the States to find out?' Paul cut in with great exasperation. Marina noticed oddly that his right hand was shaking. 'Sorry,' he said, in a lower tone. 'I'm only trying to point out that you have been under a great strain.'

'So have you,' Marina thought, but did not say it.

'All I'm trying to say is that you must go easy on yourself here. And do try to take the Mirkovskys with a grain of salt. I've known them for – oh my, it must be well over thirty years now. It is a very turbid family. That business about your being related to them . . . well! I'm glad the old girl apologized to you last night, but it was very manipulative of her to suggest it in the first place and bound to make an impression on someone who has been through so much as you.' Throughout this speech, he shredded his toast nervously and looked at her as if he were taking little, hesistant sips of her with his eyes.

'Oh, I really did not take all of that seriously,' Marina said airily. 'In my imagination, I have come from every conceivable background.'

'Sadly, not many people are Russian princesses,' Paul said. 'Actually, it's not really sad, if you come to think about it.' He laughed.

'And yet?' Her voice ended on a high pitch that reverberated with a poignance she suddenly felt. 'It made me feel real for a moment. Sometimes, I feel on the point of vanishing.' Little dabs of light through the flapping awning came to rest, then leapt on Marina's hair.

'You do?' he asked. She looked away, fearing to witness something he had not meant her to see.

'Sometimes, I even try to remember being a small baby. I am sure the memory is *there*. A face or a voice, you know . . .' She interrupted herself. 'D'you think my face looks Slavic? Marina is a Russian name and the only thing I know is that it is my real one – the one my mother gave me. Of course, it isn't always a Russian name.' She peered at him in an effort to keep her features still and her lips masked her teeth. 'What do you think? What does it look like to you?'

'I'm afraid I'm not good at physiognomies,' he said gently. 'I should have thought you were Northern European in origin. "Marina" is the name of a lovely character in Shakespeare,' he added, 'And of course, it might have something to do with the sea.'

'Ah,' she said, soothed for some reason, 'I really do love the sea.' She added quietly, 'My husband used to say it was the only mother I should want. He hated his own mother.'

'Aphrodite? Born on the foam? Oh, *Marina*!' His voice was caustic.

'He had his ashes scattered on the sea,' she said. 'Have you read his poems? My poems?' she added, oddly wounded that he seemed to mock Arthur's legacy to her. At the same time, she found it refreshing to hear the legend debunked, her legendary self distinguished from the person she was.

'Should I read them?' he asked.

Somehow, it was a very challenging question and she thought about it. 'No,' she said with clarity at last. 'I am a different woman,' she said, and it surprised her.

Helena had locked herself into her room with her journal. It had Florentine binding and creamy, watermarked leaves. She sat at her escritoire, unscrewed the cap from her pen, then wrote:

How can I describe what is happening about M? At least, I can describe the sensation of what it is to write about her here. It it like trying to scrawl a message on water. Past entries would go to support this thesis. My present dilemma is that I cannot pin her down. In fact, her very substance has eluded me this morning. She has vanished – gone for a walk, she said in a scribbled note. Cannot imagine M. walking, though have seen her walk. As a figment of the mind, she floats, diffuses, reassembles herself – might manifest herself as rain or snow. A vigorous hike might do her good, one must suppose.

I have been up half the night trying to work out what she is up to. She gives the deep impression of being virginal, yet she seduces one into intimacies . . . not the absence of experience, but the presence of purity *suggests* itself. As illusory as everything else about her? Unconsciously enigmatic, she draws one on? Fails to write and say when she is coming? Leaves little notes as trails.

An example: yesterday, she gave me a blow by blow account (I fear) of her marriage to Arthur. A pitch of honesty seemed to have been reached – the moment ripe to tell her about Arthur and me. A dreadful intensity, an awful pressure, I tell her – bang goes the trap! I should have seen it all along. But what could I have done? I had to tell her if we are to get anywhere with this biography. What else can come of that devastating marriage but a book? I know that she needs it and know too that she invited my confidence. I am sure of it. Ah, 'If we had world enough and time/This coyness, lady, were no crime.'

Again, I thought I had some purchase on the marriage, then find I am in want of a Rosetta Stone to decipher what went on between them. Why did it last so long when they were so wholly unsuited to each other? A. was primarily sensual. One can see it in the way he used language. Poetry was another way of touching. I think he came to write it in the first place because of his repressive background. Though God knows I carry no brief for Freud, I reach for Freud when thinking of Arthur. And that is the contradiction (or, is it a contradiction?) to say that there is something Victorian about Marina. Of course, there is that odd sonnet in the *Cycle* where A. evokes the goddess renewing her virginity each time. A painful process for M., perhaps? It does, of course, beg a large question to think it is M. at all.

Was watching M. and Mason together last night. Very aware of each other. Are they aware of the awareness? If so, how do they perceive it? Quite sure she thinks him 'spiritual'. Does he see Miss Sadie Thompson? A flash of red garters under the soulful gaze. What a thrill for him! For her, the full revelry of guilt that Catholics seem to imbibe with mother's milk. All of this cloaked in pious self-deceit? Or is it possible neither could ever be physically consumed.

Somehow it was torture to hear M. say she had never loved Arthur 'in that way'. She admitted it. To me, that was the one thing with A. I seem to be able to remember only this about him, that for a season everything was subsumed into my erotic connection with the man. An irony. I certainly never 'loved' him, whatever that means . . . Actually, it strikes me as plausible that Venus lacks desire because she *is* desire. Perhaps it was she who coldly did the consuming of him, otherwise, why did he stay? Why did she when she had no reason to endure what seems to have been a wholly abusive situation? Did she frustrate him?

Tear him apart with unslaked longings? Did he have her but not have her?

Maybe the key to her is her power to suggest alternative selves. Yesterday, Aunt Sonya got it into her senile head that M. was a relation. M. told her an adoption story. Little Orphan Annie. Aunt sat under the tree like an ancient prophetess casting runes. Having thought of her myself as Goddess Marina, I suddenly found myself seeing Princess, Countess, Archduchess Marina – idiotic as Aunt's 'revelation' was. She is Chameleon Marina. Perhaps Arthur discovered this too late and hung on out of pride. He was quite capable of that. In the Monastery yesterday, she appeared in yet another incarnation – Holy Marina, Saint Marina – perhaps for the benefit of Mason? Perhaps for Aunt? Not that it's a conscious fraud. Sad to say, I think she really believes. She looked unbearably lovely. It has been nagging at me that she chose to wear *white*. There she was in her transcendent self, transfigured in the light of a candle lit, I daresay, for Arthur. Her brow was furrowed with devotion. She tells me that Arthur was oppressive. What, may I ask, is the Catholic Church to women? It borders on an international scandal. But one can never get round them. They say 'Faith' and all else magically disappears. Anyway, there she was, looking as if angels were breathing in her ear, and I thought, You have to *know*. You have to come down from the clouds and acknowledge who Arthur really *was* before you can get over him. It is essential she should know about us. She really did have to know about Arthur and me.

Helena had a broad, flat hand and wrote fluently with thick, calligraphic strokes, elliptically and to herself. She could hear Tanya scuttling around her aunt in the garden below. The levee of the Princess took hours every morning. Helena considered that it would make life easier for everyone if her aunt would sleep downstairs in the little parlour next to the garden, but no. Every day, Aunt Lear had to be carted up and down precarious flights.

It is too tiresome to consider all of this yet again, she continued. Altogether it has already been a very tiresome day and it is nowhere near noon. Yesterday morning Serge was drunk, today I had to endure him sober at breakfast. On the whole I see Lipitsin as being rather an addition to our morose little crew. Serge has got the whole thing back to front as usual – a difference between deductive and inductive reasoning here. Serge starts from the romantic premise that somewhere in the haystack lies a Romanov Tsar, waiting to be activated. If so, why not progeny, who live and breathe and presumably give dinner parties in whatever Elba they inhabit. But, no, it's all a plot to S. – the existing Romanovs in cahoots with each other, the KGB the implacable nemesis of the Bolsheviks still. Lipitsin, however, starts with the letters, and I must (if grudgingly) admit they carry some conviction. Saw them last night, or some of them and they do convey that tremulous, religiose, Edwardian sensibililty with which I am all too familiar. But he needs proof. S. does not want it. He has become an hysterical mystagogue. Scratch any Russian. God's holy icon is the royal personage – totem, touchstone, spirit-bearing figure.

I put it all down to Uncle Boris. Would that one could convey a shudder in print. It was said that he carried a miniature of Nicholas II with him everywhere he went and saluted him with his dying breath. He most certainly believed the Tsar to be dead, however. It was only Uncle Pasha, who was half-mad anyway, who was convinced that Admiral Kolchak had spirited the Rs out. The whole nation lived on denial and still does.

Serge is going to Canada to look for Olga. This I must record. I looked at him this morning and thought, 'You are insane.' He has gone rushing off to Skala now to fetch Lipitsin so that they can show the letters to Aunt S. at lunch. As far as I am concerned, it makes no difference whether the Tsar was shot or died of dyspepsia in Winnipeg. But my aunt is bound to react, especially as this unfortunate business has to do with Olga. I dread the repercussions, unless, of course, she wants to believe it. If not, there will be hell to pay for the rest of the summer. Like M. with her prayers and candles, Aunt needs to believe something about Olga, but what it is, I cannot ascertain. Perhaps a confrontation like this will shake her out of fairy-land for once and for all. This is what it all boils down to in M. and Aunt – a weakness and intellectual dishonesty one can no more blame than one can a child, whose need for reassurance in an empty universe constructs a god.

Helena blotted her entry and then closed the book. She looked at her watch and she wondered where Marina had got to. It suddenly struck her that she might have run into Mason, whose custom it was to hike around the island every morning. Perhaps she had met up with Serge and Lipitsin, but they would certainly not detain her, so absorbed were they in each other. A thought flashed across her mind, but she dismissed it. There was an intensity between the two men, but nothing more. Helena thought about Mason and Marina. She thought about Marina and Arthur. She had an urge to open up her journal again and write more about Marina and about Arthur, but denied herself.

It occurred to her that it had been a mistake to wear the green sundress. She stood, looking in the mirror and decided that she must retire it altogether. The flesh around her shoulders had become stringy and slightly wattled and she could not imagine what had possessed her to put it on in the first place. Had Serge glanced at her neck with an unkindly eye this morning? She unzipped it, and uncharacteristically let it fall to the floor around her feet. She had an impulse to take off her pants and stand completely naked in the room and for a moment, she almost obeyed it. What was she now? What had she been to Arthur? A terrible nostalgia surged through her veins and flooded her. She wanted to weep. She held her fallen breasts in the palms of her hands. A fragile light from the window illuminated the hollow of her neck and she heard her aunt coughing crossly below in the garden. There was a woman who thought sex a mere function of ancestral continuity. In all too short a time, Helena thought, she would deteriorate like Aunt. She looked for haggard marks around her eyes and found them. Next came the teeth, the joints, the eyes, the hearing, but all in all the skin bothered her most. Helena crossly went to the cupboard and chose a rose-coloured frock with a flattering neckline. It was a bright, airy thing and when she put it on, she felt better. Green had never suited her. From her jewellery box, she chose a bold pendant to distract from her throat. Had she started to reassess Arthur at the onset of the menopause? She had not expected it to cause her trouble, but it had. With hot flushes, she had thought and thought about him. At night, when her whole body had seemed to blush and her bed had become drenched with sweat, she had tried to bridge the distance between herself and Arthur with imaginary conversations. As her body betrayed her into moods and tears, the memory of him became an immense, unreachable thing. And more than once, she had been tempted to ring him in the middle of the night, perhaps to know if he, too, had had some intimation of dying.

'You like the Princess, don't you?' Paul asked. They had left their coffee cups and were strolling down the pleasant quay past shops fluttering with racks of scarves. Cheap copies of icons and postcards were already set out. Heavy, woollen hand-knit sweaters swung from hangers in the breeze and Marina's hair whipped and danced about her face. He observed, cautious about the pleasure that it gave him, that Marina was covertly enjoying herself. He wondered if she had a capacity he had admired in others to be happy in small ways at odd times, even in the face of personal difficulties. She eyed the scarves.

'I love her,' Marina said simply.

'Do you get the impression she is dying?' he asked. 'I know it is an odd question coming from me. Her vital signs are good. It is simply that I have seen people make up their minds.'

Marina seemed flattered, and she thought about it. 'She mentioned it to me last night. She is preparing for it, but it frightens her so much that I think she'll put it off until the last minute, if you see what I mean.'

'Serge says she is!' He had not meant to confide this in Marina, but when he had done so, he realized that it had nagged at the back of his mind.

'I know why,' Marina said suddenly, 'but I'm not sure I should say.'

'Does it have to do with these papers Lipitsin was supposed to have brought?'

'Oh, you know about them!' she said, relieved.

'Have you been sworn to secrecy? So have I.' He burst now with a wish to share his thoughts with Marina, but held himself in.

'I have a feeling everything will be common knowledge soon enough,' she said and he found himself admiring her reticence. 'I would hate to talk about something I was not meant to hear. They forgot I was in the room.'

'I find that hard to credit,' he said, feeling a little silly at his unaccustomed gallantry. She reassured him with a quick smile.

They were strolling past a municipal building with Turkish arches. Beyond them was a church with two expressive Eastern domes. The whole port seemed to bask in the morning sky. He guided Marina towards the road that led to the Cave, but he forebore to take her arm. 'You are very pale, you know. You'll burn. Melanomas develop on such fair skin. You should be careful.'

Inspired, she held up her index finger, then extracted a filmy shawl from her capacious handbag and threw it round her shoulders. It caught the gentle breeze like a sail, but she pulled it firmly to her. 'You're right,' she said. 'I go like a lobster.' She paused. 'I suppose I might be Celtic. I read somewhere that Celtic people had the worst reaction to the sun. Paul, you don't think I'm a racist, do you? Arthur used to say I was obsessed, and thought it vaguely suspect. I'm really not, you know.' Again, she peered into his face for a reaction.

It struck Paul that she might be at least partly Irish. Again, a hidden similarity to a former patient of his emerged, not a rabbit at all, he decided, but a person, and there were so many Irish in his practice. Who? He decided against saying so. 'Of course, I don't think you are a racist!' he said instead. He sometimes thought the whole world was guilty of this crime – that concentrated indifference to black people had starved them – but he found himself exonerating Marina out of hand. 'It is very common for adopted children to become preoccupied with such things as ethnic background. It provides a clue.'

She gave him a wan but grateful smile. The graded road went upwards and they began to climb. 'My mother – my adoptive mother – had a peculiar dislike of Irish people,' she said, half to herself. 'It did not do her credit.' There was a muffled edge to this remark, as though the remembrance gave her pain.

'I'm Irish,' Paul said.

'Oh no!' She put her hand quickly across her mouth. 'I didn't mean . . .'

It was unlike him, but he let her flail on this hook, perhaps to see how she would get off it. They strove up the hill and around a hairpin bend.

'Actually, you could be Tibetan as far as I'm concerned,' Marina said with sudden vehemence. 'You have the luxury of knowing who you are. If I had shared any of my mother's attitudes, I would have married a stockbroker and settled in Hohokus, New Jersey.'

She looked so fine in this sudden blaze of spirit that he laughed. 'To tell you the truth,' he said, 'I have about as much claim to be Irish as you do. My family were Ulster Protestants, but settled in England two generations ago. They rather washed their hands of me. As for knowing who I am, that's a moot point.'

She eyed him mistrustfully, but her shoulders released and she relaxed once more. 'Why did they disown you? Mine certainly disowned me.'

'It was a political decision,' he said, surprised that this did, in fact, encapsulate it, 'disguised as a theological one. I'm a convert.' On the broad, uphill climb, they had reached a flat stretch. A motorbike, bearing the two Patmian teenagers, roared past them, breaking Paul's concentration. He moved slightly away from Marina to whom he had unwittingly revealed this information.

'I could say the same for me – about its being a political decision, I mean,' she said, 'only in my case, it may have been justified. You ran to the Church and I ran away from it.'

'I am not sure that the rejection of a child is ever justified,' he said, and could not help saying it with feeling. She gave him one, swift illuminating glance, and they trudged on in silence up another steep curve. So she had run away, had she? He thought briefly of her sex being confined in New Jersey. She laboured up the hill, perspiring, not what one would call a beauty now, intent as she was on keeping up with him. He felt a curious exhilaration at his own strength, but slowed down to accommodate her. Suddenly, he thought of Helena again, as he had seen her through the window in the watches of the night. Perhaps he was using the wrong method in trying to make the sum of the two women come out. Perhaps it was not an arithmetical thing. More surely, it had unknowns and variables.

One thing was fixed, however, Paul thought. It had surprised him to hear that Marina and Helena had not known each other for very long, and certainly did not know each other well. This clear fact ran quite contrary to the impression Helena herself had given before Marina had arrived. Maybe the simple explanation for the clear disjunction he observed between their two characters lay in the possibility that they were not friends at all, but associates. Surely it was possible to write a book about a literary figure in the same impersonal way that one might treat an ailing body. Helena was, after all, a respected academic, and if she were to write a biography of Arthur Holt, surely she would have to consult his family, all living members of it. Why did he automatically suppose that this would displease Marina or upset her? On the contrary, she might see it as a fitting memorial to her husband, and why not? It might also be possible for Helena to get very wrapped up in her project and feel spurious intimacy with Marina in the heat of the moment, as it were. Marina was, to say the least, engaging. Certainly, between them there clung a peculiarly intense atmosphere, charged with very deep and indefinable emotions. Perhaps Marina's openness was only a guise for extreme reserve. It was a good deal easier to read Helena's involvement with Marina than to ascertain what Marina's might be with Helena.

'Are you all right?' he asked, for she seemed to be flagging slightly.

'Oh, I'm fine! I'm having a wonderful time, really. I'm sorry I'm so slow, it's these ridiculous shoes.'

She had pretty feet and fine ankles. He wondered if she were drawing attention to them. 'Well, they're not brogues. Do they pinch?'

'Oh, they're like bedroom slippers. No, the only thing that really bothers me is Helena . . .'

He was alert to this apparent mind-reading. 'Yes?'

'I feel I have rather abandoned her. I hope she won't mind. I've been rather longer than I intended, but I really am keen to see the Shrine or Cave or whatever.'

So she was avoiding Helena. 'Oh, I shouldn't think she is even awake yet. Helena was up very late last night, very late indeed. When I woke up at three, I saw her sitting in the garden fully clothed. So still. She did not see me.'

She glanced at him . . . fearfully? Then kept her eyes on the smooth black road that snaked upwards. Every time he mentioned Helena's name, and he was afraid to admit that he had been digging around since breakfast, Marina withdrew into a perturbed silence. Her sandals made a slapping noise on the tarmac. At length, they reached a point where the road crossed a dried riverbed. Above and to the right was one in a series of the island's interminable chapels, perched on an outcrop of rock. He had tried the door before and found it locked, and unable to penetrate it, he had walked away feeling desolate for some reason. Now, he felt curiously serene, his spirits lifted by the presence of 'the notorious woman' who accompanied him. It had thrown him that morning to hear her describe herself in this manner and had embarrassed him; but there was an antique charm about the phrase that somehow revealed innocence rather than the guilt she had meant to convey.

'I guess Helena was worrying about her aunt or Serge or Lipitsin,' Marina said at last and uncomfortably. 'Don't you think?' Her eyes showed that this remark was precariously founded on a resolution to be kind or on a wish for it to be so when it was not.

'I expect so,' Paul replied. He suddenly thought that she needed to rest on that conclusion and that he ought to let her be. Notorious or not, she was tired and had found the ascent difficult. Clearly, she needed to rest her feet as well as her mind. 'Look!' he said, 'There is the Cave – or rather the Shrine that contains it.' He pointed beyond them at the small complex of ecclesiastical buildings above them and to the left of the road. 'Let's stop for a minute and catch our breath, shall we?'

She sat gratefully on a low wall. The municipal bus wheezed up the road and passed them. The harbour below was incandescent in the lovely day and Paul and Marina were shaded by the feathery pine trees that grew in stately profusion along the road.

'That,' he said didactically, 'is where the Book of Revelations was supposed to have been written. When he was exiled here, St John did live in a cave and tradition says it's that one . . . the place where he had his apocalyptic vision. Of course, there is a church built around it now and a little monastery. You have to go down to get to the Grotto or Cave or whatever. See the bit that sticks out? That's where it is. There are two tiny chapels interconnected, one to St Anne, the other is the Cave of the vision. He is called St John the Theologian here, and may or may not be the Evangelist. No one seems to be quite sure.'

Marina gave gratifying evidence of absorbing this instruction appreciatively. The white Shrine, refulgent in the morning sunlight, seemed to hang almost without support in the sky. It was built on a sheer drop and the foundations went deep into a steep cliff.

'"I, John . . . was on the island of Patmos,"' she said dreamily. 'Can you imagine him really being *there*?' She pointed at the Cave of Revelations. 'He really *was*, you know. I feel it!' She shivered and looked up at him, her eyes filled with excitement. 'I re-read the Apocalypse before I came here on the airplane from New York. The Spirit and the Bride . . . the Marriage of the Lamb . . .'

It struck Paul as unusual that she should mention the Spirit and the Bride. He himself always associated the Book of Revelations with its horrors – the Beast, the Four Horsemen, the Seven Seals, and the Whore of Babylon.

'Yes, it is very beautiful,' she continued. 'Very moving, God wiping the tears away from our eyes. Isn't that wonderful? Every time I think of it, I begin to cry myself.' But she laughed. Then seriously, she said, 'While Arthur was dying, I went back. I went back to church. I went secretly to church.' She was blinking a lot, whether at the sun or in an effort to contain tears, he did not know. Having sat beside her, he slapped his knees, got up, proffered his hand. She took it and rose. Together, they continued up the road. He felt a heaviness of heart emanating from her and he was sorry he had evaded her, for he had.

But she went on. 'I went to the Oratory, though I don't really like it very much, but it was close to where we lived. Arthur was an atheist. I never went on a Sunday and I never told him. The Church upset him and he used to tell me it had crippled me. I felt terrible the first time I sneaked back. It happened to be All Souls Day . . . and I had forgotten . . . All Souls, the second of November . . . all those dead things in me clamouring for attention, and it was no longer in Latin, but I didn't mind too much, it simply felt strange. But then they read that passage, you know, about God wiping the tears away from the eyes of those who had survived their tribulation, and I knew I was back for good.'

Paul was stunned by this confession of faith, as if it were wonderful

179

news he had personally wanted. There was something thrilling and touching about her as she made her way up the road, her steps light now. Her face and hair seemed to be caught up in the blurring light, as if she had been rapt by a certitude that had pierced her and left her hanging like the Shrine in mid-air. They were nearing the side road that led to the white, domed buildings. A taxi whizzed by. 'It wasn't until Arthur had died, though, that I really returned. I had to get the nerve up to go to confession. That was the difficult bit. Twenty years,' she sighed. 'I had not been for twenty years – twenty years in which I should have broken with Arthur but couldn't.' She looked at him a little wildly. 'I couldn't abandon him. I could not.'

Suddenly, Paul felt the blood thudding in his temples. His neck and face flushed. 'And they made you feel rotten about that, did they?' The outburst surprised him. There she stood, atremble like a small flame or one beseeching alms. She had the aura of one on whom the weight of the law had descended, of someone about to be hanged for thieving, of someone who had stolen bread because she was hungry.

'What one feels surely doesn't come into it,' Marina said. 'But I have come to haunt confessionals since then. I keep saying the same thing over and over again. It's a compulsion – like washing one's hands, like Lady Macbeth. And that's wrong too. I know it's wrong. It's just that I keep feeling I have left something out, something crucial even though I know I can't have done that. I can't seem to get beyond my life in the past, if you see what I mean.'

For some reason, he got it into his head that she was the outraged victim of cold Pharisees. He could picture her on her knees, clutching a rosary to her breast, heart in throat, dry at the mouth in an unending stream of remorse. She seemed to stand before him, a mass of contusions inflicted on her by insensitive bigots. The Shrine lay before them down a gravel track. Paul felt goaded. He could not understand it. The whole centre of him felt volatile and he exploded. 'You mean to say that you have repented and yet have to go back and back!'

'I think I go back because I am not sorry enough.'

'What do you mean "sorry enough"? How sorry do you have to be? You, who have shown virtue in humility! Most people don't give a damn what they do, or they spend their whole lives justifying themselves or are totally callous about the effects their actions have on others. Goneril and Regan get the kingdom and Cordelia gets it in the neck!' He spluttered and fumed, taking in deep breaths through his nose.

'But . . . I . . . they . . .'

'I can't bear it! Here I've been all this time stacking corpses in that infernal desert! Do you want to know about evil? Sin? Corruption? It is the tyranny of self-interest, the despotism of sacrificing other people to your own ends, however great or small those may be. I have seen such awful things that you could never imagine them if you were to try for years and years! I block them out most of the time. There are terrible things that happen and they condemn the whole world, not you. Whatever you have done, at least you are sorry. Casting the first stone is not something I would readily do.' He realized that he was in a paroxysm. 'I'm sorry,' he said, lowering his voice. He was aware that she was watching him. It was not tenderness, precisely, that he saw on her face, but a strange availability to what he was feeling. He felt like a sun-spot or a child with a tantrum. 'I don't know,' he added miserably, 'but I do get to feel that all these good and holy people have no idea what suffering really *is*. What people have to bear is insupportable sometimes!' He finished in a near shriek, the veins standing out on his neck and forehead.

All of a sudden, she took his hand, pressed it to her cheek, then let it go. He held it in the air for a moment and looked at it in astonishment, as if it were not attached to his arm. 'There,' she said. 'It's all right.'

At the top of the track to the Shrine, there was a little kiosk where a large and solemn-looking Greek was selling postcards, copies of icons and cold drinks. Unoccupied by any other visitors, his veiled glance fell askance of the shouting Paul. Paul wondered if he thought he had slapped her, or if they were a married couple having a row.

'You see,' he mumbled, 'I feel so awful that I could do so little. I know it's pride and that anything is a help, but it hit me that way all the same. I am sorry that I shouted in that way. I really am.' He felt deeply chagrined, but she cocked her head to one side and elicited a smile from him. 'It is very hot,' he said. 'Would you like a cold drink?'

They bought cans of lemonade from the embarrassed Greek. Paul thought he recognized him from the Orthodox Mass he had attended on Sunday, and he felt he should somehow apologize to him, if only indirectly. 'I hate losing my temper,' he said. He looked fondly at Marina, hoping the man would realize that he had not been angry with her.

'You would not be human if all that you have seen did not make you angry,' she said softly and they went to drink from their cans. They sat on a stone wall. 'But you should not be angry on my account. What you said earlier – about sacrificing people to your ends – that is precisely what I did and maybe what I couldn't articulate in all those confessions. You see, I took Arthur away from his wife and two children. She subsequently died of drink. That was my callousness, if you like. It mattered terribly to them, you see. It was not the trivial marriage that I thought it was, his first one. And the children have never forgiven me because what I did was too wounding to them.'

'You talk about him as if he were a helpless baby you snatched from a pram!' Paul wondered if he were taking the wrong side, but he ventured on. 'I suppose he had no moral responsibility in the matter. What little I gleaned from Helena was that you were the baby and he the snatcher.'

For some reason, Marina flinched. 'Well, I was quite young,' she said, 'but Arthur had no sense of right or wrong, you see. He thought creative people were not subject to rules and laws and that it was only uncreative people like myself who got caught up in them. I was caught up in them, I did believe, and I knew the difference between right and wrong. So, no matter how young I was, I knew better and ought to have prevented the whole thing.' She took a final swig of her lemonade.

'Well, cling onto your guilt if you must,' he said, 'but you should not if God has forgiven you.' He wished he could have found better words to express an inexpressible mixture of feelings. It was as if some secret chaos of his own had been made manifest in her so that he could see before him something of himself unmasked in a bitter refusal, perhaps, to let self-hatred go.

She stood briskly and brushed her lap. 'I think you are probably right,' she said. 'And now I want to see this famous Cave.'

XV

MARINA HAD BOUGHT HERSELF a Bible in New York, only to find that her hotel bedside table contained one already. She had decided that she ought to read it through, but got bogged down in Leviticus. She went frequently to weekday Masses at St Patrick's Cathedral, kneeling amid strangers. She found it hard to grasp that the city had become so shabby in her long absence. The sheer numbers of the homeless poor disturbed her and no matter how much money she gave to beggars, it seemed an almost irrelevant gesture, incommensurate with their plight. In her room near Columbus Circle, she thought she ought, perhaps, to try the Psalms and Prophets. She plumbed 'De Profundis' with King David and measured cubits with Ezekiel. She had no clue whatever as to why she was doing this or anything else and went through muffled nights and days wandering. Having dealt with her business affairs and the detective agency, she had stayed in New York buying hot-dogs at Nedicks and postcards at the Metropolitan Museum. She gazed at 'St Francis in Ecstasy' in the Frick. A lot of urgent walking had gone on, and once she found herself in a Spanish-speaking church in 14th Street, where she had told a festooned Madonna of her crimes. She had stood outside the Women's Prison in the Village and had felt a peculiar impulse to serenade its inmates from the street below.

Marina made herself a promise that she would read Joshua, Judges, Kings and Chronicles when she was more rested. She read The song of Solomon and Isaiah. That was how she had spent her time. It occurred to her that she ought to read the Gospels and the Letters of St Paul as a matter of some priority and so she read them. Speed-reading miracles in Columbus Circle, the lepers and grotesques appealed to her, as did all penitent sinners and the Prodigal.

Outside, under the yellow April sky, sometimes laden with snow, at other times balmy, she seemed continually nudged by crowds. Twice, she was accosted by fundamentalists. On the television in her hotel room, she saw Oral Roberts and Jimmie Swaggart, then switched them off. She snatched first at this phrase, then at that. 'I am the Resurrection and the Life . . .', 'Come to me all you who are burdened . . .', 'In my

Father's house, there are . . .', but she could not fix on anything. She found she could remember nothing of it from her childhood. It was as if everything had been wiped out. The Mass, now in English, seemed bulky and disquieting to her, stripped bare of ceremony. On the whole she liked the simplifying innovation, but it meant she had to think about it and express belief . . . 'descended into hell, the third day . . . the Holy Spirit, the Lord, the Giver of Life . . .' She had not attempted The Book of Revelations until her flight to Athens.

Perhaps it had been a mistake to read about Armageddon on the airplane. She was afraid of being blown up by fundamentalists of another religion. She had tried to conceal the Bible from her neighbouring passenger. As she had bought it at Brentano's, it looked quite new, and without its dust-jacket, it could have been a thriller or romance. On the long trip to Greece, she had tried to puzzle out the story of Last Things. The Apocalypse overwhelmed her with its inscrutable symbols. However hard she tried, she could not understand the prophecy with its many-headed Beast, its plagues and wars. Only the images themselves made a vivid impact. She could see the Four Horsemen, the Woman clothed with Sun, the dragon and archangels, the blood-drinking Whore of Babylon. These figures made a bizarre kind of sense to Marina, like figments of a profound dream that one cannot remember on waking. In the end, the only thing that seemed important was the final descent of the heavenly Jerusalem, the triumph of love in the Marriage of the Lamb. She had read and re-read the revelations, and then had slept dreamlessly.

The Monastery enclosure which surrounded the Cave where these apocalyptic visions had taken place seemed ordinary enough. In fact, a venerable-looking Orthodox priest with a full, grey beard was busy watering plants at the end of a light-filled ambulatory. He only glanced up as Marina and Paul entered, and assured, perhaps, by the propriety of her clothes, fell back to his task. Marina was suddenly embarrassed at the way she had behaved with Paul. During their long trek up the road, she had felt the thawing of an impulse which had become so rigid over the years that she had forgotten it existed, and it had culminated in her taking his hand and laying it on her cheek. The gesture had risen spontaneously out of a warmth of feeling she had conceived for him during the morning's conversation. Somehow, they had seemed to occupy a common ground. For as long as she could remember, her life had been peopled with those to whom she felt she owed gratitude or respect and she was generally filled with awe at the accomplishments and achievements of others. During the long ascent to the Shrine, however, she had forgotten her earlier apprehension of Paul's proven high moral qualities, and had found herself completely at ease in his company. Now, she drew back, for it struck her that he probably thought her touching him premeditated, either that, or as an unconscious desire to seduce him. He had so brightly fulminated against those whom he saw, quite wrongly, as condemning her that she wondered if it were not he himself who did. All at once, she felt like a deserting foot-soldier who had put herself on equal terms with the hero of many campaigns and the presumption in her declaration of faith ashamed her. What was more, she sensed him as a sealed person, who normally contained his feelings under an atmosphere of great pressure, like a vacuum, and it occurred to her that he might subtly blame her for the leak of rage he had let her see. Out of the corner of her eye, she tried to ascertain his mood. He moved rather awkwardly out towards an atrium, his face in an uneasy smile.

Out underneath the sky, a steep flight of stone steps led narrowly down past a complex of white walls and domes, belfries and curious elevations. Passageways seemed to go off in mysterious directions, and shuttered windows seemed to sequester monks in cells away from prying eyes. A faint smell of incense rose from below and mingled itself with the scent of flowers, flowers that must have been secreted in unseen gardens. A sign pointed the way to The Sacred Cave – Hiero Spielo below. Marina and Paul stood silent together for a moment. A casual observer would have thought them more to each other than they were. They began to descend carefully down the steep steps into the white enclosure. It seemed now brilliant in the risen sun and yet, the maze of walls and arches dazzled, as if by their own illumination against the deepening blue of the sky. Marina's eye travelled upwards. A rim of violet hung about the roofs. Beneath them, all was silent.

'We seem to be in luck today,' Paul said. 'There are usually hordes of tourists. They come off the boats and cruise ships and stay for about ten minutes.'

Marina nodded. Together, they threaded their way down the steep steps and as they did so, her spirits began to flag and sink. Almost as if in payment to Arthur's shade for her brief space of near happiness that morning, he seemed now doubly present to her thoughts, invigilating them. He would have disliked Paul as Helena did and would have seen him as a person without literary merit. He judged people in that way, as if they were poems submitted for a prize of his considered good opinion. In any case, he would have kept her from the shadowy underworld of religious shrines and holy places, fearing that her nerves would give under the pressure of an old obedience to a remembered set of images.

She had, indeed, broken down after Maddy had died, a long time ago, that was. Arthur had been all for shock treatment, but she had refused it, preferring, he said, to seclude herself in a fantastical world where God and His angels invisibly poured scorn on her adult choices. By that, he had meant her sexuality. It had been a long and painful episode and she was not sure why she thought of it now except that she was descending to the Cave with a male stranger who, for a short while, had made her pleased with herself. The memory of hunted and confused fanaticism came back to her and with it Arthur's warnings that religion was a poisoned apple for her. Had she really told Helena about her breakdown? It gave her a little jolt when she remembered that she had, though she was sure she had not told her about the theological dimension to the problem. Suddenly, she felt her bones fragile on the stairs, as if she might fall and crack an ankle. A sacred cave might be capable of anything. She wanted to grip Paul's arm, but she gripped the banister instead. Marina became aware of a tight feeling in her chest. It was as if the emotional pain she had said she was numb to had started to throb through stunned nerves. The farther they descended, the more the pressure of a nameless, expanding void squeezed at her and when they reached the bottom of the steps, it was all she could do to keep herself from fleeing up them again. She was gripped by an awful knowledge that she was about to cry.

Paul removed his hat in the porch at the base of the steps. The gesture in its English correctness seemed to forbid tears. She swallowed, remembering how Arthur had abhorred the heavy emotions she had splashed on him, especially in the early years of their marriage. He had called her demanding and manipulative when she cried. At first, she had stood up to him and had even asked him how he could write poetry if he disdained feeling so, but he had told her this was a naive way of looking at the craft. Slowly and subtly, she had realized that he was incapable of writing except through a filter of irony and this had made her oddly docile. She was sure that Paul, too, would see tears as a mawkish sign of a weak, unstable nature. She glanced at him and saw that he had been watching her.

'Well, here we are, Marina,' he said in an awkward, courtly fashion.

'I'm sorry, I suddenly feel a little giddy,' she said. 'I think I had better sit down for a moment.' Three stone steps from the bottom, she sat.

'A touch of the sun, perhaps,' he said, putting a professional palm to her forehead.

'I think it's just a mood,' she said, meek under the cool palm. She laughed it off and felt restored. The pain of tears receded from her throat and muffled itself in her bones.

'I'm afraid I upset you back there. Carrying on like that.'

'Oh, no!' she said earnestly, looking up at him.

He fumbled at his hat brim, then picked up a leaflet from a box inside the church porch. 'Listen to this!' he said. 'I found this the other day. This will cheer you up.' Marina looked past him in through the door of the Shrine. It seemed an ordinary Greek church, not a depth from which the Alpha and Omega of things had emerged. She closed her eyes and rested her head against the stairwell as he read:

'A GREAT MIRACLE GIVEN BY GOD ONLY TO THE ORTHODOX CHURCH,' it says here. I suppose that lets you and me out!' He continued, 'The ceremony of Holy Light in Jerusalem . . . takes place in the Orthodox Church of the Resurrection in Jerusalem in such a way as bewilders the soul of Christians . . . !'

'My soul is already quite bewildered enough,' said Marina, suddenly seeing it.

'Let me finish! On Easter Saturday, apparently, a Holy Light . . . flashes from the depth of the Holy Sepulchre in a supernatural way, miraculously, and lights up the little lamp of olive oil put on the edge of it. It then gets distributed to pilgrims, who receive it with great emotion, accompanied by the pealing of bells, acclamations and unbridled enthusiasm . . . It emits from the Sepulchre having a gleam of a hew (*sic*) completely different from natural light. It sparkles and flashes like lightning, it flies like a dove around the tabernacle of the Holy Sepulchre, and lights up the unlit lamps of olive oil hanging in front of it. It whirls from one side of the church to the other . . . !' He stopped reading.

Marina suddenly found the clumsily expressed leaflet touching. The thought of miraculous light flashing and whirling and flying like a dove made her shiver. 'Do you suppose that really happens?' she asked. She had, indeed, been distracted by the tale.

'I think it is refreshing to meet someone who believes it might,' he replied.

187

'I think I feel better now,' she said. Marina tried to make herself unconscious of his sympathetic regard.

'We'd better make a dash for it if we are going to see it,' he said, pointing the way into the Shrine. 'There will be coach-loads of people before long.'

It was all very simple, spilling with light. In fact, far from being sealed in gloom and claustral with numinous shadows, the little complex of twinned, interconnected chapels seemed serene. Bright sunlight streamed through a casement window onto the stone floor and it gave an almost cheerful air to the rich icons and hanging silver lamps. To the left, there was a straightforward Orthodox nave, ending in a small and brilliant iconstasis. To the right, an overhang of rock seemed to indicate the Cave as advertised. Marina and Paul were alone save for a solitary deacon, who sat in one of the oak choir stalls that lined the left-hand wall. He acknowledged their presence with a smile, then fell back to his own thoughts. They stood still for a moment in the quiet place, which for all its ornate caparisons, seemed oddly austere.

Against the wall of a kind of vestibule to the main body of the Shrine, there hung an icon of St John himself. The painted saint fixed Marina with a fiery eye. There were boxes of tapers in the vestibule and still more leaflets. Marina stuffed drachmas in a slot and extracted a fistful of tapers. She had always been a great one for lighting candles and she offered one to St John. Her votive light spluttered in its holder and then began to burn evenly. 'I still don't see what it was that hit me about Arthur,' she said silently and with painful feeling to the image, but it failed to be oracular. 'Why did it go on for so long? And why did I never have the strength to escape him?'

Paul had moved tactfully away and appeared to be inspecting a large tome open on a lectern. Marina felt that he was uneasily aware of her regard. He wandered to the casement near the iconstasis at the end of the left-hand chapel. He seemed both vigilant and tense. He probably had misgivings about her now, she thought. Surely in a place like this he must see her for the sort of woman she was. Again, she felt the agitation of tears behind her eyes. She turned to the icon again and strove to have positive thoughts, thoughts of what it must have been like to have seen the heavenly Jerusalem descending in pure gold like clear glass, all in the uncreated light where sun and moon no longer shone.

She closed her eyes and tried to see the Bride descending in her mind's eye. Instead, a reeling memory of her own wedding to Arthur came back to her. They had been married in Chelsea Town Hall.

There had been piped music at that occasion too, piped music as at his funeral. Nothing less than Bach. But Maddy and Daddy had not come. No wonder, she thought now. It had hurt at the time, though, and actually still hurt. It had given Arthur everything he needed to undermine her continuing loyalty to them. Henry and Claire had not come. There had been a clutch of people Marina barely knew and had not seen subsequently until Arthur's funeral. Also, now dead and more famous poets had arrived, tricked out in a subtle style of haute bohème. Had there really been a lot of flowing hair and floppy ties? She did remember women got up by Biba. A psychedelic flux of souls in baggy corduroys. Marina herself had worn a brave hat, brazenly cocked and smart, white gloves and a very short, smart, black and white suit. The Muse, the Bride, the penetrated Aphrodite, just twenty-one years old, but bold and sure.

Why could she not remember Arthur on this of all occasions? She could only see herself in black and white Mary Quant with severed hair. Jane, the first wife, had been the enemy then, the domestic Medusa who had turned his gift to stone. Marina had thought she had knocked castrating shears out of the woman's hand. What with the head-turning reviews of the *Cycle* and her own picture in one newspaper, Marina had felt amply justified in this opinion at the time. It was not guilt she felt so much now but shame. Jane had written her a letter begging her to release Arthur and restore their marriage. Marina had not even answered it.

It was for this reason, of course, she told herself now that she had wanted to flee from the Shrine. Marina looked down and found herself fiddling with her wedding ring again, revolving it as her thoughts revolved around the unholy chimera of herself. She looked at Paul standing at the window, his back to her. Was it out of high-mindedness that he did not condemn her? Goodness? Arthur would have said that he found her attractive. Marina could not think why people, why men looked at her in this light, but they did, she with her cellulite thighs and frowsy hair. Why had she misled him into thinking she had been grudgingly absolved? On the contrary, she had been spared, her fears of Hell allayed. Even the one priest who had been harsh with her had no deeper misfortune in store for her than Purgatory. Marina knew that she was thrashing out a lot of things about Hell, trying to update her vision of it as she was told she ought. Maddy had been a keen believer in Hell, but now things weren't so certain. Did this mean that not so

189

many people went there as before, or that they had been mistaken about numbers in the past?

Marina knew that she was timid as a rabbit in a certain kind of snare. She had married Arthur under the assumption that she was going there already – to Hell that was – and in that respect, Arthur's atheism had been a comfort. After a few years, however, it had been God's goodness she had missed, not that she sensed that it was spent, but simply that it stood in an irregular relationship to her. She felt a great longing for God now, almost as a mystic might feel it. Clutching her bunch of tapers, she proceeded up the nave towards Paul, thinking not to tangle with the Cave part of the Shrine until she had balanced herself. She was arrested by a large icon of St Anne in the iconstasis. Marina was pleased that she recognized it. In childhood, Maddy had often taken her to Mass at a church near Park Avenue where there was a shrine to St Anne, a statue not an icon, of the Grandmother of Christ. The crowned saint had held a tender arm around her daughter, the Virgin. This had been one of Maddy's absolute favourites, mother and daughter linked in mutual trust. Here, though, the Byzantine icon glowed with rich, red robes. St Anne, whose face was striated with formal lines, depicting her great age, held the Virgin, a scaled-down, miniature adult, who proffered her mother a flower.

Hurriedly, she stuffed two candles into the taper-holder, then, for a moment forgot why, then remembered. 'For Maddy' she said, and said a 'Hail Mary' and thought how pleased Maddy would be that she was doing this. 'And for my mother,' she added in her mind. As the candle spluttered upwards in contact with the flame, Marina wondered if, in the light of eternity, Maddy would forgive this betrayal. Marina looked searchingly at the saint's face. 'Whoever my mother is, she must need . . .' She felt a dark and heavy thing brush at her heart, as if she had woken a night-bird, which cawed with unceremonious cry. Where was her mother now? Where was her mother now that she needed her? Perhaps she was even now straining at the golden bars of Heaven like the Blessed Damozel mutely appealing to God for Marina. She felt a sudden need for her mother to be an angel, that she needed angelic intervention.

And the thing she had tried to thrust out of her mind since the previous afternoon removed the barrier of her conscious will and stood before her inner eye, as if asserting its own right to be there despite her fearful prohibition of its presence. Helena and Arthur had been lovers. Marina stepped back from the flickering tapers she had lit and withdrew her eyes from St Anne. Having conjured up the image of her wedding, it now occurred to her that Helena had not been there. Nor had she been among the occasional guests of Arthur's for whom Marina had cooked elaborate meals during the first few years before purdah had descended and they had not seen anyone. Yet he had spoken of her. Most certainly he had spoken of her.

No, she must not brood on it or think of it. She stuffed in another candle after an ungenerous hesitation. For Helena, she thought, then realized how absurd Helena would think her to do this. The placating taper did nothing to burn or dispel Marina's evil thought of Arthur and Helena, Helena and Arthur.

She quickly looked at Paul, who still stood at the window looking out. He was probably in high communication with God. He had lit no candles and she was sure he was above this childish form of devotion. She did not wish to interrupt his immense thoughts, but for safety against pointless outrage, she joined him at the window. She ducked her head in embarrassment, but he turned and smiled. 'Look!' he whispered. From the casement, there stretched a scene of blue in every tone and inflection of the colour, indigo harbour, ultramarine sea, navy pine trees clustered underneath a cerulean sky almost purple at the horizon. They did not speak, but stood there for a while. A vision of Arthur and Helena in bed together jabbed at her mind. Maddy would have considered that a bad thought for the sex, but not for the uncharity of jealousy. It should not matter to me, she thought, but it filled her with revulsion and when she remembered Helena telling her about it, she shuddered as if she had been fondled by a stranger in a crowd.

Marina looked down the dizzying escarpment on which the chapel seemed to hang. Had she not only yesterday confided her marital problems to Helena? And in the months before, other intimate things? Surely, Helena had only wanted to spare her and had done so until honesty had been required. It had been brave of her, really, to tell and it was absurd to think that they could really talk about Arthur unless they had a basis of truth between them. Arthur. Why had Arthur lied to her? Why had he said there had been no one else but Jane? Why had he bothered to do this when he had never shirked at any squalid thing as a matter of principle? His thoughts, uncensored and unbridled, had never spared her, so why had he concealed Helena? She tried not to think of the stuffed drawers of notebooks and journals awaiting her in London, fragments of verse and unpaid bills. Was there evidence of Helena smeared on his exercise books? Was she hidden in the leaves?

Abruptly, she checked this line of thinking and turned to Paul. His eye was caught up in the scene before them, his face in an expression of content. The view of the island and the sea was held in a light so clear that it seemed to melt the hills and the water into a haze, which gathered its forces and distilled itself as if streamed onto the floor of the close, enclosed chapel. Her throat ached. She was still clutching unlit tapers in her hand. 'I've been lighting these,' she said apologetically. 'It somehow seems the right thing to do in here.'

'Well, it's nothing like the Greeks themselves,' he said. 'On Sunday, the place was ablaze with candles. They kiss the icons too with great devotion.'

'I suppose you think it's old-fashioned and silly,' Marina said, not meaning to sound as defensive as she had.

'Why should I think that, Marina?'

'I don't know.' She had a great wish to unburden herself to Paul, but she concealed it. 'Why don't you show me the Cave?' she asked, her voice uneven. She cleared her throat.

'Oh, haven't you looked at it yet?' He turned with her. The smaller chapel was framed by a heavy abutment of rock, a cave indeed, with rough, natural walls and ceiling. Paul pointed to a deep crevice in the lowering overhang. They passed under it and he pressed his fingers into the crack. 'It is said that when the Angel of Revelations appeared, the living rock split here. The Orthodox put their hands to it and cross themselves.' He was smiling and kept on smiling at her.

Marina put out her hand instinctively and felt the rough stone surface where the cave had split. It suddenly seemed wonderful to her to be in such a place where vision was not considered to be an aberration but a way of seeing. She ducked her head and went under the abutment into the smaller chapel where another iconstasis was tucked away in the rough wall. Marina stood still in the sacred, secret place. It was vivid with a complexity of images and hanging lamps, but somehow it seemed imbued with a curious singleness of meaning which emerged from the protective depth of shadow. The icons, the silver, the heavy, grainy rock were all unified into one, pure impression of sombre beauty. 'Oh!' said Marina. Not knowing exactly what to pray for, but in need of prayer all the same, she kindled her two remaining tapers and stuck them in a holder.

Paul was busy pointing out first this thing and then that thing in the Cave, a little altar to St John along the wall, a silver-lined indentation in the rock where the saint was said to have lain his head, a similar indentation where he had placed his hand, the Virgin as the Tree of Jesse, the saint dictating his vision to a scribe. But for all of that, Marina found herself mesmerized by the large and dominating icon of the Apocalyptic Vision itself. At one end of the little chapel, there were some low benches set on the uneven Cave floor. Marina sat still in contemplation and Paul sat beside her in silence.

Cast down in a swoon lay the bearded figure of the visionary John, while above him, wreathed in gold and fire sat the Angel of Revelations, aloft in smoky cloud. The hair of the Angel was whitened and his right hand held seven stars, his feet rested on the heads of cherubim, his seat was a rainbow. Around his waist was a golden girdle, before him, seven candlesticks aflame. A sword from his mouth signified piercing utterance, and he was thronged with seraphim, who offered him seven churches from the cloud. In his left hand, he held weighty keys. Suddenly, as if by association with the fissure running through the Cave, quaked by the revelation of the sealed book, Marina felt an awful loosening of her last reserve and she began to cry. The pressure of pain, fully thawed now, seemed to invade her and she knew she could not ward off this vast release of spirit even if she wanted to. She made to conceal her face with her hands, but huge, guttural sobs came from within her and unstoppable tears poured down her face. She had no idea why she was weeping, but it came as unutterable relief. It was as if she were caught up in some elemental force which had its own momentum and designs. She seemed to be huddled there in the arm of some much larger thing that seemed to transcend her prayers and tapers with Paul sitting beside her, rigid, she knew, with embarrassment. She decided that this did not matter. 'It was my life. It was my life. It was my whole life,' she kept on saying to herself as she wept, even though this in no way expressed what she was feeling. It was more as though she had tapped a deep source of compassion for herself and it seemed to come from beyond her as if it had been waiting for years to be unlocked and as if the only thing to do was to abandon herself to it completely. After a while, it seemed to abate, having passed its consummation. She fumbled at a handkerchief and blew her nose. Paul sat very still beside her. She rose, then knelt on the rough stone floor of the Cave, then got to her feet. 'I'm sorry,' she said, clearing her throat. 'I really am. I didn't mean to do that.' She waved her hand at the icon as if the blame were to be placed on it.

'It's understandable,' he said, looking askance, and then directly into her eyes, reddening a bit.

'I'm not sure it is understandable.' She shrugged a little helplessly. He rose and together they made their way back to the door of the Shrine. 'I don't know quite what to say,' she added. She felt abashed and happy at the same time, linked to him through the experience. Her general sense of acquittal seemed to include him in it.

'I don't know what to say either!' he said with a sudden humour that relieved and pleased her. 'Are you all right now?' As they struggled up the steep steps, a busload of Scandinavians crowded their way down the stairs past them, forcing Marina and Paul into a corner against the wall.

'Yes, I feel a great deal better, in fact. I suppose the least I can say about it is that I got a lot off my chest.'

They squeezed their way past blonde, pink tourists.

'What was it that upset you?' he asked. The tourists wore cruise clothes and carried cameras like guns in holsters. They funnelled down the white, enclosed stairwell while Paul and Marina struggled to ascend.

She felt buoyed over the tide like a salmon knowing its way upstream.

'It's no one thing,' she replied. 'And I wasn't really upset.'

He gave her a sharp look, but said nothing. They carried on upwards until they reached the surface. A bustling tour guide seemed to have herded the last Scandinavian down and, clipboard in hand, dived after them.

'I frightened you,' she said, suddenly giddy in a rush of self-confidence. She felt liberated to risk this remark. She wondered if what she had experienced had been a kind of vision or a sign.

He stood in the light-filled ambulatory, encircling his hat with his fingers, turning it round and round. 'I suppose you did frighten me,' he said after a pause, 'But to do me justice, I was frightened for you as well.'

'I wasn't accusing you,' she said, but she knew that she had been lumping him with Arthur in her mind. 'And there is really no need for you to be frightened for me.'

'Oh, there is,' he said, putting a hand on the wing of her shoulder. They strolled out into the light and down the alley of feathery blue pines that led from the Shrine to the road. There was a modest block of flats set in the hillside above them in the trees. From an open window came a clear air by Vivaldi. Someone having to do with the Shrine, perhaps, had a stereo and the Italian music floated out, both apt and incongruous. Marina was grateful for his light touch. The pines tossed and sighed in the breeze and light dappled on the road. She felt an unaccountable gaiety and lightness of spirit.

'What danger do you see, then?' she asked, almost flirtatiously.

He frowned in concentration as if struggling to grasp an elusive thought. 'You are so open. I could not abandon myself in that way for fear of what might find me if I lost myself.' The words came out halt and complex. Marina observed a kind of wistfulness in his expression.

'It simply took me over, the Cave. After all, such a holy place must be safe.' And she realized that she had felt safe – utterly safe – not at all as she had feared on her descent into the Shrine. And she felt safe now, secure.

He laughed. 'Isn't that a bit of a contradiction in terms? I have always thought holiness and safety antithetical to each other.'

Marina flushed. 'One must trust God,' she said a little starchily. 'And other people too, I think.'

They had left the Shrine and the music behind them and were slowly ascending the winding road to Hora.

'If you trust everyone, you end up trusting no one,' he said.

Marina listened to this. 'What do you mean?' she asked.

'I know it's really none of my business, but I've been wondering if you haven't made a hasty decision about collaborating on this book about your husband. Please forgive me if I have overreached myself. I found myself thinking a great deal about it in the Cave.'

'Collaborating? I don't understand.' Marina was genuinely mystified.

'Did you not come to Patmos in order to write a book with Helena about your late husband? She talked endlessly about it before you came.'

'Oh,' Marina said uneasily. 'She did mention something about a book yesterday in the Monastery, but I didn't really take it in. There were rather a lot of things she said.'

'You mean you didn't know when you came here? She has already interested a publisher in London and I got the strong impression that you were supposed to be helping her.'

'I had no idea,' Marina said, feeling helpless once more.

He stopped walking. 'You must have a very natural urge to talk about your husband now. Have you told her a great deal?'

Marina put her hand over her mouth. It had never occurred to her that Helena might use her confidences.

'Maybe she wanted to surprise you,' said Paul with faint irony. 'Of course, it would be a wonderful way to celebrate your husband's life.'

Marina reeled at the thought of the ample evidence she had given to Helena for Arthur's condemnation. She made a snap decision. 'Paul . . . ?' With some difficulty, she said, 'Paul, I have told her a lot and I'm afraid to say it was not a happy marriage.' She trembled slightly at having made that admission to him.

'That was my intuition and that is why I mentioned it.'

'Did she *tell* you?'

'Well, I don't think she's going to write a hagiography of your husband. I got the feeling that it was going to be a hagiography of you!'

'Oh, how awful!' Marina cried. 'Does Serge know about this?'

'Well, she would hardly have told me. She was discussing the book primarily with him.'

'I can't believe this. This is awful,' Marine repeated.

'You see,' he said, 'there is a danger in too much openness.'

'I feel like a specimen under a microscope!' Marina wrung her hands. 'There will never be an end to it. They will never leave me alone, will they?' She thought of Arthur and of Aphrodite. 'It's all my doing, too! Without knowing it, I do it. I get them to *look* at me . . .'

'Marina!' he said, extending a hand.

She shook her head sadly. The light which she had shed for Helena on the deepest interstices of her marriage showed up its flaws in bold definition now to herself. 'Oh, poor Arthur,' she said.

'I think she means to establish him as a major poet,' said Paul.

Marina groaned.

Paul dropped his hand and looked down at his feet. 'I do see that puts you in an awful position. I'm sorry. Perhaps I should not have interfered, but . . .'

'Paul, I had to know! You have no idea what I have said. If I'd thought . . . I would never . . .'

'Well, I should weigh my words in future.'

'But she could! She could establish him. Poor Arthur. That's all he wanted.'

They resumed their ascent up the graded curves of the road.

'Well, you do have some control, after all,' he said. 'And she is a reputable writer by all accounts.'

'I have some control now!' Marina exclaimed with indignation. 'Now I know. And to be blunt about it, I have his journals and unpublished poems.' It suddenly sickened her, the thought of Helena going through these. 'I am his executor by default, I may say. He did not appoint me, but apparently, I inherit the task.'

'I suppose you've had the miserable business of going through it all,' Paul said. 'After my mother died, I had to go through awful things, old love letters from my father, locks of my own baby hair. It was dreadful.'

Marina looked down and watched her sandals slap and plod up the hill. 'There's a whole desk full. I couldn't bear to touch it.' She sensed him looking at her narrowly and with concern. She felt his concern touch her almost palpably, looked up and saw that it was truly there. All she could think of now was Helena's admission to her the day before that she and Arthur had been lovers. Her tongue strained to reveal it to Paul, but she stifled the urge.

'Well, that gives you quite a lot of leeway and time,' he said, his voice bright with false optimism. 'You can say to her, if you are at all doubtful, that you have to go through everything before you make up your mind.'

'But I'm afraid of her!' she found herself saying. They had reached a hairpin bend in the road. Beyond them was a clear vista of the sea. They stopped walking again, and stood on the gravel verge.

'Why?' he asked kindly. He seemed to exude a gentle intensity.

It struck her that she was threatened by that marvellous hegemony of the brilliant and gifted, Helena and Arthur, a pair fixed forever, poet and critic, linked not only bodily but by an inviolable necessity of the intellect. There was no guard rail to the road and Marina stepped back, only to plunge with heady daring into confidence with Paul. 'Arthur and Helena were lovers,' she said. 'She told me yesterday and this was why I missed the point about the book. She told me yesterday. At the Monastery.' Her stomach lurched with the awfulness of having said it to a virtual stranger.

'How revolting!' he cried.

'I should never, never have said.' Marina felt dizzy with panic.

'You mean you didn't know about the book *or* this until yesterday? I knew something unpleasant had happened, but I had no idea it was that bad!'

'To have told you! I'm so weak! How could I?' she said miserably and half to herself.

'It's a terrible abuse!'

'Oh, you don't understand them,' she lamented. 'It wasn't an abuse in her eyes. Can't you see? She confessed it to me and that puts me under an obligation to exonerate her or accept her.'

Paul gave a soft growl from his throat, took off his hat and rubbed his head. 'But that is where the abuse lies!' He replaced his hat and glowered at the scenery.

'Poor Helena,' said Marina, shaking her head. 'You see, you have to adjust to their moral universe, that of Helena and Arthur . . .' She waved her hand in a broad gesture at the sea and sky before them. 'Emotional honesty is everything. Hypocrisy, the worst crime. Sexual continence is not an issue, really. She was seeking to liberate me from Arthur. She thinks I am immolating myself to his memory and in a way that is true.'

'If there were honesty in the woman, then why didn't she declare her interest from the outset?' Paul said sharply.

'It has to do,' Marina said mystically, 'with her feelings for Arthur.' She swallowed. 'And that I can forgive.'

Paul adjusted his hat brim smartly. 'I admitted you frightened me. And you do frighten me. Don't you see the risks involved in all of this? Your memory of your husband is something that belongs to your integrity. I don't think I've put that very well, but it's the best I can do. Can you imagine what a mind like Helena's would make of your marriage? Once she has pawed it, you will have nothing sacred to salvage from it.'

'What do you mean by that?' Marina asked, startled by the word 'sacred'.

'I don't know what you have said to her about him. He might have been a monster for all I know. Maybe you should have left him, but you did not and in not doing so, you made a choice. Perhaps that was a choice to love him. I really have no idea. It could have been cowardice. How do I know? But if the choice was to go on loving him, supporting him without any gratification, without even a blessing in return, then it had to do with something more important than Helena could make out. And the sort of mind that cannot understand this, that cannot understand what a strange gift unhappy love can be, could never do your husband any real justice. Myself, I wouldn't put a dog through it, that kind of suffering, but having undergone it, the experience belongs to you.'

'Don't make me out a martyr,' Marina said crossly. 'That's what Helena thinks . . .'

'So, I suppose her agenda includes the idea that such sacrifice is outmoded? I tell you, she will turn the whole thing round so that you have nothing but failure and waste to extract from it!'

Marina closed her eyes and said nothing.

'I hate to see people's experience revised for them. If you suffered, you suffered. If you loved, you loved. What does she have to do with it?' he continued.

'But, if Arthur's reputation as a poet is at stake, and I am afraid I think it probably is, how can I, in any justice, refuse her?' She blinked at the sun, happy at his hot defence of her, but slightly uncomfortable with his reading of the situation. She could not help but add, however, 'She knows everything . . . the most intimate details of our married life. She knows all sorts of miseries, how Arthur wouldn't let me have any friends. She even knows about my breakdown. I had a breakdown, you see.'

'Well, you mustn't have another one!' he said vehemently. He took her limp hand and shook it back and forth as if to jostle her into life.

She looked directly at him. 'I cannot spare my own reputation in exchange for his. I wanted a Mass offered for him, but this is what was really required of me. I am sure she will be passionately, scrupulously fair.'

'I should be absolutely sure before you give her any access to further information that you demand precisely that, her scrupulous fairness.'

'She wants to *share* Arthur,' Marina said with sudden horror. 'That is what she wants.'

'Aha!' Paul cried. 'That is what bothered me, though I could not define it! You will simply have to be a Portia, give her her pound of flesh, but not one single drop of blood.'

Marina paused for a moment, thinking this all pontifical. He was, she supposed, used to solving other people's problems and, to do him justice, she had all morning leaned on his opinion and had gazed up at him as if inviting such wisdom. Suddenly, her instinct told her what to do. Swiftly, she embraced him, giving him a little kiss on the cheek. 'I am very grateful to you,' she said, 'Very.'

He looked abashed and pleased.

'Friends?' she asked, putting her head to one side.

An involuntary smile lit his face and he laughed self-consciously. 'Yes, I think so,' he said, 'I really do.' As he spoke, a white Mercedes taxi swished around the corner bearing Serge and Lipitsin up the hill past them. Either they were too absorbed in conversation or they had no wish to stop for Paul and Marina. 'Oh dear!' Paul added. 'I myself may be in need of a friend before long against all this silliness. 'I'm afraid it is nothing less than the Tsar of all the Russias we have to contend with now. I only hope they keep it well away from the poor old lady.'

Marina raised an eyebrow and shook her head. Changing the subject, she said, 'This has been a lovely day for me, despite everything. Thank you.' And quickening their pace, they made their way back up the road to Hora.

XVI

SERGE MIRKOVSKY knew that he often played the fool. Indeed, behaving foolishly was a painful, conscious choice of his at times. For as long as he could remember, he had had the strange ability to stand outside himself and watch his actions as if they belonged to someone else and were not performed by him personally. Even, and perhaps especially, the most solemn moments of his life had been imbued for him with a sense of absurdity and of all absurdities, he thought the worst was to take oneself seriously. It was almost as if his life had been pre-ordained as a joke. He was a prince, but without a principality. Born with a first-class intellect, his circumstances, he felt, had deprived him of the use of it. Handsome, he found sexual encounter ridiculous, and wealthy by marriage, he could think of nothing to do with money but to waste it on drinking and the occasional gambling spree. He had had, to be sure, a surprising fondness for his children when they were young, but as adults, he found them grown into recondite beings, graced with a dignity that he himself rather lacked. He often thought of himself as a man in a mirror, a clear but detached image, incapable of feeling what he touched, and voiceless when he spoke.

As a child, he remembered trying to feel fear and experimenting with it. He had been very frightened of his father, but this had had a paralyzing effect on his limbs and mind. At school, he had sought acute sensations. There had been a tall pine tree in a copse by the playing fields and he had once climbed to the highest branch and had bounced on it, swayed upon it, watching the crack next to the trunk widen. A weird exultation had come upon him as he realized his own, self-inflicted peril. As it happened, they had fetched him down and beaten him, but the sense of having known himself beyond the dread of death had made the escapade worthwhile. It was the same with his drinking bouts now in middle-age. The more the doctor and Fiona warned him to stop, the more he felt impelled to risk himself. At the perverse climax of each drunken episode, he seemed to fly beyond the limit of ordinary existence. From the plateau of inebriation, just as on the pine branch, he would contemplate, with philosophic equanimity, meaningless, aim-lessness, emptiness, as if this vision were the sheer fall into the dark air from the tree. As he blacked out, he would descend into the freedom of oblivion.

To his family, both immediate and extended, Serge played the role of an overgrown child. He sensed it as a popular demand. He had frittered and fooled and sulked and capered, knowing that it gratified his mother and even more subtly, his wife. She would scold and then indulge him. His mother did neither, but pranks and boyish grins had always been rewarded, whereas a firmer manliness had not. To his sister Varya, he remained an eternal playmate as he was to Paul, although Paul did not acknowledge this. It was only with 'la belle Hélène', as he privately called his cousin, that he shared the occasional streak of the bold brilliance of his larger conception. Serge admired Nabokov above all writers and sometimes he was possessed of the bleakly witty notion that this author had invented him. Like Pnin, he seemed to himself to be the literary construct of a displaced Russian émigré. And yet, he was even more open to ridicule and disbelief than this character, for his own experience of exile was at one remove. If one took into account the literary removals of narrative design, his life was even twice or thrice removed from its origins.

For many years now Serge had been so preoccupied with void and blackness that he could not chart them. He meditated endlessly on death and on the randomness of his existence. Oddly, he was no atheist and would sometimes take refuge in something akin to prayer; but if he did not discount God's existence, he certainly laid at God's door a self-negating universe. Sometimes, he thought of God as the omniscient ironist, the author of his character with a plot in mind of traps and double-blinds. Perhaps because his family had brought him up to think of himself historically, he had grown into the habit of tracing the configuration of his psyche as if it were the development of an idea thought up by someone else, an idea that had grown out of Oblomov or Platonov. Serge had been a fiction to himself.

It should have been easy for Serge to mark the time in which he had fallen from this literary mode of being into history, but perhaps it is the nature of all Edens that they are only recalled in a wistful nostalgia for mythic times and cannot be directly summoned up. Not that Serge's career as patient rather than agent had ever held any bliss for him, he had simply enjoyed the freedom of being provisional. He had been fond, for instance, of gambling, as if the very material means by which he lived a comfortable life were immaterial to him. Although not addicted to games of chance, he had been captivated by the idea of fortune, its wheels, its black and red. Besides, it charged him up to perpetuate the role of a drunken Russian prince with gambling debts. From the safety of an habituated marriage, he would sally out sometimes, go to London and have a fling at Crockfords, stay at his club, that sort of thing. It amused him to watch himself tastelessly posing as parodies of himself. It is rather a moot point why that particular night, almost a year before Lipitsin's visit to Patmos, Serge chose to ignore the signals he usually obeyed. Having lost up to the limit where he knew his delinquency could be pardoned by his wife, a switch had been thrown somewhere in his head and he had gone on until his losses had been quite considerable.

What to do? He owed and he had to pay. Having recently arrived at one of their frequent truces, Serge lacked the nerve to call on Fiona's personal reserves. On his return to Northumberland, both the debt and the guilt haunted him and he cast around in his mind for what to sell.

The one recollection of that time which disturbed him was how airily he had been prepared to sacrifice the thing which now meant most to him, his father's only bequest, a miniature portrait of Tsar Nicholas II. It was hardly as if Serge had loved his father, a severe man from whom he had felt almost infinitely remote. He had always thought and still thought that Paul and Fiona made too much of his father's death. Of course, he had wept a lot and gone to pieces over exams, but Serge had seen the whole episode as vaguely unreal and had never given a moment's conscious thought to the event since. It was hardly as if he had ever held the Tsar in great esteem either. As an historical figure, Serge had always thought him an interesting but tragic anachronism, but he had never considered him as a man or as anyone having more personal connection to him than his father had. Both had seemed part of his genesis in some way, but neither had had any more meaning to him than Zeus. The miniature itself he knew to have been painted from life and it was beautifully framed, but apart from this, Serge's contemplation of its sale did not constitute a betrayal of anyone but his own son, also called Nicholas, who might have expected it as a legacy. Nonetheless, as he had taken the miniature out of the wall safe in his study, he had experienced a thrill of horror at the thought of what he was about to do. Far from being outside the experience, he felt it throb within himself like a nasty cut and an old terror associated with his father's measured punishments crept around his stomach and seized it with nausea. It had been a kind of direct feeling he had not had in years.

Perhaps because of this, he had persevered. With that willed hopelessness, that odd, eerie disdain and disregard for danger or of dread itself, he had inquired among his more dissolute acquaintance as to how to get rid of the thing at a good price. A gambling crony had come up with Lipitsin's name, for he had made a few bob on some family paintings and had preferred, for tax reasons, not to go through Sotheby's. On the swift, electrified train journey to London, Serge had touched the oval portrait in his pocket as if it held some power in reserve to strike him dead.

It had been exhilarating, taking the thing out and unveiling it from its shroud of black tissue paper before Lipitsin's scrutinising eyes. From the outset, he had found Lipitsin both fascinating and repellant. In the bare, clinical rooms, he had experienced a kind of déjà vu. So, it had come to this, Serge had thought to himself, to the end of things. As Lipitsin handled the portrait, Serge recognized it as a summing image of tangled memory and enmeshing, deep emotion and it seemed almost impossible that it could fall off the edge of his world into Lipitsin's shadowed limbo.

Lipitsin had an eyeglass like a jeweller. He unscrewed it. 'How much do you owe?' he had asked abruptly.

'How do you know that I owe money?' Serge had asked.

'No one would sell such a thing unless he did owe money,' Lipitsin said in Russian. Oddly, Serge had not made any connection with this obviously Russian name. It caught him off balance and he had told Lipitsin the sum.

Lipitsin wiped off his fingers with tissue like a doctor. In a crisp, matter-of-fact tone, he had said, 'I will lend you the money free of interest. You can use the portrait as collateral if you like, but the frame alone is worth much more than you owe.' Together, they had looked silently at the pearl-encrusted oval surrounding the delicately executed face with its whiskers and its yachting cap, its sad blue eyes. All of a sudden, it seemed an act of mercy to Serge, a reprieve. 'What is more, if you are interested, I have word of some quite unusual papers having to do with the Romanovs,' he said carefully, 'and if you were to see your way through to helping me obtain them, then I might pay off the debt for you. Consider it my retainer.'

So, that had been the beginning of his association with Lipitsin, an association that had begun mainly out of Serge's huge relief at having been spared the consequences of his actions. The debt was spirited away and in its place came the highly amusing prospect of adventure.

Lipitsin intrigued him and the half-suggestions of remarkable discovery led him on. Although he told his wife a vastly edited version of the truth, she had initially been delighted that he had a new associate and a new interest in life. His new role as a sort of research assistant took him out of town and to London often, but even so, he drank less and anything that made him drink less influenced Fiona on its behalf.

In the beginning, there had been no talk of the Archduchess Olga, all that had come later, but fairly early on, Lipitsin had confided in him that they would be dealing with papers that seemed to suggest that there had been a successful plot to spirit a Romanov or all Romanovs out of Russia. The whole notion of searching for such proof, especially in the company of the urbane Lipitsin, had at first struck Serge as being entertaining. It seemed like trying to set out to prove a Greek myth or like building edible sculpture. It all had to do with the law of probabilities and the incertitudes of fate.

On 16 July 1918, in the city of Ekaterinburg, which lies in the foothills of the Eastern Urals, the Russian royal family and their few remaining servants were woken from their narrow beds in 'The House of Special Purpose' where they had been held captive for four months. They were told that they were to be moved to a more secure hiding-place as the White Army was attempting to rescue them. Accustomed to these movements since the Abdication and to the small indignities of their nomadic life, the family washed and dressed. The Tsarina was forty-six years old, her eldest daughter Olga, twenty-three, her youngest daughter Anastasia, had been eighteen. The women sewed their jewels into their travelling clothes, a hopeful gesture, anticipating freedom. The Tsar was fifty, and Alexis, the haemophiliac Tsareivitch, fourteen years old. There was a doctor, who tended the sick boy. There was a valet, a cook and a parlourmaid. There was even a family dog called Jimmie. From airless rooms, they descended into a cellar with barred windows where a Bolshevik official named Yurovsky told them to wait. The Tsar asked for chairs for his wife and son and they were brought three. The four daughters stood behind their parents, the ailing child leaned on his father's arm. The servants grouped around. At first, they were told to expect motor-cars to take them away. In this photographic ensemble, they listened. Then they were told that they were to be shot. Olga, Tatyana and Marie were shot. The maid was shot, but did not die, so they bludgeoned her to death. Alexis moved and was kicked in the head and shot through the ear. The doctor, cook and valet were also shot. Then Anastasia, who had fainted, moaned, so they bludgeoned her and bayoneted her to death. They crushed the head of the spaniel with their boots. When it was done, they carted the bodies to a mine shaft marked by four trees. It took them three days to hack the corpses to pieces. They burnt the limbs on a bonfire. What would not burn, they doused in sulphuric acid, and what would not dissolve was thrown into the shaft.

Or, on 16 July 1918 in Ekaterinburg, the family and servants were woken, prepared, then shot, save Anastasia who, having fainted, was rescued by a peasant named Tschaikovsky and taken to Bulgaria. Or, Olga was saved, or Tatyana, or Marie, or Alexis and spirited out.

Or, on 16 July 1918, 'The House of Special Purpose' in Ekaterinburg had been raided by the White Army and the Bolshevik Yurovsky had been left with the terrible necessity of covering it up that Tsarist desperados had captured and saved Nicholas, Alexandra, Olga, Tatyana, Marie, Anastasia and Alexis. Or, Nicholas but not Alexandra, Olga but not Tatyana, Alexis but not Marie, or Alexandra, Tatyana, Marie and Anastasia. Or, simply Olga, from the kitchen, from the garden, from her bedroom. And, either Nicholas or Alexandra or Olga or Marie, Tatyana, Anastasia, Alexis in any combination had been sighted dressed as peasants on the train to Vladivostock, or Harbin, had not been given away by loyal subjects who had recognized them and whispered 'God speed!' as they had bumped past the august figure or figures in a third class carriage making its way to China, Mongolia or Japan.

To Serge, the problem was, at first, the mathematic art of permutations. He changed each character about like a stage director with a monstrous grand finale on his hands. How operatic, it seemed, the first scenario, how like James Bond the story of escape. In the beginning, he made a feasibility study for Lipitsin and took up his option on membership to the Cambridge University Library. It was good to be back at the scene of his youth and he felt younger in consequence. He made several trips and bought file-cards. He scoured memoirs and histories both in Russian and in English . . . Botkin, Pares, Mosolov, Anna Vyrubova, Lili Dehn, Baroness Buxhoeveden, Gilliard, Wilton. He read Massie. He read accounts of Anna Anderson, who had claimed to be Anastasia. He had even read a far-flung claim by a journalist on behalf of a false Alexis.

Stumbling on Olga Romanov in the all-too brief accounts of her, he felt the agreeable shock of familial recognition. She was linked with his earliest memories. From his mother's favourite and most famous tale of their meeting, he had derived, he found, a potent sense of her innermost being, and now he was able to attach a face to a name, as it were. What, after all, had she been like in the non-spiritual sense? Olga had been intelligent and had liked reading. She had had deep feelings and had been close to her father. Rather an introspective young woman, she had been particularly fond of poetry. She had had blue eyes and brown hair and had been sought in marriage by the Rumanian King. Had she not refused him, where would she be now or where would she have been?

Serge became intrigued with the whole family. He read of the young Archduchesses' wild behaviour, their over-fond parents' indulgence, the slightly claustrophobic atmosphere of the household (Serge knew that one). He read of the Tsar's profound fondness for his children and for Alexandra. He read of Rasputin and of haemophilia, of icons, of Easter eggs, of the royal yacht. In the library, he experienced a stillness, a grace, it seemed. Woven into the fragmented narrative were names, not only Olga's, that he recognized from childhood. Even the name Mirkovsky cropped up tangentially. The evidence for survival was slim but it had a vector. Although it made no sense to a casual Western eye, it seemed quite feasible to Serge that the Romanovs could have made it past a border and remained silent. His own mother had been imprisoned in Tyumen, but about Tyumen and her release, she had uttered only the most minimal words. None of his family, including his Aunt Masha, Helena's mother, had ever referred to escape routes from Russia, nor had the particulars of any heroes or rescuers been enunciated. The fear of compromising those who had helped was an extreme and real one and the terror of revenge killing in the West had been a near mania. Had this been the case with the Romanovs? Had they not gone to Ekaterinburg at all? Why *had* the Bolsheviks gone to such trouble to burn the bones of the victims in the cellar? Who could say whether or not the jewels found on the forest floor near the mine shaft had been given as ransom? Was it not possible that the Tsarina had paid off Yurovsky who could indeed have strewn a few over the hacked-up bones of substituted bodies?

Serge started to think about his mother. He started to think about his mother's fears, her fear of death. Since he could remember, she had been alive to the possibility of murder. To her, it did not seem an unusual way of dying. It was to be formally expected like cancer or heart disease. She had brought him up on a litany of martyrs, unblurred in a line from St Boris, St Glcb and St Vladimir. From these were derived those persons of conscience who had been frozen to death in camps or shot. Her father had been shot. From the walls of Nero where Christians had been used as torches to light the Emperor's parties, through to the Grand Guignol of Lenin and down to the camps of Stalin, she saw a vista of burnt, wracked, tortured, shot, bludgeoned, sacrificed, and hacked-to-pieces witnesses to truth. He and Varya had been catechized in memories of murdered cousins, uncles, grandparents whose sufferings were inextricably mixed with those of the Crucified. There had been times in his life when he had not been able to look at the map of the Soviet Union without the paralyzing notion that a martyr's crown was being prepared for him. The name 'Prince' to which he was entitled had seemed another way of spelling 'suffering' or 'sacrifice'. Nobility and Russia *meant* a tearing in the lion's cage, the thumb screws, the Peter and Paul Fortress, the Lubyanka. It meant at the very least the front line of battle or going down in flames. His father had expected it, his mother subtly, had expected an icon to emerge from her son, one as powerful as his namesake, St Sergius, whose prayers in days of old had miraculously turned back the Mongol hordes from the gates of Moscow. She had adored him in this iconic form and during his childhood, he had taken her devotion as devotion to himself. Of course, in a way it had been and still was real devotion, but as an emblematic son, he had let her down. It saddened Serge to think that he had once even looked like her, for she had been a real beauty. In his fifties, however, Serge physically resembled old Boris. In the Tsar's fiftieth year, he had died. Or had he? Had he really died? Perhaps he had not.

In the Blue Boar where he stayed in Cambridge, Serge had ordered a few stiff ones at the contemplation of his similarity in age to Nicholas II. If he had always thought of the Tsar in ancestral terms, it now slowly occurred to him that the man whose portrait he had been about to sell might be a long-lost familiar. He, too, had had weaknesses, fatal flaws in the eyes of some. He, too, had had redeeming features. Suppose he had not been killed at all. Suppose his mother the Dowager Empress had arranged for his escape. She had been safe in her native Denmark and rich and well-connected enough to conceal her darling boy. Had this been the reason she had refused to meet with Anna Anderson who had claimed to be Anastasia? Because she knew where the real Anastasia had been hidden? Serge could see Nicholas retiring to the country or even the Canadian wilderness, as Lipitsin's gleanings seemed to be saying already. In fact, Serge could easily see Nicholas retiring gladly, happy to be free of his burden. He could see the tragic Tsar managing, perhaps, a farm as Serge himself did.

He thought these things and then unthought them. He stood outside himself and saw his growing interest as risible and pathetic. He remembered old Uncle Pasha, a colossal bore if ever there was one, whom Maman had insisted they visit in his dank rooms in Paris. Uncle Pasha had worn fingerless gloves and had seemed to subsist on nothing but Russian tea and his memories of old campaigns. To him, Admiral Kolchak had the heroic stature of Prester John and it was his senile conviction that Kolchak had rescued the Tsar, then stayed on to fight and be killed in Irkutzk as a blind to the Bolsheviks. Then there had been Cousin Zina, who was a bit simple. She had had Messianic hopes of the Tsars' return in glory. At that stage, Serge had thought he could write a fiction about himself pursuing this fiction.

Shunting from Cambridge to London, from London to Northumberland and back again, Serge became entangled in the question: could history itself be other than provisional? Could it be other than novelesque? How, in retrospect, could the Tsar be known as anything but a category, an emblem of evil to the Marxists, an emblem for God to the Monarchists? How could he be judged as a man even by those who had known him in his lifetime? How could his life and influence be objectively analyzed? Given that he was 5'7", of something more than average intelligence, fond of tennis and riding, very orderly and religious, monogamous by nature and of a gentle disposition, how was it that the end of his empire was brought about? Through him? How was that possible to say? In the great catalogue of decisions and indecisions, where was it possible to ascribe motive with any accuracy? Apparently, he enjoyed taking tea of an afternoon in the English fashion with his family in his wife's lavender drawing-room. But *did* he enjoy it? Did he eat the occasional biscuit because he liked biscuits or because eating them pleased his wife? What did he think about his wife's friendship with Anna Vyrubova? Was he troubled by the allegations of homosexuality against them, or did he dismiss such rumours? Did he observe the relationship distastefully or not? Did he notice? Did he care? And what did he make of Rasputin's entry into the family circle? Did some inflection of the man's character betray him as a demon? Did Nicholas notice this and fail to act? Or did he fail to notice? Or was there nothing there to notice of evil in a semi-barbaric Siberian shaman with a mere smattering of uncertain Christian understanding?

History, Serge thought, with all of its knowledge of outcome, weighted all actions into plot, structure and design. It slanted planless life. History made all human error into sin, committed with malice aforethought, when even at the time of the Fall itself Adam and Eve had no access to the weight of consequence. Serge decided the story of the first parents was apt to his theme. As far as Nicholas was concerned, each character in the plot of his downfall must have acted on the basis of imaginative leaps springing from fictional assumptions. Each must have read his or her own subjective attitude for truth. To Rasputin, Nicholas had been 'Little Father'; to Lenin, 'Bloody Nicholas'; to Alexandra, 'Nicky', but beyond these designations, what had been the true thoughts of Rasputin, Lenin or Alexandra about Nicholas II? And by the time the apple itself had been crunched, what in him had changed? Who had been and who was the Tsar?

The possibilities were endless. Nicholas the despot was crushed by history itself on its juggernaut path to the dictatorship of the proletariat. Nicholas, autocrat by divine right, was martyred. Nicholas, a hesistant human being, had done the best he could in bewildering circumstances not of his own making. Nicholas, weak and henpecked, had indentured his free will to his maniac wife. The choices seemed inexhaustible. He plunged Russia into the First World War in order to disguise his own deficiencies as its Emperor, *or* he led the country into a just conflict as an active and selfless hero. He was cuckold to Rasputin *or* a devoted family man who would stop at nothing to relieve his son's agony by the power of Rasputin's prayers. He left millions secreted in bank accounts all over the world *or* he died a pauper. He was shot *or* he was not.

As the months went by, Serge became more and more preoccupied by the events surrounding the downfall of the Romanov Dynasty and with the Romanovs themselves. All of this was very much encouraged by Lipitsin to whom Serge began to report with increasing frequency. Lipitsin said why not sleep at his place and continue his research at the British Museum, which was, after all, in walking distance from Lipitsin's flat.

At night, they drank vodka, Lipitsin not very much. Serge did not bother Lipitsin with his abstract theories. Instead, he fed him information. He took Lipitsin for a practical man, a man who sensed the world through his delicate fingertips. He was a man who liked to touch his prizes, stroke them. Lipitsin tended towards silence. He gave nothing away about himself, but listened, tilting his head to one side, almost like a psychiatrist, Serge sometimes felt. Of course, they would be speaking about rumours of sightings and historical details, but things about himself and his own family and the general émigré scene crept in. Serge found he had not been able to speak with anyone quite as freely since he and Paul had been young. Lipitsin's neutral rooms became a grey place which blotted Serge up.

But what exactly did Lipitsin want from him? This from the very outset had been unclear. For quite a while, Lipitsin kept him in the dark about the true nature of the papers he sought to buy. It seemed a golden moment to Serge when Lipitsin finally confided in him that, of all players in the Romanov drama, it had been Olga who was said to have survived. Serge had felt this a dawn of mutual trust. Lipitsin told him he had exceeded all expectations as an associate and hinted at possible collaborations in the future. He then revealed to Serge how difficult and delicate a task it was to extract these papers from the vendor. Serge had been thoroughly in the dark about this and was hungry to know. Apparently, Lipitsin had heard of the papers through a middle-man in Amsterdam, a trusted colleague, who had indeed seen them, but who had sworn blood-oaths not to reveal their provenance until a trusted buyer was found. Lipitsin had been given only the sketchiest idea of what the letters contained. All he knew was that they had the unmistakable whiff of authenticity about them. According to the Dutchman, Lipitsin said, the vendor was an impecunious Russian lady of good family, who had received the cache of correspondence second-hand from a person much closer to the court of the last Tsar. The letters had resided in a bank vault for something like forty years, for they had been entrusted to the lady in darkest secrecy. Her reasons for wanting to reveal the contents now, it seemed, were twofold: the political situation in the Soviet Union provided the opportune moment for her revelation; and her circumstances were of the direst poverty. It was imperative to the lady that the letters should be given into safe hands. Neither her name nor her country of residence could be revealed until she was confident that any and all who handled the correspondence were pure of any base motive. Money she needed desperately, but not at any price.

This fit into Serge's considerable working knowledge of Russian ladies of a certain age and class. A kind of high-minded avarice afflicted them. He laughed, but Lipitsin became suddenly solemn. It appeared, he said, that the vendor might well have reason to fear. He supposed that if one trusted 'glasnost' and 'perestroika' one did, but how far did Serge think such openness would extend to the shattering news that the heir to the throne might at that very moment be paddling a canoe in the Canadian wilderness or working in a bank in Toronto?

Serge's breath was taken away by this. His mind balked at belief, but all of his senses stood on their very ends. Lipitsin said it was a long shot and shrugged, but as Serge demurred and expostulated, he noticed a shade of boredom and contempt in Lipitsin's face. It was as if his failure to believe this exposed a cowardice and lack of breadth. Of course, it was not probable, Lipitsin said with a kind of finicky scorn. And Serge, with all of the survival stories he had read in mind, became at once alive to the undeniable fact that it was possible. If one could ask 'why', one could also ask 'why not?'

It was at this point that Lipitsin brought up the half-forgotten subject of Serge's debt. It sort of slipped into the conversation in a tangential way. Serge, he said, might not be in for a whole, full-blooded search, but it would straighten out their financial arrangements considerably if he were to write a letter addressed to 'To Whom it May Concern' in which he acknowledged his belief in Lipitsin's irreproachable reputation as a dealer and which he would sign with his full name and title. Of course, as a rule he needed no such affidavit, but in this particular and sensitive case, the name 'Mirkovsky' might do wonders to lessen the old woman's paranoia. Serge was appalled that what he had come to regard as a friendship should now be reduced to such formal and pecuniary straits. At once, he flourished his fountain pen and wrote a warm and generous note on Lipitsin's behalf, asserting his active participation in the matter of the letters and praising Lipitsin's probity to the skies. Sealing it, Serge did hope that Lipitsin still counted him in. Lipitsin gave a thin smile and clapped a manly hand upon Serge's shoulder. In a few weeks time, the Dutchman had phoned Lipitsin saying that the lady had been greatly persuaded by Serge's letter. It had been by Divine Providence that he had written. For Olga's correspondent had been none other than his father's first cousin, Anna Fyodorevna Mirkovskaya, who had been attached to the court for a brief period as lady-in-waiting to the Tsarina and who had died in California childless and alone in 1947. Serge was stunned. Indeed, although he had never met her, there had been such a cousin, who had become a kind of mystic and had ended her days a recluse in an old beach-house overlooking the Pacific. But to his astonishment and oddly terrible disappointment, Lipitsin had thanked him for his help as if that were more or less an end to it. Yes, a price was being discussed and he would get back to him if any further assistance were required.

Poor Serge had limped back to his life in Northumberland to face the blank aimlessness of his former days. The whole thing had made him curiously restless and unable to settle. He had no wish to confide in Fiona, and as far as his mother and sister were concerned, it was an impossibility even to mention it. It never crossed his mind to talk to Helena, and Paul had vanished into Ethiopia. Serge replaced the miniature in the wall-safe where it seemed to throb out at him whenever he entered his study. To his astonishment and even to his joy, Lipitsin finally rang, but happiness was to be short-lived. The deal had fallen through! It appeared that the Dutchman had acted unilaterally and in an attempt to verify the papers, had shown them to two remaining Romanovs, both cousins of Olga, who declined to be named. The first had flatly denounced the letters as frauds, the second had been very unsure. The elderly vendor of the letters had, at this point, been completely prostrated. The very thought of having her word doubted had virtually killed her. She had had a mild stroke and was recovering in a convalescent home. She had received the letters on Anna Fyodorevna's deathbed as a sacred trust. How could she now cast these precious pearls before the swine of the world's sceptics? What grieved her most of all was the horrible thought that the rightful heir, the Tsar's grandson, might never be discovered. But she flatly refused to show the papers again to anyone but a completely disinterested party of noble birth and of unimpeachable integrity.

How about Serge's mother? Lipitsin suggested this.

It had never crossed Serge's mind that his mother might be involved in any of this. The very idea disclosed to him an atavistic terror of upsetting her. He had said 'no' involuntarily as a gasp rather than a denial.

A silence had ensued at the other end of the telephone. Why had Serge assumed that it was cold? Why had it frightened him? But Lipitsin had rather left it. Perhaps there were other émigrés to whom he had access, he had finally said. Yet with this doubt hanging over the correspondence, surely Serge could see that Lipitsin wasn't going to take a risk unless he had himself some reliable confirmation of their probable authenticity. And surely Serge could see that only an old acquaintance of the Archduchess could really tell, the Archduchess and/or Anna Fyodorevna.

Serge responded to this telephone call with a huge bender from which it took him three days to emerge. Nothing was settled by it, but some of the emotional connections to the matter were numbed and damaged and he was unable to speak to his inner self. He took the train to London. On the way, he began to worry about the letter he had written on Lipitsin's behalf. 'To Whom It May Concern' might concern anybody, he thought. He dismissed his misgivings, however, the moment he saw Lipitsin. The moment Lipitsin opened the front door to his flat, Serge realized how ridiculous it was to suppose that a man as dynamic as Lipitsin had any need of the signature of a dipsomaniac, dispossessed prince ... or even money, for that matter. There was something about Lipitsin that made him seem like a self-generating force, an energy and not a man like himself who was vulnerable to temptation.

They ended up having a meal at Serge's club. Lipitsin had delicate manners, and this surprised Serge for some reason. Lipitsin discreetly hailed an old friend from across the dining room. It had been at the back of Serge's mind that the club might put Lipitsin in perspective. It had certainly seemed the appropriate place for interrogating him about these Romanovs who had dismissed the papers. And yet, Serge found that Lipitsin resembled a Romanov himself in his immaculate suit and snowy linen.

Suppose Olga had survived and were even alive, said Lipitsin. Suppose she had had children. Was Serge not familiar with this history of kings? The little princes in the Tower? Boris Godunov? From time immemorial until the present day, uncles and cousins had betrayed true heirs. Why should Olga's relatives be an exception? Even if it were not a plot on the part of the émigré Romanovs, surely it might be a result of the painful Anastasia episode that one had so flatly denied that Olga could be living. There had been so much reasonable doubt on the part of the one Romanov relative that really all Lipitsin needed was one more corroboration before he bought the letters – that was, if the vendor would sell.

Back in Lipitsin's flat, they had a good bottle of Stolichnaya brought properly chilled from the fridge. Serge was in Heaven to be restored to the bosom of Lipitsin's confidence. Lipisin said he hated to ask, but whom could he turn to but Serge whose connections in high places might still uncover the desired corroboration and someone whom the elderly lady would trust? The handwriting, of course, would need an expert if they could actually get to the letters and read them, but it was personal details of Olga's life that really needed checking. As a native speaker conversant with the manners of a rarefied lost world, Serge might go on being Lipitsin's invaluable assistant.

Serge began visits to ancient members of ancient families. They gave him tea or drinks and shook their heads at yet another resurrection story although he had been careful to qualify and muddle the whole thing in order to protect his source. Lipitsin had been right. It was a lost world and one that shocked Serge obscurely. These former landowners and grandees of Petersburg or Moscow, friends of the Emperor or friends of the Emperor's friends, lived in a shadowy twilight, stowed away in Chiswick or Bayswater in little colourless rooms. It gave him an extraordinary perspective on how much he and Helena had been assimilated into English life in a superficial way and how little they partook of it in the depths. He felt an extraordinary affinity with old countesses and elderly princes. Many of them remembered his parents. Bit by bit, a number of Olga stories emerged and there was even a cameo he looked at hungrily but could not copy nor keep. It came to Serge that he was wandering in the shades like some Greek hero, searching among the fitful, flitting forms for a redeemable portion of the past. Ah, Olga! She might as well be Eurydice, Semele or Alceste.

Serge began to dream about Olga, whose fault the Russian Revolution certainly had not been. Sometimes she seemed to cry to him from limbo. Sometimes she disappeared. It occurred to him that she might well be living and might well not want to be found, not from fear of her own death nor of her children's death. What a business she had been through! Talk about a troubled childhood, a fall from paradise! Perhaps as a refugee from the grandiose plot of opera, Olga had no wish to sing. Perhaps she had taken up an interesting hobby and enjoyed trips to a shopping mall in some small Canadian town. Perhaps her deepest wish for her children was or had been that they should find a simple peace in anonymity.

It had been in March, just a few months before he was due to start his annual stint on Patmos, that the devastating news came. The vendor refused to sell-point-blank and no explanations. This, despite the steady progress Serge had been making in the gathering of information which Lipitsin had so encouragingly received. All of this had made a good composite by which they could judge the letters when they got them, but the delay in finding a witness the old lady would trust had apparently broken down her will to undergo the whole process. The funny thing was that Serge, who had thought he regarded the whole business as an increasingly absorbing pastime, broke down. In Lipitsin's rooms he cried, burying his face in the grey, nubbly wool of the sofa. Looking up, he thought he caught the veiled scorn of Lipitsin in the dim light slatting through Venetian blinds and a flicker of amusement. This chilled him into recovery. Still, he was oddly alarmed to see how far his hopes and expectations had gone without his knowing it. 'Couldn't she at least let us see the papers?' he had asked. And Lipitsin had said he would try.

It had not been in that moment nor in a series of moments that Serge had discovered his detachment gone, his obsession absolute; but, having lived life, as it were, outside of himself, he understood the imprisoning difference only when it was too late. He had spent months hunting with Lipitsin and they had lost their quarry. As he watched the illusion flee, it became a reality of utter desire for it. His visits to Lipitsin stopped and with their cessation came a wild sense of irritable anxiety. He snapped at Fiona and spent hours staring at the fire, or at the wall safe in his study, or at the miniature inside it and drank. Although Lipitsin had not mentioned anything further about the debt, he began to worry about that. At the same time, he would have been almost grateful if Lipitsin had started dunning him. Lipitsin, too, began to preoccupy him. Where did he come from? He would never say. Who was he? How close Serge had become to Lipitsin and yet how far he was! How many admissions he had made in the half-light of that neat and dreary flat! Often, he went to the phone, compelled to ring Lipitsin's number, but then he would stop, abashed for some reason. In early May, just as he had given up all hope, Lipitsin rang him. He had induced the old lady to give him photocopies of some of the letters but only on one condition: that the Princess Mirkovsky herself should evaluate them.

Well, why had he worried? Why had he bothered about this one small detail? If the woman was prepared to put her correspondence through the rigours of his mother, if, as Lipitsin had reported, she valued only his mother as a trustworthy judge, she must have chosen her because the letters were genuine. And if they were, wasn't it reasonable to suppose that his mother would be overjoyed? This was Lipitsin's argument and it stuck with Serge whenever he could get himself to think of his mother as an abstract quantity. This he did with the aid of great quantities of alcohol, for when he truly considered her probable reaction, it dismayed him.

Half-shadows formed in Serge's head and blocked dreams came to him at night. He had virtually missed the lambing that spring and as he stood watching the new flock gambol and skip about the ewes of his pasture, he found himself rambling over memories of childhood he had suppressed while Fiona, in Wellingtons, grimly clanked galvanized buckets. There had been such terrible rows at night. It was not as if his parents had hated each other. In a profound way they had understood each other. Snatches of raised, muffled voices came back to him like an unpleasant tune. He had once caught his father slumped over the kitchen table, passed out. Serge at four years old had thought him dead. His mother's strength, her preternatural will, had got them through a situation for which there had been no ready absolution, for the Tsar had never been dead in the old Prince's mind, only murdered and unavenged. And so for her Nicholas had to be dead? No, that wasn't quite it. Secret totem of the family shrine, he had haunted them, his authority cracked and run out all over the place like a broken egg or a genie dismayed at the crushing of its bottle. His death was implied in the sadness of the eyes of the Mother of God. The blasphemy against his anointed personage imperilled the enthroned Saviour. Between his parents, the murder was re-enacted in a thousand ways, implied but never stated, felt but never seen. It was as if the cold and engineering hand of Lenin had signed warrants for a spiritual death and had left his parents in a transcendent state of infinte regret, a Hell, really, where demons of terror and despair choked off all growth. His mother never spoke about his father. She had abandoned him for Patmos and the saints. And he had abandoned her for the unmarked grave of Nicholas. In fact, a whole theology had been erected around this non-event, Serge thought, with his parents hurling anathemas at each other over the finer points. If his mother were to see the letters proving that martyrdoms had not occurred, then what would be the consequences? And there was more and worse besides that did not fit into this lacy construct of thought. Something in her was locked up too tight for his imagining.

In one, slow, revolutionary turn however, the consequence to the Princess had become no more a consequence to Serge. Was this what Helena had always been needling him about? His dependence on his mother's dependence on him? Was it what saddened Fiona's eyes when every year he prepared to set off for Patmos? There was no question of having any argument with himself. He really had to know about the Tsar. Had to. Had to put his hand in the side and see to believe. And whether she liked it or not, his mother was going to listen, for she could not be protected indefinitely from things distasteful to her.

XVII

IN AND OUT OF THE HOUSE all morning! Up and down those stairs! Tanya, go and fetch another loaf from the baker's! Tanya, fetch my bag! Now six people to lunch when only five had been expected! Poor Evangalia! And poor Dmitris, too, she supposed. Tanya, who was, after all, an interpreter and not a skivvy, swung through the green baize doors with the moussaka. Her efforts to politicize Evangelia had seemed almost in vain, but maybe she would see the truth of Tanya's exhortations if Tanya herself demonstrated that she herself honoured menial labour and when push came to shove would help another woman out as a matter of course. What a summer! She had assumed, when Dr Taggart had asked her to help out with a Russian-speaking family that it would mean light chores and conversation. Dr Taggart had arranged it with her tutor that she could miss the last few weeks of term in exchange for this valuable experience, but now Tanya wished she had stayed in England. By all accounts, Dr Taggart was herself a real scholar with a good record on sensitive women's issues, but now Tanya was beginning to think balefully that her politics were of the head and not of the heart. To be fair, Dr Taggart had warned her that the work did involve looking after an old, aristocratic woman, one who might be demanding and cantankerous. Tanya had envisoned scenes drawn from *The Queen of Spades* with herself in the role of oppressed companion to a despotic patrician, but she had also expected affirmative support from Dr Taggart.

As it happened, a reversal had occurred. Her exhaustive and exhausting nursing of the old lady had brought her in touch with something akin to love and her treatment at the hands of Helena Taggart had polarized in her a hatred so extreme that she would have downed tools and left if she had not known how much the Princess depended on her. There was no question in her mind about who, of the two women, was the elitist. Every time she heard Helena's voice crying, 'Tanya! Tanya!', she felt the humiliating urge to jump and scuttle after her bidding. What was more, Dr Taggart was a powerful force within the college. A bad reference from her, a word in the ear of her tutor that she had wasted those special weeks, might affect her future plans.

Tanya had a passionate wish to be given a grant to study in the Soviet Union for a graduate degree and this took some organizing, for her work was brilliant but erratic. Tanya had always had a soft spot for old people and she wondered if this were not colouring her judgment about the Princess. Her attitudes on every issue under the sun were completely incongruous with Tanya's chosen path. Nonetheless, she found herself peacefully employed whenever they were alone together and despite the brutish opinions the old woman held, Tanya knew them to be fellow-sufferers, and at the same hand.

She plonked the moussaka down on the table under the plane tree in the garden and eyed Lipitsin mistrustfully. It was good moussaka, bloody good moussaka, and she hoped they appreciated Evangalia's toil in this sweaty weather. She hovered round the table, her eyes becoming slits of meanness in her preoccupied indignation.

'Tanya? Aren't you going to sit?' Sophia Petrovna asked a little crossly. Tanya supposed she could not help that attitude. With the status of companion, she ate at the table while the servants ate in the kitchen. If she had not known it was a hopeless cause, she would have tried to explain to the Princess that there was something intrinsically arrogant about people who had never done a hand's turn. The disjunction to the Princess between the table with its fine china and the cooker on which the meal had been prepared was absolute. If only Tanya could demonstrate patiently and carefully that a whole food chain was involved, then maybe the Princess would spiritually extend herself to the farms and fields where produce grew, to the abattoir and to the sink. Instead, she lived on a selfish little island of her own, Tanya thought, and this was why she was so chronically unhappy.

'I'll be back in a minute, Sophia Petrovna,' Tanya said. 'Evangalia is *very* busy,' she added and for emphasis strode off towards the kitchen again. For some reason, having to cope with Lipitsin at the last minute was the limit. Something about his suit, his snowy linen, the presumption in his urbanity, made her angry. Indeed, everybody looked troubled or stirred up by his presence. Who was he, anyway? No one ever told her anything. They had all been drinking sherry in the garden before lunch out of a special bottle brought from England. What was the occasion? Serge smarmed over Lipitsin, Lipitsin smarmed over the Princess, the Princess beamed at Mrs Holt, Mrs Holt cast worried glances at Dr Mason, and Dr Mason glared at Helena Taggart, who alone stood to one side observing the scene with that cold, mandarin air that stamped her as the arid intellectual she was in Tanya's eyes. And yet somehow underneath it all Tanya sensed a baleful power emanating from Helena, for sure enough she had been in one of her tyrant moods before the arrival of Lipitsin and the return of Dr Mason with Marina Holt. Tanya had in mind some sketches for a theory about Helena and Marina, but she hadn't the leisure to think of them now.

Tanya slammed back into the kitchen where Evangalia had been preparing extra vegetables to eke out the moussaka. Dmitris was sitting in his vest in a rocking chair, about as far away from the tiled stove as he could get. It was a lovely, big kitchen, hung with aromatic herbs. Tanya sighed and breathed in the free air of drying oregano and piquant sauce simmering on the hob. Dmitris rocked and read his newspaper. He had been a sponge fisherman from Kalymnos in his youth, but his wife's people were Patmians, and he had given up this dangerous occupation upon his mariage and followed her to her native island. Evangalia was a strong, wiry woman in her sixties, a little deaf, but otherwise a model of stamina. If what her employers were saying to her did not suit her, she simply took out her hearing aid. At the approach of Dr Taggart, she almost always stashed it in her apron. She said it screamed and whined anyway. Above the old-fashioned cooker, there was what Tanya considered to be a lacrymose icon of the Virgin Mary. Indeed, tears spilled quite literally out of the Virgin's eyes. It was a soupy, idealized nineteenth-century painting, but Evangalia often looked at it. Dmitris had told Tanya that it came from Ephesus. He had given it to his wife as a name-day present. Tanya had her own view of that!

She swooped up the beans in oil and more bread. She had, grudgingly, to admit that they were a devoted couple. A real linguist, Tanya had started to acquire Greek from them and was making progress. Dmitris supported PASOK and shared some of her views, though not, she was afraid, on the exploitation of women. When Tanya started on politics, Evangalia took the hearing aid out. Nevertheless, they had invited her to a family wedding on Sunday and Tanya was very touched by this. The bride was their niece and she was getting married in the Cave. As well as everything else she had to do, Evangalia was baking against this day. In any spare moment she had, she carried on embroidering a sumptuous tablecloth for Sophia. That was her niece's name. Evangalia loved Sophia almost as if she were her own child and would show off snapshots at the slightest provocation. Evangalia had sons but no daughter and Sophia rather filled that gap, Tanya thought. Sophia had gone all the way to Athens to receive an education. She was coming back to Patmos to teach school. There were pictures of Sophia with crocodiles of children. Her husband-to-be, also Patmian, was an engineer. He had worked in the desalination plant on the island before it closed, but now he had a less good job elsewhere. Evangalia was very frightened they would move away in search of work. Well, back to the nobs, thought Tanya, and sighing, she traipsed back to the garden.

To a complete, stunned silence.

Looking back on it, Tanya was to think of it in terms of a photograph from the last century. Later, she was to think of the whole summer as an excursion into the nineteenth century itself – an extraordinary hiatus in time into which she had been pitched and from which she had derived much. The scene in her mind became inextricably mixed with Chekovian drama and she had the illusion of Marina Holt in particular wearing a white, bodiced dress as she leaned back silent in her chair, as if trying to take the strain of whatever had happened in Tanya's absence from the table. Serge Mirkovsky braced himself forward on his elbow. The doctor, another necessary Chekov adjunct, she recalled as if he had been wearing a flowing cravat, his sad eyes languishing at Mrs Holt. Like the powerful and insincere Mme Arkadina, sat the distinguished Helena Taggart, though why Tanya associated her with the narcissistic actress, she could never really say.

The two central figures in the drama were, however, difficult to associate with Chekov. His tolerant attitude towards humanity somehow excluded a character such as Lipitsin, whose chilly smile struck Tanya to the bone; and as for the Princess, her face had a look that Tanya always would remember, perhaps in the light of subsequent events as an implosion through the frame. It was as if an inward bursting had occurred, creating a vacuum into which all literary reference vanished. She looked like the shocked victim of a mugging. Her skin had become translucent, as if with a little imagination Tanya could see her brain and her organs. A blue vein trembled in her skull. What on earth had happened? Tanya moved swiftly to the old lady's side, and putting the beans on the table, sat down alert.

At length, the Princess spoke: 'Olga did not survive. The Tsar did not survive.' The pupils of her eyes were dilated and black. The skin around the bridge of her nose seemed to shrink so that her face looked entirely made of bone. Although she spoke in English, her accent had thickened to an almost comic degree. She looked and sounded like an old peasant just off the boat.

Mirkovsky jerked his elbow from the table and slapped his hand down. Tanya had often imagined him hunting down serfs with borzois or harrying ghettos with Cossacks. She had always seen in him a latent violence. 'Mother, you must at least read them!' he cried, his voice choked with fury. Tanya was completely in the dark about what was going on, but she curled her hand towards the Princess in a defensive motion against his threatening tone. She looked round to see if she could glean a hint from the frozen expressions around the table as to what had transpired. Was poor Marina Holt undergoing another episode in her identity crisis? Had it been mooted that she was now related to the Tsar? Tanya had taken a liking to Marina and felt sorry for her, but wondered if she wasn't a little naive.

Lipitsin shot in with a hasty reprimand. 'There is nothing your mother *must* do, Serge,' he said. In Russian, he added, 'Forgive me for upsetting you, Sophia Petrovna, but if the letters are forgeries, we must prove that they are.' His Russian was perfect, which surprised Tanya, who, despite his name had thought him English. The Princess, too, was surprised, for she looked somewhat mollified by the beautiful accent.

'I can tell you already that they are forgeries,' she said in English.

Mirkovsky stared hard at his mother and she stared at him. Tanya had always found it hard to assess what really went on between those two. When they were alone together, they seemed profoundly linked, almost as if they were still one being. In the presence of others, however, they seemed unconnected and almost hostile. 'What letters? What forgeries?' Tanya wanted to ask, but the electric look that passed between mother and son silenced her.

Helena Taggart suddenly spoke. 'Tyotya! Aunt Sonya! Mr Lipitsin just said they might be forgeries.'

'I thought you knew no Russian, Lenochka,' said her aunt. Normally, it amused Tanya to watch the old lady slide out of harm's way. She did so by introducing irrelevancies and non sequiturs into the conversation when she disliked the turn it was taking. But her face was paper-white, her voice terribly strained.

'I understand a few words,' Dr Taggart said. She really detested her aunt. Tanya thought of a little scene there had been only yesterday and of previous scenes no one else but she, Tanya, knew about. There had been times when she had been afraid that Helena would do the old lady an injury.

'You *knew* the Archduchess, Maman, and Cousin Anna!' Mirkovsky's voice adopted a wheedling tone. He spoke in Russian. 'Mamochka, please!' He closed his eyes and shook his head. Something moved Tanya to judge this as genuine despair. Suddenly, it occurred to her that they had been discussing the Romanovs. Earlier in the year, Tanya had seen a telly program about someone claiming to be the Archduchess Anastasia. The gooey romance of it had set her teeth on edge. Tanya would have killed the whole diseased lot of them with her bare hands. A constant irritant to her was the photograph of the Royal Family on the Princess's bedroom wall and she had waited for an opportunity to discuss them with the Princess, to guide her to her senses, really, by means of telling questions. How could she respect them? Young at the time of the Revolution, she must have been victim of Tsarist propaganda. To Tanya's mind, Nicholas the Hangman should have been given no quarter.

Suddenly Tanya realized she was hungry. She had been up since seven and working all day. No one had touched the moussaka Evangalia had slaved to make from her own special recipe and it was cold. Quite surprising herself, she reached for the dish, spooned up some of the aromatic aubergines and plopped them on her plate. Tearing a piece of bread off the loaf, she swizzled it about in the sauce and ate gratefully. So, they were trying to pass off an Olga story, were they? Olga, indeed! Then she felt bad for having reached for the food. 'Sorry,' she said.

The old lady turned and stared at Tanya for a moment, as if the remark had shocked her back to normal life. 'Why do you always say you are sorry?' she asked. 'What is the point of being sorry when you have done nothing wrong?' Tanya flushed. 'Do you understand what is going on, Tanya?' She looked round the table. '*Ponimayesh*, Tanya?'* she asked.

'They say they have found Olga Romanova?' Tanya asked.

'They say,' the Princess said conversationally, 'that the whole family survived and that Olga Nikolaievna is alive.'

'I am not sure you should be telling everyone this, Sophia Petrovna,' Lipitsin said in a chilly voice.

For a moment, Tanya thought he looked like a grand shop assistant. 'I am everyone?' she blurted out. '*Kto Ya? Nikto Ya!*'* Maybe that is why I always say I am sorry.'

'If I thought Olga were alive, I would speak to no one. I would not even tell my confessor,' said the Princess. 'As it is, Tanya is always near me.' She leaned closer and peered at Lipitsin. 'She cleans me off. I am an old woman. We are on intimate terms, you might say.' She looked at

* 'Do you understand, Tanya?'
* 'Who am I? I am nobody!'

Tanya through her hooded eyes. 'Your Russian is improving, my dear. The awful accent is better.'

'Maman!' Serge cried. 'Do you think I would risk their lives? Don't you think I have gone into this? I have researched it thoroughly. There is evidence. There is plenty of evidence.'

'Seryozha, they died,' The Princess said this in almost a wail like someone keening.

All the while, Lipitsin sat with his hands poised in front of him like a practised poker player. Good Grief! Tanya thought. Can't they see this man is a complete charlatan? The old lady was weeping now quite openly.

'Look, Serge,' said Paul, suddenly intervening. 'Can't this wait?'

'No, it cannot!' Serge suddenly scraped his chair back and the rasping noise made everyone start. 'Either she reads those letters or I am leaving this house never to return.' To his mother, he said, 'Helena looked at them! Helena gave them a chance. Why can't you? Though why I want you to, I can't really understand as it is clear that you will dismiss them completely without a proper reading. It's so like you! So like you! You've simply made up your mind!'

The poor old thing, Tanya thought, would have drawn blood out of a stone. Her tears had abated, but she looked at her son with an awful trepidation, more terrible in its utter meekness. It was like seeing a magnificent animal broken and saddled.

'It isn't a question of mind.' Everyone looked around, astonished at the clear voice from the end of the table. 'It is not her mind she has made up. It upsets her,' said Marina. When she saw everyone looking at her, she said, 'I'm sorry. It isn't any of my business.'

Serge's indignant glance was softened by Marina's rider.

'She's right, you know,' Tanya found herself saying. She looked down and found she had been compulsively squeezing the Princess's hand. 'You are right, Mrs Holt.'

All of a sudden, Tanya realized that Lipitsin was giving her a look of pure hatred. It seemed such an odd thing to do that it gave her a start.

'I don't care,' said Serge, 'and that's the truth.'

'Helena?' Marina asked, as if it had occurred to her that a solution might be coming from this quarter. 'What do you think?'

'Anything I say will be taken down in evidence against me,' Helena said unpleasantly. 'But I don't see any harm in your just reading them, Aunt.' She paused. 'If they are genuine, you are the one who should be most pleased. If not, then isn't it better that the whole thing should be exposed?'

The Princess ignored Helena for a moment, but Serge looked gratefully at her.

'Will you . . .' the Princess asked after a pause, 'will you say you will never see me again if I pronounce the letters false?' She looked straight at him and he could not avoid her eyes.

'No,' he said quietly, looking down at his hands.

'Then I will read them.' She turned her head to Helena. 'It is you, you who have arranged all of this,' she said in Russian.

Helena pretended not to understand, or maybe she did not. Tanya wondered. All the same, she noted that a crease in Lipitsin's cheekbone deepened, indicating a slight smile.

'She did not, Maman.'

'Serge,' said his mother, 'I would like to speak with you in private. We must discuss this in private for I will not read the . . . letters otherwise.' She turned to Lipitsin. 'You have not had anything to eat, Mr Liptsin, and I believe you have a boat to catch. We really mustn't detain you.'

Lipitsin said that he was not hungry and that he must, indeed, make the packet for Samos as he needed to make the connection by plane to Athens.

Somehow, the social 'rigueur' of the Princess restored her command of the table. Although Tanya was usually enemy to these niceties, she thought, wryly, that they had their place and she was secretly proud of her charge.

'Tanya, you may wheel me into the ground floor office,' the Princess continued, 'where I will talk to my son. I will show you the way.'

Tanya stood and flourished her hands over the creaky Bath-chair and together they made stately progress into the house and down a forgotten corridor.

XVIII

THE LITTLE OFFICE was on the ground floor overlooking the front courtyard and the street. It was supposed to have been used as a counting house for a Venetian merchant in the seventeenth century, but nobody knew for sure. There were elaborate wrought-iron bars at the window and they cast intricate shadows over the cool, stone floor. The Princess had not been in there for years, for it brought back memories to her of her sister Masha, who had conducted the business of the household from this little room. Very occasionally, Helena would sit at the old, roll-top desk where the accounts were kept and pay bills, just as her mother had done before her. Where this piece of furniture had come from was anybody's guess and it might have contained anything.

The Princess had no idea why the thought of the office had flashed into her mind. Perhaps it was its association with practical matters, perhaps the room seemed neutral ground. More likely still, it was the fleeting inner glimpse she had had of Masha, her head bowed over ledgers. Sometimes, she had pored over a Greek grammar in there. In any case, the Princess had vividly seen her sister as a presence. What would her sister have done with this exigence? She did not know, but felt the office a safe place to be. Curiously, in her mind's eye too had come the vision of Helena as a gangly adolescent, sitting on the dilapidated old leather chesterfield, scuffing her shoes against the floor and glaring at her mother. It had been discovered after her death that Masha had been unwell for a long time but had told no one. The Princess tried not to wonder if Helena's return from Canada after the war had killed Masha, but she did not always succeed. Helena had been a cold girl, given to bitter resentments and outbursts of rage. Of the fact that Helena now wanted her dead too, the Princess was quite convinced. Or drive her insane. Maybe that was it. Maybe Helena had plotted with this Lipitsin to turn Serge against her and drive her mad so that they would have to put her in St Geneviève des Bois.

She felt a little mad. She felt as if she had straws in her hair. She was sitting in the office alone. She was waiting for Serge to say good-bye to Lipitsin. Perhaps she should not have dismissed poor Tanya, but should have asked her to stay with her in the room. The sun cast prison

226

gloom weakly through the bars at the window. There were bars all over her lap and wheelchair. It reminded her now of her incarceration in Tyumen. These were places not to think about. She had been in prison, that was it, on account of her origins. Was she bad because of what she was or what she was because she was bad? What had a young girl been supposed to make of all that she had seen there? Abruptly, she unsaw it.

She was wandering and that was bad. Olya? The confined office seemed a place for toiling spiders. It had been a mistake to come here for the vision of Masha had deserted her now and there were spiders only, that genus of plotters, connivers and web-weavers. The Holy Scriptures had a lot to say about 'those who made and loved a lie'. She forgot what it was now, but it comforted her somewhat to remember that things went ill for liars in the next world. Olga Nikolaievna Romanova, what would you say if you saw me sitting here waiting for the gunshot wound? Why had news of Olga arisen at this time? The idea of Olga came to her in iconic form, hands upraised like the Virgin Orans. Were the hands outflung in blessing or as the bullets hit the innocent breast? What were Serge and Helena and Lipitsin doing with Olga's memory? She had a feeling it had something to do with a knitting machine, rows of little picks shuttling stitches into whole-cloth. Maybe they did not realize that people really did die. Maybe they thought it was like something on television, only actors who later got up and dusted themselves off. She had something to say about that. Death did happen. It was not pretend. You could not go on digging up and desecrating dead people. You had to leave them to God to gather . . . and judge.

Surely, it must be Helena who had manufactured all of this. To the mind of the Princess, Helena could not share a simple crust of bread with another human being without some obscure, political gain in mind. Varya and Serge were both quite innocent of the depths to which Helena's mind could plunge. What did she have to gain from this? This very minute she was probably plotting behind her back. What was she saying? Something evil. Lena.

Worst of all were the trembling fits of hope. It had gusted through her and was gusting through her now that maybe Olga Nikolaievna *was* alive and had children. Would Olga remember her? Might they meet again? Oh, if only they could weep in each other's arms? Because they had equally suffered, it would not be necessary to tell stories for which there were no words. Suppose she could see just once again the quick, responsive eyes of Olga. Even in one's nineties, one's eyes never really changed. Would she remember the quiet chat on the lawn at Livadia? Tears welled up again. Had she really wept at the lunch table? Helena was probably using this as proof of madness and would have her put away. Even Varya had made her see some doctor or other, but she had not told him anything like the whole story. For years, Helena had been telling everyone . . . what was that modern word? Ah yes, that she was 'paranoid' with all her fears of plotting and the KGB. But she had wept because, of course, it could have been true. Because Olga could have written to her husband's cousin Anna Fyodorevna. Old Anna had indeed waited on the court and in exile had led a celibate hermit's existence. Confiding in Anna Fyodorevna would have been like confiding in a nun, the risks to Olga would have been minimal.

She imagined Marina trying to tell them she was not mad. Maybe Marina would do that. Last night she had held her hand and at lunch she had reproached them all. The Princess recalled that St Marina was usually depicted at the entrance of a church, for she was said to repel demonic forces. Maybe Marina was explaining to them that Olga and the Tsar did not make her cry because they unbalanced her mind but because they unsettled her spirit . . . because they inhabited her soul. Just thinking of demonic forces made the Princess shiver. This Lipitsin – who was he? The moment she had seen him he had inspired her with fear and when he had mentioned Olga's name, she had quickened into dread. Where had she seen him before? She could not have seen him in Russia, but she knew the gist of him and that was sure. At the luncheon table, her heart had thumped in terror at the thought that he might have access to the Royal Family, and had, in his perfect Russian, even spoken their names. Throughout the meal, a long, slow shuddering in her had manifested itself in tremors of her hands and pictures vivid on her inner eye, pictures that had to do with her father's sudden meekness when they had taken him away to be shot. Nothing – no prayers, no words, no histories – had rendered her capable of communicating what this had been like to her children . . . and to Helena. They had simply taken him away. Who was that Greek heroine? Cassandra. Cassandra had stood on the walls of Troy, shouting herself hoarse to the deaf ears of her bewitched countrymen. Helena had actually told her once that she rather admired Lenin. The Princess had truly not known what to do. No, she must not think of that. She must be credible and pulled together when Serge came. She uttered the Holy Name 'Jesus', and felt calmer.

She thanked God she had never told anyone about the 'returns'.

At long last, there was a knock at the door and Serge slipped into the office carrying a grey portfolio. Suddenly, she realized what she had expected of him and that it had come to this. He was a middle-aged man, his hair was grey, his muscles were slack, his face puffy from too much drink. Little capillaries were broken on his skin. As a dear little boy, she had had such hopes for him because of his cleverness and good looks, such fears for his safety. It was true that she had always loved him more than Varya, as Varya was wont to say. His baby purity had redeemed so much when nightly she had expected Herod. But somehow, the abjection of his shoulders before Lipitsin had told her the story he had obscured from her for years. The more dutiful he had become, the more remote from her he had grown and she saw he had substituted birthday cards and telephone calls for what had existed between them. As she now looked into his eyes, she saw something she had never seen before – dislike. She was sure that he loved her in his way, but he watched her from the doorway with a distaste that until this point he had concealed. From time to time, she realized, she had seen its shadow, but now she saw its substance.

'So,' he said. 'You have now extracted the maximum sympathy for this. In return, can I ask you to give this a fair trial?' He smiled somewhat wolfishly and swaggered to the old sofa, where he sat, one leg crossed over the other in a nonchalant balance. He threw the portfolio down on the table between them. It was a dusty, rickety affair with ring-marks.

The Princess was suddenly afraid of him. Nonetheless, she said, 'How can you trust this man – this Lipitsin?'

'Why should I not? What relevance does it have whether he is trustworthy or not?' He rubbed a spot off his boot with a licked finger.

Together, they looked at the portfolio, then at each other. 'Suppose,' she replied, gaining strength, 'one of the Romanovs were alive. Suppose there were children. Of course, it matters who knows about it. I do not trust a man who could tell a whole luncheon party full of people!'

He looked evenly at his mother. 'Lipitsin is as sceptical as you are, Maman.' His eyes looked bloated with the threat of tears. 'It is he who discovered these papers and it is he, too, who is negotiating to buy them.'

'Suppose you are being cheated,' she said. She thought a good deal about money.

He looked as if he were about to say something, but checked

himself. After a pause, he said, 'How can I be cheated? I just said that Lipitsin is thinking of buying. It is I who am in the position to cheat him – or rather, it is you. A great deal depends on what you say. This morning, he told me he was not prepared to take the risk without your verification.'

'Have you seen them?' Her nerves sang in her ears, she hoped so much from his reply.

'There are only a few here, photocopies, but I have read them and re-read them. I almost know them by heart.'

'What do you think?'

They shared a curiously hostile but intimate look. 'I think it is Olga. I think that it must be.'

She thought she could hardly bear it if this were not to be true.

'And you say Lena has read them?' Suddenly, she remembered Helena's plot to put her in St Geneviève des Bois.

'Oh, she just skimmed through them last night. She thinks it *possible* that they are Olga's, but not likely.' He made an ironical face.

'Helena wants me to be mad! She wants to put me away!' the Princess blurted this out, suddenly aware of the apparent non sequitur and worried by it.

Serge leaned back and smiled antagonistically. 'She thinks you already are. But your future is up to Varya and me.'

'Do you think I am mad, Seryozha?' She was in a state of great agitation about Olga. She kept wanting to grab the portfolio and devour the letters and yet she was almost physically prevented from doing so by the terror in her stomach. Perhaps she had told someone about the returns without knowing it. Perhaps she had spoken to someone in the midst of one of them and had been reported like a sleepwalker.

'Cra-a-zy like a fox!' as the Americans say. Good phrase. No, I do not think you are mad. Do you think so? Is that going to be the new thing? That I have driven you mad with these letters? Just because you don't want to believe they are true?' Something had got into him. He reminded her of her husband. He uncrossed his leg and leaned forward with something like menace on his face. 'You said you would read them, but you will not really read them, will you? I feel . . .' he said, smiting his chest, 'I feel as if I have spent my whole life obeying your secret orders and as they sometimes conflict, you see, it is very confusing. You hang onto your precious suffering and that is why you want the Tsar to remain a dream. Well, I do not. I have evidence enough already to know that I shall go to look for these people. I am sick and tired of living in your fantasy. Do you understand? Your mind is so rigid that I am surprised you do not think the earth is flat!' He reached up and clasped his temples.

'Seryozha! Why are you saying these terrible things? What is the matter with you?' She was reduced to quivering. 'Why have you changed so much towards me? I know. I know. It is that man! That Lipitsin! He has got you in his grip!'

'Do you think so? You probably think Lipitsin and Helena are in cahoots! But maybe it is I, and maybe it is about time.' He looked at her with astonishing coldness. 'I watched you weeping at the table and suddenly I thought to myself that you were using this situation as you have always used such situations. And, of course, the whole thing now revolves around you! I also realized that this is the first time I have ever asked you for anything at all.'

A vision of Lipitsin swelled into her mind now with its upswept cheekbones that stretched his mouth into a perpetual grinning. He had, to her, the pallor of one who inhabited night and shadow. 'Oh, Mother of God, preserve me!' she cried.

Serge's shoulders collapsed. 'Maman,' he sighed. 'I know I will regret this outburst and that you will make me regret it more than I actually will and that will be a lot. But please, do give me the kindness of giving these a fair hearing and please remember that I will have to live by what you say.' His voice came up through the tight funnel of his throat as a moan.

Suddenly, she gripped the arms of the wheelchair, herself in a passion. 'Give them to me!' she cried. 'Give the letters to me!' But he did not move. 'You dare to speak to your mother in such a voice?' Still, he did not move, and they were locked in each other's glare. 'Are you saying to me that you want me to verify these papers even if I do not think they are genuine? Are you threatening me?'

He was silent.

There was an old lithograph of the Cave of the Apocalypse above the sofa and she fixed her eyes upon it in an effort to abide in its engraved walls, its steely integrity. 'If I have made you unhappy, then you must find it in your heart to forgive me, but I will not tell an untruth in order to please you, nor even to thwart those plans against me!' Her eyes snapped open and shut. 'I love you better than anyone in the world, but I am not a liar and have never told the least deliberate falsehood.'

231

Her heart hammered in her thin chest, but she was directed by an inner force towards making this statement and she allowed the full impact of its power to hit him. 'That is all I have to say to you,' she said and she clamped her mouth shut.

For a moment, he sat very still, and then he rose. It occurred to her, perhaps because it was true, that he was about to embrace her, but then he turned away. 'I will go and get Tanya,' he said, dryly and he threw the portfolio from the table onto her lap.

She held the little grey, paper case and looked at it for a moment. A nauseating dread overcame her. 'I promised you I would read these letters and so I shall,' she said. 'If you wish me to think about them, then think about them I shall. I shall give you my answer on Sunday, no sooner and no later. And I do not wish to speak to you or to anyone else until that time.'

He turned again and left the room. She sat and she thought about the numbness of bad wounds, aware as she suddenly was that a portion of herself that had been he had been sliced from her. Although she wanted very much to cry, she did not. 'And I shall read them,' she said. 'I will.'

XIX

CAUGHT BETWEEN Paul and Helena after the lunch things had been cleared, Marina started thinking of her mother. They were drinking Greek coffee, very sweet, and were sitting on garden chairs around the table under the fig tree. There was an edgy silence caused by the near presence of a family row and the departure of Lipitsin for Samos.

It was not that she wanted to think about her mother, but her mother came up and seemed to invade the garden with her absence. If the detective found her, might things come to this? It was all very well to defend the Princess as she had done over lunch, but it hit Marina on the wing that a reunion with her mother might dredge up an awful rage and, like Serge, all that was unresolved within herself might explode in fury against some poor old thing, some pitiful, helpless, geriatric case. All her life she had felt it, and keenly she felt it now – a void place, a black hole where her mother should have been. The sensation extracted colour from the plump lemons on the trees and blue from the wide, burning sky, and a wistfulness invaded her. To have such a quarrel with a mother presupposed a solid chain of events dating from birth. She sipped bitter coffee from the delicate cup, hoping that the concentrated strength of the brew would jolt her from self-pity. Helena was looking at her, and so was Paul. The only sounds in the garden were the clicking of slender spoons on saucers and the omnipresent hum of cicadas in the trees. Marina felt that she was expected to say something, but what could one offer after such an explosion?

'Well Marina!' said Helena at last, 'Now, you have seen my Russian family in action.' She spoke languidly as if the conflict were of minor importance and only mildly interesting.

No one said anything, and Paul raised an eyebrow at Marina. If Helena caught this, she remained impassive. 'They swing from crisis to crisis as apes swing from tree to tree,' she continued. 'No one seems to realize that my aunt is always central to them. My cousins are always dragging me out of bed in the middle of the night with panicked phone calls about absolutely nothing at all, as it usually turns out. They go to Dostoievskian extremes when really they are straight out of Noel

Coward. They are like that emoting family in *Hay Fever*.' Nonetheless, Helena's eyes were on the garden door.

'I suppose they are inclined to be a little histrionic,' Paul ventured.

The remark was a peace offering, Marina thought, but Helena turned abruptly and looked at him. 'They thrive on it!' she snapped.

Everyone fell silent again in the highly charged atmosphere. It was becoming difficult for Marina to listen to Helena or to look at her in her rosy frock. All of a sudden, she conceived a passionate wish to be back in London. If only she had not been such a coward! If only she had, instead of courting disaster by her trip to New York, stayed, held her ground and opened Arthur's desk! One can of worms at a time would have been quite enough, as Paul had rightly suggested. If she had read Arthur's journals and poems, she would have been accurately informed about the weight he had given Helena in his life. She probably would not be in this situation in the first place. On the very day of the funeral in London she would have been able to say to Helena that she would rather not go to dinner at Poon's, that she had a headache, that she had to sleep, that she had someone coming to stay – anything at all rather than get embroiled in this dreadful business! Of course, that was presupposing that Arthur had mentioned Helena at all. She took heart at this, but then she inwardly knew. Oh, she knew the tinder-box awaiting her! If not Helena, then someone else, if not someone else, then a searing condemnation of her, of her life, of her soul, of her mind all given to him. But this was it, wasn't it? Her pattern was to avoid decisions until decisions made themselves – until she became aware that the avoidance had been the decision; until the avoidance had handed the decision to someone else like Helena.

It occurred to Marina that it would be a decision to go. Leaving Patmos was something she could do. She thought of the Cave that morning and of her walk with Paul. It somehow awed her that she had not felt so free and happy in years. It was as if, like the saint in the icon, she had simply let go and allowed herself to be borne upon the tide of an invisible will in things which had brought her to this place. It was perfectly within her power to pack her bags and catch a boat back to Athens. It was within her power to read what Arthur had left her and to dispose of it as she best saw fit. And yet it was not. It both was and was not. If she left abruptly, then what void would she leave? She glanced at Helena and Helena moved even though her eyes were on the door and away from Marina. She moved as if Marina had touched her in her sleep. Having eagerly accepted an invitation for the whole summer, how could Marina simply go? How to leave when she had just arrived? If Helena had behaved as she had behaved already, what reprisals could she take if Marina did not move very slowly, very carefully away? Yet, Marina thought, if she stayed much longer, she would compromise her whole cause utterly. Either way, she might endanger Arthur's future reputation or herself.

'I must say, Serge seems to be taking an awfully long time in there,' Paul said, musing aloud. He shifted restlessly in the uncomfortable chair.

'Oh, I expect she has gone back on her promise to read the letters, don't you?' Helena said.

'Surely, you don't think they are authentic, do you?' Paul asked. 'I confess that Serge did tell me something about them, but I had no idea that they made such preposterous claims. He only said he thought Olga had escaped and that the Tsar's grandchild was alive and that's more than enough.'

'What? Didn't Marina tell you about last night? She was there,' Helena said with an acid little smile.

'I promised I would not speak of it and so I did not,' Marina said a good deal more sharply than she had intended and was surprised by a look of fear in Helena's eyes. She lowered her own. She was unused to being aggressive in any way and it alarmed her when she was.

'Well, I looked through them myself, and I'll agree with you, Paul, that it sounds preposterous, but it is just conceivable. The tone is right and Lipitsin says an expert has already seen the handwriting,' Helena said in an ameliorating way.

'He's a detestable man!' Marina could not attach any idea she had of herself to the making of this statement. It was as if someone else had spoken. Paul and Helena looked very startled. 'Sorry,' she said, flushing, 'but I really did not trust him.'

Helena shrugged. 'He has credentials.'

'Well, that may be,' said Paul, 'but don't you think it odd that of all people it is *Olga* Romanov he says he has found? I remember hearing about Olga long ago in Paris when I visited as a child . . .'

'Oh, the great legend!' Helena said with exasperation. 'It improved each time she told it. And then she got to the stage where she refused to speak about the Romanovs at all. Some iron whim or other, I suppose. But I can't see how it is odd that Lipistin should approach her, tactless, maybe, but only natural. She considers herself the world's leading expert – and on slender evidence too. She met Olga only once, you know, and one would have thought they were sisters.'

Marina was grateful that Paul and Helena were distracted by this conversation. How could she put it? She hadn't even a cat to get back to in London. And hadn't she told Helena that she had given the detective her Patmos address? Indeed, she had but she was not sure that she had mentioned it. In any case, it seemed to make things worse to lie. I can hardly say I thought I left the iron on, she thought hysterically. All she had done for the last twenty years had been to iron, cook, shop. If she had been no equal to Arthur's practised intellect, how could she evade Helena? It suddenly came as a terrifying image to her that before Helena's mind, her own was like a mouse with a mowing machine, a 'timorous beastie' under that scything force. Perhaps she would get a cat. Marina remembered that she had always liked cats. Yes, maybe she would buy a cat for company, or rescue one.

'But that is my whole point,' Paul said. 'I can just see Lipitsin feeding back Serge's very own stories with the help of a forger. They've been working together for over a year, you know.'

'Poor Lipitsin,' said Helena. 'I rather liked him. But it makes very little difference, because my aunt will think what she wants to think.'

'That's brilliant, Paul!' Marina cried. She was jolted out of her thoughts by the obvious sense this theory made.

'Brilliant Paul,' Helena mimicked her sotto voce and he shot her a look of leonine intentness, gleaming as if at a bungling hunter.

'Well, it's of no consequence to me,' Helena sighed. She gave the air of one who had been defeated by stupidity. 'I have come to think that anything is possible with Russians. Olga might have been spared. Who knows? Who actually cares? It is an Asiatic country, really, you know, and they might have done anything with her and said anything about whatever it was they did. Personally, I can't see Lipitsin going to such lengths, but even supposing he had, I cannot imagine it would matter that much. Objective reality is not my aunt's deepest concern. There is an icon in a convent here in Hora, I forget which one, but my aunt thinks it is miracle-working. It's a Black Virgin, hung and studded with trophies, a gruesome thing. Aunt swears it healed her arthritic hip, but we have no readings on its activities in other catastrophes where the Virgin failed spectacularly to intervene, such as the death of my mother, for instance. I am sure She could have prevented that if She had really tried.' Her studied nonchalance had dropped and her voice had risen to a pitch that apparently surprised even herself, for she abruptly stopped speaking. She looked from Paul to Marina and then repostured herself. Her dainty pink dress seemed incongruous.

Marina wished for a miracle. She wished that she could find the Black Madonna and find truth and guidance from Her inviolable wholeness. What should she do? She was almost afraid to glance at Paul, for Helena seemed alert to the smallest and mutest exchange between them, but out of the corner of her eye, she caught his. Perhaps he had been exaggerating Helena's claims on the book, but somehow she thought not. On the other hand, she thought he had too glibly dismissed Helena as an insensitive cynic incapable of doing a good job. He quickened at her glance now, looked down and then fell silent. What had he said on their way from the Cave about her marriage having meaning? Certainly, he caught her meaning now, for her instinct told her that further words would lead to a very awkward contention, but somehow she thought he had got the wrong end of the stick about herself and Arthur, although she could not quite remember how.

Helena also fell silent and bit her lip. It was as if they were all poised in expectation of a scream or some other dreadful thing, for the atmosphere was subtly murderous. It struck Marina with even greater force than it had done earlier that day that if Arthur had left a large number of unpublished poems, then someone would have to edit them. How could she deny him this last rite? She had a sudden and unwelcome memory of him sitting in their frigid, beige living room, which she had never liked. Bright colours had distracted him, he said. And despite her timid interest in Art History, he had chosen all the paintings, afraid that she would choose figurative designs. She could see him now in her mind's eye looking murderously at her, although he had never struck her. She could see herself quailing before his displeasure as he sat with half-closed eyes in that armchair he had liked, silently, endlessly smoking, lighting one cigarette off another, end on end, in the bleak, alien room, fugging up the double-glazed, centrally heated, generally overwarm atmosphere and poisoning himself with disappointment.

She had not been allowed to speak to him when this sort of mood was upon him, nor would he allow a television, nor could she do anything with her hands that might irritate him, like knit or sew. How had she put up with this? It was as if she had been under a spell. Some evenings, he would be like this for hours at a time so that she did not know whether to go to bed or read or what. Sometimes she read Bernard Berenson, but her mind could never stick on it. And why had

237

he behaved in this way? It was a paradox to Marina and had been for some time that Arthur had wanted to be a public lyre and had craved a panoply of laurels. It was a paradox because she knew him as a man so desperately private that being in anyone's company for any length of time, save her own, drove him frantic.

Yet, he was eaten. The thought of his more successful contemporaries tormented him. He could not bear to hear about Ted Hughes, for instance, whose work had something in common with Arthur's. Robert Graves, though much older, was a forbidden topic. Sometimes he sat in the dark with the blinds drawn. It was almost as if he could not endure the light of day to hit his eyes that he might see how little he had been valued in comparison to others. Blind Homer had bit by bit become his patron saint, whom no one but he could understand. Horrified by this thought, she thought it nonetheless: that he had never made the necessary voyage to Troy, nor sacrificed the right maiden, nor stayed out the sirens, nor left Circe soon enough to gain his ends. It was ironic, really, she thought, now that she found herself daring to think, that he should ever have believed that his eccentric gift for words might be trusted or accepted by a generation committed to lucidity. His had been a black and curious art with largeness and violence to it. At worst, it was heavy, brutal stuff full of spondees and sarcasm. At its best, it had odd, teasing juxtapositions with patches of breathtaking lyricism.

For years, Marina realized, she had not allowed herself to think. It was as if her head were aching now to let out thought. At the time the *Cycle* had been published, it had seemed unkind and ungrateful of her actually to think about it. The division of labour was that he did the thinking and she did the being. In any case, from very early on, it had seemed her function merely to reflect his rays as the moon did the sun. One might as well have seen Beatrice taking Dante to task for errors in taste and judgment. Had this been why his affair with Helena had foundered? Because she had parsed a few verbs? Marina wondered this, but thrust it to one side for a moment, in pursuit, as she was of finding something to say for herself about his work. He was, she realized, a violator of words. This had been his main distinction. He had forced his way into his poetry, and like a ravisher, had commanded his readers' submission, sneering at anyone who failed to enjoy it as a second-rate sensibility, a third class mind. Marina found herself trembling inside at her own audacity. It seemed somehow necessary for her to add the rider that of course he had been a genius. Of course, he had been. It astonished her now to realize how she had taken it for granted that he had had the right to resent not being chosen as poet laureate. They would never even have thought of him. His name would not have occurred. Marina suddenly felt like saying out loud that she could have just as soon seen the Queen Mother limbo-dancing as she could have seen Arthur composing odes on tidy royal happenings. He would have torn poor Princess Diana viscerally apart and lauded her strung-out intestines, or would have seen, in the investiture of Prince Charles, the 'flaying of Marsyas' . . .

Marina grounded this flight of fancy almost at once. If ever there had been an occasion for unselfish behaviour in her life, it was now. A biography from a woman of Helena's stature would fix Arthur forever in that empery, the only one worth gaining in his mind. His longing for immortality had consisted in the contemplation of this only joy, that after his death, he would be read, and discussed, and memorized, and as a corollary of this, his smallest preferences, his greatest sins, his minutest observations should be studied, acclaimed, condemned and made history. He had clung to the hope that he would be made history like a hermit clings to the Cross. He would have given anything for this and had, indeed, sacrificed all his peace and every happiness to that end. So unless someone else were to come forward with a plan for a book, which seemed highly unlikely, Marina was trapped by honour into a collusion with Helena whether she liked it or not.

Sadly now, she looked at Paul, grateful to him for his having given her, for a while anyway, the illusion of choice. No one had spoken for quite a while and the silence had become less charged with feeling. In fact, Paul was leafing through some book or other. A pang of longing invaded her. She had a desire to touch him. It was a pang of deep loneliness that could not be evaded.

As the marriage had stumbled on, she had found herself harbouring guilty thoughts about other men. When she had her breakdown, she had developed a crush on the psychiatrist and had almost stood up to Arthur when he had demanded she abandon the therapy. From time to time, she had found herself hoarding away memories of appreciative glances on the street, keeping them like mementoes, and had often imagined love. It was a case of wanting someone with whom to share the trivia of her day, she balked at sexual thoughts. She had always been walking, shopping. She had walked a lot past dreary dogs and car parks and into Marks and Spencer and out again, anywhere, like a ghost flitting, seeing in fleet glances a child with a tantrum, an old man with a stick, a pair of blowsy shopgirls on a toot. She would think of how that night she would have to stretch her body out next to his and wait. Waiting in fear for Arthur to ask response and then giving it. But these occasions had come much less often. In the end, he had almost forgotten her existence.

Had she alluded to this much to Helena? She could barely remember all of the things she had said. But surely, Helena could not forego the pleasure of reporting what she had told her only the previous afternoon before they had gone to look at the Monastery, that the marriage had been a sexual fiasco. Marina wished the ground would swallow her up. Maybe she would take the veil. Then it could be argued that she had been a celibate all along. People would buy the book. People would read it. Hadn't his obituary been in *The Times* and the *Daily Telegraph*? He had been known – really he had – but not *enough*. He crowded her thoughts now as if there had been many of him. For all his height and thinness, he had developed a heavy, jowly face. Out of the newspapers had brooded the Churchillian visage. Now that he was dead, her connection with him seemed immutable. How did she feel without him? She felt orphaned without him. Marina was no fool and she had known this all along.

'Marina?' Paul looked up from his book and she turned her head. 'Marina, this is what I was telling you about yesterday. Ephesus. See? I found a guide.'

'Oh, Ephesus,' Helena said. 'It's a bit of a nightmare journey.' Two patches of sweat showed under the tight-fitting sleeves of her rose-coloured dress. Somehow it made her seem vulnerable, a thing Marina had noticed before. Paul waved the guidebook in Marina's direction. It was thin and brightly coloured. 'Here,' said Paul. 'I want to show you something.'

Just as he spoke, however, Serge Mikovsky suddenly appeared in the dark, inner hallway of the house. Going past the door as if to remain unnoticed, he looked at Marina like the shadow of a bough moving in a sudden wind. On seeing Serge, Helena started then hailed him.

In later years, Marina was to think a good deal about Serge and about how she should have paid him more notice at the time, but as it was, she retracted slightly from the sight of his heavy, pallid face as it emerged from the gloom of the hallway out onto the dappled terrace. 'Lenochka?' he said.

The Russian diminutive seemed wildly out of place to Marina and she saw Helena twitch with irritation at its use. He seemed intent on speaking to his cousin and looked neither at Paul nor herself.

'I know, she's changed her mind!' said Helena.

'No, she has not changed her mind. Nothing changes her mind, does it? But she will not deliver the verdict until Sunday, an act of petty sadism, it seems to me.'

Paul made to speak, but evidently thought better of it.

'I would have surprised and pleased you, Lena. You cannot imagine what a task it is for me to stand up to her, but I did.' He looked at Paul for a few seconds, but said nothing. 'Look,' he continued, 'I'm going to fetch Tanya and then I must hurry down to Skala to see if Gregory has left yet. I think I'll just have time to catch him before the boat goes.' Abruptly, he vanished.

'Do you think your aunt is all right?' Marina asked.

'You might do better to inquire about Serge,' Helena replied. 'My aunt has the strength of ten . . . Neither of you has the slightest idea, have you?' Her tone was sad rather than angry and it reverberated in the air.

After a moment's hesitation, Paul stood. 'I'll go see to her,' he said. 'Don't worry, Marina. She really is a tough old bird, just as Helena says, but nonetheless . . .' And Helena looked after his retreating figure narrowly as if to assess the meaning of that last, diplomatic statement.

Marina felt trapped and she determined to say nothing. During a few, taut seconds, they were silent, but she found herself unable to avoid Helena's eyes. At once, Helena raised a fine eyebrow and smiled. It was a deep, intimate look – quite direct. 'Marina!' she said, breathing it. Marina gave what she hoped was a temporizing expression, pleasant, remote and neither here nor there. She picked up the book on Ephesus and fanned herself with it. Paul returned almost at once, to Marina's great relief. 'She chased me out! She'll only have Tanya with her. Poor Tanya looks very confused.' He shrugged. 'I can't do more.'

Helena looked annoyed at Paul's return. Suddenly, Marina felt an unbearable discomfort at the whole situation on Patmos with its thick undertones and Byzantine hierarchies, its rigid rules, its claustral feelings and a stunning headache hit her. She felt the heat oozing through the leaves of the lovely trees in the garden, oppressing her and clinging to her. All at once, she thought of the water she had seen that morning from the window of the Shrine, its azure purity, and she could think of nothing better than to dive, abandon herself to its depths, swim and splash around, churning up the foam.

'If it's all right with everybody,' she said, 'I think it would be nice to swim.'

'What a lovely idea!' Helena exclaimed with a fresh, crackly laugh. Enthralled by the notion, she clasped her hands together.

'I must say, that would be nice,' Paul agreed. Helena sat back, slightly recoiling, and there was the flash of a glare between them.

Marina felt like saying that she had assumed she would go alone, but it seemed churlish to do this. So, after collecting the paraphenalia of costumes and mats and sunhats and lotion, they took a taxi from the stand below the Monastery to Kampos Beach, where a wide expanse of sand lay exposed to the fierce, low-hanging sun.

XX

HE WAS SURPRISED to see that she had a somewhat dumpy figure.
Helena, some fifteen years older, had a better one, although her skin
had aged. It surprised him, but it did not altogether displease him.
Marina wore a green, cotton bathing costume and a shirt over her
shoulders to protect her fair skin from the sun. She had already
slathered her face in lotion, and her nose had a comic, white dab down
its well-moulded length. 'I go like a lobster,' she said again as she had
said that morning. She took off her shirt and tried to anoint her
shoulders, but Helena gracefully took the oil from her hand and started
rubbing her back with a light, feathery touch. Marina leaned forward,
head bowed, and allowed this to go on, sighing as Helena massaged her
back with oil. Helena knelt above her, eyes angled down and there was
a little smile in the corners of her mouth. Incongruously, this gave Paul
the impression of an old Italian painting he had once seen of the
annunciating angel, but he could not remember which one, the kneeling
figure with its shining, cropped hair, brooding with mild, inner rapture
over the crouched, retracting form of Marina. Having been urged down
by Helena, she lay prone on the towel now. Closing her eyes, she
allowed Helena to dribble oil onto her legs and rub it in. Paul resented
this palming and slapping, so he looked away.

He, too, was fair-skinned and burnt easily. Although his face was
leathery now, his hands and forearms dark, his back and chest were
pale. He asked for the oil and felt awkward putting it on. Helena turned
her face out to sea and gazed at the blue water in the middle distance.
Marina rose. She had large breasts and they stretched the cloth of her
bathing costume tight. Her waist was snug, though and the costume
was belted to reveal it. She made an offering gesture with her hands,
took the oil from Paul and gently rubbed it into his shoulders and down
his back. He felt close to tears. Her sense of touch was sure and gifted
with instinct. He turned away from her and lay down on the sand in
order to conceal evidence of a sudden, sharp desire. The hot sand hurt
his stomach and loins. Feeling confused, he said, 'Thank you' abruptly
and she stopped, but he looked up at her in an effort to see if she had

known what she had been doing and his throat caught as she quickly turned away.

'Here, Helena, let me do you now!' she said in an efficient sort of way.

Helena was wearing a curious, old-fashioned two-piece, but it set off her lithe, fit body. Marina plastered the oil with diligence. Her face was furrowed with concentration as if she were painting a picture. She rubbed brusquely. Paul propped himself on his elbows and watched. He wondered if she were thinking of her dead husband.

She finished, giving Helena a pat like a horse, stood abruptly and said, 'Oh, look, my hands are all covered in oil! I think I'll swim now and wash them off. It's so hot!' Indeed, although the sun was well past its zenith, it hung heavy and glared reflection off the sand and water. The bay before them was large and shallow. As Marina walked down to the sea, she appeared to shimmer in the mirage that rose in waves over the sand. She picked her way, hopping from scorched foot to scorched foot.

Before Paul could get up the nerve to follow her, Helena called out, 'Wait!' She gave him an urbane little smile. 'You won't mind looking after our things, will you? My credit cards are all in my handbag.'

Helena set off after Marina and Paul sat upright, drawing his knees up and circling them with his arms. He perspired and crawled with irritation. Far out in the water were children in paddleboats and beyond them, windsurfers becalmed with slack sails. To the left of him and some way down the beach, there were platforms erected for sunbathers and on these young girls with bare breasts lay still as idols being worshipped on pink cushions. The young men with them seemed wholly oblivious to their nudity and chatted idly amongst themselves or lay supine, soaking up the sun. Nearer to Paul were two groups of people. A Greek family had come down to bathe. They were numerous and related to each other, a grandmother, a mother, a father, some children and an assortment of uncles and aunts. They had, as a precaution against the sun, a large umbrella poised in the sand and they had brought a hamper with them too. It was filled with bottles and sausages, tomatoes, fruit and pitta bread. Nearby, on a blue lilo not fifty feet away from these, sat a couple in their fifties . . . tourists from some Northern European country. The ample woman took off the top of her bikini, jerking the halter off with an air of defiance. There she sat, immobile in the burning sun, looking for all the world to Paul like a cult object, some Nordic fertility goddess. The Greek grandmother, dressed in black, fiddled with the Orthodox cross around her neck and gave the other woman a hard stare. She took a grandchild by the hand and set off for the water. Paul watched as she walked fully clothed into the sea with the child, immersing herself as in a baptism until the two were nearly covered by water. Far out, he could see Marina and Helena, their heads bobbing in the sea.

Suppose I fell in love with her, he thought. What would happen then? He could not imagine what would happen. Maybe I have already fallen a little in love with her. He reasoned that on such short acquaintance whatever it was he felt for Marina could not be love but only its analogue.

In the past and since Julia it had been only married women or patients who attracted him, those whom he was honour-bound to avoid. But here Marina was. She simply was. She was without proscription, unfettered in her green bathing suit. Why not? he thought. If she would have him. Yet, everything about her showed short access, her melting eyes, her deep, unguarded bosom. She quickly opened, flower-like, to smiles. He felt restless and a little ashamed of himself and looking behind him, he saw some bushes edging the road, maybe tamarisk, he thought. He picked up the towels and valuables and moved into the shade of the bushes and sat there for a moment, considering what to make of her. What was he thinking of, risking an involvement with a freshly widowed woman and one who, by her own admission, had ambivalent feelings to say the least about her husband. Were not these things usually fifty-fifty? What had his side of the story been? He had done some rough-and-ready marriage counselling in his surgery and one tale of woe often left out the salient points of the other.

He reminded himself that the only accusations she had flung at anyone had been at herself, but was she one of those ruinous people who go around causing emotional carnage without the slightest idea they are doing so until it is too late and the dead bodies start floating down the river? Suppose she ruined his life. What more ruin was there to do, he thought, that he had not done already? Suppose, on the other hand, he ruined hers. That was possible. He could do it with only a little effort. He had a way of slamming doors on fingers. He dimly knew this and winced to think of pain he might have caused.

Why was he thinking this way in the first place? She was a natural and spontaneous person who probably treated everyone the same way and here he was bolting to conclusions like a fool. He realized that he was thinking this way because he had not thought about Africa, nor

245

Serge, but only of her, not of himself, since early that morning. Not since the night before had he thought of any other thing but her.

In the Cave, with her tears falling to the riven stone floor, she had held him in the circle of some emanating prayer. He had sat so still, hardly daring to breathe as the tapers had danced and flickered over her head as she bowed it in her hands. The little tongues of flame had almost seemed to surround her. He had suddenly felt huge dimensions, as if he had made a great pilgrimage, or rather, as if she had made it into one for him. That was how he had felt, but he foundered on doubt. Was he not only too ready to be dazzled by this spectre of beauty made innocent as fresh roses? He had needed to weep and she had wept for him. Her tears seemed to speak of a beauty fresh and innocent, pre-existing guilt in its freshness, a primary innocence born on a rushing, fresh tide. He could not conceive of guilt ever having been near her or having touched her. But had she not created for another man just such an illusion, though perhaps not that one? He ached when he thought of that, with fervent, incoherent love and a terrible pity for her.

Oh, this is foolish! he thought. Pull yourself together. He tried to change the subject and think of Serge. It frightened him that he could not even picture Serge's face, only hers. Even the poor old Princess's efforts not to cry when he had gone to the office to check up on her, even those suppressed tears, had done little to distract him. There she had sat with the portfolio of papers held tight to her chest, as rigid as a nun with an undiscovered Dead Sea Scroll, the contents of which might challenge an article of faith. He had wanted to say something to her, to express his solidarity with her in her doubts, but nothing had been adequate to the expression of inner dilemma on her face and he had been, on the whole, thankful to have been summarily dismissed from her presence. He had found himself making his way eagerly back to the garden and Marina.

Paul gazed out to sea. There she was with Helena, bobbing about. She swam the breaststroke in short, uneven thrusts (would break his heart, would break his heart). Helena lay on her back in the water and kicked up a spume. She wore a bathing cap over her close-cropped hair. (Or would evaporate – vapid – and leave him arid and starved.) Marina swam a little way from Helena. What had Arthur Holt been *like*? Why had she stayed in the ectopic marriage when an annulment would have been so easy to achieve? Why had he exerted such a fascination over the two women who splashed about together uneasily in the sea, circling to avoid each other, heads awkwardly turned from each other?

He had a fantasy of Arthur Holt pulling them under like a crocodile with ducks, a cold, impersonal appetite of a man. No, it was he, not she, who had been the destructive one.

He shook his head as if trying to dislodge the buzz of her from his ears. One should not squander oneself on idle speculation. He wondered if it wasn't prurient to think about her marriage, for the obvious conclusion to his questioning was that Marina had been sexually enthralled to the man and that made him feel angry and jealous. Jealous and suspicious of her motives. And he had no right to be. He had blithely called her a martyr earlier, but it could be that she was one of those pathologically guilty people who confess crimes to the police that they have not committed, people who long for punishment in order to feed a complex. Surely, a woman like that would do better to free herself from men altogether . . .

He did not even know her. How could he dare such thoughts? What was more, he felt a sudden panic at having been drawn in so far against his wont. Since he could remember, he had felt compelled to put large distances between himself and other people, and the idea of spending his latter days in silence with crusts appealed to him. During his African days, the idea of such solitude would come to him as a healing thought and he would apply it to his imagination like a cool poultice. He had had visions of himself alone in a grey cell, speechless and abstaining from everything unnecessary, free from disquieting association, lapped in peace and purity. Sometimes this thought had welled up from a source within himself, sometimes he had been able to summon it at will in the way a man of a different disposition might summon thoughts of Tahitan islands with beaches full of willing girls. But I am completely unworthy of that now, he thought. Why did he think that? Surely it was not a merely altruistic horror at the starved which had crow-barred and jemmied its way in. Other things had forced him open and had driven him to Patmos where now he sat on a beach sprawling, indeed, with women in various attitudes of casual availability. I am no longer my own man! he thought despairingly and then thought again about Marina in the water. An image of her blamelessness came to him again like a freshlet in the brine. He suspected that he needed to see her this way, but he was beginning not to care. Suddenly, a reproof of Arthur and Helena welled up within him. How could they? How could Arthur have

247

used her? How could Helena be using her in this way? She had been and was being used and manipulated! Was it up to him to stop it?

Paul could understand how Arthur and Helena had become fascinated by Marina. But what mattered was what one did about it. With an impulse to protect her, his mind enclosed the thought of her and there it was again, his old vision of a simplicity of life, transformed by her so that walls danced with light and windows hitherto closed opened onto a garden voluptuous with flowers and with bees. He had not felt so for twenty years, no, maybe longer. Maybe he had never felt this way. It was as if his voice had broken again and had found new depth and range of utterance. To think about Julia now was to think about imprisonment in a delusion, cracked wide open by Marina. The remembered sense of her fingers on his back, the reverberating thought of her huge tears earlier in the Shrine, the recollection of their breakfast together earlier still under the voluminous blue awning where she had sat demurely, charged him with an intensity of feeling which he thought people reserved for sacred moments. There she was fixed in his mind. How could he accuse her? In the piney forecourt of the Cave, she had resolutely eschewed all excuses for her past and had confronted him with hard honesty and self-knowledge. It was himself he had to blame for the weird rage she had drawn from him, a rage he knew had been bottled there for years and still fumed within him, not at her nor at social injustice, nor at anything else but the whole frustration of his own life. She had seemed almost a Biblical figure, scarved and scented, a Magdalene. So strongly had she represented this eternal figure to him that his own reserve had broken down and seemed breached now beyond recall.

Here, he sharply recollected himself to himself. A motorbike, going along the road behind him, blurted out its mechanical noise and made him start. He suddenly thought of himself as ridiculous in his swimming trunks, exposed, concave, helpless and disempowered by his need. For her? For her approval? Oh, what high romance! He picked at a weed in the wall, twiddled it and felt embarrassed by imagining such nonsense. What had he revealed of himself already to Marina?

He began to wonder from his vantage point under the low, unnamable bushes, why had she and Helena been in the water for so long? With a reflex action for danger, he wondered if she had drowned and had visions of Helena holding her head under the water until she did. But, no, Marina was swimming idly towards the shore and Helena was swimming after her. Perhaps they had been talking about him. Perhaps it was only too obvious and they had been laughing at him. He was ashamed of this puerile thought, but wondered if he ought to get dressed at once. No, of course they had been talking about Arthur Holt.

He was under a vague impression that he had once seen a picture of the man and strove to recall it. A boney face and white hair? It eluded him. In the water, they had spoken of him, the man who had so merrily ploughed into first one and then the other. A rush of disgust came to Paul at this goatish thought and his face reddened. With anger? Of course, she had loved him and she loved him still. Marina. Hadn't she embraced him when he had implied the same? Had that been a release of guilt, an affirmation of the truth, or an unconscious attraction to himself? He was sure that Helena had been filling the gaps in Marina's knowledge with blow by blow details of her affair. Was he thinking about this because he would like to know too? He felt a sudden urge to smoke a cigarette, a thing he had not done for twenty-five years.

Marina moved herself fishwise up from the little waves, then, clutching modestly at her costume, she rose from the sea. He shook his head and tried to watch her ascent without a view to these thoughts and then he gazed out at the broiling tract of sand that separated them so that she could come up the beach in peace from his gaze. It suddenly struck him that the well-fed bodies of the half-naked tourists looked like basted joints of meat and he realized that they were all literally roasting. The irony occurred to him so sharply that he gave a little bark of laughter. They were not dead from famine. They were even oiled for cooking. And so was he. He shut his eyes and swayed a bit at the nauseating thought. There were flies in the bushes and he heard them buzzing.

He opened his eyes and Marina was upon him, her hair dripping. 'You must be dying for a swim,' she said. 'I fear we have deserted you. It was so lovely in the water that I lost all track of time.' Helena came up behind her and evenly peeled her bathing cap from her head.

'Marina,' he said. He was acutely conscious of his white torso and of muscles gone slack. He felt shelled like a crab and as vulnerable. Marina lowered her eyes. She bit her lip and cast a sidelong glance at Helena, who briskly rubbed herself dry with a towel.

'Now, that was heavenly, Marina!' she said. 'Wonderful idea coming here! I daresay I shouldn't have bathed all summer if it had not been for you.' She slid her long, dancer's feet carefully into sandals, shaking her toes like a cat. She walked down the beach to where Paul had abandoned their mats. 'I am going to *collapse*!' she said.

'Paul?' Marina replied. With one hand, she held her towel, the other she extended towards him as if for alms, then let it drop loosely to her side. It was almost as if she had heard his thoughts as summons and had obeyed them. Confronted with her, he felt paralyzed. Her hair snaked in long ringlets around the chain of her neck. 'I think I'll go and sunbathe,' she said awkwardly, as if sensing a refusal in him.

Ah, the Beast from the Sea, he thought strangely and it shook him that this crowned image of apostasy and doom had emerged from his mind in response to her pleading. He stood, walked down the beach, picked up pace and ran across the burning sand, then plunged into the water where with long strokes under the surface he swam with a sense of joy and horror mixed.

XXI

'MARINA, we must talk,' said Helena. Together, they watched Paul's back shimmering in the sea. 'We really must, Marina.'

'About what?' Marina asked. Her hair was frizzy and sticky and she was hugging her knees, her head hunched over them. Helena noticed with sudden anguish a curl of hair on the curve of her cheek. Having decided to be magisterial with Marina, she melted into an urge to smooth and touch her. In the water, Marina had dived and spluttered, making conversation jerky and difficult. She had made a good deal of being out of shape and out of breath. Now, she sat looking Heavenward at the declining sun from which the earth retreated and then at Paul, who was displaying a strong Australian crawl before them.

'You like Paul, don't you?' Helena asked.

'Is that what you want to talk about?'

'I want to talk about *you*,' Helena gasped. 'About you and me!' She had not meant to put it this way and certainly not on an intake of breath, but suddenly she had seen that the space between them could not be easily broached. Marina had withdrawn from her farther than she had thought. She turned her head at this and gazed at Helena in an enigmatic way. 'I've hardly seen you since you arrived,' Helena continued.

'I think I find it hard to talk about Arthur,' Marina said, looking away. She gripped the sand with her toes and fell to strewing it with her fingers in little, meaningless piles. 'In any case, my time-clock is completely shattered. Having slept till noon yesterday, I woke at five this morning. It seemed stupid to wake you.'

'Do we have to talk about Arthur? I thought you liked talking about him.'

'I do sometimes,' Marina said with pent-up breath. She caught her lip in her teeth. She was digging about in the sand and making a little hill with it. 'I enjoyed the Cave,' she said. 'I loved it.'

Helena did not know what to say. 'Last night, you said that it bothered you to hear that Arthur and I had been lovers. I'm sorry if I upset you.'

Marina looked round, her eyes softened.

'I think you are probably right. I think I must be mourning him myself, although I can't quite say why.' Helena felt uncomfortable with this admission, but it made Marina flow towards her.

'I felt better about things in the Cave. The Cave helped me to resolve a few things,' Marina said. She had found a little stick and was drawing circles round the hill she had made.

'You prayed?' Helena had sudden energy for this. 'Marina, I think we have very different points of departure. I don't believe in God.' She found herself wanting Marina to accept this, but Marina said nothing. 'But I have known enough people who do. I think you have been involved in a kind of . . . process . . . that I do not understand.' Her words climbed out of her painfully and uttered themselves differently than she had intended. 'It seems to me that getting things straight about Arthur is paramount for *you*. Maybe it is for me too. I did not love him. You do realize that, don't you?' This failed to express anything she had wanted to say. She watched Marina's face carefully and was caught up once more in an exquisite sense of its arresting beauty.

After a pause, Marina said, 'I did. I did love him.'

Oh, no, you didn't, Helena thought. You did not. You didn't, my dear. My dear, my soul. But she let it pass. 'Look,' she said, 'Arthur performed a function for me. My marriage was . . . I don't know . . . loveless, I suppose. Arthur simply supplied a necessary transition for me or a transfusion. A way out, really. I don't see sex in a believer's terms and even if I did, I can't see why it should disturb you so much if he was not actually being unfaithful to you when he and I were together . . . especially. . . .'

'. . . .when I broke up his marriage?' The sand was becoming shadowed with a dun colour, although it was not yet dusk. Paul had left the water, but he was walking along the shore, picking little things up and inspecting them. Helena noticed that Marina kept looking at him. Perhaps aware that Helena observed this, Marina turned her head to the Northern European couple, who basked in the late light. She spoke to Helena about the woman whose heavy breasts sank onto rolls of fat around her midriff. 'Even with my figure, I wouldn't dare do that.' The woman started to replace her halter. They were evidently going back to their hotel. 'And I haven't a very good one,' Marina added. She became abruptly attentive to Helena once more as if it had taken her a while to decide what to say. 'I know it is irrational, but it is simply the feeling it gave me – that we had shared him. It makes me uncomfortable.'

Helena started to quiver with an unlooked-for emotion. She almost put her hand on Marina's shoulder. 'But it *unites* us,' she wanted to say.

'I'm sorry. I can't help it,' Marina continued.

Helena cast up a hand. 'At least we are talking about it,' she said.

'What is there to say?' Marina asked. 'I would not want to know what it was like for you and, in some senses, I do not want to remember what it was like for me.'

'But you were so unhappy! I would have thought it was worth working out why if you don't want it to happen again.' Helena knew she should leave it alone, but she could not.

'Maybe I should be psychoanalyzed,' Marina said somewhat sharply. 'Heaven knows I have enough time and money to burn.' She looked at Helena carefully and evenly, maintaining the glance as if it were the result of much sober reflection, but the faintest barb of buried hostility in it all put Helena on her guard. 'You have been very helpful – please don't get me wrong – in fact, so helpful that it's made me realize how complex the whole thing was. I've said so much and I'm not sure if any of it is really accurate.'

'Your feelings seem pretty coherent to me!' Helena exclaimed. She was reduced now to a state of cold, muffled panic, but she could not say why. It was as if Japanese doors were being slid quickly into closures and disclosures according to some mathematical plan.

'Well, they're not. I thought about it a lot in New York. Going to look for my parents put some things into focus and blurred a lot of other things.'

All the time Marina was talking, she looked ruminatively down the beach. Helena could tell that from time to time she checked on Paul's position. From around the arch of the bay, he was now coming idly towards them, but he was still a long way off. It was he. It had been he that morning who had implanted these thoughts in Marina's addled skull, for, Helena thought acidly, there was little in Marina's own nature that could give rise to this small but significant change of direction. Psychoanalysis indeed! There was the rumble of something else afoot, but she could not locate what it was. Of course, the attraction between them was not lost on her, but after Arthur it was improbable that Marina could take him seriously for very long . . .

Why did she think that? Only this morning she had recorded something slightly different in her journal. She had watched Paul herself, thinking him no catch, certainly no Adonis. Did not the poems themselves give evidence of Marina's luxuriant appetite? Just to look at

253

her now, half-naked gave one an idea of her rich endowments. How had Arthur arrived at that pitch of sensuousness without her cooperation? Perhaps she was right. Perhaps she had not been 'accurate' about the marriage. A proper little convent girl in her head, she was maybe not so in other respects. No . . . she might waste a little time with Paul in an attempt to bolster up some sanctimonious notion of herself, but one had to face it – she had chosen Arthur and this was incriminating evidence enough of whorish needs.

He, for one, had had little inhibitions. He had liked to be an outright barbarian. He had unveiled to her the coarse weave of real life which had lain beneath her meagreness of imagination, her fastidiousness. He was hardly likely to marry a cold fish. Marina with her hypocrite's propriety looked up at the reddening sun from the calm, broad sand. That body would not content itself with Paul. And yet, with the craft and cunning of one who saw a rival in herself, Helena thought, Paul would be quite capable of inducing Marina to caution. Because of course he would see her as a rival! Such men were always possessive and resented women's freedom to be meaningful to each other!

What had they been hatching together, then? Had they talked about her book? About her? It was odd that Marina had not referred to the book. After all, she had revealed her plans to Marina only yesterday, plans that were far more important than all of this incidental business about an ancient, buried love affair. Oh, she was getting as paranoid as Aunt Sonya! Either Marina had not taken it in about the book or the business about Lipitsin had erased it from her mind for the time being. Nonetheless, as she saw Paul curving up towards them along the beach, it occurred to her that the subject of the book must be broached more fully before his interest in Marina eclipsed Marina's attention. Suddenly, Helena felt she could not endure one more evening in his company. It suddenly occurred to her what to do.

'You know,' she said, 'I have a splendid idea. Why don't I treat you to dinner tonight at the Patmian House? It's our only gastronomic claim to fame here on the island. It has even been written up in *Vogue*. The proprietor has relatives here and he comes back from the States every summer. I've been meaning to take you and after all that brouhaha with my aunt, it would seem a good idea to get out of harm's way. It would be so lovely, just you and me. What do you say?'

Marina had buried her face in her arms, which were cradled round her knees so that she gave a whole fetal impression. She said nothing for a moment, then turned her head. 'Oh, let me take you,' she said, her voice nervous and uncertain. 'I would love to be able to thank you for your hospitality.'

'Well, if you like . . . but, you see, I'm longing to talk to you about my book. We haven't even begun to think it through yet and there is so much to say.'

Either there was no helping the twist of pain on her face or she had intended it as a signal to Helena, but she quickly hid her head again, sheltering in her drawn up knees.

'Marina?'

'Oh, yes, we must talk about it. Yes, you are right,' Marina said, muffling it. Oh, God! Helena thought. She's crying. Without knowing she was going to do this, she reached out and curled a drying ringlet from Marina's shoulder onto her finger and fanned out the fine hair.

'Do you not want a book?'

Marina shrugged away her touch as naturally as a small child or animal. Her eyes were full as she looked into Helena's face. 'Arthur would have wanted it,' she said.

Every kind of warning was borne on this. Helena's heart thudded. 'Well, your cooperation is *essential*. I mean, I can't imagine doing it without you.' She gave what she knew to be an over-eager smile.

Marina said nothing. She propped her chin on her elbows and looked out to sea.

Suddenly, Helena felt an acute sadness. She had not felt so for many years, if ever. It was as if the wide, flat chilling bay gave portents of a veritable ocean upon which she voyaged alone, stranded. She tried to shrug off the feeling. It was unlike her to be sensible of herself. 'It's getting late,' she said, and it came out hoarsely. She started collecting belongings. 'Let's gather up Paul and go back to the house. There will be taxis coming back from Lampi.'

Marina looked up at her and their eyes met in something akin to sorrow . . . or at least, Helena interpreted sorrow somewhere in Marina. She said, however, with sudden humour, 'I don't think it is that easy to gather Paul up!'

'Would you like to?' Helena could not imagine why she had said this arch thing.

'What do you mean?' Marina asked with yet another warning in her voice. 'I admire him very much. I think it wonderful that he has done such a great deal in Ethiopia. Don't you? More than that, I like him.'

Helena made no reply to this and she suddenly felt exasperated with Marina. The eternal schoolgirl, she thought, gawping after the great humanitarian just as she had gawped after the great poet. Always an aspiring handmaiden to a great man! She ought to use the Nobel Committee as a dating agency. Perhaps next time a famous scientist or musician would floor her, Helena thought, and nearly laughed aloud.

'Marina,' Paul said. He was suddenly upon them. 'Helena,' he added. She noticed how quickly he pulled his towel around him, grasping it with a clenched fist. His other hand was a fist too. She observed with what covert hunger he looked at Marina, who gazed up at him from the mat with poignant seriousness. Of all things, it was this that alarmed Helena the most, their shared expression in the chilling, rosy, late afternoon. It alarmed her and it angered her too. In fact, from deep within her, there came something akin to explosion, as if far off a mountain had exploded in the sea, or as if something live and hitherto mute inside her had been wakened by torture.

Marina, sluicing the sand from her hair and reddened body, let the cool shower pour across her eyes in order to eliminate the last, green afterglow of the furious sun. The impression stayed with her of fire.

In the clear, lit depths of the bay, there had been little fishes shifting in small shoals, their small, silvered forms flitting in parallel formation. She had felt ungainly swimming above them and would have given anything to have had their peaceful, innate knowledge of the right direction to take when threatened. Should she talk with Helena about Arthur for Arthur's sake? Or, for his sake should she remain silent? What was required of her? Was it possible, as Paul had earlier suggested, to give Helena information about their life together with one hand and then extract it with the other? This whole thing gave her great pain and it seemed quite impossible to know how to do what she knew she must do. She had felt the sun on her back and the natural ebb and flow of the current and then Helena had plunged in after her, and as the fishes had circled her own feet, so she had circled Helena and then there had been the thought of Paul on the shore. She had felt first a wave of pleasure, then of shame, that he had seen her so exposed in the unbecoming bathing suit.

Now, she considered the evening before her with great misgiving. So much would depend on how she played it. She was not used to playing things, plotting moves, deliberating outcomes by tactics and design. Already, she was exhausted by the conversation she had had with Helena on the beach. It was as if the older woman engulfed her in a volume of something heavier than water – mercury or glue. When they had returned to the house, they had found the garden empty and had sat drinking lemon tea on the terrace. At Helena's announcement that they would be dining alone together at the Patmian House, Paul had given her a look of such alarm and reproof that she had started. But then Serge had wandered in, sober and nervous with news of his mother. Through Tanya, he had been informed that she had retired to her room, refusing to see anyone at all until Sunday when she would make her announcement about the papers. No readings, no Paul, no garden, no nothing. What was more, she had sent for Father Nikon in Athens, or had tried, only to find he had taken off to Mt Athos for the week and would not be available even for a telephone conversation until next Wednesday. All of this seemed very dire and alarming to Serge, who had fidgeted and pranced about the terrace, plucking blooms from flowers and sighing.

Finally, Marina had fled, declaring that she must change and get the sand out from between her toes, and bundling the dripping evidence of the swimming party, she had withdrawn into the house. At the top of the carved stairwell, she had turned for some reason and had caught Paul standing at the bottom, clutching the newel post, looking up after her. She had caught his eye in the relative darkness after the fiery blaze of the sun.

She patted her sore skin dry, then wrapped herself in her large kimono. It billowed after her as she went to her room. Paul's door was ajar and as she passed, she saw him reading at a table. At once, he closed the book and rose. 'Marina?' Evidently, he had been waiting for her.

She clutched at her sponge bag, but pushed the door open and stood on the threshold. His room was very simple and there seemed nothing in it to identify him as an individual but a battered suitcase tucked from sight under the table and a pair of military hairbrushes on the chest of drawers. Her kimono was covered with golden chrysanthemums. She had bought it in Tokyo on her tour of the Far East with Arthur. He had told her, then, that she looked like a butterfly in it, a rare compliment in those days, and she wondered if she looked like a butterfly now.

'Marina,' he said. 'Will you go to Ephesus with me tomorrow? Or do you want to stay here?'

She retracted slightly at the brusqueness of the question.

'I've checked on the boats by telephone. Unless we want to stop over in Samos, it seems that this will be the only one for quite a while.'

Marina was uncertain about the workings of Greek tragedy, but she had an idea about the arrival of a 'deus ex machina' – an arbitrary force coming down from the flies to relieve the situation. Was this as an intervention in favour of herself? 'Oh, what a wonderful idea!' she said, laying her hand on her breastbone. Paul was looking at the hand and Marina dropped it to her side, aware of the heavy wedding-ring. He looked down and frowned with concentration on the Greek rug at her feet. Her fingers remembered, with a little chill, the feeling of his skin underneath them, the sense of his distance at her presumption. 'If you really want me to go, that is,' she added. 'Don't feel you have to ask me.'

'Don't come if you don't want to!' He sounded edgy and angry. She surveyed the room, not so much neat as bare. It was as if he were not staying but borrowing the space allocated to him. And yet, she sensed again a density of pressure built up that seemed to permeate the atmosphere with himself. But he looked up and at her, his eyes expressing need.

'Of course, I want to.'

'Well, then, come.'

'What about the Princess?' Marina asked, realizing that she was making excuses now. The likelihood of being trapped into extremes with Paul appeared peripherally to her. 'I mean, you might be needed.'

He sighed. 'Just now, I tried to get in to see her. Tanya is guarding the door like Cerebrus. I'll look in before bed, but I don't think she will see me. Besides, all things considered, she is in very good health.' He paused, then added meanly, 'Maybe you feel that Helena cannot spare you.' He looked wretched. 'I'm sorry,' he said. 'That was unfair.'

In the pause that followed, Marina had the desire to throw her arms around his neck and sob, being between, she felt, the devil and the deep blue sea. I do not know this man, she thought. There is no chart. She was both aware and unaware of what such a journey together might bring. 'It was unfair,' she snapped. 'Especially if you are right about what she plans to do with this book, I must talk with her. And after all, she invited me here. She has been complaining to me that I've been avoiding her.'

'Well, in fact I have just told her that I am soon going home,' he said a little wildly. 'I must say, she took the news rather . . . well.'

This sank Marina. 'You are going home? To London?'

'It seems a bit much to make one's hostess actively miserable. And Serge is seething at me because I won't play along with this obsession of his. It is probably a good thing he and I are having dinner together alone tonight. I haven't so many friends that I can afford to lose them.'

Marina found herself leaning against the door jamb, her hand to her throat like a torch singer in her kimono, then stood upright and quickly started fiddling with her sash. She realized that she had gobbled up the crumbs of the morning they had spent with each other like a real 'lonelyheart'. She had trusted both Arthur and Helena and had longed to be at one with them. Was it Paul, now, upon whom her imagination fixed? Always on the lookout for St George or Perseus. Perhaps she should have a look at the rock and chains, instead. It crushed her that he was going home like a schoolgirl who has discovered the misdirection of a valentine. 'I am sorry you are going home,' she said evenly.

'I must face it out sooner or later,' he said. She had hoped he would have said that he would see her there . . . in London.

'Well,' she said, 'Ephesus seems an awfully good idea then.' She covered the falter in voice with a bright smile.

He studied the air above her head. 'The boat leaves at a dreadful hour – five. Have you a clock, or shall I wake you?'

'I'm a marathon sleeper,' she said. 'Wake me.' She turned to go.

'Marina?' he said after her. 'Do be careful talking to Helena tonight . . .' And the strain in his tone followed her as she made her way to her own room down the hall.

XXII

IN ITS QUIET WAY, Patmos is full of wealthy people. Perhaps its defended air gives them a sense of security; perhaps the white labyrinth of Hora gives them anonymity. The Aga Khan owns no less than three houses on the island, and for a while, the Onassis family had a summer residence there. Maybe they still have. No one would ever know from the ultimate discretion of walls.

Helena had booked a table at the restaurant which reflects the presence of such international clientele, an excellent but by no means pretentious place set in a position that overlooks the west of the island. One of the chief pleasures of dining there is to watch the sun go down over the barren sweep of hills dotted with hermitages. As Helena and Marina approached The Patmian House, the panoramic view of slopes and dwellings seemed aflame with the dying glow. From inside, there was an educated murmur of voices, and as they entered, Helena vaguely recognized some of her Patmian neighbours, gentry from Athens, who had perhaps made the escape from the unnaturally early heat. In years gone by, Helena had politely refused invitations to drinks or dinner from these, pleading her aunt's ill health. Nonetheless, a kind of fealty was owed to the Princess, and from time to time, they would call, making it inevitable that Helena should call in return. This she would do briefly, punctiliously, or not at all. She surveyed the garden where they were to be seated, and was glad to see that there was no one there to whom she had an obligation. Mostly, the tables were filled with yachting foreigners. On the whole, Helena disliked being with people of her own class. Tonight, however, she suddenly felt like being surrounded with them, surrounded so that she might be protected from saying too much to Marina or from saying anything at all in too loud a voice.

Marina was going to Ephesus with Paul the next day, slipping through her fingers like water. The thought that he would be leaving soon afforded her more relief than she could say, but to imagine them off alone together in Turkey was like a neat, impaling pin around which she was helplessly forced to revolve in an almost preternatural pain. What could she do? She could hardly suggest that she accompany them.

To suggest to Marina that the projected trip displeased her was not only a social impossibility, but a glaring psychological error. Far better, she thought, to put on the air of detached interest. 'He wants me to see the house where the Virgin was assumed into Heaven,' Marina had said, her eyes sliding away in clear evidence of guilt. 'Ah, the Great Artemis – the Great Mother,' Helena had replied, adding, at Marina's faint look of indignation, that in addition to the Christian Shrine, the goddess was a sight not to be missed.

So, they seated themselves at a little table in the courtyard, invisible from the street. In the hidden, muted ambiance of the restaurant, it was almost impossible to believe that by day the island crawled with tourists. A woman whom Helena recognized as an opera singer sat a few tables away from them, and near her sat a Greek tycoon and his scrupulously well-behaved family, who remained obediently silent while he held forth. Their own table was covered with thick damask, peach-coloured in the light of the setting sun. A shaded candle stood between them, and by them, lilies and amaryllis bloomed in a marble tub. Marina's sun-burnt face, the flowers and her white, silk shift all seemed ignited into rose colours. Her expression, however, was as hooded as the candle.

'What a beautiful place!' Marina said. She studied the menu.

'I simply could not endure another evening with darling Serge,' Helena replied. 'Leave him to the doctor, I thought. He's a head case.' She said all of this in the lightest possible tone. 'Besides, I have been longing to explore this book with you.'

Marina studied the menu harder, as if she needed glasses. 'This all looks very good,' she said.

'It is. I recommend the mezze,' Helena said. Suddenly, it occurred to her that she badly needed a drink. She rarely drank, but the medicinal quality of wine in quantities appealed to her now as never before, a potion to smooth the stark edges of Marina's obvious resistance to her. She determined to buy a good litre, of Samian wine, perhaps. She scanned the list. 'That frock suits you,' she said. 'Where did you get it?' Again, she observed that Marina was wearing white. All at once, a waiter appeared at her elbow. The restaurant was beginning to fill a bit more as the sun went down. It suddenly sank below the horizon. A German and his wife, whose thick, streaked hair was pinned up with golden combs, came and sat near them. Helena found herself thinking that the woman's appearance was common, but the couple, obviously rich, ordered champagne.

Helena and Marina ordered the mezze and wine and fish fresh caught.

'I'm glad you like my dress,' Marina replied. 'I'm not sure where I got it. I did a lot of aimless buying for years . . . I have been thinking about what you said yesterday quite a lot – what you said about a book on Arthur. What have you planned so far?' She smiled. Her hair was the colour of opals and the moon was rising over the hills, casting opaline beams over the fastness of the hills beyond. Over the water, over the sea.

Whenever Helena viewed Marina in one way, she seemed to re-gather herself at another point of definition. This way, it was difficult to trace her process of thought. Having seemed scattered, dreamy and withdrawn, she now spoke crisply. With elbows lightly on the table, she touched the ends of her fingers together as if she were about to make a trenchant point about an essay or discuss sums of money. The waiter returned quickly with the food and wine. Helena poured a glass and gulped it. She took a bite of the lightest of cheese pies and began to feel the knot in her stomach unwind.

'I haven't outlined anything yet,' she said, although this was not precisely true. 'But even before Arthur died, I had it in mind to do something about him, to put him in context. And then the idea of the biography developed from there.' This was true.

Marina ate an olive and nibbled round the stone. 'I suppose you mean to do his ancestry, his childhood, the marriages, things like that. What is going to be your approach?' Her face was impassive. Behind her, the moon was sailing higher almost immediately after the sun's plunge from sight.

'Well, there are a number of ways of tackling it,' Helena replied carefully. 'The larger part, of course, would be a critical reappraisal of his work.' She leaned back and sipped wine, golden and from Samos in the goblet, wine from the island of Hera and Dionysus nearby. 'Among other things, I thought it might be exciting to take a feminist approach – not entirely, but it is a standpoint that interests me.'

'A feminist approach to Arthur?' Marina said with a trace of irony. She trailed her fingers across the cloth and chose one of the excellent dolmades, stuffed with rice and pine-nuts, simmered in stock and oozing with lemon sauce. She took a large sip of wine. 'Gorgeous wine, Helena,' she added.

'Does that worry you? A feminist approach?' Automatically, the catalogue of Arthur's crimes against Marina manifested themselves before her inner eye as if on the screen of a word processor.

'To tell you the truth, I have been so cut off from the twentieth century that I hardly know what it is. As you might imagine, Arthur dismissed feminism outright. I take it that such an approach would highlight his misogyny, wrongs you felt he had done me, for instance.'

Helena thought it wise to deflect this last. 'I could hardly glorify his misogyny.' She chose and ate a meatball. 'Surely, you yourself do not! As for your role in his life, well ... this is where your cooperation would be so valuable.' She shot a deep, conspirator's look across the table.

Marina retracted slightly, and herself ate a meatball. She helped herself to aubergine pate, which she spread on thin bread. 'So, you mean to explore the political content of his life and work in the main? I'm afraid I know nothing about criticism and modern theories are quite beyond me. I am sure, however, that Arthur would think he was in safe hands with you, though. I do remember his admiring your literary acumen.' She paused. 'You do think highly of his work?'

This piqued Helena slightly. 'I would hardly write a book about him if there were not much to say in favour of his poetry. No, my thrust is not mainly political, but it will contain that aspect. Just any old anodyne stuff would not serve Arthur's reputation. Nowadays, these questions must be addressed, believe me.' She speared a small fish drenched in oil.

'But you are doing his life?' Marina paused and drank some wine. 'It would be quite colourful, you know. I think Arthur's life was colourful. He didn't write like Byron in the least, but I think he had an unconscious identification with Byron, you know, his limp, Greece, or rather, Greek mythology.' She flushed. 'Then there were the women. You, Jane, I ... perhaps there were others. I think it would sell very well.'

'Oh, Marina!' Helena really was stung. 'Marina, I hardly see it as a commercial venture. I had it in mind that you ...' She was not angry, oddly enough, but hurt. To disguise this, she polished off her glass and poured them another.

'I'm sorry. I simply meant to say that it was a good idea for a book. Perhaps I am afraid,' Marina said. All the same, she lifted an eyebrow in an expression Helena had not yet seen.

'Afraid of what? Afraid of what I might say about you?' She knew this had come out as hauteur, but she felt pain.

'Although I deserve it, there is nothing very agreeable about having one's sins exposed,' said Marina. 'Nor one's life, for that matter, one's privacy.'

'I have no intention of exposing your relationship with Arthur as a sin!' The German couple looked around at the sound of Helena's explosive hiss. They were eating fish, detaching flesh from bones.

'So, Arthur takes the blame in that case.' Marina seemed undeterred.

'My darling Marina. . . .' she started and surprised herself by this tender expression, and thought to herself that it really was only an upper-class affectation anyway, 'why blame anyone? What is the point? You seem to see everything in terms of shame and blame. It's too ludicrous for words! I could only portray you as having a guilt complex.'

'My guilt *is* complex,' Marina sighed. 'Guilt is a very complex thing.'

'I never feel guilt,' Helena said, and she realized this was true. 'If I make a mistake, then I make a mistake. That's too bad. Put it in the past. I think my mother died of guilt. I think it killed her. She felt guilty at surviving my father, though God knows why. She was very religious like you.' She did not know why she had digressed in this way. She realized that Marina reminded her of her mother. It was odd. They both had a little gesture of flinging out their hands when they spoke, as if bracing themselves for a fall. 'But I do not want to write about the sort of thing that so preoccupies you. I do not want to write about guilt, but about writing itself. I see Arthur in terms of his vision and there are traces of that vision in you.'

'Helena, I embodied Arthur's vision, as you call it, for only a very little while. If I had known who I was, where I came from, where I was going, if I had only known who I was, I would never have allowed him to do it.' She paused. 'All I am asking you is that you do not make me out to be something that I am not!'

'Does one allow a poet to sing one's praises?' Helena felt a little buzzed by the wine. 'You did not allow it. It happened.'

'I was a Galatea in reverse! He preferred the statue. And I'm not even sure that is true! Sometimes I feel that the *Cycle* had nothing to do with me at all. But I don't want revenge on Arthur. I don't want to be glorified at his expense.'

The waiter brought them sticky couscous and fish, barbarous, bloated-looking creatures that were nonetheless delicious. They both drank more wine and set about eating the fish. Marina's passion over the book was oddly healing to Helena's earlier wound. What was more, she could not seem to help but reveal more and more about her relationship to Arthur and his work. In the pool of shaded light from the candle, she felt held to the same orbit as Marina. However great were the ellipses they severally travelled, the centre of them both belonged to dead Arthur.

'Look, Marina,' she finally said, after the charred skin of the fish had been removed to disclose its delicate flesh, 'why is it you seem to assume I would write a fiction about you and Arthur?'

Marina discarded her backbone and put her head to one side. Perhaps she was not simply attempting to be fair. Perhaps she was listening.

Helena continued, taking a bold approach. 'I am beginning to think that the truth about your marriage to Arthur lies somewhere in the religious differences between you. I am sure you were in full flight from your upbringing when you married him, just as most people are at that tender age. But as you grew older, your true character emerged as very separate from Arthur, who was already quite formed when you met him.' She was pleased to watch Marina's interest deepen. She felt like a gypsy reading a palm, astonishing its owner with the obvious. 'As it happened, you turned out to believe after all, and it put you in one hell of a pickle. I'm quite sympathetic to the fact that it must have tried you sorely to dance barefoot on that particular griddle. You had to reconcile two completely opposing views.' She shrugged.

'That is true . . . and it's very helpful, Helena. Thank you,' Marina said, although not in that earnest manner of gratitude that had seemed to be her wont.

'What is more,' said Helena, waxing and enjoying yet more wine, 'all this self-flagellation you go in for strikes me as odd, considering what you have already suffered at Arthur's hands. Open your eyes, Marina!'

'I suppose the inference I must draw from what you are saying is that I enjoy punishment. On losing Arthur, I recreate the situation . . . is that it?'

Helena looked up into Marina's clarified eyes. For a moment, she was struck by the raw intelligence of the woman, and it was a quality she had not expected to find. 'Isn't there an element of masochism in Catholicism? There certainly is in Orthodoxy.' She found she had turned this corner without knowing it, and felt a subtle thrill of danger at the cliff's edge. 'Women who care are inevitably the losers. I'm not accusing you of some perversion.'

'I'm very glad to hear it, Helena,' Marina replied. Marina had withdrawn into her chair. She was white as the moon behind her – blanched in spite of the sunburn. 'I would find it disquieting to say the very least, if you were to write that about me. What, do you think, women win when they do not care? Or what is it they fail to lose?'

'Allowing oneself to be verbally assaulted by an obscure poet is not my idea of caring!' Helena snorted this, glad at the whiff of this particular battle.

'Did you care for him, Helena?'

Automatically, Helena drew herself up at this impertinence. Marina played nervously with the backbone of the fish on her side plate. 'It's important,' she added. 'Did you care what happened to him? Do you care now?'

Helena disliked this line of questioning extremely. 'I care about the truth,' she said. She looked for more wine. The bottle was nearly empty and so she refolded her hands, thirsty still and wanting to upset things somehow. The tension of the last few days had been, she suddenly saw, unbearable. 'Don't assume you have the moral high ground.' She could not help sounding surly and truculent. She felt a kind of troubled adolescent furore within herself.

'Oh, Helena, I'm not!' Marina cried softly, squeezing her eyes shut. She dropped her hands into her lap, an expression of exhaustion. 'And I'm sorry if I have seemed that way.' Helena blinked at the apology. 'The point about my guilt is that I actually did wrong, and though I may have ended up damaging myself in consequence, my actions destroyed Jane Holt and a family. Jane Holt took to drink after Arthur left her, wrecked her liver and died. Did you know that? You did know that, didn't you?'

Helena was quite taken aback. 'God! No, I didn't know that.'

'Well . . .' said Marina, looking relieved and as if they were gaining ground after all. 'You see? Am I really the victim of some Papist plot? I deeply regret having hurt her, and having done so, it put an appalling pressure on the marriage to be – I don't know – a blissful and eternal honeymoon.'

Helena thought of Jane suddenly. She had not thought of her, except as Arthur's unsatisfying wife, for years. A model but unsatisfying wife, a real trudger and plodder. She had forced a move to the Home Counties out of a pathological need to be middle-class. The children had done gymkhanas and Jane had treasured her herbaceous borders. Arthur had never disclosed his reasons for marrying Jane in the first place, and Helena had never thought to ask. Before they had had children, she had done something . . . what had it been? Ah, yes, Helena thought, she had done languages at university and had translated some of Arthur's poems into French and had sold them as a collection to Stock, in Paris. They had had a party with the French money. On having her first baby, she had become a total womb. Helena remembered sitting in Jane's drawing room (there was no other word for it) at the height of her affair with Arthur. She had observed its house plants, its feathered sofas with distaste. Sunday lunch . . . Jane had always liked a foursome and would dispense coffee with full ceremony. She would 'pour'. Helena raked the cold ashes of her memory for episodes of Jane drinking. Had she had the odd glass too much? Cosseted a bottle near the Aga? It was extraordinary to think of her stretched out dead with a cirrhotic liver. It was a wildly incongruous vision. One might as well see Mrs Tiggy-winkle roped into the Mafia. At best, she had been a mother-figure to Arthur, chivvying him into clean underwear and visits to the dentist. The idea of her passed out cold seemed almost risible to Helena until she saw the plausible vindictiveness in such slow suicide. Now that, from Jane, would be entirely possible.

'Did you ever *meet* Jane?' Helena asked. 'You see, I knew her very well.'

Marina shook her head. She looked very subdued.

'Well, I shouldn't go on berating myself on her account. I can promise you that if I do the book I shall have a lot to say about *that* situation.'

Marina's eyes stretched slightly, but Helena went on, fired with an interest in Jane's self-immolation and its corollary in Marina's. 'The marriage was a hopeless cause long before you knew him . . . and though it's sad she had to die in that way, she could well have done so without your assistance. Deep down, she was a very boring woman, not a fit consort for dear Arthur.'

Marina muttered something. She looked slightly mad, as if she were talking to herself or prophesying on the Tube. 'What did you say?' Helena asked.

'Nothing!' she paused. 'Actually, it was something. It was. I was wondering about the great crime of being boring and the heavy penalty it seems to draw down upon itself. In what way was Jane more boring than I am?'

'Marina, you are not boring!' The wine Helena had drunk spilled into this expostulation, making it a free expression of feeling. 'Jane was into matching towels.'

Marina looked uncomfortable for a moment. 'That is not the way I sensed their marriage,' she said after some deliberation. 'She loved him. That is what her children say. And at base, I always thought he loved her.'

'What do children know?' Helena extended a hand with a broad sweep.

'Do you have plans to talk to them? Henry and Claire?'

Far, far above them, the sheen of the moon in the sky all but dimmed the stars. Constellations began to pick themselves out beyond the tranquil air. Marina's bosom swelled with a sigh like that of a heroine, Helena thought of *The Blessed Damozel*. 'I would never hurt you, Marina. I could never,' she said softly. 'You seem so afraid.'

'Helena,' Marina said, 'I have no authority at all over what you intend to say and, in a sense, Arthur made himself public property.' Her words had an edgy pomposity and she gathered and ungathered folds of napkin in her hands. 'But I do have a responsibility over his papers. He left stacks of journals and unpublished poems . . .'

'Have you read them?' Helena had not meant to be quite so forceful.

'I have not, and until I have, I do not see that any discussions about a biography can be fruitful or realistic.' She let the napkin go and folded her hands on the table, quite composed.

'What are you suggesting?' Papers! Arthur had left journals, poems!

'I am suggesting that neither of us yet has evidence to back up any of these conjectures about him. I am also going to put it plainly to you that I have strong feelings about Henry and Claire, about what I owe them. Jane was their mother, and though she may not have been an exotic dancer, I cannot and will not cooperate in any project that starts from the premise that she was only a middle-brow, middle-class housewife.'

'Are you bargaining with me?' An impact of outrage hit her.

Marina looked straight across the table at her. 'Yes. Yes, I am. I am doing just that, bargaining with you.' Her eyes glowed. Joan of Arc. 'When he was ill and hallucinating, he spoke to Jane. He thought she was there in the room. He never recovered from her death. Don't you see? We both betrayed the woman. We betrayed the woman, after all.'

*

268

Serge looked out over the water at the risen moon. He and Paul were eating calamares at a quayside table down in Skala. There was no doubt about it, Paul did have, as he always had had, a calming effect. It was nothing he obviously said or did. He had always had a way of simply being there, abstracting himself from whatever fury Serge had given way to until it blew over. Having felt abandoned by Paul earlier, he now caught glimpses of that old and reassuring manner. They were not talking, of course. It was really impossible to broach the subject of his mother with dignity, but at least Paul seemed to have withdrawn from that new and ugly, moralistic pose he seemed to have adopted since his time in Africa. So, together, they speared little ringlets of octopus and drank ouzo, Paul watering his to an almost infinite dilution.

There was a bright fire next to the doorway of the restaurant, and dead octopi hung limp on a washline, tenderized and waiting to be grilled on the charcoal blaze. Serge had known the proprietor of the ouzerie for years. Someone in the family had been killed, but he could not remember who it had been. Bouzouki music crackled gaily from little speakers high up on the poles of the awning above them, which went flap, flap in the evening breeze. They were playing a tape of Zorba, and the elephantine rhythm picked up speed until it reached its predictable, furious pace.

Where was Lipitsin now? Far from Patmos and the dark harbour. The water lapped against the quay and slapped the little boats moored there. From the opposite hill, the huge, blue neon cross cast an oddly baleful reflection in the bay. It had always seemed like an advert to Serge and disturbingly un-Orthodox. To him, the water now had a black and unredeemable quality, as if it were crude oil or poison. He ate and drank, however, as if this were not so.

He had never had such a fight with his mother. He still could not quite believe that he had spoken and acted the way he had. Oh, there had been conflicts before, but these had always taken the form of sulks on both sides until the wind changed and all was forgiven. Somehow, he could not shrug the feeling that he had uttered infamous blasphemies against her that afternoon. Had he really told her she believed the earth was flat? Of course, he could retract. Indeed, he would retract. After all, she did love him best and had even said so. Yet inwardly, and in a very sore part of himself, he was filled with foreboding. Her eyes, her expression had shown her blown by his passion into the eye of a storm quite central to her mind. Somehow, he felt as if he had taken all her clothes off and left her exposing a reality she had always dressed in

269

symbols. And having laid her thus bare, it was almost as if she accompanied him now, released from her carnal being as a spirit more powerful than ever. She seemed to haunt the harbour in ghostly presence. He preferred not to think about that. He tried to exclude such thoughts. She was lying in bed, reading the letters or not as the case might be. And surely what Helena had always said was right, his mother had an almost infinite capacity for bullying and manipulating people.

They had ordered salad and bread with the octopus, a light meal, and Serge picked at these. Paul's eyes dreamed over the water. It had been foolish, really, to get so angry with him. Paul was Paul and had always put the brakes on. He was looking out at the harbour now as if some inner thought possessed him about the mysteries of fishes. He had often been thus in the past, trance-like and unreachable. Without preamble, he suddenly spoke, as if by intuition he had caught Serge's shift in attention. 'What do you know about Arthur Holt's poetry?' he asked. 'You said you had read it.'

'Ah!' said Serge. He suddenly saw how Marina Holt might attract Paul. Paul looked up and cocked an eyebrow at him as if in warning. Serge crumbled a bit of feta cheese onto his fork and tasted it. His anxiety about his mother rose again and held him in its throes. Holt's poetry. He tried hard to think about it. But Paul was looking at him in the old way, his eyes direct in an admission of feeling.

'You said you liked it, admired it, something like that.'

'Oh yes, I suppose I did.' He had to admit that Marina had surprised him. He had expected a seamy, corrupt woman from the sketchy memory he had of the poems. 'I suppose you mean *The Hephaestus Cycle*.' Paul nodded. 'Well, I would not think they would be your cup of tea,' he said carefully. 'The *Cycle* is a narrative of the life of Aphrodite seen through the eyes of her obsessional, crippled husband, you know, the smith god, as if she had told it to him in bed. Actually, I can't remember it terribly well. I was only trying to be polite to Marina. But the beginning of it is quite startling. Aphrodite's father was a Titan, and she was born from his severed phallus, or at least the sperm from it, as the result of some battle in heaven. That is why she is shown emerging from the foam . . . oh, it's all rather basic . . . not at all Botticelli, nor even Sappho.'

'Ugh!' Paul said, and Serge took an interest in the revulsion on his face.

'I seem to remember,' Serge continued, 'that the imagery is quite powerful. The most celebrated poem in the *Cycle* is a rather touching portrait of Aphrodite exposed. The myth goes that Hephaestus rigged up a net in order to catch her "in flagrante" with Ares. The whole thing is sort of voyeuristic and tragic because it is voyeuristic, if you see what I mean. She is seen as elemental and beyond him, but in need of his forgiveness. It's odd stuff.'

'Is it erotic?' Paul asked. His tone was impersonal, but he sat with his hands on the table, fingers revolving and tightening around each other. Serge was wondering if his mother had yet read the letter about Admiral Kolchak. Perhaps she had read them all, perhaps none.

'I myself don't have erotic feelings,' he found himself saying to Paul without thinking about it. 'So it is hard to say. Isn't that strange? Hardly any ever.' Everything safe in his head. In the mind. He lived in the mind except for the pleasures of the table. 'But I don't remember an outcry when they were published. There is a puritan streak in them in any case. The goddess unfolds, but in the end, she is rather a blunt deity, an instinct. It is as if she is all there is left in life, a blind energy, a sterile force. As if there was no faith possible to the human race save in this goddess. And that, of course, is supposed to be a huge irony.'

'Did you really like the poems?'

It was a relief to talk about something else, something that preoccupied Paul. There was Paul on his own hook and Serge smiled. 'I only read them because Holt was a friend of Helena's once.' Paul made an involuntary face at this. 'I've always had a lot of time for my cousin, but you don't like her, do you?' He supposed this was a bit unfair. After all, he had kept them apart for years in the knowledge that they would detest each other.

Paul looked as if he were about to say something, but he checked himself. 'I'm not her speed,' he said at last.

Serge could not help but laugh at the truth of this remark. 'She is a very complicated woman,' he said. 'I assume you like Mrs Holt, because everyone seems to. I do myself, actually.' He nearly added that Marina had said the only kind word to him about his hunt for the Romanovs. She had been the only one gentle enough to see it. But he decided to leave that. Taking a risk instead, he leaned forward. 'But Helena is quite obsessed with her.' The speaker was playing a loud song now, a Greek dance which Serge knew and which involved a lot of complicated steps.

'Does Helena normally become obsessed with people?' Paul asked.

He speared a ring of octopus with his fork, inspected it and put it in his mouth. He broke some bread and swizzled it in oil.

'My cousin's private life has always been a mystery to me. Who knows what she does? Who knows what she feels? She was almost forty when she broke up with her husband. I remember going to see her in her new flat. Bloomsbury, of all places! She was sitting amidst crates of books sorting them. Her face was deathly pale. I never saw anyone quite so angry, but her anger certainly wasn't directed at me. She gave me no justification for what she had done and I did not ask her to, but I rather assumed there was someone else. No such person emerged, though . . .'

Paul looked down and frowned.

'You think it was Holt? Could be. I'd never thought of that.'

Paul said nothing.

'Well, that makes a lot of sense then. Anyway, I remember her showing me an antique desk she had just purchased, worth a fortune. And actually, I thought this had replaced Mungo. She had stripped the floors bare, too, and had covered them with polyurethane. The whole place smelt of it. And Holt or no Holt, she has lived there ever since – quite on her own, and I think by choice. In some ways, she is a bit like you, Paul, self-sufficient.'

Serge half-expected Paul to be angry, but instead, he sighed. 'I'm not so sure I am anymore. I used to think I was, but I think it is what I dread the most about going back to London. That mean little house – two-up, two-down.'

He looked so sadly now out over the water, that Serge had not the heart to insist on further connections he saw between him and Helena. It struck him, though, that Marina Holt must appeal to them for a similar reason.

'Which brings me to the point of saying that I really do think I must go home now, Serge. It's been good of you to have me, but I have to face it out.'

This gave Serge a small jolt, as if he had been rebuffed. Although he had wanted Paul to go earlier, he felt loose and unearthed without him.

'It's not your fault, if that is what worries you,' Paul said.

'Marina . . .' Serge said, then wished he had not.

Paul looked away. 'I'm taking her to Ephesus tomorrow. He erupted. 'Why did Helena bring her out here?'

'You don't want to get involved,' Serge muttered, happier at this than he wanted to suppose.

Paul glared silently at the calamares. 'There is nothing wrong in my taking an interest in her,' he said somewhat hotly. 'Everyone is a little confused at the moment. Everything is. It is always best to minimalize confusion.'

It was odd of Paul to react like this. He had always kept himself to himself where women were concerned. Serge remembered his early, broken engagement, but he could hardly credit Fiona's romantic notion that Paul was a tragic hero, whose pure singleness of heart could not sustain more than the love of one woman in his entire life. 'Why should you see things in terms of right or wrong all the time?' he asked a little crossly. 'And what does Helena have to do with it anyway? She wants to write a book on Arthur Holt. That is why she asked Marina out here.'

'You yourself just now said she was obsessed! In any case, Marina did not *know* about the book until she arrived. Now I have decided to go, I feel I must tell you that much. She did not know until she had revealed many things she would have preferred not to if only she had known!' He stared angrily at Serge, but not angry with him. Serge wondered for how long Paul had been angry. He wondered if it had been a long time.

'Well, well,' he said. Serge was not precisely shocked by Helena, but it did surprise him that she should have taken quite this expedient. 'She has always been a woman of extremes. I don't know quite why I say that, because superficially she is too controlled. But I have always thought, that undiscovered to herself, she had a passionate nature.' He paused and then gave a short laugh. 'You see, it seems cruelly ambitious, but it could be just cruel. She would not see it in that light, of course. She would see Marina as something to be made sense of – you know, take it apart and see how it works like a watch. But she could be feeling all sorts of things, God knows what!' He poured himself another tumbler of ouzo. It tasted weak to him and he longed for something stronger. He hoped that Paul was not going to ask him to look after Marina. His own qualms heaved back into his stomach and he thought about Lipitsin on the quay earlier that day saying goodbye. He thought of Paul saying goodbye and felt abandoned. Lipitsin had given him an address in Athens and it was crumpled in his pocket. His thoughts went fleeing up and down that city, like shadows searching for Lipitsin into alleys, around the Plaka, around the Cathedral Square. The idea that the plan would fail seized him. Apart from his mother, there was no way at all to verify the letters, and of that Lipitsin had made him certain when he left Patmos. If only he could speak to his mother again! But he knew it was hopeless to expect this. He wondered what it was in both Helena and himself that made them the way they were. He shook his head. It was as if they had both been formed out of the same, arid intelligence, both odd, misshapen people. He sank the drink and brooded. 'Why don't you take her away with you?' he asked. 'Or why don't you stay, if that is what you are feeling?'

'I didn't say I was feeling anything,' Paul said. There he was, with his distinct, panicked reserve. His unwillingness to compromise had always made a solitary state almost a necessity. Even he and Fiona, Serge thought a little smugly, had worked out a system of give and take.

'Well, maybe that's for the best.' He suddenly saw the woman of Holt's poems burgeon out, the quintessential sexual expert, lubricious and contemptuous of masculine failure.

'Why do you say that?' Paul's voice and expression were animated by an almost desperate air, and it would have been comic in other circumstances.

'I don't know. Is she your type? Your simple life is the one you have chosen.'

'You think she is frivolous?'

'I don't know her.'

'Venus on a half-shell.'

Serge put up his hands in mock defence. 'I have really no idea whether or not she is the woman of the poems at all.'

'Well, I'll decide what to do after Ephesus, I suppose.' Paul looked horribly glum and introverted and bit his lip.

'I should be cautious if I were you,' said Serge, 'although I know that is fine advice coming from me.'

Paul gave him a troubled smile.

'I can't think what Maman will say if she knows you are going,' Serge said. And he thought about her hands upon the counterpane, skeletal and leafing through the thumbed photocopies, her white, powdery fingers sifting and weighing like fate.

She was surprised to see that Marina had such a hard streak in her nature. Her mouth tasted metallic from an odd excitement it gave her to feel this moment so acutely. In fact, every sense was heightened into a new kind of awareness of Marina, whose eyes flashed out of the darkened terrace in an utter connection with her own. Was it fear? Was it antagonism? Was it an assent to the bond between them? In that very defiance, Helena sensed its opposite. The idea that this woman should cross her opened up in her a pure emotion like hatred, and yet she felt her forces concentrate around it, dispelling mere sentiment. Her consciousness sailed cold and illuminated above the whole dilemma as if she were at one with the moon above them. She saw how easy it would be to kill someone and she felt very powerful. That Arthur had left journals, that he had left tracks, traces seemed almost a mandate that she should find them and finally do what was necessary. She was unable to think in this moment what that was, but inwardly, she knew.

'Look, Marina,' she said, 'we are only in the initial stages of this thing. I am certainly not attached to the idea of rubbishing Jane, and, after all, your feelings about her might prove very interesting. In any case, I hope you don't suppose that I would jump to any conclusions. One's education has predisposed one to back up statement with fact.' She hoped that sounded sufficiently dry, sufficiently injured, sufficiently dispassionate.

Marina was crying, and one of the Greek tycoon's children was staring at them both transfixed. 'Oh dear!' Helena said, not quite knowing what to do with this.

'Helena, I am so tired,' Marina said after a while. She reached into her handbag, took out a tissue and blew her nose. Her mascara had run and left dirty streaks under her eyes. 'I know Arthur would have wanted you to do this,' she said, 'and I'm not impugning your scholarship. It is simply a very great strain to talk about it. Don't you see?'

Helena did not see. Marina looked dishevelled and appalling. Whatever she had expected of Marina, it had not been this continual outpouring of emotion.

'You see, I think of all three of us, Jane was the most significant to him. I can't express to you why I know this.' Her voice was a soft wail.

'Never mind,' said Helena. 'It is absurd to talk about it now. As you suggest, the diaries will probably solve the whole problem.' How Arthur would have loathed those tears! One thing was clear to Helena, he had married two fools, two weak sisters. And yet, the slope of Marina's shoulders caught her throat, the nacre of pearl on her hair. She shared out the rest of the wine and smiled. The waiter came, encircling them with attentions, and the Greek family moved off, leaving the spoils of their meal behind them. Helena asked for the bill, and Marina, apparently somewhat mollified, smiled in a fragile way and fell to musing.

Almost as if Helena had conjured him, Arthur seemed there beside her, present at their meal. He jagged vivid against her mind's eye, his tall, bent form, the heavy spectacles he sometimes wore, and she was bounced back with an absolute lucidity into the day she had broken with him, but the memory of why she had done it strangely eluded her.

She had asked him to meet her at the British Museum. Or had he told her he would meet her there? On whom had she been doing research at the time? On Auden? She thought not. She had abandoned the project, whatever it had been. At any rate, they had met there one summer weekday afternoon. There were American tourists in shoals, in obedient little parties. The library had been filled to overspilling too, with American academics, demanding in loud tones the laundry bills of Meredith, editions of Marvell or Aphra Behn. It being the sixties, they wore badges of moral earnestness or plaid trousers, depending. And Arthur had swanned in with his mop of red hair in a whole dazzlement of cultural superiority to these.

There had been something to do with feelings. What had it been?

Never mind. She was wearing a dress, patterned with abstract checks, that was it. Helena had always been a dresser. Mary Quant or Jean Muir? Mungo had liberally bought her clothes. Style, boldness. At the time, nearly forty in the sixties, she had liked to put pay to the image of mousiness in women's scholarship. This was before the sackcloth and ashes had begun.

What had her feelings had to do with this? Had he hurt them? Surely not. The thrill of the affair had been its ecstasy of cold blood. It had smoked like dry ice doing things to a sealed retort. But he *had*. How? On the one hand there had been Mungo, on the other hand, Jane. Her heart. Helena's heart.

In the sixties, they had been no longer young but trying . . . Arthur harder than she. Being young had never mattered to her. Being there mattered. There were always huge parties. Quiche and brie were new then. 'Plonk', Conrans. Bumping into Edna O'Brien, the Mortimers (as then they had been), George Melly – all with Mungo. She had bought clothes at Biba. Why was she thinking about clothes now when she wanted to be thinking about feelings and about Arthur?

What had they done that day? They had had tea at the British Museum and had gone to a special exhibition not Tutankhamun. She would have remembered that. Then they had looked out autographs of famous writers. Who else had been in vogue at that time? R. D. Laing and Brigid Brophy. That was it. Brigid Brophy had written a provocative book about authors she (and some pal) could do without. Arthur and she had played this game, peering into cases and swearing softly at Americans (even though, in abstract, everyone was striving to be one in a way). Arthur disliked Keats. Helena disliked Dostoievsky. But they had argued over Emily Brontë and that had been fun and they had laughed. It was not important. Their tryst in the fusty old BM had been.

Now, why was the Buddha the occasion for what she had done? She and Arthur had wandered into the Oriental section for some reason, perhaps to get away from sticky children looking at the mummies. There arose the great column of the Buddha from the bottom of the stairwell, three storeys high. It had been a Monday after one of their weekends in Orford, or maybe a few days later, but her body had ached and she had been tormented with a sense of repletion and yet more longing. They had not touched in case they were seen and this had made it all the more exciting. The Buddha . . . neither of them had ever had anything to do with him, rose from the stairwell, his feet from a cloud or a lotus. He seemed to ascend in pale stone, his face splayed and broad, compassionate. He had a third eye in the centre of his forehead from which she derived a sense of him. His other two eyes, if you could call them that, were blank stone. She had looked up and down the long column of the Buddha, and she remembered the words 'feet of clay' coming to her quite clearly.

Why on earth had it happened? No wonder she had failed to recall it. Standing next to the Buddha had made it crystalline that she was absolutely finished with Arthur. There was no conjecture, no hesitation. It had been a hot day and the high windows had been dirty and sunny. It had been like jacking herself out into the eternal, cold stars, cutting the cord from the space ship far, far above the atmosphere. Even though she had no interest in the Buddha, nor his writings, nor his philosophy, and had only read about him in regard to T. S. Eliot, she had realized what she had subtly known all along, that any continuation with Arthur past a certain moment would be unendurable. And so, she had told him. It had been like a form of insanity, this seemingly random but crucial move. Something curious had happened high up in her nose.

The effect of shock on Arthur had soon worn off. Was she inventing it now that he had *understood* this? He had rebalanced his heel on the museum stair carpet and had engaged his interest in a Chinese bell. There was some relief to her in his having taken it with urbanity. Had he said something to the effect that it would be a relief to stop cuckolding old Mungo? He had asked if there was another man, but she had denied this and had denied sparing Mungo. In fact, from her new, high, crystal point of view, she had told him that she planned to leave Mungo. It surprised her now to realize that this had been the time she had made up her mind to it. Had he mentioned a nubile American student at this point? Marina? Surely not. But maybe he had. Near the Buddha, on one of the landings, there was a model of a juggernaut, a huge carriage with vast wheels, bearing a Hindu god.

Later, she had gone through physical torture without Arthur. She had had to get up in the middle of the night and sit very still in the dark living room sweating it out. What had Mungo been after all? A sensitive, neurotic man, afraid of Helena sexually. Arthur had become a narcotic to deal with this. Yet, how had he hurt her? She had told Marina that he had been oppressive, but he had never put her down or flaunted other women in front of her, or hit her. What was missing? Something.

It had been the year, though, when she had shorn off all her hair so for a while she had looked like a Pharoah's daughter with her well-shaped head. She had pierced her ears and left Mungo. And here was Marina, banging on about Jane when Arthur had come to her in a shower of gold, in the form of the form of the form of such riches. Helena knew that she would have to think about it now, how Arthur had hurt her, but not yet, not just yet. Perhaps the recollection of the Buddha and the checked mini-dress would bring it back. Jane! Jane, indeed! Jane had been of no more consequence to them than a dead body.

'Ah, I don't know, Marina . . .' she said. She was dealing with the bill and had fobbed off Marina's strenuous attempts to pay. Helena offered American Express. If her aunt were to die this year, perhaps she would sell the Patmos house. Helena wondered if she would find life hard to maintain. Perhaps something smaller on Naxos would do. She would prefer to contemplate the fate of Ariadne than saints frozen in their hierarchies and it would be much less expensive. 'I don't know at all, Marina. One's early plans for a book are always so amorphous. Of course, you see Arthur in your own way and I in mine, but these two points of view may, in the end, converge. Who knows?'

Marina brightened at this. 'Oh, I'm so glad we have talked about it,' she said. 'At least, we have talked about it.'

She *was* so American. As if 'talking about' things moved mountains, Americans uttered this phrase like a mantra. Still, Helena was glad that the storm had passed.

'I think I probably had too much wine,' Marina said when they were out on the pavement. 'And such lovely food! Thank you. I am sorry I got so emotional. I was up at six this morning.'

'I am sorry I upset *you*,' Helena said, although she was not. Why should Marina be exempt from the tax of all of this?

Helena realized that she had no wish to get back to the house. She was out abroad in the moonlight now with Marina and it was true that both of them were a little drunk. She felt more at home in the empty, silvered maze where in her adolescence she and Serge would clamber, little Varya puffing to catch up, as if they had all been about nine or ten. They had had night hunts. It had been a way, she supposed, of dealing with the complicated fractions of a veiled and slightly morbid interest in each other, she and Serge. The thing had been to simplify and act as if puberty had not been reached. Well, they were bored with each other now and that was the truth. She had no wish to run into him and Paul, so she led the disoriented Marina by a circuitous route, pleasing herself with the mathematics of direction. And, having been shuttled back to a time well before Arthur and the Buddha, the poise to slip like a shadow unnoticed returned to her. Along with this lost ability, the realization came that Marina's tears reminded her of her mother's continual crying after her father's death. Her mother, once so competent had become competent again before she died, but the price had been exacted. Low, stifled sobs had shuddered through the night instead of at the breakfast table, and in place of torrid prayers and the clutching of Helena to her bosom, had come grief as total absence in which her mother had been isolated. She became wonderfully fair and gentle to everyone without exception, and without emphasis too. It had been as if she became unable to differentiate between people, their closeness or apartness. She had gone to church a lot and then died. Helena had also missed him – missed her father. And she also missed Arthur. All that sentimental gush diminished it. It levelled grief to a thumbed, common thing, whereas, she thought, one should maintain one's own private door to the tomb to come and go at will and to be made marble there. They threaded their way through shadowed arcades.

'No, no, it's all my fault,' Marina said hastily.

What was? Helena could not think or remember what they had been saying. Oh yes, who had upset whom. What a ladylike exchange.

'I think it is rather soon after his death to be talking about this, you see,' Marina added. 'And you know what? I have a really bright idea.'

'What is that?' The silvery Marina in the moon sounded to Helena like a college girl with her 'bright idea'.

'I think that rather than make each other miserable with . . . so many heavy feelings about Arthur . . . I might change my plans just a little and head on back to London. You see, I could read it all and when you yourself return, we could discuss things then.' She paused. 'Actually, if I had known you had this book in mind, I would have gone through Arthur's papers before I came rather than rush off stupidly to America. Only, it never occurred to me . . .' She stood wide-eyed against a wall at the top of a flight of white steps, almost camouflaged in her surroundings. Go home, would she? The moonlight streamed over the flow of white silk, her pale aureole of hair. Apart from the illusions she was able to create, was not Marina just a little second-rate? Everything she did and said betrayed her middle-class morality, and, one must face it, taste. She had even given Helena scented drawer-liners when an interesting pot-pourri would have been far more acceptable. And the word 'betrayal' itself, the word she had used in regard to Jane did not that usage give her away? Marina had a suburban mind.

They descended the long flight of stone steps and arrived at a larger street with a blind chapel at the end of it. In the past, there had always been votive lights in that window but now they were snuffed. Her heart was exercising hard. It had developed a syncopated rhythm like jazz. Marina must not go home. 'Well, do go if you like,' she said airily, 'but as far as I'm concerned, we can drop the subject of Arthur from this very moment. I assumed the idea of the book would please and interest you, but if it doesn't, then let's not talk about it. After all, you were supposed to be coming out here for a rest.'

Marina squashed a wadge of silk skirt in her hand and kneaded it in an attitude of social embarrassment. 'Oh, no, no!' she cried, 'You were absolutely right to think the book a good idea. In fact, it's such a good idea that I'm rather bowled over by it, confused. It is only that I think I would probably think about it better on my own for a while, you know, get adjusted to it. If you don't mind, I'd like to mull over the journals myself, then I could give you a realistic idea about what the biography might involve. It would be a shame to leave this beautiful island . . .' here she made a large gesture with her hand, 'but I don't think I can really rest until I've got to the bottom of it all, the truth, as you so rightly said.'

Quite a speech, Helena thought. Marina was such a little tit-bit. She had heard a neologism for it the other day. What was it? Ah yes, such a 'bimbo'. She was chasing Paul back to England. They strolled, leaving the patch of moonlight for darker alleyways. Helena's head felt tight and large on the stem of her neck, bigger than her body. She felt a slight pricking in her brain. She thought of Paul's body, draped in a towel and quivering earlier that day on the beach. She thought of Marina's wattled thighs, her awkwardness and his, and she remembered her own elemental grace with Arthur, the thrusting force of him and then release. Together, Marina and Paul would hatch a way of destroying Arthur's journals – or the relevant ones. Had not the wife of the explorer Burton been a faithful daughter of Mother Church? Had she not torched his diaries, his erotic writings at his death? Oh, she could see them hand in hand consulting some Jesuit, who would in all probability advise them to tip Arthur's work into the sea. She thought of Marina rippling in the sea and then imagined her unclothed. The lush body and the prim mind. She could not help but be provocative, daughter perhaps, of a courtesan or whore. How had Marina been conceived? Helena wondered that now. Up against a wall by a navvy and a drunken tart? A tart with after-thoughts and scruples.

They were strolling aimlessly now over silvered flagstones and had arrived at the gates of the convent, 'Zoodochos Pighi'. As an adolescent, she had found the Greek name hilarious, but had been sharply told by her mother that it meant 'Life-Giving Source' and was a title of the Virgin. Her mother had consulted the nuns. 'Pigs in a zoo! Pigs in a zoo!' Helena had hissed to herself through her teeth, as she had watched her mother abase herself before the fat, black-clad women. It was said that they gained weight because they sat spinning all day. Helena always thought that it was cakes and secret nips of the Communion wine. Her Aunt Sonya swore by them, but Helena had noticed that they had not been exactly beating a path to her door this summer. 'They pray for me. They don't have to come,' she had said in response to this observation.

'Well, see what you think when you get back from Ephesus,' Helena said. 'It seems such a shame to come out here – all this way – and stay for only three days. You haven't even seen this extraordinary convent yet. It's rather lovely and famous in its way.'

Marina looked up at the lintel of the gate where the Greek words were scrawled. 'Well, we'll see,' she said uncertainly, uncomfortably. 'I think I have really taken on too much you know, going to New York, travelling around.'

'Are you planning to leave with Paul?' She hoped she had said this lightly and evenly. She started to stroll back in the direction of the house. Maybe she really was a little drunk. She felt she had lost control of her words and feelings and might do anything.

'For London, you mean? Oh, no. No, I . . .'

'Oh, I would have imagined he'd have asked you,' Helena said, feigning surprise.

'Well, I'm not following him, if that is what you are trying to imply!' Marina sounded defensive. It was too dark to read her expression, but she turned her head away with a queer little jerk.

'I wasn't implying anything . . . Marina you are so nervy! I was only thinking that if you found Arthur heavy going . . . well, I've heard things.' They started to ascend the claustral pathways in the general direction of the Monastery. What was she saying? She had heard nothing. Nonetheless, as they groped their way upwards, she tried to feel for some damning but untraceable word. It made her feel cold and thrilled to do this, but she told herself it was only a preventive measure against the worst malignancy of all, the suppression of Arthur's diaries. It had taken so long to dawn on her that obviously they intended this. And perhaps this was even the explanation for their exchange of significant looks earlier that day.

'What things?' Marina asked after a long pause. They were passing along a level walkway lit with streetlamps, but her voice sounded muffled all the same, and her face looked sheltered by an impenetrable expression, as if they were still gliding along in the dark.

Helena was triumphant that she had risen to it. 'Oh, I don't know. He's a bit mad, I understand. There's something very peculiar in his attitude towards women, or so Serge told me. I would have thought it was out of the frying pan and into the fire with him, but of course I may be mistaken. Not that you are thinking about him in that way. I mean, how could you at such a time?' She wondered to what depths of hypocrisy Marina would sink.

'What form does this madness take?' Marina asked. 'Is he a rapist or something?'

Helena laughed as if Marina were making a joke, even though her tone had been sharp and strained. 'Oh, nothing like that. Rapist – can you imagine! No, he simply behaved very shabbily at one point to someone I knew. Ah, it was a long time ago and perhaps he has changed. I have always thought that saints had a kind of ruthlessness.' The concept of an abandoned friend began to amuse her. 'Perhaps he was not aware of the mess that he caused . . . then Serge told me some other things and a pattern seemed to emerge. I'm sure he is quite unconscious of it.'

Marina said nothing for a while. They were picking their way up some steps that led towards the house. Out of the corner of her eye, Helena observed a preoccupied look on her face. 'So you think he is a saint,' Marina said.

'On paper,' Helena replied. 'Maybe in fact. Who knows? I always think a lot of denial goes into all of that conspicuous virtue. You know, the little dark corners of the mind get shut away, but they find a way of expressing themselves nonetheless.'

'Indeed they do,' said Marina. 'Indeed they do.'

Helena did not know how to construe this expressionless remark. As they ascended, the western wall of the Monastery loomed at them. 'Well, you ought to enjoy Ephesus at any rate,' she said. 'You can't possibly see all of it in a day, but do make sure Paul takes you to see The Great Artemis in the museum. It's only a Roman copy, but it is quite extraordinary.'

All at once, a deep, hooded memory of the Artemis, the Great Mother, came back to Helena with its many breasts and sacrifices, its rigid, archaic head, passive above its beast's body. She smiled to herself. 'She's a real fertility goddess! In fact,' she added, 'the acropolis here, where we are now walking, used to be sacred to her. I wonder what she would make of all these monks running around with their little rules and narrow lives.'

'It is not a narrow life,' said Marina.

Helena let this pass. She thought of Marina and Paul, skittering over the belly of the Great Mother of Ephesus, the Turkish hills as tumid as her breasts. How innocent they were of nature's forces! No, not innocent, ignorant of them. She thought of the famous amphitheatre, and wondered if, in Ephesus, they had not thrown a Christian or two to the lions. She rather hoped they had, and an image of blood spurting from torn arteries assailed her. How Arthur would appreciate the irony in this, his wife on pilgrimage with a new man to an old, old place. It struck her that only his mind could really have comprehended the depths of that ancient savagery and the hilariousness implicit in his 'goddess' walking there.

'Actually,' said Marina, 'you mentioned her to me before dinner, this Great Artemis. She must have made a deep impression on you in some way.'

Was there a hint of sarcasm in this? Helena could not be sure. It unnerved her slightly to think she had repeated herself and annoyed her that Marina had pointed it out.

'. . . So I shall be sure to see it. You can rest assured.'

They had reached the house. Helena wished it were within her means to invoke some deity, to enlist some supernatural power. She must, she would have what she wanted of Arthur, and of Marina too.

XXIII

JUST BEFORE DAWN, the Princess was alerted to the noise of someone moving about in the hall. A door closed and she heard the pipes clank. Someone was washing. The Olga papers lay strewn about her, as if in the wake of a burglary. She had read them. Of course, she had read them. There were no more than twelve pages of them. She had read them again and again, and there had hardly seemed any point in putting them away, for she knew she would read them a hundred times more. On the coverlet, the grey light irradiated them. Her cold right hand picked aimlessly at the sheets and then at the papers themselves. She wondered who was washing, but she knew it was not Serge. Behind the wall between their rooms, she sensed him breathing, the suspiration of a soul in expectation.

> Of course you know Papa and I were very close. What with Maman's death, we have become closer still. How he loved her! And what terrible lies they told about her! Darling Alyosha has been in such agony this past week that we all long for the time when he will be released to join her. She was an angel, and is an angel now, I am convinced. Poor Papa is becoming very confused and thinks she is still with us . . .

It was like table tapping or some horrible witchcraft, calling up the dead.

> It seems to lack gratitude to God to say that sometimes one wishes things had happened in the way they said. Alyosha was too ill to come to Papa's funeral, and I think his own end is very near. We have our Russian priest, of course, but I dare not tell even you his name. Tanya and I had to lay Papa's poor body out all by ourselves, as we do not trust anyone. The funeral was private, but we shaved his beard because we were too afraid that someone might see him, recognize him and tell. Dunyasha went all the way to Toronto to buy us black dresses from a large department store – clothes so anonymous that no one could tell that we are who we are. I can barely write to you about Papa. Seeing him on his bier clean-shaven recalled to me the time at Tsarskoe Selo when they took away his epaulettes. In death, he had

the same immobile features, and the peace on his noble countenance made me happy that he is now at rest . . .

Why could she not believe? On first reading, she had embraced the letters with tears, as if Olga had actually been there, reading them to her.

> . . . Alyosha died last night of a major haemorrhage. He called out for Maman and for Father Gregory . . .
>
> My own darlings know so little of the pain we have suffered. I want to tell them. I long to tell them, but they do not yet know who they are. Nicky must go to school this year. We have decided that engaging a governess would invite too many questions. In one way, this woman who claims to be Anastasia has helped us enormously. I actually wonder if it is not a part of X's plan. You see, I cannot bring myself to write the name of our saviour. Perhaps it is a plot to draw off the scent from us and the woman is a hired actress . . .

And on they went. It was as if Olga poured out her soul, not to Cousin Anna, but to the Princess herself. Imprisoned in a prairie town, she seemed to shelter there in the minutiae of daily life recorded. Olya had learned to cook. Marie had learned to garden. But the letters were streaked with lines of terror that stood out as bold as bars. The patience of Olga was there. The sensitivity of Olga was there. The piety of Olga was there, but it was not Olga.

What was she going to do? There was nothing, no word which she could pin her doubts upon. At first, the letters had seemed flawless, the details perfect. Even the handwriting looked credible. There was an old-fashioned style to it and the Princess could almost feel the nib of her school-room pen in her hand. The letters were partly in Russian, partly in English, the language which the Romanovs had spoken at home. As for the writer's diction, it seemed highly appropriate to a person of such noble birth and feeling. There were the right words for pain and the right words for suffering, the right words for endurance, and it almost crushed the Princess's heart to read them. But how did she know it was not Olga? There was some detail, some little thing. It was as if an insect disguised on the leaf of a tree had flown up in the flash of a second. She still doubted she had seen the flaw.

Earlier, she had had Tanya ring Athens in hopes that Father Nikon would be there. He would have listened and would have known the truth of what to say. Now, she tried to imagine him in his cell on Mt Athos. She could see his face frowning into his white beard, fanning snowy on his chest, his pure hands in prayer. Perhaps he would be praying for her. Perhaps in his wisdom he could see her dilemma.

She knew what he would say. He would advise her to crush the serpent's head, that father of all lies, and undeceive Serge about the letters. But how, when she had no proof, and when she longed so painfully to believe in them herself? She longed to believe, but she could not believe. What was there? There was something.

Through the wall, she heard Serge groan and thrash upon his bed. A dilemma more painful had occurred and kept occurring on and off throughout the night, this time, a truly sleepless one. If only the dumb spirit of the Archduchess would cry out to God and save her son! The martyred girl. Slowly, she reached for her prayer-book, but knocked it off the bedside table. It lay sprawled open on the floor, its thin, thumbed pages squashed. This seemed ominous to the Princess. She was unable to pick it up and tears of frustration and fear collected in her eyes. Surely, with faith he should be able to see that Olga had not really died at all, though dead. Were the saints powerless? Was the authority of God Himself to be mocked? Perhaps she should not even wish for Olga to have been spared. Perhaps that wish itself was the result of diabolic action in her soul.

It was all very well to follow this line of reasoning, the sort that Father Nikon might use, but the fact remained that her son had no faith. Oh, he would make the sign of the Cross all right and would attend various liturgies with her in order to appease her, but he failed to see the radical aspect of the supernatural world, how they were all surrounded by the unseen being of God. She struggled with this thought for a moment. If one did not see it, then how could one possibly surrender the dead to death? Let go of them? Their spirits could only be protected by fame in men's eyes, by history, by the selective remembrance of history. And if so, what should happen to those not crowned, not fabled, not starred by genius or good fortune? The Princess supposed that she herself would go unchronicled . . . but she was drifting from the point, the crux upon which she most suffered. If Serge had no faith except in Olga and the royal progeny of Olga, then what would happen to him when and if she failed to authenticate the letters? Did not God temper the wind to the shorn lamb? Did God break the bruised reed? With that umbilical connection she should perhaps have broken long ago, she sensed his fruitless anguish through the wall. They all expected her to denounce the letters, but expected her to do so out of base motives, out of obstinacy or out of superstitious awe. But it was worse than that – more serious than that. She could neither perjure herself nor destroy Serge.

What was the evidence? Where was the truth? It was something so small. She picked up the wedge of papers again, then let them fall. Even if she found the mistake, what would she do?

On board the excursion boat at dawn, Paul and Marina watched Patmos disappear from view. The engines churned and shuddered. There was an oily swell and the smell of the sea. Even though an expected party of holiday-makers had failed to materialize at the exact sailing time, the boat had got away punctually, leaving the decks virtually empty. A few sad-looking Turks stood about, evidently returning home. A Canadian woman, who spoke a fluent sort of pidgin Greek, had been very much exercised about whether or not the boat would make the return trip. She wrangled with the first mate on the deck, who assured her with much Aegean shrugging and philosophy, that the boat would be back in Patmos by midnight. She made it her business to inform Paul and Marina of her findings, as if they had sought the information. She was a tall young woman, bold and angular, with frank eyes. She had an independent air and was travelling with two men, one of whom, she said, was her brother.

'I wasn't really worried about it,' said Marina to Paul. 'Quite honestly, I dread going back, especially after last night.'

The morning was cool with a wind and the sea was choppy. Wavelets slapped briskly at the hull and spume shot up. As the sun rose, the froth shone like crystals. Very soon, even the Monastery with its vast bulk looked tiny on the horizon.

'Was it as bad as that?' Paul asked.

'It was awful!' Marina shuddered and from the railings of the ship, she bleakly regarded the sea its agitation. Her mouth and eyes felt gummy from the wine she and Helena had drunk at dinner. 'Do you think they have any coffee?' she asked him somewhat wildly.

He laughed. 'I'll go and see.' He made his way uncertainly across the rolling deck and vanished into the cabin.

He had woken her at first light from a deep sleep, and she had been shocked to find him standing over her. For a moment, she thought it was Arthur returned, wanting his breakfast. She had been dreaming about a woman hidden behind an old gate with a curious, round window in it, and the figure had been rapping insistently with gloved knuckles.

As soon as she had realized that it had been Paul who had gently shaken her shoulder, she had been overwhelmed with relief. Her first impulse had been to cling to him, for the dark character in her dream was familiar to her psyche as her mother. Instead, she had leapt up with apologies and had hurriedly dressed without the slightest attention to her appearance. Together, they had left the house as if fleeing in order to make the sailing time. Now she felt she even looked like a refugee. She ruefully grabbed at her hair and rummaged in her handbag to see if she could find anything with which to repair the night's damage. Finding nothing, she shrugged. She should have welcomed Arthur. If Arthur were to come back, she should welcome him. Swimming into consciousness now, she wanted to swim back where this thought would not occur, and where the fresh lesions caused by Helena the night before could not throb as they were beginning to do now. Resolutely, she decided that she and Paul were both owed a nice day. Whatever Helena thought of him, she liked him.

He returned triumphantly with two scalding cups of blackest coffee and even some hunks of bread. They sat under the lee of a little corner on benches out of the wind and quietly consumed their modest meal.

'That's better,' she said. 'I'm sorry, I must look a fright.'

He had been thinking, however, that he liked her this way, without artifice or guile. He had been annoyed that he had had to enter her room and wake her, but on seeing her asleep, he had felt a shaft of tenderness towards her. Her slumped form had made her seem almost ugly, her dreaming face had held secrets, an absorption so profound that it had seemed a sin to wake her. But, as he had jostled her into life, she had given him a look of surprising, deep familiarity, and it stayed with him even now. There was something about Marina that made him feel he had always known her, such was her immediacy. 'You don't look a fright,' he said dryly, thinking she was fishing for a compliment. She had an irritating narcissism, and it annoyed him. 'How did things go then? In what way was it awful?'

Marina blew at her coffee. 'We talked about the biography,' she said. 'And I told her about Arthur's journals, thinking as you said that it might give me a measure of control over the situation.'

'Well, it does, doesn't it?'

'It should.' Marina closed her eyes. Helena seemed vividly present to her. 'But it seemed to have the reverse effect. The very knowledge of the diaries seemed to send her quite out of control.'

'What? Did she rant and rave at you?'

'Hardly that. It was her face, the atmosphere. I felt as if I had thrown a switch. What could she and Arthur have meant to each other? I felt as if there would be no stopping her now.'

'I'm sure she can be stopped,' said Paul firmly.

'How? I suppose I could burn his journals or forbid her to look at them. In fact, in the end, I did impose a kind of condition. But I can't see being able to use that threat and it is not what I mean by "stopping her" in any case. I suddenly saw it, sitting there with her in that restaurant. She will go to any lengths to repossess him. If he is there in black and white, in her words, she can have him as she wants him. I know she thinks I am chiefly concerned about what she will say about me and I am concerned about it, I suppose, but that is not what frightened me, what disturbed me. The minute I told her about those journals, I felt her plunging headlong into Arthur.' Marina felt wonderfully lucid all of a sudden. The ship rocked them gently. The wind was dropping and there was the soft creak of ropes. 'I am convinced that whatever lay between them was quite terrible . . . and so, she must have him, she will take him, and she must distort him and his life in order to make sense of him to herself.'

'Marina, you are not an object. You can't let yourself be used to that end.'

'I have no choice,' Marina said. 'It is the last and probably the only decent thing I can do for Arthur.' Suddenly, she felt freer for having uttered this out loud and for having really meant it. 'But I do not know how long I can take her awful intensity and I don't know how I shall ever . . .' she did not know how to put this. She had been about to say that a successful book on Arthur would trap her within his confines forever. 'I don't think I shall ever be able to talk about him with her again,' she said instead, lamely.

'But you said you had imposed a condition.' He swallowed the dregs of the coffee.

'Oh, I don't know . . .' Marina said, sighing. 'I suppose it came to a head in that way. We started talking about Arthur's first wife, Jane. I told you about Jane. Well, Helena had not known how she had died, or even that she was dead. The only reaction she seemed to be able to muster was a kind of contempt for the poor woman. The point is that I went in for that attitude myself when I ran off with Arthur, to ease my own conscience, I suppose, and maybe that is why Helena made me so angry. I told her I would withhold the journals unless she promised to be fair. After all, I have Henry and Claire to consider. She seemed so callous!'

'Look, Marina,' Paul said briskly, 'if Helena cannot claim objectivity about Arthur, she should not write about him unless it is a memoir or a straight work of literary criticism. She has no business prying into your life or into the lives of his family. Surely, she should know this.'

'Should, should, should!' Marina cried, flailing her hand out. 'Like Arthur, Helena seems to feel that the laws of the universe are not based on moral imperatives unless, of course, they apply to other people's behaviour towards themselves!' She looked away. 'I'm sorry, I should not have said that. It probably is not true, but it is the way I felt last night. I could not appeal to her reason. I felt there was no way of acting reasonably with her. I know it sounds crazy to say that about someone so cerebral as Helena, but that is how it seemed.'

'Actually, it tallies with something Serge said about her last night. And I can't help but feel I misguided you yesterday when we spoke about the book. I should have kept right out of it.'

'Misguided me! You saved me!' Marina felt a little wild. 'At least it is out in the open now. And it gave me a perfect excuse to get away. In the end, I told her that I had to go home and read his journals myself – now, without further delay.' As if she had been spinning and spinning throughout this conversation, she suddenly stopped, wobbled and faltered. 'I hope you don't . . . I mean, I'm sorry. I mean I don't want to horn in on your departure.' In an agony of embarrassment, she wrung her hands on her lap. She was aware that she should never have begun to justify her decision to him.

Paul both looked and felt suddenly uncomfortable. It made him nervous to think of Marina at large in London. Would he be expected to pay her court? All at once, she appeared to his inner eye in an English context. He supposed he might take her to a concert or a meal, but the idea of this made him feel constrained. Somehow, he could see her frozen in cultural attitudes at the Festival Hall, or toying with a bread roll in a restaurant that he could ill afford. Against the London skyline, her sorrow and beauty would transpose themselves into a different key. He could imagine thinking her self-pitying and blowsy, a drain on his meagre emotional resources.

'I am sure it is a wise decision,' he said in an impersonal tone.

She said nothing. For a horrible moment, he thought she might cry.

'When do you plan to leave?' he asked, ashamed of himself now.

The idea of her leaving Patmos had been implicit in all that he had said about Helena.

'I'm not sure,' she said. She rose and jettisoned the plastic coffee cup into a bin, then turned and walked to the ship's railings.

Was she angry? He most certainly did not want her to be angry at him. He felt convicted by his conscience. Here she was, alone in the world with no one to befriend her. He pictured her forlorn on the boat back to Athens, abject on the airplane back to London, hesitant, a little lost, humiliated by the failure of her visit to Helena and threatened by her. Why could he not simply be loyal to her? Generous? He did, after all, like her and he was, in fact, moved by the curious dilemma in which she found herself. He himself would not have wished to have to make the choice she had to make, between becoming prey for Helena and obscuring her husband's name. He rose and joined her, somewhat sheepishly, and together they looked out at the calming sea. The sun was rising higher now and it looked as if it would be a very hot day. 'We could go back to London together,' he said.

'Oh, no, no, no!' she replied, hastily. 'I'm sorry, I hope I didn't give that impression. In any case, I think I must choose my time carefully. I think I offended Helena and I really cannot afford to.'

He knew, however, that his hesitation had hurt her feelings.

'I tell you what!' she said brightly. Why don't we meet for a drink sometime back in London. When Helena herself returns and the plot thickens, I shall need all the help I can get!'

He melted at her false brightness. It seemed like a little flag of courage she was showing in the face of her own precariousness. Somehow, too, he liked the idea of meeting Marina in a wine bar or pub. He could almost hear her breathlessly recounting the exploits and predations of Helena in the shaded lights of evening. By the river, they might sit and unfold the thickening plot. 'That's a grand idea,' he said, 'Nonetheless, it seems stupid to travel separately, and I suppose I ought to stay on to keep my eye on the Princess as well.'

'We'll see,' she said, and tilting her chin upwards, looked out to sea. Paul wondered if he had not been arrogant in thinking she wanted to be with him. A bleak mental image came to him of his own front door in London. He had let his little house for a year, but it must be vacant now. He imagined the junk mail silting up the hall and the clammy rooms. His brother Rufus had agreed to check out the property from time to time and perhaps he would have done. More likely, he would have sent Julia. He could see Julia squirting 'Pledge' over his desk and tables, her hands impersonal on his things. She was grateful, he knew, that they had never married. Rufus suited her and they had been very happy together.

As for Marina, she looked at the shifting, deep, blue water beyond the churning foam of the boat. It was so like her, she thought, not to think through the implications of things. Always she had trapped herself in sudden words or actions. She had thrown herself at Arthur, all right, as if he had been a Beatle. And here she was, with a virtual stranger, leaning on his proffered kindness like an arm, offering the availability of her empty nights to come, arranging things so that London became a new point of focus, egging relationship on, orchestrating a prelude perhaps to romance. All of a sudden, it hit Marina what a task reading Arthur's diaries really would be. That was another instance of her impulsiveness, saying that she would do this. Another instance still, had been her trust in Helena. Whatever occurred to her, she did; whomever she met, she embraced. She could hear Arthur saying that. She could feel him thinking it, and found her shallow heart accused by him.

Marina tried to contemplate the deep. In places, the sea seemed almost purple in the growing calm, 'wine-dark' as Homer had described it. Well, she was unfurling her sails towards Troy. Homer, Agamemnon, Arthur, all might have made this trip, taken this route to the Anatolian plain. He had travelled widely in the Greek archipelago before their marriage and had been to Turkey. He had spoken of Turkish delights, of veiled women with mysterious eyes. Perhaps even then, he had been dreaming on Aphrodite, the giver of an ambiguous reward to Paris, and Helen, the cause of the trouble.

Helena. The coffee and the breeze were clearing Marina's head. Helen. Helena. Oh dear, it was opening and would not stop. Helena, Arthur, the diaries. She could see Arthur at his desk, a modern, deep-drawered, high-tech thing from Heal's, writing, exploring, exposing, exploding her own carefully treasured myth that somehow, despite her inadequacies, he had loved her. Maybe he had written another poem – a long epic. Maybe he had written about Helena.

And what would he have said? Oh, she had strewn his ashes on the sea, all right, but what lay buried and corrupting in the desk? In the dreaming moonlight of the night before, Helena's face had been livid with emotion. Passing down a long flight of stone steps by a little chapel, Marina had wanted to rush into it for sanctuary against that pitched and terrifying need, that awful intensity. For a moment, she had thought that Helena was going to push her against the wall, pound her and bloody her. It had been an atavistic fear of animal instinct as if at the approach of footfalls in the dark. It was this irrational feeling that lay beyond the sense of what she had told Paul, a curious kind of panic. Perhaps it had not been a nostalgia for Jane at all which had drained the life-blood from their marriage. Perhaps it had been Helena all along. Marina shuddered.

'Is it too breezy for you?' Paul asked. Why, he wondered, had he made her withdraw into herself like this? She was fretfully picking at her hands, her wedding ring, revolving it. He had noticed her doing this before. In fact, she did it all the time. She responded to his question with a quirky little smile, and it reassured him.

'No,' she said, 'I think it is going to be quite hot, in fact.' The fresh salt breeze played with her hair almost skilfully, as if it knew what strand to curl and whip across her brow. Despite himself, her strange, transient beauty moved him and suddenly, he saw the aptness of that association with the goddess of love that her husband had made.

There she was, framed by the hills of some nameless island they were passing, bathed in the aureole of rising and burning sun which pierced the mist so that it seemed pregnant with light. All of a sudden, she seemed almost incandescent to him, hardly substantial, like a spirit or bird hovering out over the water. It came over him in a wave of feeling, which he would have called the pain of nostalgia if he had ever experienced anything like it before. How could her husband have written what Serge said he had written about this woman? Paul found himself struggling to get a grip. He had not read the poems, but he would read them. His first act on British soil would be to go to the library and get them out. He felt as angry at their putative coarseness now as he might have felt at a dragon which had captured her and which he had to thrust through the heart.

'Marina?' he found himself saying, surprised that he had spoken at all and only half-aware that he had.

'What is it?' she asked. She turned her head to him, and the curious inflatus that had surrounded her profile left her. Again, she looked almost ordinary, an attractive, middle-aged tourist on a boat trip to Turkey.

He faltered around for something. 'Marina, did you *like* the poems your husband wrote about you?' As soon as he said this, he realized that he really did want to know. He wondered if anyone had ever bothered to ask her before.

She put her head back and thought for a moment.

'I'm sorry, I don't want to put you on the spot,' he said and did not.

'I never really thought in terms of liking them,' she said at last. 'They frightened me and I did not really understand them.' She flushed. 'I could never really associate them with myself. They are very powerful . . .' She was blinking hard and looking at the deck. 'Arthur was a genius,' she said. 'There is not a shadow of a doubt. I'm just stupid,' She fussed around with her handbag. 'You know, if there is coffee, there must be a "ladies". I think I'll freshen up. Can I bring you another cup?' And she fled into the ship's cabin.

XXIV

IN SOME WAYS, Helena was pleased to breakfast alone on the terrace and relieved that Marina had left the house. In another way, she felt obliquely crushed. She was certainly angry and more than a little disappointed with Marina. Apart from anything else, it was part of a pattern of slovenly manners she had observed. Bad manners, actually, to go skiving off to Ephesus for the day without even including her in the invitation. Not that she would have accepted. Helena supposed that Americans were lax about these things.

Helena rarely drank and she had slept soundly for the first time in ages from the wine. She had a little headache now from an excess of it. She sipped her coffee and bit into her roll, then noticed that the lemons were ripe on the trees at the end of the garden. Her mother had put a pretty cluster of them near the wall. She made a mental note to ask Dmitris to pick them. They were so fresh, they would almost taste sweet. Evangalia and Tanya had been almost churlish to her this morning. She could hear the to-ings and fro-ings on the stairs as they tended to her Aunt Sonya. It was a relief to Helena that she would not be taking up battle-stations in the garden. From Tanya, she had received the intelligence that her aunt was sticking to her resolve not to see anyone or to move from her room until Sunday. On this day, Tanya said, she would require some form of transport to take her to the sacred liturgy at the Cave or failing that, the Monastery. She would hear Mass said, she would receive Holy Communion and then she would deliver her opinion on the papers. Helena sighed. How like her aunt to make a ritual out of the whole thing. How like her to manufacture mystery and then reveal it. Most women of her age, she thought, would be pleased to be included in an historical project like this one. Not Aunt!

'Lenochka!' It was Serge. He came into the garden carrying the paper, the post and a cup of coffee.

'Don't call me that! You know I hate it! ... You're up bright and early.' She noticed that he was sober. His hands were shaking.

'I know you hate it. I couldn't resist. You look like the old "Lenochka" – like you did in the old days – when you had secrets.'

She blinked at him like a cat.

'I can't bear this tension, you know!' He flung himself onto a rarely used chaise longue with a little fringed awning. He lay there and closed his eyes. 'I did not get a wink of sleep.'

'No vodka?' she asked.

'That's my old Helena! Out of sorts today? The divine Marina off with poor old Paul?'

'Shut up!' she snapped.

'They are probably discussing us now – this minute – judiciously, compassionately. Don't you think?'

Helena shrugged.

'Paul thinks I am mentally unbalanced. Not that he has said so in so many words.'

Helena shrugged again.

'What do you think? Do you think I am unbalanced?'

'I think you are bored and I think you drink too much, maybe because you *are* bored. I can't think why Russia obsesses you.' She waved a hand. 'You've never actually been there. In fact, you have always seemed more English than Russian to me. Why do you want to restore the Tsar? The whole thing is meaningless now.'

'You read those papers! You even suggested to me that you thought they might be authentic.' He urged himself slightly from his sprawl and sipped coffee. 'God! I feel awful!'

'Well, there might be some truth to them, I suppose, but I don't know how much of it you can derive from photocopies from a concealed source. But that's not the point. The point is, surely, that it doesn't matter. What do you want the Romanovs *for?*' Helena heard her voice crack with irritation, but it sounded distant to her. Her mind was on the boat to Ephesus and Marina.

Serge sat and looked at his cousin with an obscure gaze she could not quite fathom. 'What do you mean "for"? Do you mean what use are they?'

'There's a Greek king,' Helena said. 'Constantine. No one wants him back. What point would there be in getting him back? It's an outmoded concept. The British royal family is a waste of money.'

'That is not what I mean. What use is poetry? What do you want poetry *for?*'

'For kicks,' Helena said. She found it hard to concentrate on what Serge was saying.

'You're impossible!' He lay down again, supine. His lashes fluttered on his cheeks. 'What do you and I really want, Lena?' he asked.

She thought of the prow of the boat, plying the Aegean, Paul and Marina discussing her. 'Oh, I don't know. Very different things, I imagine.'

'We do not belong to the world as it is, Helena,' he said with a little gasp. He sat upright again, this time, swinging his legs off the chaise and clasping his hands between his knees. 'Our grandfather was a feudal lord with a little kingdom. I am not saying it was a good thing, but it was a true thing. It is a disappeared world, like Atlantis, sunk without trace almost overnight. It is as if you and I had been hatched, not born at all! We do not come from anything real. The English have at least gently eroded. You and I were just stopped.'

'I've always voted Labour,' Helena muttered.

Serge laughed aloud. 'Helena, you are such a fraud! As far as you are concerned, everyone is a peasant but a few chosen souls. My bad character has, at least, given me some insight into that! It would be hard for a person like me to see himself as anyone's "better". But the whole thing stems from our being displaced people. We have been kept from the common life because of our ancestry, but in the present tense, we have had to muck along like everyone else.'

'You! With Fiona's fortune! You make me laugh!'

'Our grandmother wore diamonds big as pigeon's eggs sewn into her ball dress . . . no, it is the psychology that counts. We have the psychology of masters and the condition of slaves. We are dependent. I depend on Fiona.'

'Well, you won't when Aunt Sonya dies!' she said sharply. 'Despite her meannesses, or perhaps because of them, I feel you will inherit a tidy sum.'

'Oh Helena! You are deliberately misunderstanding me. We have no authority.'

Helena gave a short laugh. 'Speak for yourself!' she said. Her eye was not on him but the lemons. 'You could have a better life! You could have done something with yourself. You simply chose to abdicate when Uncle Boris died. Not that I blame you. I put all of this down to Uncle Boris. All of it! Your father, now there was a little tsar if you like!'

Serge groaned. 'Why does anyone put up with you, Helena?'

'I tell the truth.'

'Then you don't mind hearing it?'

Again, she shrugged.

'The fact is that I'm quite aware I could have had a better life. For God's sake, I've been up all night thinking about it! But I think it's a bit much your implying that you have authority while I have not. All you are in stronger and cleverer than everyone else, and you hold yourself aloof from people because you actually think you are superior. That is not what I mean by having authority and it is not what I want out of the Romanovs. If they held themselves apart, it was because they thought they were consecrated. They had meaning to themselves as anointed beings. You like power.'

He was half-smiling. 'What a lot of junk!' she said. The Tsarina was mad and the Tsar was a fool, quite a combination! There is no divine, so there is no right. They were playing at kings and queens while Russia starved.'

'Helena,' Serge said patiently, 'I hold no brief for their behaviour, but I honour the reasons behind what they *thought* they were doing. If anything, you are the family autocrat. You are the one who plays the Tsarina here. I simply want to find one – Olga. I want to see myself in some sort of context . . .'

'You want power yourself!' she snapped.

'I don't. I want to understand our exile. Who better than Olga and her children could tell me about that?'

'You want "to sit upon the ground and tell sad stories of the death of kings,"?' Helena asked archly. '*Richard II.* You sound like Richard II, a little out of date.'

Serge put his head in his hands. 'Helena,' he said after a while, 'why have you never been able to see what matters to other people?'

'That's rich, coming from you!' Helena replied. The tone of the interchange was not charged with feeling, but waspish. 'What your mother feels about all of this is clearly of no consequence to you. It is hardly as if you did not know what an emotional subject it is for her, her "friendship" with Olga, her meeting with the Tsar . . .'

'Helena! It is you who have consistently told me that I let my mother dominate my life. Where *are* you in all of this?'

'Look!' she said. 'There are other things! I was in love with Arthur Holt, he is dead now.' And she felt the shock go through her of having given away a confidence that she had not fully betrayed to herself.

'Oh, Lena, Lena,' he said after a few moments. 'How did you get yourself into this mess? Having his widow to stay?' He stood and went to her, put his arm around her hard, smooth, little head, and kissed it. 'Poor Helena,' he said.

She would have liked to have responded to her cousin, but he had said some things that hurt her. He quickly released her from his embrace.

'We were talking about Holt's poems last night, Paul and I. He was asking me about them and it forced me to remember them . . . Helena, has it ever occurred to you that they might not be about Marina at all?'

'What do you mean? It was the reason they married. He must have started on the *Cycle* at the end of our affair, right after he met her.'

'Those poems are never about that woman!'

'How do you know? Poetry is usually not *about* anyone in any case.'

'Helena,' said Serge, 'I know we are first cousins, but there was a time when I had an eye for you myself.'

She was jolted by a weird certainty. 'You mean, you think they are about me?'

'I don't remember them well enough to say, but as I was trying to evoke them to Paul, it suddenly struck me in a half-conscious way that for a character study of Marina, they are certainly way off the mark. Then, just now, as you were saying you loved Holt, it clicked. I am sure she was a beauty when young, but never a primordial goddess, not that one. Is that why you left poor old Mungo? Because of Holt?'

Helena said nothing. Her heart beat with a slow and heavy thud and her hands shook. Arthur? she thought. What an exquisite revenge his doing that would have been. My God, she thought, to sustain twenty years of loveless marriage in order to get revenge . . . She shook her head, denying this possibility. In any case, would she ever find out? She said, 'Well, by your own admission, I am hardly primitive, being, as you say, a closet aristocrat.'

'Oh, but you are, my darling. Dorogaya. You are as barbarous as an ancient queen, complete with racks and torments. I did not say you were common, but you are primitive. I can see you lopping off heads. In fact, I can see you sharpening up your axe now. Leave that poor woman out of it, Lena. Let her be.'

'What do you think I have in mind to do to her? Whose head have I cut off before? I've left yours intact, in spite of all temptation.'

'I really do not know,' said Serge. 'It is simply a feeling I have about you. Whatever it is you have in mind, don't do it!'

She had put up with this – all of it – for old times' sake. The enervated railing had always been something like a summer game they had played. In earlier years, they would sit on the terrace and snipe at each other aimlessly, without its having any effect, but now she felt a sudden anger at her cousin dominate her whole thought. If he was so sure of his powers of observation, why could he not see into the folly of his tsarist ramblings. Into her relationship with Marina, she was sure he could not see at all.

'Suppose Lipitsin denied you access to these famous Olga papers you are so keen on? Suppose your mother denies that they have anything to do with Olga? How will you feel about that? What will you do? You know very well I have planned a book on Arthur. Last night, after I had bought Marina dinner, after I have brought her all the way out here and lavished her with kindness, she told me that she would not show me Arthur's journals and unpublished poems unless I promised, in effect, to let her edit the material. Wouldn't that put you in a rage?'

He shrugged. 'That's not it, Lena.'

'It bloody well is!' she shouted.

'I can't contend with this,' he said, running his fingers through his hair. 'I know you so well, Helena and you are a very odd fish indeed. I think I will have a drink after all.' He picked up his coffee cup and left her alone in the garden.

She screwed her eyes shut. 'I hate this. I hate it so much,' she said. She breathed deeply and quietly through her nose, a technique that she sometimes used to quell rage. Sometimes, these storms struck, with colleagues, with students, and even for no really cogent reason she could name. As children, she and Serge, during that brief period before the war when they would visit each other and play, would do each other down, face each other out with whose temper would snap first. It had terrified gentle Varya, who had later admitted to Helena that she had dreaded trips to England with her mother. Of course, the Mirkovskys had stayed in England during the war itself, after Helena had been sent to Canada . . . Why was she rambling on to herself about that?

She sighed and bent to sip the cold coffee – only dregs in the pottery cup. She squinted at the headlines of *The Times*, which was always a day late, but which was delivered anyway, at some cost from Skala. And then, on the wrought-iron table, she spotted the post that Serge had brought in. In all their squabbles, they had forgotten about it. She picked it up. There were a few bills in Greek, an air-letter to her aunt from Varya, and then, she saw it – Marina's news. It was in a large, fat, expensive-looking envelope covered with air-mail stamps and stickers. It was addressed to 'Ms Marina Holt'. Helena turned it over and over in her hands. The return address, 'Ashton Associates', was discreetly embossed in the upper left-hand corner, and the letter came from New York. Helena made to put it down again, then thought, Oh,

Christ, that's it! She turned it around in her hands once more. Then she thought perhaps it wasn't. Perhaps it was from Arthur's American agents, then again, she thought it was not. It was, surely, the firm of private investigators Marina had hired. She weighed the letter in her hand as if to guess at the contents. Well, Marina would be late home tonight. Helena thought about it again. She put it in her pocket. It was quite heavy and must contain a good deal of news. Had they found her parents? Her mother? Surely, it was too soon to tell. These searches sometimes went on for years. Whatever it was, Helena decided to keep it with her. She supposed she would give it to Marina in the morning.

At the Turkish port of Kusadasi, Marina and Paul had their passports checked by a suspicious-looking official, who stood with military stiffness under a florid portrait of Attaturk. At least, Marina assumed it was Attaturk, for she vaguely remembered his name from a history book. He frowned down upon them in a statesman-like fashion, but his rich, flowing moustaches made Marina think of a production of *Cosi Fan Tutti* that she and Arthur had seen at Glyndebourne. 'Women Are All Like That' Arthur had translated for her. The two heroes of the opera, dressed in Turkish costume, had twirled their false moustaches and sung of the fickleness of her sex. Even though Arthur had been in a benign mood that evening, even though they had dined from a hamper on the lawn, Arthur had truly believed that women were endemically faithless.

Perhaps it was true, Marina thought. The giddy Fiordaligi, trilling and tripping through her arias in clouds of wig and rococo dress, had reminded Marina of a time before marital wars when she had been escorted to balls by the scions of rich families. She had whirled and waltzed and had been spoilt for choice in the matter of suitors. She had not so much sacrificed this memory of her power for her marriage, but buried it undead. Often the urge to be admired had broken past her conscious will. She cast a sidelong glance at Paul and hoped that she was not using him as a mirror. Towards the end of their journey, they had watched dolphins leaping and feeding and playing near the boat and a spontaneous gaiety had seemed to catch them up in each other, almost as if the fish had been a sign. He had removed his hat lest it be blown away and the breeze had ruffled his hair and freshened his complexion. Together, they had delighted in the snorting, muscular fish, who had almost seemed to smile benisons upon them, and she had felt buoyed by the presence of Paul, who had made her feel young, and attractive once more.

When the official had stamped their passports, they were herded into the presence of a guide. Paul protested, but he seemed an inescapable adjunct to their visit. Ephesus itself lies a few miles inland from the harbour and so they were coralled into a minibus along with the Canadians who had been on the boat. The guide was a heavy-set, middle-aged man with a gloomy appearance, and he pointed out the elegant, eighteenth-century fortress of Kusadasi as they set out. Marina looked about her, inspired by the sense of being in so foreign a place. The Canadians talked among themselves. The woman seemed to be the binding force in the trio. Both her brother, whom she strongly resembled, and their friend, a man with a bushy, red beard, appeared to defer to her, and listened to her remarks in a docile, attentive way. They were trying to determine whether or not they should return to Delos, which they had evidently much enjoyed. Yet, as the minibus left Kusadasi with its minarets, the woman abruptly interrupted the flow of conversation and turned to Marina. 'Do you realize,' she whispered, 'that you are the only other woman I have seen since we arrived in Turkey? Do you think the men keep them under lock and key?' Marina was a bit nonplussed by this remark. She had not observed a lack of women in Kusadasi, but she supposed the Canadian woman was right.

They sped out, up a curved thread of new road upon which there was no traffic. The guide praised it extravagantly and spoke of the importance of tourism to Turkey. He explained how ancient wonders and modern progress were perfectly combined in his country. There were deep pine forests on the hills, almost navy against the azure sky.

The guide seemed to have worked out their itinerary according to a set plan and when they reached Efes, the modern village which bore the name of the ancient city, he told them they would first make for the Agora. The Canadian woman complained that she wished to see the Artemision. They had visited, she said, the birthplace of Artemis in Delos, and now she wanted to see her major shrine, one of the seven wonders of the ancient world to be sure. The guide explained that it was merely a column in a swamp these days and that she would find the market place more interesting.

It certainly was too hot for anyone to fight. By degrees, it had become grilling, just as Marina had predicted on the boat. As they disembarked from the minibus, the impact of the sun seemed almost alarming, and it was an effort to walk the short distance from the road

303

to the once huge, but now ruined city where ghostly struts of column and white, toppled capitals lay wrecked.

Marina had forgotten to bring a hat in the excitement of getting to the boat on time that morning. A trickle of sweat escaped her brow and dripped off of her nose. 'Oh, I wish I had a parasol!' she exclaimed and the Canadian woman laughed. She had a slim, athletic body and looked cool in shorts.

'Where is your scarf, Marina?' Paul asked. She rummaged through her handbag, but it was not there.

'It is a 102 degrees today,' the guide said, obscurely proud, it seemed, of this extreme.

'I'm so chaotic,' Marina said helplessly to Paul. Her flowered dress was sticking to her at the bodice. At her waist, a belt nested in her flesh.

'Here, have my hat,' Paul said. She shook her head, but he took it off and placed it on her hair. 'There!' he said, 'you look very smart.' It crowned her head, perching there. As he touched the wiry filaments of her gold hair, he felt again a sharp desire for her, this time, bordering on desperation.

She laughed and thanked him and cocked the hat at an elegant angle. 'We'll share it,' she said, 'as we go along.'

They stood at the top of a long and ancient street. The marble pavements stretched intact down a long hill and terminated at the façade of a ruined building with graceful arches, which rose in skeletal fashion against the sky. The sheer size and obvious importance of the city lay spread before them, delicately defined in its remains. 'Why, it must have been enormous!' Marina cried.

The guide smiled at this affirmative remark and launched into an explanation of the site and the history of Ephesus. It had been founded by the mythic Amazons, he said, inhabited by Ionians, Lydians and Persians. The legendary King Croesus, it seemed, had helped to found the Temple of Artemis. The guide spoke of the Roman presence in Ephesus, of Caesar Augustus, of Domitian, of Hadrian, and of the buildings they had caused to be built on the very spot where they stood and where they would walk.

Perhaps because of the heat, there were few tourists about. Everywhere Marina looked, some relic of antiquity loomed or leaned. Somehow, the town seemed newly abandoned to her, as if in the fierce glare of the sun they were the first witnesses after a nuclear holocaust. So fine and wide were the empty streets, so lofty the buildings, that it appeared to Marina as if she were in a dream. Heat wavered over the marble slabs in a phantasmogorical way. It was here that St Paul had come. St John had been here, and the Virgin Herself was supposed to have lived here. Marina found it unimaginable that she should be walking in the footsteps of the Virgin. She tried to think of the Virgin going to market, shopping here, but she could not. She could only think of Arthur in the furnace blast of rays, incinerating in his coffin. She adjusted Paul's hat, feeling unworthy of the loan of it. It gave off a musky, pleasant scent of him and she thought maybe she should take it off.

Despite the ministrations of the Turkish guide, Paul was reading a guidebook, which he had purchased in Kusadasi at the port. He read with furrowed concentration. 'This is the Street of Curetes,' he said. 'Down there is the Library of Celseus, that big, marble façade . . .' He showed her the picture in the book. The photographs were blurred. Their arms touched and they looked at each other. As if fused in the heat, they stood for a moment, unmoving. Marina was alarmed and cleared her throat. 'It all seems a little unclear,' she said, gesturing at the book. 'Let's go and ask the guide.' He had gone on with the Canadians and was half-way down the street. As if hearing Marina, he turned and beckoned them to follow and they continued down the columned way.

'Oh, look, that must be Hermes,' Paul said, himself uncomfortable. He pointed to a bas-relief of the naked god, who held a caduceus in one hand and stroked a ram with the other. The graceful guide of dead souls, accepting sacrifice, perhaps. Paul searched Marina's face, shaded by the hat. Her wiry hair, escaping it, shimmered in the heat, fine-spun, unearthly.

'Come and see the brothel,' the guide said, sniggering.

The sun, striking marble, rose in waves of mirage. 'We are walking the earth as spirits do,' Marina thought. She felt unreal in the molten fury. Paul reached out his hand and touched her waist as if to support her and she felt a jolt of pleasure then of guilt.

'You will slip on these stones in those sandals. Those sandals!' he said.

The brothel was a tumble of fluted columns and distended brick arches. The guide muttered something about the god Bes or Priapus and promised to show them his statue later in the museum. Marina thought it embarrassed him to speak of such things in front of women, for his tone was more coy than smutty.

It really was too hot to see the site properly and they flitted from shade to shade, trying to avoid its blistering rays. Marina returned the hat to Paul, who took it only on the condition that she should have it back when she wanted it. Even the Turkish guide seemed taken aback by the heat and he commented on how unusual it was for this time of year. 'It has been terrible,' said the Canadian with the red beard, which must have prickled him fiercely. He started to recount some tale of furnace temperatures in Crete and talked in a rambling way about global warming. The woman in shorts smiled continuously, like an archaic kore, Marina thought. 'You are going to get a terrible burn,' she said to Marina, and produced a tube of Ambre Solaire from her rucksack. She briskly smeared some on Marina's face and exposed forearms.

Paul thought of the touch of her waist. I am taking advantage of this woman when she can least resist me, he thought. I am no better than Helena. And his head became irrationally filled with a sharp memory of shiny birds of prey, busy atop the body of a child. Their sleek feathers had glowed with health. Alone of the creatures of Ethiopia, they had seemed healthy.

'Thank you,' Marina said to the woman. They briefly inspected some Roman public lavatories, a neat row of privy holes near the brothel. The guide said there had been running water through them, plumbing in ancient times, and he proceeded to discuss aqueducts. They trailed after him, past the ruined library with its civic Roman arches, and drifted down a long, marbled way set at neat right angles to the imposing main street. The guide described the library. He described the Romans. He described how the sea had come up nearly all the way to this spot and how the greatness of Ephesus had depended on its harbour. There seemed to be an interminable walk past long walls with stubs of columns based upon them. 'It must have been a very fine street,' said Paul. A few vast Corinthian capitals lay about on the ground nearby. They were twined with acanthus leaves so ornately carved that one might have imagined bees to visit them.

In her mind's eye, Marina saw vistas of columns intact, a grand promenade with a broad, mercantile sweep. Suddenly, the idea of St Paul made his way into her crowded thoughts, as if elbowing through them to her conscious mind. All at once, it seemed to Marina, very brave of him to have taken on this rich city. She could see him, a little man, vital and waspish, hectoring a bored and cynical populace on the evils of idolatry. 'Just imagine,' she said. 'Imagine St Paul preaching to the Ephesians! It must have been like going to New York and telling people to stop making money.'

Paul laughed and she laughed with him, then it came back to her how she had seen Wall Street topple in her mind's eye when she had visited it no more than two weeks ago. The thought of New York made her feel ill at ease and she put it out of her mind. She looked at her feet. 'The pattern of these sandals is being branded on me,' she said. 'When I took them off last night, I saw that my feet were all criss-crossed.'

Paul thought of her naked, branded feet, her aureole of hair.

He jammed the hat on her head again and she ducked but laughed and accepted it. 'Your turn,' he said.

'It was stupid,' she said, 'to have forgotten mine.'

At length, they arrived at the Amphitheatre which swept up a hillside, immense with tiered rows. The guide, once more taking things in hand, began to instruct the small group as to its seating capacity. 'It was here that gladiators fought,' he said, 'and it was here that the artisans who made images of Great Artemis assembled and made riot against St Paul.'

Marina struck out for the centre of the stage. She stood there solemnly for a moment and thought of wild beasts tearing at limbs, of clashing swords and spouting blood. Against that, the ardour of St Paul's courage seemed to speak boldly and it made her feel ashamed.

'If you had met me, you would have been horrified by me,' she said privately to the saint. 'I know I shouldn't have got mixed up with Arthur in the first place, and I certainly shouldn't have married him, not that you would have recognized it as a marriage. You would have had me stand up to him at the very outset, die resisting him. Instead, I just went along with everything. But once I was there, do you think I should have left him? I always thought he would feel so terribly abandoned, but I suppose I'm just making excuses for myself. The only trouble was that I felt too guilty to give myself fully to him and too guilty to leave him, having caused all that havoc in everyone's lives. Forgive me for saying so, but I wish I could really have loved him.' And she tried to envision the saint who had been taken up into the seventh heaven.

'If you speak only in a natural voice,' said the Turkish guide, making her start, 'the others will be able to hear you.' She looked up and was surprised to see that Paul and the Canadians had climbed far above her into the tiered seats. 'The acoustics are very good,' he said. He seemed pleased with the erudite word. 'Go on, say something!' He smiled at her in a nice way.

'Hello,' she said obediently. 'Hello, Paul,' she said, 'Thank you for the hat. Can you hear me? Hello,' she said to the Canadian woman, 'Thank you for the suntan lotion.' Her remarks seemed lame and feeble things to say.

Paul sat in the shade of the fourth tier and heard Marina's voice. She stood there, small and far away from him, alone, save for the guide, and with loose hands at her sides. 'We shall see what we shall see when we get back to London,' he said to himself. 'There's no point in rushing things.' But there was something pitiful about her standing there, diminished by the size of the arena. He could imagine her as an early martyr with lions, but this romantic notion irritated him. 'Hello, Marina!' he called back, smiling despite his reservations, which had caught him once again. From this vantage point, he could also see the dried-up harbour and the strewn marbles of the ancient world, which jutted like insignificant gravestones of strangers long dead far below him. The sky was almost white with heat, as if there were no atmosphere anymore between themselves and the sun.

XXV

HELENA SAT at her escritoire, but she did not write in her journal. She was trying to read the book in front of her. A slight breeze blew in at the window. The sun had passed its zenith and was on the other side of the house. Evangalia had annoyed her by asking for the afternoon off in order to help her sister with her niece's wedding, but she supposed it made the house quieter with the kitchen empty of servants. Tanya, she knew, was with her aunt. Earlier, Helena had heard the muffled sound of a quarrel in the hall, Serge's voice, strained and sloshed, at odds with Tanya's fierce hiss. A while later, she had heard the clatter of his feet on the stairs and then the slam of the big front door. Helena had kept well away from that. She imagined Serge had gone on a vengeance binge. By nightfall he would be incapable, slumped, she assumed, in the arms of some other votary of Dionysius, who would probably ensure that he got home. Through the walls, she heard the faint sound of stentorian snoring. Maybe he had returned already, or maybe it was her aunt. It was an odd, monotone noise, quite unpleasant. Helena decided to ignore it.

It was a struggle trying to concentrate on her book. Almost at random, she had decided to do some work on Auden. She did not know why, but she decided that she ought to change the emphasis in her lecture on him in the coming term. Above her on the shelf lay her copy of *The Hephaestus Cycle*, but the idea of re-reading it repelled her. It was to shut it out rather than to let it in that she leafed through the paperback before her, but sitting down to it, she found she could not make sense of even the most well-known poem.

> 'Lay your sleeping head, my love,
> Human on my faithless arm . . .'

She drifted from it, thinking how Arthur had admired Auden once. He had admired Yeats.

> 'Time and fevers burn away
> Individual beauty from
> Thoughtful children, and the grave

Proves the child ephemeral:
But in my arms till break of day . . .'

Had they slept like that in Orford? She remembered waking in the inn to the shock of hair boyishly dabbing his face. His features had not seemed heavy then. Either he had had a curiously light beard or he had cleverly shaved closely, but he had always had the appearance of being smooth-skinned, and this had added a piquancy to his domination over her, the way he could make her entire body weaken and collapse.

'Let the living creature lie,
Mortal, guilty, but to me
The entirely beautiful.'

Had he been entirely beautiful? She had certainly not seen him as guilty – immortal, rather, perhaps. He had seemed fixed, not mobile in time, when she had first met him. He had always smoked a lot, which made him thin. She had found herself crushed next to him at a party, then Mungo had introduced them. Rings and wreaths of smoke had circled him wherever he went. Later, Mungo had suggested they invite Arthur and Jane to dinner. There had been a lot of long, cotton dresses about at that time and Jane had worn one of them, sprigged and with ruffles. Helena had once been a good cook, good at 'daubes' and 'ragouts' long simmering. Everyone seemed to eat in the kitchen in those days. She and Mungo had a pine table from Habitat and Helena had bought a formidable 'batterie de cuisine'. She kept it glinting. She kept it polished. Arthur had challenged her throughout the entire evening. He had got wind of it that her aunt was a Russian princess. At the time, he was getting a lot of poetry published, in the *TLS*, *Encounter*, the *London Magazine*, the *New Statesman*. She had known the colour of blood in her veins, all right, when she had got through with him.

After that, she and Mungo and Jane and Arthur had met fairly regularly. He had never seemed attached to Jane in any sense at all, but completely beyond her. He had had a potent and furious mind. Especially after Jane had engineered their move from London, he had sometimes asked her to read drafts of his poems and comment on them. Mungo had been rather pleased that the lion had favoured her critical judgement so. And from time to time, he and she had met for drinks alone when he came up to London. It had been really casual and loose-knit, they had shared the same world.

Helena could not really remember the crisis into which they had fallen or how. But of course, she did! Things had reached a head in a pub, somewhere smart, she could not remember. It had been long before wine-bars. Where? Never mind. It had been around Christmas, she did remember that, for it had been freezing cold and he had helped her on with her coat and his arms had caved around her, and she had caved into them. What had been sudden, agreeable and boozy had turned into inflexible decision. Then and there, it had fallen out in perfect pattern on the floor before them like a concealed rug opening and showing an exotic design. His face had been pale. He had been vain about his looks. It had never crossed her mind that it was not the right thing to do. It had just been there, there it was. Mungo and Jane were excluded by the very fact of its existence. Thinking about it now, she realized that neither her husband nor his wife had ever found out about them, nor had they ever suspected, she was quite sure of that.

Imagine Marina trying to get at her over Jane! Even Mungo had said she had been no match for Arthur! Arthur had been ebullient, charged with energy. He radiated thought and became quickly bored. It was almost impossible to call up Jane's image now. She had been a thin, fretful creature with pale, wispy hair, enamoured of her children. Sometimes at dinner, she would escape the table and take refuge in them on some pretext or other while plates congealed. Or was she hitting the bottle in secret? Arthur never blinked at this and would continue to hold forth. He had always loved good company, and it had initially surprised Helena to hear Marina say that they had seen no one and had had no friends.

Why had she told Serge that she was in love with Arthur? She had never claimed to be in love with Arthur, nor had she ever said 'I love you' to him. Were those poems about her? Certainly, they were not. She felt both sick and delighted to conceive of that possibility, bald, and priapic as they were. She had never seen them quite that way before. Applied to herself, that was how they felt. Had she been of another age or in a another social milieu, her reputation would have been in ruins.

Helena was sure it was not so. She ploughed on with Auden. Why Auden now? Well, why not? Working at the scheme of poetry soothed her. Working oriented her. Crosswords and geometry. Rhythmic and a-rhythmical tones. Had Arthur had Auden's restraint. . . .

> 'Soul and body have no bounds:
> To lovers as they lie upon
> Her tolerant enchanted slope

In their ordinary swoon,
Grave the vision Venus sends . . .'

Oh, she had forgotten Venus. She had forgotten Aphrodite embedded
in there. Had he been working on the *Cycle* during their affair? Surely
not. Would he have mentioned it? He had loved her long back and her
shining fair hair, her slender figure, her irreducible fastidiousness,
surely not barbarity. But he had mentioned that line about Venus, that
stood out crucially in her memory. Oh, but there had been no boundless
soul and body with them. What gravity of vision had there been? What
had the goddess sent . . .

'. . . Of supernatural sympathy,
Universal love and hope; . . .'?

What had been the context for his mentioning this verse?

'While an abstract insight wakes
Among the glaciers and the rocks
The hermit's carnal ecstasy.'

Of course. Now she recalled it and Orford too, when it was and why
that Arthur had quoted this poem. Presumably, her unconscious mind
had led her to take up the task of Auden on this day rather than to
plunge into the *Cycle* for further clues. In any case, she knew it by heart.
With its burnings, with its blood-soaked goddess, with her sacrifices,
and her wolfish, terrible beauty. Wringing the sheets, she had cried out
for Arthur. It had not been *a* night, but *that* night (among many other
nights) when a conflagration had appeared to her in a dream and
everything had gone into it. She had been gleeful at the bonfire of
Mungo, her safe marriage, her dead mother, her father's airplane which
had gone down in flames. In this one night, orthodoxies of every kind
had been burnt, a space in which soul and body truly had no bounds.
She had woken feeling boundlessly powerful. She had not told him
about the dream.

She had known never to give him that dream. Everything on fire,
herself purged and irradiated.

They had sat together at breakfast, Arthur tucking into an enormous
meal of eggs, sausages, bacon, tomatoes, toast. He had been so thin he
could eat anything. (It distressed Helena that his face had become
rather portly. She had thrown away his obituary picture). Helena had
had the sensation of being a fire-eater eating with another fire-eater. A
nibble of toast and a sip of coffee had partaken of the dream in some

312

way, and she had remembered the tale of Shadrach, Meshach and Abednego walking in the heart of the furnace. No affectionate mutterings, no sentiments had passed between them and of that she had been wholly grateful. They had eyed each other like practised acrobats across the table. Of course, she had not been in love with him.

After this combustible collation, they had walked. She had felt linked to herself at last, and if Helena had ever had a sense of holiness, this had been it. At last, at last in touch. Young people were taking drugs at the time. Helena felt young and on drugs. They had walked to an old tower, a medieval keep with a wicket gate and a National Trust leaf and a box for pennies. 'Soul and body have no bounds . . .' ah, yes. Had the Auden poem come then or later? Whenever, she had thought he had meant to emphasize the faithlessness of his human arm or to mock her awesome swooning of the night before. 'Grave'. 'Visions'. No, it was not that. Venus-sent-them-what? Oh, it was all too long ago, and it blurred in her mind. The main, empowering thing had been that she had surrendered without giving anything away. She had found out what she had wanted to know. Through him, it had been revealed. Arthur, limping, had dragged his foot up the slope to the tower. Ah, now she remembered the limping. It was important to remember the limping because of what had followed. Arthur had known unconsciously about the vision of fire that Venus had sent, for when he had mentioned it, she had been sure, not of universal love and hope, but certainly of his supernatural sympathy.

Here Helena abruptly stopped. She put a flat, polished stone on the pages of the book to keep them from ruffling in the breeze that came into the window. She stood and paced a bit, then crystallized her mind on his maimed claw of a foot. It was a mangled, stunted portion of himself that needed to be dealt with. Arthur's sexual needs were only too palpably bound up in the misfortune of his foot. Limping along, he had told her of his cold, pious mother with her vaulting social ambitions, his dry, pious father, who had beaten him, out of justice, of course, for small flaws. He had told her too of the livid, frustrated sexuality he had felt running as a malign undercurrent through his parents' suffocating marriage, and then they had reached the tower where he had bought a guidebook. Together, they had climbed laboriously to the top of the keep and there he had read to her from the leaflet, there, he had discovered 'The Merman of Orford'.

She could not recall all of the details from this distance in time, but it seemed to Helena that the townspeople had discovered a feral man in the Middle Ages. He had lived by the shores of the inlet and had survived by catching fish with his bare hands. He had been wild and naked, covered with matted hair, and he had been unable to speak. They had taken him into custody, thinking him diabolically possessed, and having deliberated at length what to do with him, had finally subjected him to an ordeal. If, they reasoned, he failed to acknowledge the crucifix, the case against him would be made. They produced it, he ignored it, and they had him put to death. Helena could not remember how.

So that was the reason Arthur's ashes had been scattered there, that was why his body had been burned! The story had had a profound effect on him, Helena remembered, and flinched at the memory for some reason.

She returned to the escritoire and looked down at the fluttering leaves of the book, not wanting to read any longer of how

'Certainty, fidelity
On the stroke of midnight pass
Like vibrations of a bell.'

She snapped the paperback shut. It was pointless even to attempt to think of Auden when Arthur had so . . . so . . . humiliated her. Why on earth did she think this?

Helena sat quite still, her elbows on the little desk, her fingertips touching. It was as if the concept of humiliation had arrived unbidden to her conscious thoughts where it lay sprawled on the floor of her mind like an operatic ingenue ruined by a rich young wastrel. If it had not run counter to the truth of the situation as she had perceived it then, and as, indeed, she perceived it now, the clear image of her own degradation would not have startled her. She began to think that her reason was becoming unmoored. To herself, slowly and aloud, she said, 'It was I who ended the affair. It was I who broke off all communication with him. It was I who remained in control throughout.' And, almost antiphonally, as if another voice were to be heard in the matter, she repeated the words in a whisper.

Twenty years ago. What had happened? It was like trying to remember the war from which she had been absent. It was like returning to a razed London confused with bouncing jeeps and rubble, as if a disturbing power of magic had been at work. Perhaps that was how Serge felt about not knowing the Revolution, about not knowing what had hit them. And she felt a momentary twinge of pity for him.

After Arthur, she had reconstructed her life so radically that virtually no trace of the self she had been remained. She had excised all inconvenience. She taught, she wrote, she oversaw the doings of her Russian family. She ferried back and forth from London to Patmos, Patmos to London. And all the while, brimming in his desk, lay the corruscating evidence of Arthur's point of view. Perhaps it contained nothing at all of her, not reminiscence nor stanza. Perhaps it cruelly exposed her. Either she would never know, or Marina would know too.

Walking to the tower, he had limped. They had climbed the medieval keep. Over the battlements, they had gazed out at the inlet, and caught up in the drift of Arthur's power to see, she had almost caught a glimpse of him, the Merman, scuttling naked on the farther shore, an obscure, baboon-like shadow, spearing fish with his long and filthy fingernails. She was possessed with a shudder of horror. No, it was not as if Marina stood between them, it was as if some primal cause had made her necessary.

Without really thinking about it, Helena's hand went to her pocket where Marina's letter lay. She took it out and put it on the blotter, then propped it up against the inkstand. 'Ashton Associates', New York. No, she really could not steam it open, could she? That would be a childish thing to do and besides, someone might discover she had done it. Who had picked up the post that morning? Had Serge taken it directly from the letterbox or had one of the servants already placed it on the tray in the hall? Would Serge remember it? And where was Tanya? The house was completely silent. Of course, she could not steam open the letter! Nonetheless, she picked the letter up again and turned it round and round in her hands, as if to weigh the consequences for, rather than against, her compelling need to know its contents.

'We will visit the Basilica of St. John after lunch,' said the guide, 'but right now, we will visit the museum, where there is very much interesting to see.'

Helping her into the minibus, Paul had grasped Marina's arm. As they drove towards Efes, the smoothness of it remained on his hand like an impression in clay. She had turned to him and smiled, pleased and malleable. Serge had told him to be cautious. As they jolted along, he thought she seemed an unlikely siren, but then, so had Julia, now plump and earthed in marriage to his brother. Were all those qualities of life and warmth he sensed in Marina illusory? Were they treacherous?

She looked damp and wistful in the hot, plastic seat next to him. Why did she inspire in him a blind rejoicing when he knew the probable outcome, the consequences of such unrooted feeling?

He spoke sternly to himself. She was clearly still wracked over the memory of her dead husband. If she had married him and stayed with him despite even disliking the poems he had written in her honour, then she must have been in the grip of some more powerful, erotic compulsion. His own intervention could hardly dispel a history as deep as that. And so, he should stop thinking about her, her hair, her face, her waist, her little hands and feet. If he had no clear intention towards her, he should curtail the activity of his senses altogether. So he closed his eyes and fiddled with the lock on the door of the minibus.

They arrived at the museum and as she descended from the minibus, he saw that her flowered lawn dress had adhered to her thighs in the heat. In that limelight of a sun, her slip and legs could be seen through her thin frock. He had an awful desire to lunge at her and found himself calculating when they could be alone. I must be going mad, he thought.

Marina felt weakened by Paul and open to him. Troubled feelings caught at her, adhered to her and confused her thoughts. She felt dreadfully exposed, dropped and cracked, the soft part of her unguarded. Even her flesh felt raw. Her arms had been burned in the Agora, despite the Canadian woman's sun-cream. As she stood on the pavement, the sun bit further into her reddened skin. Was it her destiny to respond to any man who liked her as a living sacrifice? She did not mean to lead Paul on, but she felt herself doing so nonetheless. Was this not how Arthur said she had behaved with him? With a clean, lithe, pure movement from the minibus, Paul alighted. She could not fathom his expression, so she looked away. The contact between them, however, both gratified and frightened her. She wondered if she could really ever love anyone. If it were possible.

They drifted into the Turkish museum.

She had wept after Arthur had seduced her. She had been a virgin. He said he had never met any. She said he would not respect her. He said that such a thought could never enter his head.

Glorious virginity, fruitful virginity, the immaculate enclosure of her integrity. She said he would not respect her. Indeed, he had not respected her, but she had wept, thinking her soul dead. Arthur had turned on an anglepoise lamp and had insisted on looking at her nakedness in the light. He had told her that her natural impulses were good, not evil. He had seemed very surprised at her as if she were some kind of rarity. He had been both touched and amused by her tears that first night, but finally had pointed out, though really not with malice, that she had been asking for it. And of course, she supposed she had. She had always been knocking at his door, taking him her poems, dreaming up questions to ask him, bumping into him accidentally-on-purpose. To Maddy – Mother, the loss of virginity had been 'the adequate of hell' before and (Marina knew intuitively) even after marriage. And just see where her oafish crush on Arthur had got her! When later she had discovered he was married, her doom had seemed sealed.

Marina did not want to go on thinking about this and so she stopped. The Canadians, quite rightly, were complaining of thirst. She was parched too and felt demoralized by memory.

When Paul felt Marina's eyes and mind drift from him, he wanted them back. 'Please look at me,' he thought. She blankly sucked cola through a straw. He felt an irrational dislike of the guide, who had brought them drinks, and wished he would get lost. He thought, What am I doing here with this woman? I should be back in Africa. The heat, at any rate, was Ethiopic, and he felt curiously at home with it.

Together, they started to drift past cases and together seemed to fall behind the guide and the Canadians. She stopped to inspect a huge pottery urn of the Mycenaean period. It was covered with scrawls, immeasurably old, and had been dug up from some grave. In such a very ancient vessel had bones been hidden, crouched and tenuous, made cobweb by time? He wondered this and the urn made him feel more peaceful

Marina thought of Arthur's dust flying back at her from the sea. I've become obsessed with him! she thought, and felt the dreadful constraint of this limitation around her. He had become, quite literally, a cloud of motes, speckling her vision so that all sights returned her mind to him. The love of her body had never really pleased him and her attempts at affection had bothered him. She turned to Paul and gave him a weak smile. How quickly she had been drawn into the orbit of a new man! His features appealed to her in every way.

They had lost the guide and the Canadians, who had gone ahead. 'Where could they be?' she asked.

'I expect they have gone to see the goddess,' he said, checking his book. 'That seems to be the main attraction.'

Perhaps incongruously, a party of nuns dressed in blue habits came into view. They were earnestly speaking French in quiet, suppressed voices, and they were making for the exist. '*Excusez-moi, mes soeurs,*' said Paul, chancing his unfamiliar grasp on the language, '*mais, où est la déesse?*'

'*L'idole de Diane? C'est là-bas,*' said one, as if to correct a false impression that Artemis was still worthy of the reverend title of 'goddess' he had just given her. '*À droite!*' she added, then the group moved sturdily on.

'Are they Marists?' Marina asked.

'I don't know. I never got the hang of nuns, being a convert . . . except, of course for the sisters in the camps . . .'

Marina laughed. 'And I lost the hang of them! At school, I was always terrified that God would call me to be one. Sister Louis Mary had a beard. But they were very kind, really. It seems amazing now, but they had high hopes of me academically. Maybe I should think of it now, the cloister. I think a nun is what my mother really wanted me to be.'

They passed an antique bronze of a boy on a dolphin in a hall lined with Roman statuary. Generals and consuls frowned from the wall. Somehow, the story of her fear of the nun with the beard touched him. He realized, yet again, that he actually liked Marina. There was something touching, too, about the damp curls at the nape of her neck. 'What was your father like?' he asked, suddenly curious.

She stiffened slightly, though not against him. 'My real father? I haven't a clue. As for my adoptive father, he seemed almost as absent. He was what Maddy used to call "a man's man". He went fishing a lot and belonged to a club. He was either there or at the bank and I always felt I was Maddy's project really. The only reaction I ever got out of him was when I married Arthur. Apparently, he nearly cut me out of his will, but in the end, didn't. It is odd, I never think about him, nor much about my real father. I think it makes me too afraid.' She laughed nervously. 'I did go through a phase of dreaming about my adoptive father once, a recurring dream where he was always shouting angrily at me through a plate-glass window. I could not hear a word that he was saying. I suppose Maddy cut me off from him a bit.' She hesitated. 'I dream about my real mother all the time. When you woke me this morning I was dreaming about her, which is why I was so relieved to see you.'

He found himself eager to explore her thoughts. He wondered if the crude force of his earlier feelings did not evince a clumsy desire to love her and hoped that this was true. 'Perhaps you were smothered off in a little convent alone with your mother, "Maddy" as you call her. Maybe that is what the dream of the angry father means. Maybe that is why he was angry. It's only a guess.'

'Oh, you are a very Daniel!' she exclaimed, pleased with the interpretation. 'Did you do your training in psychiatry?'

'I did have quite an interest in it once,' he said, 'but my religion was so intense at the time, that I immolated myself in general practice.' He was surprised at how bitter this sounded. 'Not that it is an immolation, it simply seemed to be one to me.' He laughed wryly, lightening his tone. 'The only trouble with humility, in my experience, is that you have to become humble in order to endure the consequences of your sacrifices ... I don't know why I said that. I feel foolish talking so personally.'

She rewarded him, however, with an admiring, intimate look.

'I've given up on being noble,' he said. 'I'm not a very good GP. In fact, I think I lammed off to Africa because I felt such a failure at it ... but ... it didn't ...' For one horrified moment, he thought he was going to cry. He had not spoken to anyone about himself for years.

'Are you going back to Africa?' she asked gently.

'It all depends on what I feel when I get back to London,' he said, recovering himself.

'I haven't thought past this trip myself,' said Marina. 'Everyone else seems to have a purpose or theory or aim, but I have only dreams and imaginings. I always wanted a baby, but I'm sure that was only for selfish reasons. I suppose I shall try to find some good cause, maybe finish my degree.'

I love you, Marina, he thought strangely and with no emotion. It simply occurred to him. He let it drift away with no attempt to catch it. It was a habit with Paul to lift what lay in his heart to a shelf in his mind so that he was safe from whatever he felt. He looked about at the pieces of statuary in the room without really seeing them.

Marina felt awkward at mentioning babies. She remembered her mad connivings over a pram in Sainsbury's, the sudden impulse to bundle up the child and run. She was far too unstable to have had children, she thought, and might have harmed them in some way had she had them. Maybe Arthur had pierced the heart of that truth and saved her. There were sarcophagi about and small bronzes.

'Where on earth is it?' Paul asked, 'This "idole de Diane"?'

'I think we're lost,' she said. 'You don't think the guide has gone off without us, do you? We'll never get back to the boat without him.'

Just then, however, they spotted the Turk standing with the Canadians in the centre of a large room ahead. They seemed to be enjoying a joke together. Relieved to be free of a tension they felt in each other's company, Paul and Marina made for the party from which they had strayed.

'I see what the good Sister meant,' Paul said as they entered the room. 'It *is* much more of an "idole" than a "déesse"!' And he laughed uneasily.

Two female deities stood on opposite sides of the room. Iconically identical, they were, nonetheless, executed in a different fashion, one in crumbling ochre stone, the other in glistening, white marble.

'It says here that they are copies,' Paul read from his guidebook. 'The original stood in the great temple here.'

Marina looked from one rendition of the goddess to the other. Her hand moved to her chest. As if bidden by it, she moved towards the statue on the left. There she was, the Great Artemis, the Great Mother, supreme goddess of the ancient world. Marina felt as if she should be wearing a hat and gloves. She also felt slightly sick. The archaic idol stood free without support, but rigid and immeasurably crude. Somehow, its shabbiness and crumbling gave it a larger potency. It looked as if it should be standing amid leaves, creatrix and protectress of spiders and spinning, toads and all manner of unearthly oracular beings. It rose from its base like a column or caryatid, though it supported nothing. Its features, nearly obliterated with age, were not exactly grim; they were more impassive and impersonal. Its blank eyes seemed to see everything and nothing at the same time in one, huge, cynical regard. Corrupt and pure, fecund and death-dealing, there it was. It had a sense of surreal otherness from all feminine attributes, a wisdom of an animal nature. Chiefly, there were its many breasts, row upon row of stone paps arranged neatly and formally around its bodice. Marina shivered with revulsion at these. The breasts seemed obscene to her and yet the sight of them absorbed her. Rising from the idol's head was a sort of crown, stiff, hieratic, high, it was carved with blurred, emblematic figures. Symmetrically, by the wedge-shaped, thick-lipped face, hung two hanks of hair, again carved with obscured figures. Below its many breasts, ranging down its tight, ceremonial dress, were still reliefs of animals, the identity of them almost lost in the erosion of time. She could not make them out. Were they birds, sows, deer? Creation seemed to be represented. Maybe the breasts were eggs, for they were ovoid without nipples. Marina stepped back and closed her eyes. So Helena had wanted her to see this. What was it that she had seen? She felt a buzzing in her head and sat down.

'It says here,' Paul said, fiddling with the guidebook, 'that one must not confuse this Artemis with Apollo's twin, although they have something in common. This is an Asiatic deity, Cybele . . .' His voice trailed off. 'Marina, are you all right?'

Marina shook her head. The guide and the Canadians were eyeing her from across the room. 'What do you make of it?' she asked.

'It seems a thing for which there are no words,' he said. 'It is rather magnificent, though, don't you think?'

'You asked me earlier what I thought of Arthur's poems,' Marina said. 'They try to make that statement, say that thing,' Marina shuddered. Marina felt herself weak and foundering, as if her name had to be mentioned over and over again like a charm to make herself separate from the goddess. She felt that she had been caught up in its unconscious power, as if it had pronounced secret dooms and fiats in her ear.

'But this is a fertility . . .' he stopped, feeling stupid and tactless.

'I know,' she said sadly, shaking her head, 'but that is how the poems made me feel, nonetheless. As if I had put Arthur in mind of some terrible abstract urge.'

The letter was fat. Helena had prepared a cup and saucer for herself and dried herbs for a tisane in case anyone came into the kitchen. The water began to hiss in the kettle on the stove. The house was utterly silent save for this noise. At the kitchen table, Helena sat with her head in her hands and cried. She had never before steamed a letter open and she knew she ought not to do it. She also knew that she did not have to complete the action she had set in train by descending to the kitchen with Marina's letter burning a hole in her pocket. She, with a life-history of self-control, could and should end this and return the letter to the table in the hall or put it in Marina's room. She should do this and sleep the impulse off, but she could not stop weeping and yet she could think of no reason why she wept. Somehow she had raged on ahead of her mind and found herself in this pitch of misery. She had to know who Marina really was. Who was she? That seemed to be the only question.

The kettle reached a boil and screamed. Helena jumped at its piercing whistle and removed it from the stove with a tea towel. She hoped to God that she could do this without staining the paper and that she would be able to reseal it. She removed the whistle, returned the kettle to the stove and let it simmer. Gently, she exposed the glued flap of the envelope to the steam. At first, it would not open, then tentatively, she started to pry the flap loose. To her surprise, it came away with melting and satisfying slickness. She had an urge to take out the contents and read the letter there and then, but on looking inside the envelope, she discovered a second one enclosed. With mounting impatience, she repeated the steaming operation, but her hands trembled and she made a little tear in the paper. Oh damn! she thought. She then filled the teapot she had prepared and, concealing the opened letters under a woven mat, swept tea and all onto a tray and scurried back up the stairs to her room. As she left the kitchen, her eye caught the icon of the Virgin of Ephesus, presumably put there by Evangalia. Garish tears poured from the image's almond eyes. This debased convention of suffering rather proved a point to Helena. She wondered what Marina would make of the mawkish picture when she saw it.

At her escritoire, Helena poured tea and the pleasant scent of camomile rose up into the room. Carefully, she removed the letters and began to read:

Dear Marina (began the first),

I am writing to you much sooner than I anticipated, and have decided to so so because you said you were staying with friends and were anxious to know. I have found your mother and I enclose a letter from her. It was not a difficult task. Just as I thought, you were privately adopted. Your biological mother gave you up on the condition that you should be told who she was if you ever wanted to know. This may have been the reason for your adoptive mother's extreme reticence and will almost certainly be the reason why she discouraged you from asking questions. Your biological mother assumed that you did not want to find out about her until I contacted her and she is overjoyed that you have made the effort. You may be very angry when I tell you that your adoptive mother left the information that you sought with her sister Theresa, making an added condition that the secret should be kept from you until the dissolution of your marriage to Arthur Holt. I am sorry to have to tell you this, but in these cases, feelings do run very high on all sides. Do please get in touch with me if you want to know more. In any case, I have spoken to your biological mother myself. As I am convinced that she has very strong feelings for you, I am forwarding her letter. Please let me know if there is anything else I can do.

Sincerely,
Frances

322

Helena scanned this quickly, then slowly pulled the second letter out. She eased it from the envelope. It was written on lined paper:

Dear Marina,

I wanted to hear from you for so long. I miss you my baby girl. I know you had a hard time recently and lost your husband. This is probably a real shock to you, but try to forgive. Your nice detective told me you wanted to know all details and now I can tell you what has been in my aching heart so long. I was in high school when I fell for you. It's a long story. My Mom worked at the estate of your adopted Mom's folks in Mendham, NJ. My heart was broke when I had to give you up, but Mrs Horner said her daughter would give you a really good home and they would bring you up as a good Catholic and send you to college and give you all the advantages. My dad took a strap to me when he found out. I wanted to marry the boy, but he wouldn't have nothing to do with me when he found out. Mr and Mrs Horner made it easy and sent me away so I could have you. I loved you so much, but what could I do?

Your father's name was Stephen Grabowski. He joined up and went off to Korea later and was killed. I graduated from high school after all. I wanted to be a baby nurse, maybe to make up for you, but we didn't have any money. Mrs Horner wouldn't tell me anything about you after they took you and she fired my mother. But that is water under the dam. When you had your deb party in New York, I cut your picture out of the paper. You are so beautiful. I heard you married a divorced man. Don't worry, Marina, God forgives all. I almost went to see you when you had your deb party because it was in a hotel and I thought I could hide in the lobby, but I thought you would be ashamed of me. Maybe you are ashamed of me now. I am ashamed of what I did, but I am glad you are alive. I love you.

I got married to Mike Doyle in 1959 and we have our own business. I am not good at English, but I was always good at math and so I keep books for him. He is a contractor and we have a split-level ranch home in Basking Ridge, NJ. Mike built it. We have five kids – Mary, Teresa, Kevin, John and Mike Jr. Everybody knows about you. It was silly to hide it, and Mike tells me to say Hi to you and so do the kids. Teresa went to college like you. She went to Rutgers. She is very smart and she says your husband was a famous poet and that he wrote poems about you that would upset me. I didn't think so, so I read them. I don't think sex is evil, do you? It's just the way we use it. Mary is married with a baby on the way. Kevin is a mechanic. John wants to work with his Dad, but Mikey could go to college. He is just that age and he is top of the class in Biology.

The detective told me you wanted to know where you came from. My folks were called Maloney and they came from Ireland. I was born in the USA. Your dad's parents were Polish, not that they could care less, and he was very bright in school. He was shy and that was what made me fall for him. You get your looks from him. He was very handsome and blond. He liked to write poems. I called you Marina because of secret reasons to do with our romance. I think he just got scared off. I was really upset when he died. I think he would be real proud of you.

I think you are probably very angry at me. I don't blame you. I want to see you very much. For years I worried that the Horners didn't treat you right, but I guess that's silly. I trusted you to the Sacred Heart of Jesus and I believe in that. Whatever happens, I pray for you every day, and I won't ever stop, and even though I was wrong to do what I did with your father and get pregnant, I did love him. I thought I did, but I was fifteen. Please write to me.

Your loving Mom

P.S. I realize I haven't told you my name. It is Maureen.

XXVI

PAUL, who was by this time irritable and fatigued by the heat, had decided that he and Marina would on no account miss the Holy House of the Virgin. Over a lunch of pilaf and watery beer, the guide had sketched out an itinerary that included a trip to the Byzantine ruins of St John's Basilica, the Mosque of Isa Bey, and a Turkish rug factory. Although she had said that she very much wanted to see the shrine, Marina seemed sadly compliant. The Canadians, however, barracked for the Artemision. In the end, they had all wrangled with the distraught guide.

'Look, we have all come an extremely long way to see these things,' Paul had said, taking the lead with masterful firmness. 'I really cannot see why my friend and I can't take a taxi to the Virgin's house while you take the others to see the temple!'

'There is no temple,' said the guide,

'That is for us to decide,' said the Canadian woman.

In the end, the guide had had to give way. Perhaps it was too hot or his sensibility too eastern to force the issue. A taxi had been found, and Paul had been left very much out of pocket. In a way, it gratified him to have won the day for Marina with such evident gallantry. In another way, he wondered why it was that she could not assert herself over the smallest thing. It was clear to both him and the Canadians that the guide had bamboozled them into taking a tour in the first place, perhaps in order to sell rugs. While there was no point in being strident, surely Marina could have mounted some objection. However, when she had offered to make a contribution towards the expensive taxi, he had not wished her to do so.

It was a six miles up the mountainous road from Efes to the shrine. The taxi driver was a malevolent-looking man with drooping black moustaches. Worry beads and charms against the evil eye swung from his mirror. Paul thought he had the faint air of a security policeman. He fiddled with the dial of his radio and a wailing sound came out of it, a Turkish lament. It seemed to touch Marina, or she was tired, for she rested her head on the back of the seat and listened to its subtle ululations, her eyes closed. As they travelled slowly upwards, Paul noticed that the driver's eyes were on her arched neck. In the mirror, he narrowed them, glancing at her. Paul glared at the back of his neck, suddenly possessive of Marina and indignant at this insolence. Did she need to wear a veil in order to be considered decent?

Suddenly, he yearned to see a picture of Marina as a much younger woman. That eerie blamelessness she had would have marked her out as prey to mauling eyes and straying hands. She would have been a sweetmeat to tantalize the failing appetite of an older man, who, with some reason, might have wanted to keep her in purdah as his vanity's pet. She had mentioned that Arthur's children had been hostile to her. Paul wondered if he had not subtly driven them away in order to stop embarrassing comparisons between them and Marina. Although he felt some disloyalty in thinking this, it occurred to him that Marina might have taken their place. He wondered if she were not even now forcing him into the role of a father and if that were not the danger he sensed in his desire for her. Marina was not the sort of woman one embraced casually. As the taxi ascended the winding road, blue pines by the wayside shed cool shadows and the air cleared. There was something about Marina's languor beside him: she seemed to flow along the line of the undulating music, the plaintive Turkish woman's voice coming from the radio. His instinct told him that one move, one kiss, one word would be decisive.

Marina's sunburn throbbed. She had been up since five. The weak beer at lunch had made her sleepy and the music lulled her.She slipped in and out of dreams. She would have liked to have visited the basilica where St John was said to be buried. The Emperor Justinian had built it, she thought she had read, and she felt the pull of Byzantium where, Yeats had said, one should sail in middle age. She floated off in a dream of golden domes, then jerked awake as the taxi jostled round a corner.

Paul was sitting beside her, flipping through his guidebook. A cooler breeze was coming in through the taxi window. They were in a mountainous region that seemed far above the broiling plain. Waking, she felt peaceful and refreshed as if something pleasant had happened in her sleep. She smiled at Paul as he frowned with concentration on the book and was surprised to find that a queer little affection for him had sprung up without her really noticing it. He was very serious about collecting information and conveying it to her.

He glanced at her. 'It says here that the Virgin's house used to be sacred to Artemis.'

'Really!' she said.

'Apparently, Muslims as well as Christians come up here to pray to the Virgin. That's interesting, isn't it?'

She nodded. She felt abashed and pleased in his presence as if they were both very young and at a dance. She studied the book that he proffered. Beside the text was a full colour reproduction of a modern icon of Mary, who was swathed in a sumptuous robe of scarlet and gold. A jewelled halo wreathed her head, and she was set against a background of violent turquoise blue, which bore little relation to anything in nature, not even the Ephesian sky. From her sloe, Eastern eyes there poured crystal tears shed down cheeks of an incredible bloom. She and Paul inspected the picture together. He took the book from her and turned back the pages to the photograph of the Great Mother. She stared eyeless from the muzzy picture, her chthonic form sporting the breasts of a sow.

'I don't confuse them really,' Marina said simply with a shrug. 'One is the friend of my soul, the other would seem to condemn me to my body.'

'That's a pious statement!' Paul said with sudden humour. 'Perhaps my being a doctor makes me question the division.'

'I suppose it is a rather starchy thing to say,' Marina laughed too. 'Sister Louis Mary inhabits me still.'

'You allow people to possess you, Marina!' he said far more sharply than he intended.

'I know I do,' she said gently, 'and it worries me.'

He was sorry he had been harsh, but he said nothing. He stared at the picture of the goddess and remembered her reaction to it in the museum. Again, he found himself flying into an inner rage at Arthur, this time for literally idolizing his wife. He had turned her into mere words, perhaps so that she would not threaten him with her humanity. Not without his own sense of irony, he wondered if he himself were not frightened of becoming enslaved to Marina. Although he had never given much conscious thought to idolatry, it occurred to him now that it must be much more comfortable to fix the essence of a thing in stone and worship it, for then the only demands it would make upon you were those you created yourself. To fall into the hands of the living God, however, was a fearful thing, as the adage had it and as Paul knew. For this reason, he withdrew into himself again watchfully. Was it from this he had fled into the desert or to it? Was Marina a means to meet God or to hide? He changed the subject in his mind.

In any case, Marina took the book from his slack hand and flipped idly back to the soupy icon. There was a scent of pine forest fresh through the window and he inhaled it. On it, was the perfume of Marina, mingled with her sweat.

'This picture reminds me of my childhood, I don't know why,' she said. 'Maddy had a great devotion to the Virgin and used to carry around prayer cards, rather like this icon. My grandmother, too, used to have rather garish, laminated momentoes of saints. She had frightfully good taste, of course, but a weakness for this sort of thing.' The Turkish lament had changed and the taxi radio was now playing a martial, strident tune.

'The Feast of the Assumption used to be a big deal. We would all pile out to my grandmother's house in the country – oh, it was very beautiful – in Northern New Jersey. Out we would go on this rickety train with wicker seats every 15th of August. We even planned our holidays around it so that we would not miss it.' The memory came to her as balm like the breeze from the cooler hills into which they ascended. 'I had a number of "cousins", I suppose you could call them. My adoptive grandmother had a huge family and that was part of Maddy's trouble. I was the youngest girl, though, and so it was up to me to crown my grandmother's statue of the Virgin with flowers. It was Italian and very beautiful indeed. Someone had bought it on a pilgrimage to Rome and it was considered quite a collector's piece. There would be Latin hymns and prayers and then Maddy would hoist me up in my best dress while everyone, servants and family, would stand solemnly around while I put the wreath in place. The statue had sorrowful eyes, I always thought, but the Infant and a vast amount of gilt seemed to make up for it. Maddy always cried. Every year I would get a new dress for the occasion. I remember an especially pretty one, white and very fine, with smocking and rosebuds embroidered all over it. I smeared grass-stains on it in my grandmother's garden where the flowers for the wreath came from. She was a force majeure in the local Garden Club, notwithstanding her rabid Catholicism. It is a WASP area, believe me! Anyway, I remember asking the Virgin to protect me from the wrath to follow the grass stains and I thought She had because no one seemed to notice! And so, I have trusted Her ever since.

'I have a rather unclear memory of my grandmother because she died when I was still fairly young and the house was sold, but I shall never forget the garden which is why it is hard to believe after all that

328

lushness that the actual Assumption might have taken place here in this dry, Asiatic place.' Marina stopped and studied the wistful tears of the picture on her lap. 'It seems awful that they associate Her with a fertility goddess. I think of Her as having more to do with unconditional love.'

They had reached the shrine. It stood in a little grove of leafy and venerable trees with large, distended bolls. Paul felt a lift to his spirits. He had found Marina's story rather touching, and what was more, his long sojourn in the desert had given him a dowser's instinct for the presence of water. The coolness and the trees proclaimed a spring nearby, and then he remembered reading of a sacred well. Marina stood under the complex, shifting shadow of the leaves while he and the driver attempted to communicate in sign language. It was agreed with much showing of wrists and jabbing of fingers that he would return for them in an hour. As the driver roared off, he winked at Paul, who suddenly felt alone and afraid.

Helena resealed the envelopes carefully. It had been difficult to stuff the letters back so that they looked undisturbed. She was worried that the flaps now licked and stuck, had a puckered appearance. Oh, Marina would be too avid to notice she thought. In any case, it would never occur to her that Helena would have steamed them open. Helena gave a little grunt of a laugh. Marina's naïveté had its uses. Not liking to be without it at any time, Helena kept a copy of the *Oxford English Dictionary* in Patmos as well as in London. I. A. Richards had once described it as 'Holy Writ', and Helena subscribed to this notion. She took the heavy volumes down and pressed Marina's letter under the dictionary's weight. Her hands trembled in fits as she did this. She felt the thrill of delinquency and guilt at the same time. She wondered if next she would start taking things from shops.

She could not get over what she now knew about Marina. It charged her up in an antic sort of glory. The heft of the pilfered secret lay almost palpable in her mind and it amazed her that she had never even discussed the possibility with herself that Marina might be the daughter of a servant. Or was it granddaughter? She was not about to steam the envelopes open again. It was incredible. It amazed her. The whole story was so utterly banal – the woman's letter ignorant and sentimental. It quite took her breath away to conceive of this . . . this goddess being the result of so inglorious a union. Helena felt strangely liberated. She realized that she had unconsciously seen Marina as parthenogenetic – born of a virgin – or self-propagated in some way – or created entirely by Arthur himself. When all along . . .

So this was the reason Arthur had discouraged her from investigating her origins! His intuition of the truth had kept her from destroying her mystery. He had enforced her innocence, and thus had kept her ever-fresh, forever young . . . his enigma. And she was, she *was* enigmatic. She was the hidden, secret, unknowable, unfathomable, inscrutable Marina, who far from being Aphrodite was the by-blow of a high-school prom. Helena started to laugh. Marina's father had been a Pole, but no Kuriensky – no relative of hers at all, no babe smuggled in fur wraps across icy borders with jewels sewn into her little things – not émigré, but immigrant! And that knowledge would have made a difference to Arthur. It really would. Imagine. Maureen. Helena could just see Arthur and the in-laws in a split-level ranch home, swilling Diet-Coke and eating tuna crumble made with two cans of condensed soup, a can of fish and a gratin of cornflakes. She could imagine lurid, fluffy Christmas cards coursing the Atlantic, accompanied by tins of home-baked cookies. There would have been throbbing images of Catholic kitsch as well – dashboard Virgins and light-up Christs with battery operated Sacred Hearts. Oh, but she would have liked to be a fly on the ceiling for that! To see Arthur's martyred taste would have been worth a grandstand seat.

Helena felt a bit ashamed of herself. Theoretically, snobbery offended her. Had she not cast mental malefactions upon Serge earlier that day for implying that she unwittingly endorsed elitism? She did not! She eschewed it. It was, she thought, a pardonable offence to revel just a bit in the de-mystification of Marina. She paced a little across the floor of her room and looked out at her own mother's lush garden beneath her – at the fig tree with its twisted branches and tiny buds of fruit, not to mature until August. Now she was in possession of this information, what was she going to do with it? The safest course of action was to return it to the letter tray in the hall, as if she had put it there after she had recognised it was not addressed to her. Or, she should place it on Marina's bed, or prop it on the dressing-table once the OED had done its work.

She took care that not a sound could be heard of doorknob turn or footfall, and slipped across the corridor to Marina's room. Without the letter, of course, she had no business to be there, but she wanted to take a recce nonetheless. The shutters were still drawn and the bed was in an untidy heap. Rejected clothing lay on the coverlet, and the close, hot room bore a subtle smell of Marina's scent. Helena recognized it. What was it? White Linen? Oh, that was going too far even for a pathologically guilt-driven Catholic. Helena wrinkled her nose. It was probably Miss Dior. Whatever it was, it was too young for her. Maureen would wear a Coty Body Spray.

Helena found herself short of breath and she did not quite know why. There was something terribly pathetic in the room, something she could not name. Evidently, Marina had hurried to get dressed in order to be on time for the boat. The wardrobe door was sprung open and the white silk shift she had worn the night before hung askew and exposed. In it, Marina had looked like a queen with her fine eyes and fine, gold, wiry hair. What would it do to a woman of such aristocratic demeanour, a woman half in love with the very creation of herself, to discover what she really was? What would it do, how would it strike her to be tied forever to this origin?

Helena was not so sorry now that she had opened the letter. If she found the right psychological moment to deliver the envelope, might there not be some adjustment to Marina's claims on Arthur's journals and unpublished poems? What ever was she thinking of? She could not use blackmail or barter. In any case, for that to be effective, she would have to admit that she had read the letters. She thought. She stood and chewed her lip. Could it all hang on who caught Marina's Icarus fall? One thing was clear. The letter was certainly not expected, and Helena doubted if Serge had even seen it. The posts to Patmos were easily enough explained away as unreliable. She could slip the envelope onto the letter tray almost any time she liked – or destroy it altogether. The detective would write another one, or maybe she would not . . . but the main thing to do was to get Paul out of the house and far away before she delivered Marina's news. Knowing it already, she could prepare. She could cloak Marina – comfort her. A vital reunion would be effected between the two of them. Of course, Marina would probably fly to America after that, but the emotionally draining encounter with her mother would almost certainly result in finding the papers and journals of little consequence. All sorts of readjustments would be made as a result of this discovery, but as long as Paul was eliminated, Helena could see her way clear. Marina had frostily asserted that she had no intention of going with him. If only there was some way Helena could insure this. It would come clear. It would become clear. Whatever,

Maureen, as lurid as she was, was proving to be worth her weight in gold.

Paul tried to imagine the ascension of the Virgin into Heaven, but he could not. Since his arrival on Patmos, he had planned to visit this spot, but the original impetus for the journey seemed light years away. One of the few friends he had made in Africa had been an Italian monk, who had somehow materialized in Addis Ababa. He was a peculiar little old man with a face like a wizened apple. He might have been a Tibetan lama or an Indian guru but for his peasant Christian simplicity. What he was doing in Ethiopia was hard to say, but he had talked about the shrine at Ephesus with open-hearted enthusiasm.

This all seemed very distant. It was dark inside the little Byzantine chapel, which could never have housed a woman of the first century A.D. The atmosphere was waxy and stuffy from the banks of candles standing against the rough-hewn wall. Marina was adding to the blaze along with a small party of Muslim women with veiled heads and lowered eyes. She was smiling at them with ecumenical friendliness. The altar itself was dominated by a black statue of the Madonna, dressed in flowing Western robes, her hands outstretched, her attention on a crucifix beneath. One of the French nuns he had seen earlier that day in the museum at Efes, indeed the one who had directed him and Marina to the 'Idole de Diane', came buzzing down the aisle, but she did not seem to recognize him.

It was a Catholic shrine, but this did not make him feel any more at home. The gaudy icon they had looked at in the taxi was tucked away in a niche beside the altar where it looked less florid. On the other side, there was a pile of crutches cast away under a wall of plaques claiming miracle cures.

Marina believed in miracles. Her hair was frowsy from sweat, her face pink from sunburn. Like his Italian friend, she had the guileless ability to beg for a miracle, a shift of the eternal through particles of time. She would be receptive of such a gift. Paul sat at the back of the chapel in one of the pews and experienced nothing but wave upon wave of exhaustion. He tried to pray, but he could not.

The story of her coronation of the Virgin had left Marina exposed to other memories of her girlhood, which made the shrine seem homely and friendly to her. The blue-suited sisters and the regulation Catholic Mary on the altar seemed to relax the transcendent stiffness of the

Byzantine vision to which she had made obeisances at Patmos. Having evoked Sister Louis Mary earlier, she was put in mind of her school, where she had been happy and successful. It saddened her only slightly when she remembered what had long been far from her mind. She had been the class poet and destined, in the year-book, for a niche in the annals of literature. Well, she had sacrificed all of that to Arthur and maybe it was no bad thing. She blushed to remember her verses which she would shrink from putting on a greeting card now.

Whatever the reasons for her sense of ease, she felt an urge to put aside those things antagonistic to her peace. If it had perturbed her slightly during the ascent up the mountain that this spot had once been sacred to the many-breasted Artemis, it suddenly seemed a natural flow of events now. Indeed, it seemed an ideal place for Mary's luminous revival, drawing as it did, all aspects of the feminine into the impenetrable mystery of God. Having lit her candles, she sat a little way apart from Paul and allowed herself to sink into the tranquillity of the place. With a kind of pleasure, she found herself letting go of her furious concerns. She presented them in a whole snarl to the tearful icon she had inspected in the taxi, Arthur, Helena, Helena's book, the search for her mother, even Paul, and she rested.

Paul tried to contemplate the tasteless icon. He only wished he could explain to the Virgin with the stylized tears that flowed from heavy-lidded Eastern eyes that sorrow was forbidden to him. Both sorrow and vulgarity had been denied him, and yet he knew he was bottling up a grief that had no noble proportions, nor any aesthetic merit, nor rare emotional refinement. He was miserable. To cry about this as Marina had done in the Cave in Patmos would have been to undermine himself. What was more, it would seem to mock the drought-stricken dead whom he had abandoned. For he had abandoned them. He was aware that the Virgin had a high reputation as a help in times of God's withdrawal, but this painful silence seemed so profound that even she could not get through.

It had been like the disconnection of atoms one from another in which the familiar, associative process of dialogue ceased and became a deaf incoherence. It was strange that God was known by His absence. It was as if one had to bite the dust to know the earth, but it was true. Paul would have given the world to be able to light a candle to the icon like Marina and see in its illumination some aspect of beauty or importance. All he really wanted, he thought with a sudden, overwhelming urge that stemmed from loneliness was for her to touch him – to embrace him.

Marina's eyelids fluttered as if waking from an absorption with peace. It was as if she had been carried away into a flash of darkness beyond the abode of meaning and as she gently surfaced, she saw with some surprise that there was no point in dragging her chains any further. She had come to a place where she could lay her heavy burden down and she was glad to do so. Perhaps her tears and prayers had been sufficient, but she doubted that. It simply came to her that Arthur had finally gone away. It would be all right to think about him now, and even to remember his face. What she had done, she had done. What Arthur had written he had written. To learn to accept these things seemed a painful road, but hardly as unendurable as the marriage had been. This she had borne, but she was neither crushed nor finished. Perhaps he had needed someone to bear him.

With certain clarity, she saw that she should not have allowed him to degrade her, but in what sense had he done so? He had wounded her self-esteem and insulted her and perhaps she should have left him, but she had not been able to. Was that degrading? If she had been a different person, she would have left him, but she was not a different person, she was herself. Maybe there was something else that made her feel so endlessly guilty about him, but at the moment, she could not reach it. Who was to say why people suffered or what it meant? The sight of the homey, gaudy Virgin moved her. The world did not look like Michelangelo either. Most people had a thumbed, Woolworth's appearance, and she herself had behaved quite tackily.

All at once, it occurred to Marina that she was not Aphrodite. The realization did not come as a thunderbolt, but it arrived with an abrupt seriousness nonetheless. She was not and never had been Arthur's Aphrodite in the sense that she had come to believe. It had been either a cruel or kind deception on his part, but the woman of the poems had not been intended to represent her. She saw it. The love of Arthur's life had been Helena. Evidence from the text of *The Hephaestus Cycle* came to her head unbidden, line by line, in which the startling revelations of passion unconsummated in her own married life now made perfect sense. All along she had thought she had failed to reciprocate his feelings for her and they had been for someone else, whose shadowed activities with her husband had been lauded, sung and even deified by him.

Marina looked at the altar with its arrangement of Madonna and crucifix in order to sustain this heavy and welcome blow. She reeled a little at it. With the part of her that had been catechized by Maddy, with

334

that same part that had made her a guilty and clumsy lover, she wondered if she should be thinking of such things in such a holy place. But her eye fell upon the piles of crutches and callipers near the altar and she understood inwardly that there were ways and ways of being crippled.

She was not a goddess. She had not even faintly resembled a goddess, and she did not have to be one. If Helena wanted this power, that was her choice, but here and now, Marina formally divested herself of it and was free at last.

It was true that this vanity, which had always seemed such a little fault in her, had damaged lives, especially her own. It was true that she had played deep and irresponsible games by marrying Arthur and had, perhaps, made him miserable by staying with him. But she looked at the black Madonna with its formless, conventional, outstretched arms and she realized that in order to accept responsibility for herself at last, she would have to leave her self-reproach behind. To prod the wound so often as she did was to undermine the process of healing.

Marina shifted in her seat. For some reason, the very admisson of her folly and weakness cheered her up. It seemed yet more wonderful evidence of her mere mortality. Her skin throbbed and she felt a little stiff from so much walking. She had wrinkles and was getting a little plump. If she did not have permission to die, then how could she ever accept the solace of love? She did not know why it mattered to be mortal and to accept it, but she was sure it did. She suddenly remembered Paul, but when she looked around, she discovered he was gone, and so she rose and followed him out into the sunshine.

He was standing by a tree looking at the dusty ground, his hat once more upon his head. He seemed to be inspecting a desiccated leaf that lay at his feet. She had an impulse to put out her hand and lay it gently on his arm, but he quickly turned. 'There appears to be a well,' he said. 'Shall we see it?' She drew back and nodded. They descended a neatly marked path. 'To the Sacred Spring' it said on a sign.

They found themselves by a low aqueduct surrounded by school-children. Some tall spigots had been set up and the taps were full on. The children were laughing and shoving their hands under the water as it gushed forth. It was hard to tell what nationality they were because they chattered in a language Marina did not understand. She thought it unlikely that they were Turkish, for the little girls were dressed with Western freedom and their hair flowed down their shoulders. Nonetheless, they had olive skin and deep black eyes. Some splashed in the

335

water, some drank it. The drops that fell on Marina felt pure and cold. All at once, a teacher bustled up and shook her finger at the children, admonishing them to let Paul and Marina through and, at once, they stepped aside with solemn courtesy.

She stooped and drank out of the cupped palm of her hand. Paul's throat ached and he closed his eyes. The sight of Marina and the sound of water moved him so, Marina stooping among schoolchildren and drinking from the spring. He looked again and she was splashing water all over her face, running it over her hot, burnt forearms. She had found and opened her lacy handkerchief, doused it with water and finally stood, running the wet cloth over her neck, gently pressing it to her eyes. She moved aside. 'It's good,' she said. 'It tastes wonderful.' The children peered at her, listening. 'Go on,' she said because he did not move. 'Try it. Here, let me take your hat.' She touched his shoulder blade. He bent to the tap and drank the cool water, letting it splash and trickle down his chin, run down his neck and onto his shirt. Then, like Marina, he cupped his hands and bathed his face and head, then opened his fingers wide and let the water run through them as if he had suddenly become a wealthy man. There was a trough below the tap where the water splashed and fell, and he watched its myriad, agitated and concentric rippes as they conjoined and intersected each other. He turned and stood. One of the children was running towards them from a little tourist stall with a large plastic bottle in his hand. The child gestured to Marina. 'See?' he said, and waved the bottle at the tap. 'Keep!' he said.

'For me?' she asked, gesturing broadly at her chest. The child nodded and she gave him an immense smile. 'Oh, *thank* you!' she said, taking the bottle from him. She filled it ceremoniously from the spring while the little group watched with satisfaction. The teacher gave the little boy an approving gaze, and with benign smiles all around, Paul and Marina bowed their way out of the group and stood alone together on the pavement near the road. She looked delightedly at the bottle, her gift.

'Oh, Marina!' he said, and unable to bear it any longer, he put his arms around her and kissed her.

XXVII

HELENA HAD NO WISH to dine with Serge and wondered how she could avoid him. Apart from all of the other considerations that weighed upon her mind, she had admitted her vulnerability over Arthur to her cousin and she could not bear the thought of his condescension. The sun was setting and Helena was hungry, even though she rarely felt the need for food and often skipped meals without noticing. Except for the tisane she had made and the coffee she had shared with Serge that morning, Helena realized she had eaten nothing all day. She had to have something and, in fact, she could not bear being in the house a moment longer. It was preternaturally silent and she felt a little afraid. Well, she would just have to brave Serge if she met him. If she stayed in her room much longer, she felt she would not be able to leave it at all. She had been confined there all day and the air had a stale smell of herself. She forced herself, therefore, into briskness, lit the lamp, polished her cap of silver hair with her brush, bathed her face in the hand-basin, and put on a coat of lipstick. She grabbed her shawl and crept out, locking the door behind her. It would never do to have the envelopes discovered. This was an irrational fear, she knew. She reminded herself that Serge had not even been present at the meal when Marina had broached the subject of the search for her parents. Even if he had been, he was so caught up in his mother that he would never have noticed the letter.

Helena tiptoed past Marina's door. Even though she feared discovery, she acted on an impulse to swing it open yet again and look in upon the darkened room. She was suddenly possessed of a desire to bury her face in the rumpled sheets and clothes that lay scattered on the bed, but she resisted it. Like sheet lightning, the urge illuminated something to Helena about herself, but as quickly as the insight came, it was gone, and she thought no more about it. She closed the door and threaded her way down the stairs. To her relief, Serge was nowhere to be seen, but Tanya stood in the doorway, evidently on the way to the kitchen with the Princess's tray. 'How is my aunt?' Helena asked. She found that she could not help but speak to Tanya in an abrupt manner, even though she knew she ought not to do so. The girl gave a little start.

'Poorly,' Tanya replied. 'I think she is very low.'

'Has she read the Romanov papers?' The words came like a chill breeze through her teeth. Her aunt put spells on people. She captivated and charmed them. To an unpractised eye, she always appeared to be in the right, and Helena felt instinctively that she had seduced Tanya. Helena suspected that she herself had always lacked that magic component, charm. She thought it a low quality.

'She will not talk about it,' Tanya said. 'I believe she has read them, but she will not comment on them.'

'I see she ate her meal, though,' Helena retorted, 'so she can't be so very badly off. Have you seen my cousin?'

'He tried to get in earlier to see your aunt, but she refused to speak with him. I believe he has gone out,' Tanya said.

Helena was relieved. 'Well, would it be possible for you to hold the fort while I go and get myself some dinner? I shan't be long. Dr Mason and Mrs Holt will be back sometime very late this evening. So it is simply a question of listening out for my aunt.'

Tanya recoiled slightly, although from what, Helena was unable to say. She supposed she was too hard on the young woman. If someone worked for her, she expected a lot. She made students groan and suffer, but they learned. Tanya was, after all, only a student, and what was the point of putting her back up. She might leave and then where would they be? 'Look,' she said, 'I think you have done quite an exceptional job with my aunt. Your Russian is very good. I think we could see our way clear to increasing your pay. Quite frankly, I had no idea there would be so much work.'

'As you see fit, Dr Taggart,' Tanya replied coldly, her eyes on the eggshells the Princess had strewn on the cloth. 'I am glad to have been of use.' She tried unsuccessfully to smile and backed away from Helena, as from a presence, and fled towards the kitchen.

Helena drew her shawl around her. In the shadowy hall, she felt a dull pain. She had been trying to be nice.

She made her way through the familiar streets towards Vangelis's taverna. Even though she had wanted to avoid him, she felt deserted by Serge. She supposed he was getting himself 'wasted'. This was an Americanism she had heard, but she thought it a creative one. Suppose he were already at Vangelis's? What would she do then? They might get drunk together. Why not? The alliance needed to be deepened. Why not endorse the search for Olga? No one stopped people searching for God, that ultimate, metaphysical unicorn. On the contrary, a school of theology was a well-established feature of Patmos, and her mother and her aunt had consulted its divines. Perhaps she would help Serge to establish a School of Tsarology, proving empty steppe-land to be ruled by an invisible crown. In return, what loyalty did she want from Serge? She did not really know, but thought it best to prime his fealty just in case.

On her way, she passed a little hole-in-the-wall tobacconist and bar where Greek men drank ouzo and clicked their worry beads, old, grey men, all of them: it was no place for women. Nonetheless, she glanced in at the doorway, hoping to catch a glimpse of Serge. Prince Hal, he had always kept a string of Falstaffs and the Greek community liked him. Helena was on nodding acquaintance with a few of the men in the ouzerie; they glanced up at her with a secretive, guarded look, and so she went on.

Suddenly, it hit her that she had forgotten to purchase a wedding present for Evangalia's niece, who was marrying the very next day in the Cave. Well, she would make it money and they would appreciate that. Perhaps some silver object could be found in the house to go along with the cheque. With a pang, she realized that this was the sort of thing her mother always did without thinking, or rather, it would have been unthinkable to her mother not to think of it. No question but that she would have been invited to the wedding as a welcome and honoured guest. In their midst, she would have been a partaker of that intimate procession of crowns and tapers, a presence felt intuitively, a mere princess at the feast of bride and bridegroom, who were king and queen for a day in Orthodoxy. There was a photograph of her own parents' wedding at The Russian Church in Exile at Emperor's Gate in London, her mother with smooth and silvery skin in the picture with loads of lace capping her head and caping her shoulders and her father in morning dress, grinning.

They had not been able to have more than one child, herself, and although no one would have dreamed of saying so, she had always sensed it had been a general disappointment that she had not been a boy. As a very little girl, she remembered burying her face in her warm mother's waist and feeling safe there, but as she had grown older, she had always felt jagged and masculine next to her, especially when she had returned to Europe after the war. Maman had been ruffly and feminine. She had had an elegant boudoir with scent bottles and make-up and tissues in a box.

Helena wondered why she was thinking so directly of her mother now, and decided it must have to do with Marina's news. In all things, her mother had tried to make Helena a lady. Her mother had defined the right hats and gloves to choose and had made her write thank-you letters by return until Helena had quite simply rebelled. How she walked and how she talked and what she did with flowers had been ceremonially taught, but above all, her mother had wanted Helena to have a certain sensibility. She had believed true manners to be a corollary of Orthodoxy. All airs and graces were nothing to her mind next to a reverence for others no matter who they might be. Helena's mother had regarded her aristocracy as an ambiguous gift from God, a curse if one did not flatten oneself in humble service.

With a shock, Helena realized that she was now fifteen years older than her mother had been when she had died. She had been Marina's present age. Like a lemming, she had hurled herself off a cliff of self-abasement and mortification. She remembered her mother's face after Communion, ablaze with spiritual love, united in it, she had always said, with her dead father whom she had adored. Helena had also adored him, but did not know how to say so. At the funeral, Aunt Sonya had acted as if she had been her mother's chief mourner, not Helena, who was now an orphan, alone and strange. When people were dead, there was nothing you could do about it. Although she doubted that her mother and she would ever have been close to each other, the fights she had had with her as an adolescent could never be resolved.

The sun's last burst against the windows made Helena start as she reached the taverna. The square, which it abutted, looked like the centre of a velvety rose, one called 'Peace', which her mother had loved. There was a concavity in Helena's stomach, partly from lack of nourishment. Serge was nowhere to be seen under the awning at the front of the restaurant, but the tables there were usually occupied by tourists. A number of these lounged there now, long-boned Americans and Australians, a few English and Germans. You could always tell by the way they sat. Aunt Sonya disliked Germans. She thought they had a bit of a nerve coming to Patmos as they did every year after the way they had treated the Greeks in the War. Helena disliked all tourists and noted how these stretched themselves in an affluent way, sunning themselves like dogs, immobile and cloddish, as she slid by them.

Vangelis and his wife seemed surprised to see Helena by herself. Immediately, they asked if there was anything wrong with the old lady. Abruptly, Helena cut in, leaving their kindness dangling. They were prominent members of the island community, and ran a good restaurant, but although their inquiry was pertinent, Helena chose to see it otherwise. 'My aunt is well,' she said in Greek. 'Is my cousin here?' They said they had not seen him. Helena chose dishes of lamb and beans stewed in oil. On impulse, she ordered a bottle of retsina. She had drunk too much the night before and decided that she would drink again. There really seemed no danger of its becoming a habit. She decided that she would not consume the whole bottle, but she wanted a whole bottle with her.

She descended into the garden behind the restaurant where they had eaten nearly every evening since her arrival and chose a table in a corner sheltered by vines. By now, it was almost dark, and the festive gourds hanging from the trellises had been lit. The tablecloths were chequered red and white. Helena thought she heard a frog or a toad chirrup in the bole of the large tree near her. She felt protected by the leaves of the tree and the vines that snarled and twined around behind her.

A new waiter came down the steps and brought her the wine, some bread and some cutlery. She could not place him. Perhaps he was some relation of the proprietors come from another island. He was a handsome young man in his early twenties with dark hair and a slim, athletic figure. It popped into Helena's mind that she would like to go to bed with him, and she supposed that at her age she would have to offer money. That did not seem such a terrible thing to do in order to obtain such an Adonis. She gave a wry smile as he put down the food and wondered what he would say if he knew what was on her mind. Of course, she would never stoop to such a thing, but there was a subtle charm in the idea of paying someone to gratify oneself impersonally, a sense of having absolute control. She watched him wend his way back to the restaurant kitchen. Perhaps, she thought, I ought to ask him for a lock of hair. She poured herself a drink and let the rough wine, with its taste of cough mixture, soothe her throat. 'The material world,' she said aloud, but softly, 'is all we have, and that is the tragedy.' She tore off a piece of bread and ate it, realizing that the wine would go to her head on an empty stomach. What were Marina and Paul doing at this moment? She tried to imagine them pitching and tossing on the high seas of passion and it made her laugh. Nonetheless, Marina was, beyond all expectations, a woman to be loved. It was almost as if she had been born with a guarantee that love children were the loveliest, and stood in certain hope of sharing her bed with a man until the day she died. Even on her deathbed and even if she were very old, all who came to attend her would catch the drift, like snow, of a woman with an ineffable gift. Even death itself would be so pleased to sleep with sweet Marina and devour her with worms.

Helena poured herself another glass. The young man returned with a tray balanced on his arm, a young Hermes, perhaps, or Dionysius. He had high cheekbones, which gave his face a mask-like appearance, as if he were a player in a comedy or tragedy or both. His hair curled over his forehead. He left her with the lamb, the split bone of it pointed upwards at her. It was tender and could have been eaten with a spoon. She summoned him back. He had forgotten the beans and she thought to ask him, too, for a bottle of mineral water. She drank more wine and toyed with the food, raising a forkful to her mouth. It had an almost sweet savour of aromatic herbs, and the evening closed in around her. The waiter came back, and she ate and she drank until her head buzzed and her stomach was full of tender lamb and beans and oil.

Surely, it was useless to dive into the wreck of old, dead times for salvage – a sign of being elderly, to say the least. To stretch the metaphor further than she would have allowed her students to do, Helena thought, there was much ill contained in the murk, and that unlikely to be treasure. She had not wanted to assay the past without Marina's help, but now it looked as if it would not be forthcoming. Even if Marina were to allow her access to Arthur's journals, she had clammed up about Arthur himself. Helena laughed softly at having produced yet another marine image, that of clams. She supposed it was the wine. A vision of Marina clamping her foot in a giant shell came to her, a child's fantasy of drowning. For, Helena thought, Marina had started this whole, painful train of associations. Memories bumped dangerously against her consciousness and threatened to swamp her. Yes, Marina had set off a whole process and had then abandoned Helena to dark ruminations and flitting shadows which would not embody themselves. To recover Arthur would require some Orphic feat, and while she had no desire to descend to the underworld, something seemed to call from there for her attention. It rather pleased Helena to stumble on this classical vein. It was more nicely structured and precise than woolly thoughts of shipwreck and giant molluscs. She supposed she had thought that Marina would turn out to be one of those enabling figures of myth, who would turn up with coins for Charon, sops for Cerberus, and seemingly impractical but salvific advice regarding journeys to the land of the dead and back again.

Helena sighed and wished that she still smoked or that she had not finished her dinner so quickly. It seemed to lack purpose to sit here in the dark and viney recess of the taverna garden all alone and with nothing to do but think. The gourd lamps, with their jack o'lantern faces, shed soft light upon the terrace. Save for an English couple, who dined a few tables from her, the garden was empty. They were conversing in low voices. Helena had the idea that she had seen them somewhere on the island before and decided that they must be staying, perhaps in one of the Skala hotels, for their holidays. Although she could not hear their conversation, the ease and fluency of it gave evidence of a contentment with each other. Helena reached out for some remaining bread and dipped it in a little pool of sauce that she had left, rubbed it round the plate and ate it.

There had been no salvific advice from Marina, only a shirking and shrinking and a failure to acknowledge Helena's task. Helena wondered if she had not expressed clearly enough to Marina how much she feared the descent to Avernus, how sombre and Stygian was the gloom of her old memory of love. Indeed, she felt wedged already in Tartarus, as if it had been she, not Arthur, who had died. Helena was aware that she did not always communicate her true wishes and feeling to people, and that she was often annoyed when others failed to anticipate what she wanted. She had to remember that Marina was from quite a different background from her own, as was made clear from the detective agency's letter. Perhaps she did not have an ear for nuance. Perhaps, if she spoke in personal terms about Arthur rather than in general terms about a book, then Marina would befriend and assist her.

All at once, as if in response to these classical musings, Arthur himself seemed to rise before her inner eye with all the authoritative presence of a figure in a nightmare. There he was, pale and stooped, with his drooping lock of hair. Only his eyes were not as they once had been. They seemed vanished into another world, dark, like two bruises, accusing her by their absence of light. It was a grim and impure experience. Helena tried to shake it out of her imagination. She uncorked the bottle of retsina and had a little more, but she choked slightly and bubbles of red wine appeared on her lips, fell and stained her bodice. With irritation, she took a napkin, dipped it in mineral water and scrubbed, then drank the water itself, patting her chest. The train of mythic association was dangerous to be sure, for once one started to think about Hades, the Christian overlay was certain to get mixed up in it all. Arthur might have been driven by his own, inner daimon, but he was no demon. Certainly, Arthur was not. Even Marina, from her little

343

purse of Catholic propriety, had offered the idea that there had been something sad about him. Helena wished she could put out the very last fires of her rigid upbringing, but was not sure that this was entirely possible. He really had looked faintly damned, but then she was programmed to see that. It must mean more about her own sense of him, she supposed.

Had there been something sad about Arthur? Helena wondered. She had not fully inspected the annoyance this remark of Marina's had caused her at the time. Helena could imagine just what Marina's brand of pity would have done to Arthur – the condescension of a pious girl! Even before the women's movement, Helena had always seen pity as a dangerous weapon turned at her sex and used as a great inhibitor to mobility. Once one gave birth to pity, it wreathed around one's ankles, stunting the bones with its constant begging. She supposed she had not seen this in a clear light until she had got shot of Mungo, for it had been something like pity that had entangled her with him. He had been terribly in love with her. He had started life as a medievalist and had called her 'la princesse lointaine' and 'la belle dame sans merci'. She wriggled at the clichés now, but at the time, Mungo, with his moony, trusting face, his admiration of her aloof beauty, had swayed her. In truth, she had felt out of place in the mating ritual, and could have killed Aunt Sonya for making her go to deb parties, which she had thought were de rigueur. Mungo had disclosed to her a sense of herself as being a person made for courtly love, not an awkward intellectual in taffeta drag. He had given her the power to dispense blessings or refuse them. At the time, she had not much minded about sex, and Mungo seemed to prefer it only when he could abase himself, when, in fact, she could be seen to be taking pity on him. A few years ago, she had read with wry amusement that he had published a book on Blondell and the troubadours . . . and she had heard that his present wife was a born-again Christian.

So, it had been the very absence of pity between herself and Arthur, the absolute equality of each sexual encounter between them, which had charmed her.

As the affair had gone on, they had made love with an exacting cruelty. It had been the time of *Marat/Sade* and the *Last Tango in Paris*. There had been little dalliance. Helena had never responded to fondling and had eschewed the babble of sweet nothings. For this reason, perhaps, the affair had seemed extraordinarily safe to her. Her love-making with Arthur came to her memory now as a series of underground nuclear explosions, blasting fusions of huge force, but hidden to the naked eye. As if her initial dream of fire had been an omen, the affair had fulfilled the promise of a total liberation. There had been no sacrifices to be made after the manner of her sainted mother; there had been no inhibition of her own sexual power as she had succumbed to in order to gratify her husband, only a molten pain. It had awed her then, and it awed her now she thought about it.

But was she thinking about it? Was it something she could *think* about? Instead, Helena felt, the thought thought her. Ever since his death, it had been as if the memory of Arthur had played with her and entertained her like a kitten, she as Alice in a cosy wing-chair. But now it gnawed and threatened to engulf her even though she had consciously seen the affair as only an episode.

She appealed to her reason again. This was how it had happened: she and Arthur had both been married to dull people. At one time, a stable domestic situation must have been necessary to them both. Mungo, loving her distance, had given her freedom, while she, loving her freedom, had found it convenient to be married. As a young, ambitious and good-looking woman, she had found it helpful to invoke her marriage when the need arose. What was more, she had liked Mungo and they had been good companions. He had been (and still was) a literary agent, and he had helped her to place her first book. Why was she thinking about Mungo now when she was wanting to think about Arthur?

As for Arthur, his children had been adolescents at the time of their affair. He had seemed to find this heavy going, she seemed to recall. Whatever anyone said, his wife had been a crashing bore. The affair had seemed strictly a holiday from marriage for them both. What had gone wrong?

It struck Helena as it had never struck her before that what had happened had not been meant to happen. Arthur had not been meant to end up with Marina, and although she herself might have been destined to live alone, there was some fundamental flaw in how this had come about. It had certainly been no ambition of hers to marry him, but the mutation of herself that had occurred in the process of leaving him had not been intended either. It was almost as if some alien rationale had been wielding powers that she had jettisoned Arthur in such a random way . . . All at once, Helena was back. With a great, irked shrug of soul she had returned to the stifled feelings of confusion that she had forgotten to the subtle and undefined torment that had led to her final and irreversible choice.

The Princess had not known that it would feel like this. She had been expecting something rather different. Everything seemed in order and there was a curious circumspection about it all.

The morning had been a rough passage to get through, and that had been perhaps, because she had not then made her discovery. She had managed it really by letting Tanya read to her in Russian. She had allowed Tanya to choose. Tanya had decided on Mandelstam and Akhmatova and she had read them in an impassioned way so that a glimpse of beauty and freedom had been carried not in the words, which the Princess found curiously unable to follow, but in the feeling. That should have been the first clue of angels, but she had missed it. She now wished that Father Nikon would come, but the whole process seemed more like giving birth than anything else except not so painful. One was simply too concentrated on the business at hand to care about who was attending her. Jesus bathing her, Himself? That was odd. The thinking of this went away.

What she really wished was that she had let Serge in when he had come pounding on the door around lunchtime. If she had known all of this was going to happen, of course she would have let him come in, because this was far more important than the truth or the untruth of the papers. How strange it was that an entire universe could shift in the space of just a few hours. In one way, the truth was more necessary than anything, but in another way, it did not have to do with fact alone. It was, to be sure, an elemental thing, far graver than she had supposed, for in God there were no lies. The blankness came down again, not at all unpleasant, and it seemed to have to do with the grey interlocutor to whom she had offered her observations on so many occasions. Since she had eaten her eggs, he (or perhaps it was a she) had started to take a much more active role. She felt as if her chest and mind were much more open than ever before. Actually, it was important, in the absence of Father Nikon, for her to recount step by step the last few extraordinary moments – or were they hours? Had the truth come to her before or after the blanknesses had become frequent? No matter. Was it truth or was it simply the solution to a puzzle, an outcome rather than an exposure? No, the blanknesses had come afterwards and she more or less wished for them to start again as she was feeling exceedingly clammy and sweaty. The ring had been the truth.

So much agitation after lunch she had not eaten! So much agitation because she had heard her son's voice at the door and Tanya barring him! It did now seem an extremely long time ago, but she had been very frightened of him because she had not known the answer to his question. Then, the agitation had slopped around a lot, spilling itself into her veins and organs so that they were still entirely full of it even though it had turned itself into something very calm now. He had threatened her. She had heard it. Then, she had heard the door bang, and in the banging of the door, it had occurred. The reason the papers had been forged, the reason she knew emerged from its camouflage. There had been no ring. Olga had had no ring. Now, why had she missed this when all along she had known it? She asked the greyness this question. The reason had to do with an immeasurably long time ago. 'Oh dear God, you do forgive me, don't you?' she asked. Again, there was the pleasant sound of Jesus bathing, the gentle sound of water being wrung out from a sponge, as if everything was being wiped tenderly away. She had told her son that she had never lied, but this had been a lie that she had told about Olga's ring, but it had been when Serge and Varya had been little children and she had told them fairy tales.

Weaving in and out of wondrous Bilibin pictures of legendary queens, of spirits and russalkas had come the ominous fiction into which her own life and exile had joined, and there had been a blurring and now blurred story of the Archduchess Olga and herself. The lawn of the palace at Livadia had become a very Eden, or rather, (and she was still able to make this pious correction) an enchanted castle wherein she had been offered from the very hand of Olga her pearl ring. Things were threatening to be very blank again. The room was blank and grainy grey, and the interlocutor held her now in a quiet embrace from which she did not struggle. She simply asked for permission to finish. Also, before she forgot it, she wanted God to know how sorry she was that she was not at peace with Helena and how she very much wished she had followed Father Nikon's advice to pray for her. That seemed somewhat incidental, however, to the story of the ring. 'Keep your lovely pearl ring,' she had told the children she had said to Olga, 'and when you look at it, always think of me.' It had been a magic ring, a spirit ring, a fairy ring, a harmless embellishment of symbolic detail, standing for the dream of Olga and the day with Olga and the friendship

347

with Olga that had been sealed by other and immaterial means that hour beneath the bowing, fruitful trees. As icons stood for the immortal essence of the saints, so had the tale of the ring to the children stood for the integrating wholeness of time, its closures and disclosures in eternity.

The forger had done well, so well, in fact, that if it had not been for Marina's visit to her room – when, was it a long time ago or just the other night? Marina – now what was she thinking about? Ah, yes, she had been wearing a pearl or moonstone – not on her wedding finger – and the princess had all but forgotten she had seen it until like black bats the lie had flown out at her only a short time ago. 'My pearl ring,' the pseudo-Olga had written, 'the one piece of jewellery I have not sold because it is very precious to me . . .' and it had been packed away in such a plethora of clever details that she had not noticed it, nor would she have seen it as a regurgitation of her old fairy tale had not the fresher memory of Marina's ring sprung to her mind. All of a sudden, it had come and with it the dreadful knowledge that she had been outraged by something worse. The reason she had not been able to explode the forgeries at once, the reason she had so very nearly believed them was that they were hers. The letters were hers – her spirit, her life, spieled back to her in hashed-up form, transmuted into the life of Olga Nikolaievna and written in her mimicked hand in such a way that she herself would never guess that there was no truth in them. She had found the style, the diction so familiar, the pious thoughts, the memory of happy times, the poverty of spirit in exile as knowable as a shaded figure of herself in a mirror. It had been she who had suffered thus, not in a Canadian town but in Paris. It had been she who had lived in dread.

Now, there seemed to be a long time between that realization and the present. There was something to do with eggs. Yes, there had been a very long, blank time when her egg had come and gone away with Tanya. Always had liked eggs, the taste of them and the yellow look of surprise inside, and there had been a very white pitched buzz of sound around her bed and in her presence so that she had really forgotten to tell Tanya about the ring. There was something she was meaning to tell. Ah, yes. There were two things she could think and it was really important to decide which one it was. Either Serge, her own son, had been complicit in the forgery, or he had unwittingly fed the information to someone else. There was a welling-up taste of egg, a sulphurous after-tang at the thought of this very painful cross. How had it been endured of Christ that Judas had kissed Him? She thought, He is my very own son, and then there was another blankness, this one very long. Again, the white pitched buzz came. As if individuated, there now seemed forms of being not-yet-being gathering about her in a ceremonious way. They were formal beings, interconnected with each other in some way, and they invisibly sang not-songs. It was all quite friendly. She suddenly saw that it did not *matter* that Serge had done or not done this thing as long as she forgave him. It depended on her, the whole thing. And in a moment's great release, she forgave not only him, but her husband and Helena and even the Revolution. She forgave all of them from the bottom of her heart.

And so, the white buzz and the now-openly singing grey interlocutor were pressing her and urging her nearer to the door of a return not wholly unfamiliar to her, but very very strange. She thought, I will do my meditation for them. Even though it did not matter or did matter and even though it might not matter to them, it mattered to me and so I think it will do. She seemed now to slip through and join Olga Nikolaievna at the top of the stairs in the narrow House of Special Purpose. Olga might be called Olya now, even Olenka, for she was very pleased to see the Princess, delighted really. She called her 'Sonya' and not 'Sophia Petrovna'. It was all very quiet. The Tsar was there and all the family and the dog. 'You will come with me now, won't you?' Olga asked her gravely, but with a very pleasant, gentle smile. 'Of course,' said the Princess, for she now realized that she must and that she had let them all down just a little by having refused the stairs in the past. So, altogether, they started out and it was all very quiet and white and without any fear, just gentle. And she started the steps – one, two, three – down. She thought she had better call on the Name of Jesus. 'Come, Lord Jesus, Come,' she said and she felt much better for that, and so was able to continue – down four, down five, down six steps and so on – until she reached the bottom. There was a crack in her skull like a shot, and then she was gone.

Helena remembered. Now, why had she not remembered the revulsion? The first attack had been terrifying. A time near dusk one winter afternoon came back to her when the sky had been grey and heavy with snow. She had come back from an assignation with Arthur, and was sitting on her bed, the bed she shared with her husband, but the little house in Pimlico had been empty. Suddenly, she had felt a deathly pain

349

in her womb, but it was hard to decribe to herself even now, for it had been more of a psychical than a physical pain. It had been as if she had suffered the outrage of a rape effected brutally upon herself by curious and invisible means. She remembered rocking back and forward in the grey, grainy light, her fists clenched at her groin, her knees pressed together, her chest and stomach thudding with panic. She had had the sensation of going nearly mad. When Mungo had come in, mild, expecting dinner as husbands had expected in those days, she had been grateful for him, and by the end of the evening, she had shrugged off the episode, convincing herself that it must have been some biological revenge taken on her, some vestigial need for pregnancy that had crept in with all that good sex. In any case, she had been so engorged by Arthur, that the need for him had superseded everything.

And yet, it was hardly as if she had flung everything into the affair. She had kept it very separate from her daily life. She even funnelled money into a Post Office account (to which Arthur also contributed) in order to pay for the cheap hotels they frequented when getting away to Suffolk proved awkward. Both of them liked to slum away the afternoons. Sometimes they drank together. They drank champagne and they smoked pot. Dope. Arthur had been enchanted by The Rolling Stones, but the fastidious Helena had balked at accompanying him to concerts. However, the cheaper and sleazier the hotel, the better she had liked it. He had liked her to listen to his verse in bed and they had bounced away on squeaky mattresses . . . the vicar's son and the Russian aristocrat. It had been an extraordinary experience of total glamour in Earl's Court and Bayswater, total submission, and a whole surrender to what was the body's idea to do. An abrogation of the mind. A stillness in the centre of things. A pure anarchic arc of thoughtless grace in which all power to analyze experience became uncoupled from the deed. It was as if a freighted railway car had lost its engine on a hill and moved with devastating speed towards an incalculable destination of impact. The momentum of the thing had been such . . . Helena could not help but think of mechanical metaphors to describe it. As she sat in the taverna garden, she stuck her fingers through the web of her shawl and kneaded the wodge of wool she had bunched up.

It had been impossible to dismiss the outrage at the centre of herself. Why was that? After the first episode of panic, there had been others. Why had her memory refused to release this information to her before? Why strictly classified? Surely, it would have been in her interest to recall this bleeding bruise and keep the power of its horror constantly before her. She would crawl back home and hide under the covers shivering, and then crawl back for more. The oddest thing about it was the ecstatic sensation she had had of spiritual purity yoked to its polar opposite of animal degradation. It had been like being drawn and quartered between sacred awe and filthy violation . . .

Helena stopped herself here and gave a wry little laugh. There was no need to be mystical about this. Surely, it had been Arthur himself who had been the mystic manqué. It had been he who had loved extremities – polarities, not herself. Was she not handing him power, a power she had always refused him, by remembering it all in this way? Arthur had exercised himself, made formidable efforts not to be trivial, and had longed to be madder and badder than he was. She was merely playing into this . . . this fantasy life of his where raw lust had become a transcendent principle. Surely, it was the wine and the hour that gave these ruminations such a romantic turn. And then, without her knowing how to stop it, the inner, gaping wound, so central to her being, reopened. 'No,' she said softly and aloud. It was like being tied up and subjected to the loud noise of a radio which she could not reach to shut off. Again, there was the sense of no control, the sense of being swamped.

Helena looked up at the lighted doorway of the taverna. It seemed curiously far away and she shivered. There was the sound of Greek music going on inside, the harsh sound of bouzouki and the Asiatic sound of a woman singing. There was the sound, too, of rhythmic clapping. She supposed some tourists were being entertained in that off-the-cuff, spontaneous way the islanders had when they felt like it. The music was not live, however, and it came from a juke-box. Someone – old Yiannis, perhaps, would be dancing. Last year, he had taken up with an American girl forty years younger than himself. It had been the talk of Patmos.

Helena wondered if Serge were in there, but she imagined he was blind drunk by now and sleeping it off somewhere. When she had heard him in the hall that afternoon outside his mother's room, she should have broken from her morbid introspection and followed him. By keeping herself isolated, she had laid herself wide open to this hysteria, for what else could she call this stabbing pain? Was it because Serge had said she might have been the goddess in the *Cycle* that she felt this way? Had she been? Did this powerful affliction come from tumid gods hidden within herself? Within Arthur?

All at once, it came back to her plainly, as if by looking across the garden into the brightly lit taverna, she had been given the stark illumination of truth. The truth was that Arthur had loved her. All of these masks and poses and memories of experience twisted to an ultimate pitch were antonyms for what it really, finally had been. Arthur had fallen in love. Oh, that was awful, was it not? She covered her mouth with her hand and sobered up like one splashed with cold water. What had she thought at the time? Had this been why she had panicked? She remembered she had thought, This can go on forever and ever unless I stop it. The panic had been the way to the knob – the only way to switch it off – this horrifying sense that she was known to him not in body but in being. She had never wanted that sort of thing! Never! How could she have borne the blurring of the sharp thing any further? How could she have been, for instance, his wife? Of course, they had never discussed marriage, but the secret tracks where the out-of-hand thing led to had been, she was sure of it, a conclusion of mortgages and alimony and Sunday papers in bed and a civilized solution all round. The flat with the bad abstracts in Knightsbridge might have been hers. Why did she now know she was not flattering herself? She knew. She just knew. It was as concrete a thing as having been pregnant and having had an abortion – something that the mind might tend to forget – something the body might remember.

It had all started in Orford, first the affair, and then later the love. Each time they had managed to get away there, he had talked about the Merman. Arthur was trying to write a Merman poem, but it was going badly. Oh dear, thought Helena, Oh Christ! She had understood him perfectly as half-man, half-fish. He had been the delicate balance of an amphibian thing, a thing not wholly natural, a mind and a body with the soul cut out. Both he and she had found sentiment repulsive. He would talk, for instance, in the oddest way about his teenaged children, especially Claire, like a reptile expressing horror at some warm, mammalian thing. He hated the way the child clung to him, cringed from him. He would talk of the grossness of Jane's motherhood, how he had come home in the early years of their marriage and had found her smelling of milk, vomit, covered in fluff. Helena would half-listen to all of this, propped on her elbow, eyeing his flanks as he spoke, as he talked of how his own strange nature filled him with disgust. He had opened the chambers of his heart to her, told her how he dreaded going home to the revolting adolescent girl covered with spots, too fat, eating like a pig – and his dim son, squeezing his pimples and sequestering girlie magazines. He had told her how he could not bear to touch his wife and how he became so angry. If it were not for Helena, he had said, he might do some injury at home.

For some reason, the memory of a painting in the National Gallery flashed through Helena's mind. Who was the artist? Why did it matter? The point was that a maiden was leading a dragon on a chain. Had that been herself with Arthur? There certainly had been no St George. Round and round and round she had led it as it grazed on human flesh and wept bitter tears for doing so. What had he wanted from her? To change the analogy, had he not wanted the transforming kiss? Why should she have been put in the position of having to do that? She had not wanted to do that. To do that was the dirty thing, the thing that smeared their balance with marks and thumb-prints.

Helena felt sick and cold. 'Lay your sleeping head, my love, human . . .' The affair would have lasted if only he had kept to the discipline of its inner truth. Perhaps his mother's death had had something to do with the way things had gone wrong. During the pitch of the affair, she had had a sudden heart attack. Arthur inherited quite a lot of money from her, for he had been her only child and she had come from a very wealthy family. Her husband, Arthur's father, had disappointed her ambition to be a bishop's wife. It had been as if Mrs Proudie had spawned Heathcliff and Arthur had loathed his mother. Helena gave a long shudder, for it was after this woman had died, this woman with a 'heart as cold as charity', that Arthur had crumbled and become moist and doting. He started to become dependent. Helena could not stop it becoming what it was becoming.

She remembered the last time she had tried. He had started to fall apart, disintegrate in her arms. It had been terrifying, and so it had been she who had suggested that last trip to Orford, the weekend they had both managed to sneak away, never to return there again. It had been summer when they had broken up, so why did she remember walking by herself on Sunday morning before breakfast through cold grass. She was sure there had been starred frost on the grass, maybe dew, probably it had been dew.

She had walked at dawn and all alone, aware that it was not working – the spell, the magic, the charm – whatever. She had walked knowing that it was not working, but not yet, that finally it had not worked. She had left him sleeping that Sunday morning, his fragile eyelids closed, the child's droop to his sleeping lip, his breath innocent somehow of all that was buried just beneath her mind. She was walking off the night before, because she could not stop him *becoming*, and she had thought

353

of the Merman, stuffing his mouth with berries, his unshorn talons spearing fish, his pagan and uncrucified self. She had thought to herself of his feral teeth, his sour breath, his matted hair. She had thought about the power of his death, the triumph of his ordeal. Arthur had burst through the bounds, the conventions, the whole *Oh, Calcutta!* of it all the night before with a great release of feeling. He had been in the process of becoming what she could not turn off. The lame to walk and the blind to see. She walked and thought and walked all that early morning. She had thought of fishes' tails and the white club foot, the damaged limb. And it was as if the waters in the little English bay had gathered their forces and overwhelmed her in the tide of what was personal.

She had tried to preserve things by giving reasons to them. The truth was that she had loved Arthur, but not in that way, not in the way it was becoming. She had tried to reason with herself that having lost both of her own parents at a very early age, she was somehow threatened by Arthur as a middle-aged orphan. That was how he was behaving now, but he would not always behave in that way. All the same, his new and childlike quality unhinged her somewhat.

A memory of her dead father had come to her. It had risen and bubbled at her throat, a sketchy sense of a powerfully built and elegant young man in uniform, leaving. Sitting in an armchair before leaving, cigarette smoke had curled around his head like an aureole and Helena had been awed into silence. Of course, that had been the last time she had ever seen him. He had been debonair, her father, and had always spoken to her as if she were an adult, but he had gone like the smoke eddying.

Striding onwards away from the shore, she had found herself by a ditch in a country road, the frost like flax on the long, lush grasses, but of course it had been dew . . . and iron cold in her feet. At the end of their conversation, Arthur had made love to her, his face wet with tears. Now, what could she do with that? She did not know now and had not known then what to do with that, for it had quite unbalanced her. To this very day, she was not sure he had said 'I love you', but he had. She had pretended not to hear it and they had gone on as if he had not said it, even though every meeting before that one had become pregnant with the pressure of those words unexpressed. She had kept on thinking he would return to what he had been to her at first, so fiery like the sun so brilliant, so lopsided in his odd nature. He had risen above her and burnt from her the fear, the modesty and the very pity he had asked for

354

in the end. Had it been pity he had wanted? At one point, he had told her that she made him feel real. She had understood the Merman and had made him feel real.

Helena found that she had been crying. Tears ran down her cheeks and spotted the tablecloth in the soft gourd light. Her shoulders were hunched into her shawl and her chest was quaking. Had this been the element that had betrayed them? Had, all unwitting, she destroyed the thing she valued most by giving him that access to himself? Whatever, she had been impelled to flee both Arthur and her husband, and here she was all alone.

Helena became aware that she was being watched by the English-woman who was sitting with her husband at the far end of the garden. She murmured a few words to the man, whose face was cast in shadow and Helena panicked, terrified that they would come over and ask her what was the matter. Oh God! she thought, Does that woman know me? She was sure she had seen her before. She got up abruptly, purse clutched to her, shawl clutched around her, and made for the steps leading up to the main body of the taverna with its clean, steel kitchen and its bright, overhead lights. There was, in fact, a sort of party going on. The man who sold postcards at the Monastery was buying people drinks. Ouzo glasses were being clinked, and the juke-box was blaring 'Agape Mou', sung by a man with a throaty voice. There were no tourists about, so Helena decided the celebrations must have to do with the forthcoming wedding of Evangalia's niece. Helena gave herself a shake and dabbed her nose on her sleeve. She paid the distracted Vangelis, and suddenly remembered that she had seen the English people waiting for the boat the night Marina had arrived. They had been drinking Metaxa underneath an awning at the port. It was all right. She would never see them again. Actually, she felt much better now. Yes, she thought, almost as if it were an inconsequential thing, the poems might indeed be about her, about their affair, Ares and Aphrodite, Mars and Venus, in part, at least. But she really must, she thought, have a look at those journals, especially after all she had been through.

All of this relieved her, being once again in the bright light with the brisk Vangelis totting up her bill and the faintly boozed Greeks enjoying themselves. She wondered if Paul and Marina had returned, then looked at her watch and thought, No, not yet. Of course, not yet.

And then, as she left the taverna for the short walk home, there came Tanya again, flapping in her foolish Greek dress from the other side of the square.

'Oh God! What next?' she said aloud, vexed that her moment was over, so quickly truncated before she could stroll back under the sailing moon, savouring and adjudicating upon the strong emotions that her meditation had revealed.

Tanya, on seeing her, slowed her pace. 'Dr Taggart!' she called.

'Yes, what is it, Tanya?'

'Dr Taggart?' she came level with Helena. They met in the centre of the square. 'Your aunt . . . I am really very sorry. Your aunt is dead.'

'What?'

'Your aunt. The Princess has died. I went in to get her ready for the night. She is dead. I am sorry. I am so sorry. If only I had known. I'm sorry, so sorry.' Tanya kept on saying. 'I looked for your cousin everywhere, but he is nowhere to be found. Maybe he is in Skala . . .'

But Helena heard none of this, even though Tanya babbled on. 'She can't be!' Helena cried. 'Oh, Tyotya, you are not! You cannot be dead!'

'Dr Mason has not arrived back yet . . . I don't know what to do! Please, Dr Taggart . . . oh, please, help!'

'Are you absolutely sure she is dead?' Helena felt a great crack in herself and could almost hear it as a small ping signifying the beginning of something vast.

'She is cold. She is not breathing. I cannot feel her pulse. I gave her mouth to mouth resuscitation. I massaged her chest. Maybe it isn't even her heart. I don't know! Her eyes were open, but I closed them. I don't know how she died. How could she die just like that? I'd only spoken to her an hour before. She ate her dinner. Evangalia isn't there. There's her niece's wedding, you see. Dmitris isn't there. No one was there but me.'

'We must find Serge. We ought to get a doctor, but there is only a paramedic on the island. We must get him. Paul will be back soon. Yes.' Helena said all of these things, but her mouth felt numb, and she heard a cry coming from herself that she did not associate with herself. 'Oh, no! Oh, Aunt Sonya, no!'

XXVIII

A STRONG WIND had got up and the boat heaved upon swells of dark water. The Canadians had disembarked at Samos, having decided to see it after all, and although a few, straggling tourists had boarded for the return voyage to Patmos, most of them stayed inside the warm cabin where stale cheese pies and honeyed sweetmeats, Cambas, beer and ouzo were to be consumed in relative comfort by the good sailors amongst them. Marina and Paul, however, stayed out on deck. Even with the chill of the sudden stiff breeze, they stood slightly apart, elbows balanced on the railings. They neither touched nor moved away from each other. They were held in a curious stasis.

It might have been the Turkish guide who had inhibited things between them, Marina thought, or it might have been themselves. A bright, summary moment had occurred in their embrace like the flash of a wing opening, but before either of them could stagger out a word from the shock of it all, the guide had rattled into the car park in his minibus, anxious to collect them before they missed the boat, and with an insinuating leer had mortified them both into silence.

Marina felt as if she had been caught dancing on Arthur's grave. The embrace had been an enormous release, but she was gnawed by the sense that he had not really meant it, for since their putting out to sea, he had not acknowledged it. She checked at her handbag to make sure she still had the plastic bottle of water from the Ephesian spring, and fiddled with the straps. To her surprise, she felt a sudden indignation that he had neither mentioned nor repeated what had passed between them, as if he were actually denying the whole thing. She gazed balefully at the moonlight on the swell of waves. Her scorched flesh shivered with goosebumps, but still she did not go inside.

Paul felt sure that Marina had welcomed the intervention of the Turkish guide. On the bus ride to the boat, he had not been able to tell whether it had been sunburn or flushing which had made her face so red. It was most certainly his imagination that she had been made happy by the kiss, for she would not even look at him now. She was clearly used to being admired and probably thought he was bent on seducing her, when it had all along been a fleet thing like the opening of an eye.

357

He felt trapped in himself, as if like Lazarus, he had been called forth, only to find the door of the tomb sealed and rock solid. They had stood like this in silence for a long time and now she was beginning to look annoyed. He thought he must speak, but at the same time he wondered if it would not be better to take his chances with the sea and jump.

'Marina?' 'Paul?' they spoke together.

'No you!' 'No you.'

'Go on!' she said, oddly insistent.

He looked at her and could not help but smile. Her hair tufted about in the wind in a little top-knot where her combs had been misaligned, and her face had a beaky expression. She looked a bit like a fluffy, outraged chicken and he melted for her. 'Actually, I don't really know what to say. Maybe I should apologize.'

'For what?' she asked sharply. 'For the kiss or the silence? Or are you apologizing for having made a mistake?'

He was quite taken aback by this. In fact, he really did not know if he had a truthful answer.

'Look,' she said, 'I'm not holding you to anything, you know. It's the sort of thing that's bound to happen when two people are on their beam ends. I was happy. It made me happy, but I'm not making anything of it if that's what you're thinking. Let's just skip it – you know!' She churned into a small temper and brooded into the water.

'But . . .' he said. A wave slicked against the hull and sent up white foam, splashing them both.

'You're wrong about Arthur and me . . .' she found herself winding up and jacking off into this nonsequitur and was amazed at the force of her feelings.

'What?' He was suspended in bewilderment.

Her chest heaved. She breathed through her nose. 'It's in your mind that I am being unfaithful to his memory, isn't it true? You said you thought I loved him and so you must think that I loved him and that I love shallowly.' She looked wildly at him. 'But I did not love him. I did not, I did not, I did not. I hated him! There! And I felt sorry for anyone, *anyone* who had anything to do with him, especially myself, I suppose, but most of all Jane and his *children*! You should have seen the way he treated his own children! You should have heard the way he talked about them! And I put up with it all for years, trying to pretend that I didn't hate him, but I did, and that's why I feel guilty, I feel guilty because of that. I'm not just saying this because you kissed me, because I'm sure it didn't mean anything, but when you did and because you

358

did, I saw it. I see it now. I *hated* him. Now, what am I going to do with that? How am I going to live with that? There it is – the Beast from the Sea. I loathed him – passionately, and as far as I was concerned, the marriage was one long rape!'

Paul was agog. He had never really seen anyone behave like this before.

She took a long, dramatic step back from the railings. 'I don't know what it is,' she said, 'whether it is something I ate or dreamed about last night or whether it is what happened in Ephesus, but Helena can bloody well *have* him! And why not?' She looked at her left hand, efficiently, as if she were about to consult her watch, but instead, spread her fingers wide before her.'Right!' she said, 'This is it!' and for the last time, she fiddled with her wedding ring, then pulled it off, and before he could stop her, she flung it into the sea. 'There!' she said briskly, 'the fishes can have that too – Greek fishes! That ought to please him. Don't you think?'

'Marina!' he cried.

'It shocks you, doesn't it?' she said, and then, before he knew what was happening, she burst into floods of hysterical tears. Instinctively, he moved to comfort her, but she pushed him away. 'No!' she said, 'You know very well you don't really want this.' She made to go inside, stabbing a few steps in defiance towards the door, but she got no further than a little bench under the porthole. Her midriff went concave and she threw herself upon the sea and sobbed with complete abandon. He could only barely see her in the light from the cabin window. Quietly, he went to sit beside her. He did not know he would do this, but he did. 'Look,' she said, gasping, 'you are going to say I manipulated you into something. You are. When it comes to relationships between men and women, I can truthfully say that I have learned a lot!' Effluvia from her nose ran down her lip and she wiped it off on her forearm.

'Well,' he said, 'you certainly come with a government health warning.'

'A goddess cannot have friends,' she said.

'Well, then, we'll have to sacrifice you a goat, won't we? Or do you prefer oxen?' He took out his pocket handkerchief and wiped her tears and her nose. 'There!' he said.

'Actually,' she said, laughing a little and crying at the same time, 'I like oxen, or sheep maybe. I've never been too keen on goats. Anyway,

I wasn't his goddess, you know. I'm sure of it. I know that it was really Helena all along.'

'Well, that's as maybe,' he said. 'May I?' he asked, and he put his arm around her. Mistrustful for a moment, she dropped her head to his shoulder, and before long, he realized that she was fast asleep.

XXIX

HELENA HAD NEVER SEEN the paramedic before. He was new to the island, a young medical student, nearly qualified and the chemist in Skala had rustled him up. He was doing something in the Dodocanese, some project or other, and he already had the air of a portly consultant. He pronounced her aunt dead of a stroke as if there were no room for a second opinion, and he had been dreadfully shocked that Helena and Tanya had neglected to get a priest. Taking matters in his own hands, he had rung the Monastery and advised them to expect a visitation 'momentarily'. He spoke the sort of English that made him sound vaguely like an American airline pilot or newscaster.

When he had gone, Helena, for some reason, opened up the drawing room and seated herself in the big tasselled chair next to the fireplace. She thought, curiously, of a line from Milton about 'the two-handed engine at the door', but try as she might, she could not put the words in context although she knew the line was from *Paradise Lost*. There was something about smiting. And so it had come to pass that she had lost Arthur and her aunt within three months of each other, and towards neither of them had she had any conscious feeling of affection until they had died. This seemed very odd to her. Another snatch of verse came:

> 'After great pain a formal feeling comes –
> The Nerves sit ceremonious like Tombs.'

Now that was Emily Dickinson, that she did remember. Helena thought that this must have been why she had opened up the drawing room, because of the formal feeling death gave. 'Fancy,' she said aloud. 'We haven't used this room for years. Now twice in the space of three days.'

Poor Tanya was dreadfully upset. She seemed to think it was all her fault, although it was not her fault at all. If it was anyone's fault, it was Paul's, and Serge's, of course. Tanya had never seen a dead body before. The paramedic had been particularly kind to her, even though she had not sent for a priest. He had taken pains to explain to her why it was important to have one and Helena had seen, for a moment, his eyes lurid in religious fervour. He had not been kind to Helena. She shrugged.

361

Helena had asked Tanya to come sit with her in the drawing room, but somehow, Evangalia had been called back, though by what means, Helena could not ascertain, and she was laying the Princess out because she knew how to do it properly. It was a thing some Greek women knew how to do. 'I think you might find that very upsetting,' Helena had said to Tanya. She was not too sure, but she thought it involved irrigating the corpse and stuffing orifices with cotton wool. There was something to do with rigor mortis coming and going, but apparently this problem had solved itself, as it would do. Tanya was with Evangalia, however, and it was agreed that Helena should wait for the priest. Most of all, she dreaded Serge's return. If he were to discover that the world was coming to an end at teatime on Friday, it could not possibly be more horrible for him than hearing this news. Helena thought she had better ring Varya in Paris. She would really have to do that right away, but she found she could not move. Aimlessly, she thought how lucky it was that she was wearing a dark dress. Greek women of her age wore black all the time, and it suddenly struck Helena that in view of so much loss in one's mid and later life, it was probably the frankest thing to do. Why change? Why change into something lighter when the next funeral was just around the corner? Even if there were no funerals, one's senses and passions were being systematically pressed out of one's body until nothing remained but oneself as a toothless crone, sharing an eye or a tooth with remaining friends.

There was quite a nice icon of the Cretan School, she recalled, next to the fireplace. This was one of the Virgin, who else? It showed her alone, her hands upraised in blessing or horror, Helena did not know which. She caught the serious eyes for a moment and then looked away. She heard the knocker. The knocker was in the shape of a hand and it was made of iron, for this was a style of Patmian knockers. She went downstairs to answer the door and let in, to her surprise, a fat, jolly old monk, who was wheezing and puffing, for he had had to climb down from the Monastery then up to her house. He had a big white beard and looked like Father Christmas. Helena had no idea at all what to say to him. She realized that it was all part of his routine in any case, and so they exchanged minimal greetings and she showed him up yet another escalation to her aunt's room. She smiled thinly when she realized that he thought she was a tourist, even though they had spoken in Greek. 'Aren't you going to come in and say some prayers for her?' Tanya asked, just as if she were an equal.

'You don't believe any more than I do!' Helena retorted, sure of this for some reason.

'It's a mark of respect!' Tanya said, brimming with moral outrage.

'I will respect her in my own way!' Helena snapped. Evangalia was crossing herself elaborately, and the priest seemed to be setting something up. As Helena vanished down the hall, the scent of incense followed her. Her throat was aching. Russian words came back to her from a long time ago and she felt them wanting expression in her mouth like a craving for some basic, vital food. She went downstairs to the telephone. The instrument looked absurd in her hands. It looked like a toy or as if it were going to fall apart. She heard intoning from above. She thought, Nothing has changed, nothing has changed. Nothing has changed at all. It made her feel about twelve years old. She kept wondering where Serge was and what bar she should ring first. She made a mental map of Hora, the twists and turns and by-ways and alleys that she and Serge had known together for so long. All white, all blinding white and tunnels and steps and narrow passages, sometimes leading nowhere. The whole town was interconnected as if carved out of one great block of icing sugar.

'Kyrie Eleison' came floating down. She knew the words and the tunes. 'Alas!' she said, 'Poor Helena!' She found she could not remember the names of the bars, although she could see the proprietors of them all vividly in her mind. Then she realized she could remember nothing at all. She was unable to lift the slim telephone book. She rang the police, but the policeman was not in. Everything seemed incredibly slow. She rang Varya's number in Paris and felt it urgent that the connection should be made. The sound of the French telephone bell in Varya's sitting room deeply reassured her. But there was no one at home. That really made her suffer. She sat down on a step and wanted to cry, but she could find no tears. The priest was still intoning. Helena wandered through the house picking things up and putting them down.

Wherever she went, she heard singing. It sang her. She could not remove herself from its soft insinuations of the sublime, from its polished, unmelodious Byzantine grace. 'It's tribal,' she said aloud, and wandered into the kitchen to get away from it. She flicked the switch and the neon light flickered coldly on, blenching everything in its dismal rays. She sat at the deal table, her hands folded. 'I thought she could never die,' she said. 'She seemed indestructible.' This whole business seemed to touch her so nearly. Suddenly, the bathos of all that singing hit her. It seemed absurd to chant over a corpse. She had merely been caught in the trap of not being able to see Aunt Sonya dead, not really dead. On her first desperate rush up the stairs with Tanya, she had encountered the absence of life in the corpse as if it signified the presence of her aunt's spirit elsewhere. Whatever else could be said of Aunt Sonya, she had had a crude, robust vitality, so much so that it was all too easy to perceive her body as having been vacated rather than dead. Of course, she was dead! It was only an infantile part of herself that saw the spirit haunting, hovering like the smoke of incense somewhere above the singing figures in the bedroom. Helena felt as if she were the victim of some atrocity. Her face hurt deep in the bones. How could she endure all of this loss? Terrible Aunt Sonya! Sonya the Terrible. What was she thinking of, allowing herself to get into this state? She was gone now, and there was nothing to do but get over it.

She wandered back into the hall. The priest, now finished with his offices, was huffing down the stairs, Tanya behind him. He put out his hand to Helena and it was her sudden instinct to kiss it as her mother would have done, but she refrained from this, annoyed at herself for the impulse. Shaking his hand, she said, 'Thank you very much' in English, and let him out. 'A funeral! Oh God, there has to be a funeral!' she said to Tanya. 'I forgot.' She felt she could not endure following the priest and discussing this with him. She felt a torment of nerves as if little hot insects were nipping the end of each one of them. 'I must call Varya first, I must ring Varya and see when she can come. I must wait for Serge. We must arrange things together.' She thought she was going to scream aloud for the nerves and the sluggish torpor that weighed her hands in chains and her feet so that she could not reach for the telephone on the hall table. So much for their sitting 'ceremonious like Tombs'. She supposed the unwiring of nerves was beginning.

Tanya said nothing. Evangalia could be heard keening above them. Suddenly, Helena realized that Tanya regarded her with contempt and was regarding her with open contempt even now. 'I found this,' she said shortly. 'I found this just now.' She handed Helena a letter addressed to her in Serge's handwriting. Helena found that her hands were shaking so violently that she could not open it.

'Please read it to me, Tanya,' she finally said. 'Please?' She sat down on the steps and looked up at the implacable girl, who slit the envelope and, with a thin mouth, unfolded the letter.

'Dear Helena, (she read)
    As my mother refused to see me this afternoon, perhaps you could

364

tell her that I myself intend to buy the papers whether or not it is her whim to validate them. It was foolish ever to expect her support and foolish of me ever to try to obtain it. Believe me, I am not drunk, but quite sober. It gives me a rather vindictive pleasure, I am afraid, to steal her thunder. I am cutting out of her best scene – the scene she has planned for Sunday morning – and am on my way to Athens to meet Lipitsin. You can tell her from me that I believe so strongly in the papers' authenticity that I intend to offer my most prized possession for them – the portrait of the Tsar my father left me. I know that he would approve, and apparently, the miniature is extremely valuable. I daresay when she hears this, she will refuse to see me or cut me out of her will, but I will simply have to take that risk. You were always right about her – and right about me too that it gratified me to let her take control of things. I see that now. Well, better late than never. I will ring you from Athens. Tell Paul not to worry – I shall return, but I do not know exactly when.

Love from
Serge'

Helena's stomach started to heave and she sat on the stairs in a fit of dry retching. At last, she murmured, 'Where are the papers, Tanya? What did she say about them? Did she tell you?' She looked pleadingly at the young woman. She could not bear to think that Serge had done this.

Tanya said nothing for a moment, then dryly cleared her throat. 'She said nothing about them, absolutely not a word. She read them over and over again and she was very upset. Reading them killed her.'

Helena was frantic. 'You mustn't say that! You mustn't say that to my cousin when he arrives. You won't, will you?'

'Do I need to?' Tanya asked. She paused. 'I'll go up and sit with her now,' she said. 'I grew to love her, you see. Princess or no princess, she had a good heart,' and Tanya struck her chest. With that tone of moral ascendancy she had gained, she added, 'Call Varya!' And she went up the stairs, leaving Helena adrift on a wider sea than perhaps she had scope to know.

At last, Helena reached for the telephone and dialled Paris for a second time. She let it ring and ring until the exchange itself cut the call off. Helena supposed that she was out with André. Varya was very much in love with this man and it had been touching to see her shabbiness disappear. Never mind. Here she had been sitting and thinking of the torments of love not five hours ago. How long ago? Five, three? Seven years. A millennium ago? She put the telephone down. In love. She was in love herself, of course, she thought. A flux of imagery came straight from her unconscious mind, curious and unrelated objects of a waking dream. She rubbed her forehead and it stopped. In love. She needed some fresh air. What did she mean by saying she was in love herself? Oh no, she thought. It was true. She was flooded by a painful, heartening throb, an antic, aching feeling. The numbness was still there in one respect, but in another, she was shot through with adrenaline and had a manic desire to walk. Why hadn't she realized? There was no need for shawl or keys she simply walked out onto the street. A wind had got up and her dark dress flapped like a flag around her. It had taken Aunt dying to make her see. She had fallen in love with Marina.

Well, why make such a tragedy out of it? She could not decide what the tragedy was, her aunt's death or being in love with Marina. She was over ninety, and she had died on Patmos as she had always wanted to do. Soon, very soon the black crows she had befriended on Hora would foregather in the house with pious obscenities in their carrion mouths. Was there not a Sapphic ode to Aphrodite? A lovely poem, a prayer. Her step felt light now. The streets were completely deserted. Marina was Arthur's parting gift and Arthur's hostage, the embodiment of what had passed between herself and Arthur. She had been preordained in the pure anarchy of their painful romance. Arthur had discovered and conquered Marina, but had not known how to woo that exquisite feminity.

This stupid thing with Paul could not possibly last and what was more she had the real key to Marina's identity. No one else knew. No one else could call her out. She would bestow her own nobility on Marina. Helena felt exalted. She flowed into the shadowed alleyways like a charmed dancer who could not put a foot wrong. From an upper room somewhere, there came the faint noise of Greek music, an air more refined than the coarse taverna songs, and Helena's feet leapt to the tune. She felt she was flying. She felt revealed to herself as an ancient kore with an enigmatic smile. It was terribly liberating this. Perhaps one did, after all, have a soul, a boundless, flowing thing. She felt she was climbing out into an Olympian understanding of herself. She felt extremely young. She knew the secret, had the letter, held the power and the key.

Marina would be very upset about Aunt Sonya. It should be quite obvious to her that Paul had let them all badly down and he a doctor of all things. Oh, yes, this would shame him a lot. She could see scorn

366

pouring out of Marina's eyes on him for having so badly misdiagnosed things. Together, they would repel him. Marian would never desert her at this time and on her lovely breast could Helena lie. Bit by bit, she would gain Marina's confidence once more. Perhaps they would spend the winter in Patmos. They would work together on the book; they would light such beautiful fires to keep out the cold; and they would give themselves to each other finally in trembling and ecstatic love.

She skittered through a tunnelled passage, inhaling the clean, fresh air. She got herself lost on purpose and wandered past ghostly domes and walls, descended into spectral caverns, ascended complex twists and turns, and traversed ethereal crossroads. It was white as a bride's bed, this town with the moon. Oh, silver, silver, white on white!

Suddenly, she felt exhausted, utterly wiped out. She thought she had better return home. She did not want to spend the night in the house with a corpse. Helena suddenly became afraid that she might faint. She looked up and was relieved to see she was nearly home. She had gone full circle. She trudged a little farther, then sat down on a low wall, not fifty metres from the house. It really, truly was her house now. She could set it on fire if she liked, sell it, let it. She began to wonder if she might live in it. Yes. That would reduce her expenditure considerably. She might indeed live in the house, take early retirement and let the London flat instead with a proviso built into the lease that she could make use of the spare room when she needed to do research. The London Library had a mailing service, after all, had it not? Her head felt very unclear. She would live in Slough or Toledo, Ohio just to be with sweet Marina.

Again, Helena thought she was going to faint. Her head buzzed as if there were a whirr of angry wings coming at her from far off. In a giddy calm she felt herself an oracle and she wondered if she would begin to shriek.

XXX

THE NIGHT had bled into day and then into early afternoon without anybody realizing what time it was or how it had been spent. The sun, however, stood at the meridian, having done its work and its worst. The scaling heat had turned the rooms to ovens and the body of the Princess had finally been removed. Paul had had a memorable morning arranging this. He sat now with Marina and Tanya on the terrace. He expected they were as relieved as he was that Helena was on the telephone again, this time to an insurance company in Paris. The sound of French drifted through the open windows and he was surprised to hear that she expressed the language awkwardly. She had given him hell on their return from Ephesus last night. He felt bad enough about it, but the paramedic had been quite right. The Princess had died of a stroke, he was sure, and these were quite unpredictable. He had tried to prevent Serge from forcing her to read the papers. He had done his utmost to check on her and she had been in good health, considering her age. He was not even her physician. Helena had talked of suing him, however. She was insisting, in fact, that an autopsy be carried out in Paris where she was trying to get the body returned. Apart from everything else, she seemed hell-bent on preventing the Princess from being buried on Patmos. As for Marina, she had mounted a vehement defence of him, but now she sat terribly withdrawn on the little wrought-iron chair, exchanging glances with Tanya as hostilities deepened. From time to time, she gave him a wan smile.

He knew for certain that Helena had no chance with such a law suit, but he felt it weak to rehearse his case before Marina. If she had now concluded that he was at fault on Helena's say-so, then maybe she was rejecting the hope that lay between them now for more pressing and ulterior reasons. He sighed and blankly eyed some forms provided by the policeman on the island. They were written in Greek, but Tanya had supplied a rough translation. These had to be signed before the poor, wretched body could be released. Tanya's face was drawn from lack of sleep. She was picking at a thread in her lank Greek dress. He wondered if he imagined the smell of corruption emanating from the

368

open windows, but he was aware of the heavy, greasy, fruit smell of death. Two hooded crows cawed at the top of the plane tree. They were a species quite common to Patmos, but Paul wished they would go away.

Marina was struggling to keep herself intact. She did not know what to do now and was completely at sea. Paul had troubles of his own, what with Helena's appalling attack. This had been a nightmarish, ghoulish stretch of hours. It was vital not to lose her self-control or push Paul into losing his. Tanya had agreed with her on that score.

This is how it had all happened. Returning late from the boat the night before, they had rounded the corner where the house stood, and there had been Helena. Unrecognizable at first, she had seemed like a vagrant curled up on a low stone wall. There had been something shocking and ominous about her as her dark form had unfolded and risen to meet them. Marina still felt startled and frightened by it, as if she had seen a body, trapped beneath the surface of a pond, released from whatever held it, rise bloated to the surface. Helena had had a curious, limp and desperate quality . . . and then there had been the news, the accusations. It was hard to keep the rest in mind, considering what had happened later.

There was a jumble of images – the body of the Princess, greenish and sunken in the hot room choking with the scent of incense and flowers. Marina had longed to take lungsful of air. Then there had been more quarrelling, and then yet another terrible fight had been engaged between Helena and Evangalia when it became apparent that Helena planned to take the body away and not bury it on Patmos. It had been unseemly and terrible. Helena had been shouting at Evangalia while Paul seemed to be working over the body in some way that Marina did not want to see. Helena had kept on saying that the body was putrefying. She kept on wrinkling her nose. She had seemed old and harsh and angry and had held a handkerchief at her nose while shouting in a queer jumble of English and Greek. Everyone was speaking at once. Apparently, everyone had assumed that the Princess would be buried in the cemetery on Hora the next day. At one point, Helena had appeared mad – insane or hysterical, it was hard to see which. 'But I can't get Varya on the telephone! Serge is in Athens and I don't know where!' she had cried, and all of this would have been reasonable but for the bugged look in her eyes. She had stood, she had paced, she had rubbed her hands. It had been quite terrifying. 'It is not to be! It is not to be!' she had screamed. 'Go to the Monastery and tell the priest there will be no funeral tomorrow! Go and fetch him, *please*!' The electrifying tone of real emergency – of overwhelming personal crisis had silenced everyone.

'Helena!' Marina had finally said and had gone to put an arm around her. This had soothed and hushed Helena, who had looked up at her with big, wondering eyes, lips parted and trembling. In view of present circumstances, Marina was glad that she had tried to console Helena, but the memory of that horrifying, naked, inner look still troubled her as she sat on the terrace.

The worse of it was there was no morgue on Patmos. Surely, tourists had died on the island before, Helena had said, calmed as long as Marina massaged her shoulders. Using Tanya as an interpreter, Marina had gently suggested to Evangalia that the presence of the Princess's children at her funeral was to be desired before a hasty burial. Perhaps, she suggested, sufficient ice could be found to pack the poor old lady's body until things had settled just a little. This seemed to strike a compromise and it calmed Evangalia long enough for her to explain, again through Tanya, that she had understood it to be the Princess's last wish to be interred on Patmos. She had even brought her shroud to the island and had showed Evangalia the shroud with instructions about it. Burial on Patmos, it seemed, insured blessings in the life to come. Marina found herself whispering 'Hail Marys' as she stroked Helena's shoulders.

And so it went on until someone did, in fact, fetch the monk at an ungodly hour and it had been he, puffing fatly from his climb to the first floor drawing room where they had all gathered, who had solved it all. Yes, the Princess was entitled to be buried in Hora. No, she did not have to be, especially if the chief mourners could not be found and the cause of death was not sufficiently established in Helena's mind. Why not do it this way. Why not bury her in Paris and then, after a few years had passed, why not exhume the body and have the bones sent to Patmos where her skeleton could await the Last Trumpet? All the bodies of those in the cemetery were, in any case, dug up three years after the funeral. There was not much room. The bones ended up in an ossuary anyway. This reasonable solution eased the situation considerably, and bit by bit, they worked through the night – Helena at last reaching Varya. Having been released from her scruples by the monk, Evangalia had set about helping Paul to find ice. Her cousin, an octopus fisherman, set sail before dawn. She and Paul raced down to the port to catch him. Perhaps with his help they could find freezing facilities.

At this point, Marina had gone to pray by the body of the Princess. Helena, having demanded a sedative from Paul, had gone to bed. It seemed quite peaceful in the little room now. Marina knelt and it was very still. The sad little bones of contention were wrapped away in their cerements and she was struck with the sense of the naturalness of it all. When she was through, she rose. On impulse, she gave the cold cheek a little kiss, then crept away and went into the drawing room where she had left her bag.

To her surprise, Tanya was sitting in the tasselled chair, one knee crossed over the other, swinging her leg. She was smoking a cigarette, something Marina would not have associated with her. 'Would you like one?' Tanya asked, offering her the packet.

Marina shook her head.

'You do realize that Evangalia's niece is getting married tomorrow, or would that be later today? It's the most important thing in her social calendar for years to come. I don't know . . . these people!' Tanya said with disgust.

'Poor Evangalia,' Marina managed to say.

'She likes you,' Tanya said casually. 'So did the old lady. So do I. You seem a descent sort.'

The young woman seemed odd to Marina. It was rather like accidentally coming across a well-known actress, taking her ease in mules and a robe, no longer dressed for her role. 'Thank you,' she said, not knowing what else to say. 'I'm not sure I am "a decent sort".'

The young woman peeled tobacco from her lower lip. 'I'm not really used to smoking. I hope it doesn't bother you. I'm awfully upset. I think the old lady was very badly treated, and not by Dr Mason,' she added darkly. 'I think of her as having been my friend.'

'I am sorry. I think you did a good deal for her and I know it was appreciated,' Marina said, hoping to stave off any unpleasant remarks about Helena. From Tanya's rather unhinged mood and swing of leg and her bright, angry eye, she felt something like this was bound to come. 'Poor Helena seems totally devastated,' she added. 'I do feel sorry for her.'

'Servants see things other people don't! That's what I am learning. Do you realize that I was hired as an interpreter and companion? I am a linguist. I already have three languages and I am now acquiring Greek, as you see. This *is* a proper "nest of gentlefolk", isn't it?'

'Tanya!' Marina felt forced to say in a gently chiding tone.

'Mrs Holt,' she said with emphasis but not unpleasantly. She

371

uncrossed her legs, put out her cigarette and leaned forward earnestly. 'Mrs Holt . . . may I call you Marina?'

Marina nodded. 'Of course.'

'When you arrived, you told everyone that you were expecting to hear from a firm in New York. Well, I have something to tell you. A letter has arrived.'

'What? Where is it? What!' Marina leapt to the edge of the chair into which she had sunk.

'I'll come to that. This morning after you left I picked up the post from the mat and put it on the letter tray. Dmitris usually does this, but the wedding has thrown everything out. There was a big, fat envelope for you, and I noticed it especially. "Ashburn" or "Ashton" or something . . . is that the one?'

'Yes, oh yes, oh please . . . Oh yes!' She found herself babbling and trembling and shaking all over, her throat dry and her palms sweating.

'Well, I saw it come, but I also saw *her* take it. I saw her from the window. Her cousin brought her the post in the garden, and when he was gone, she put the letter in her pocket.'

'Well, I can't disturb her now,' Marina said, collapsing back. Her legs, however, tried to obey an impulse to run into Helena's room and shake her awake.

Tanya continued. 'Marina, I said I liked you. I am going to tell you this because I like you. That woman has read your letter!'

'My letter?' Marina could not take this in. 'What do you mean? How do you know? Surely, she was only keeping it for me and the death put it out of her mind. You can't blame her . . .'

'Look!' Tanya said. 'She thought I was locked up with her aunt all afternoon. I keep thinking I should have been. I keep thinking I would have seen the signs, you know, but I didn't. To tell you the truth, I couldn't take any more of it, the poor old woman poring over those bogus papers. What was more, the son had turned up and there had been a row between us and I got to worry. So I crept down to the kitchen, actually to make myself a cup of tea, and lo and behold there *she* was steaming open your mail. I *saw* her! She, of course, did not see me. Who notices little Tanya?'

'She opened my letter?' Marina had nothing against which to measure this act. She felt it was happening to someone else. It seemed a large thing to her like the invasion of Poland or the sack of Rome. It felt foreign and peculiar and then it felt specific.

'Unless she was brewing up some toe of frog!' Tanya said hotly. 'I don't know, maybe she was doing origami or steaming open the gas bill. It looked like your envelope to me.'

'My letter. My mother. Maybe it's my mother.'

'I know,' said Tanya softly. 'I know. It's a shock, isn't it? Coming on top of everything else . . . but the thing is, we must get it for you.'

'How could she steam open a letter about my mother? How could she do that?'

'We must get it. Do you want me to confront her?'

'Tanya, you can't. I think it will have to be me. You don't think she's destroyed it, do you?' Marina panicked.

'I would have thought she was biding her time,' said Tanya, who really had reached rather august proportions in the tasselled chair. 'She'll use it somehow.'

'Where's Paul?' Marina cried. 'That's what he . . .'

'Would say? He sees through her all right! Look, I'm sorry to sort of push you around like this, but most people in your situation wouldn't be too lucid. If I were you, I wouldn't tell him about this. Actually, if you want to know the honest truth, I think he's in love with you. Do you want him to blow a fuse? With law suits already hanging in the air?'

Marina caved in, feeling her weakness entirely exposed. She put her head back on the chair and shut her eyes, and the tears rolled down her cheeks. She felt for her wedding ring, and then realized what she had done with it.

'I'm sorry. I'm sorry I upset you . . . Sophia Petrovna kept telling me I ought to stop apologizing to people, but I really do mean it this time . . .' She spoke so softly that Marina opened her eyes. 'Are you afraid of what you will find out?'

Marina nodded. It was hard not to acknowledge Tanya's quizzical and honest regard.

'I wouldn't be afraid if I were you. You can take it,' she said. 'This has been my month for observation. Now Helena, and I'm not afraid of calling her that now, Helena would have to have it all just-so . . . you know, parents made to order. She is incapable of truth, but you, you must not be deprived of it. Whatever you find out about your mother and father, you will be a better person for it. You are afraid you will be worse, but you won't be.'

Suddenly, Marina felt a strange, compassionate amusement at Tanya's youth. It reminded her of a time in which she had made declarative statements and had tried to weigh the weightless value of abstractions. 'How old are you, Tanya?' she asked.

'Twenty,' Tanya replied.

It struck her that she had been this age when she had met Arthur. His denunciations of hyprocisy had bowled her over. She could have a daughter this age now. Had they found her mother?

'Do you know what I think about Sophia Petrovna? You know what *I* think who am nothing and nobody?' Tanya was launched. 'I think she died because she did not want to tell a lie, and to tell the truth might have been worse. That's what I think. She was a horribly difficult old lady, but she got through somehow, by a whisker. Isn't that all it needs? Maybe no one is more than a whisker's edge away from being Helena!' She shuddered, but then looked at Marina with a kind of serenity. Marina thought this all a little sententious, but there was some truth to it.

'Now look,' Tanya continued, 'You are exhausted, apart from anything else. You stretch out on the sofa here and get some sleep. There isn't much you can do about the letter yet. Maybe she will give it to you tomorrow. Maybe you will just have to ask for it. If you like, I can try to steal it back for you. She doesn't know I know, you see. Maybe I can do that.'

Even though the horrible tiredness flooded her, Marina was sure she would never sleep, but she lay on the sofa to please Tanya and, like someone given pentathol, she was suddenly out.

As she sat on the terrace now, she wondered why she had not yet had the courage to take Helena to one side and ask her outright about the letter. It was already noon. She argued to herself that she had hardly had the chance, for Helena had moved the day into gear first thing with a stream of telephone calls. She had tried every hotel in Athens above a Grade C listing for Serge, or even for Lipitsin. She had rung the British Embassy and the Athenian police. She had been on again to her Cousin Varya and then the French Embassy in Athens. She had rung the French consul in Kos, Olympic Airways and Air France. She had attempted helicopter services, Flying Dolphin services, shipping companies and boats both large and small in an attempt to get the body of the Princess off the island.

To make things worse, she had kept on gazing at Marina in this deep, impenetrable way. There was something so wistful and tender about the look that it seemed almost terrible to challenge her. For the first time since they had met, Marina sensed a genuine empathy coming

374

from Helena, a real warmth of emotion. Maybe it was because she too now had suffered. At other times, Helena seemed mildly deranged. Her voice on the telephone sounded like machine-gun fire. When she was not phoning, she doused Paul and Tanya with excoriating looks of hostility. She kept on clapping her hand to her forehead, clenching up her eyes and grimacing. Marina was not sure whether she did not have the heart to disturb her further or whether, in truth, she did not want to know.

The thought that the letter must be somewhere in the house now possessed her. Every time she thought of asking for it, she became immobilized with terror. She had to do it, but she did not think she could. She felt oddly as if the process of dreaming and waking had been reversed and wondered if she were still asleep. She felt as if she were making a huge fuss about this relatively unimportant thing. All the furniture on the terrace, the flowers in pots and bowls, the vines and the trees looked improbable like a bad stage set. And yet the leaves held menace as they rattled and whispered in the occasional gust of dry wind.

Maybe Tanya had got the whole thing wrong. Maybe Helena had been making a cup of tea in the kitchen while reading a letter of her own. On the other hand, her tender looks might mean that she had, indeed, read it and was trying to shield Marina from some really grim news, news that had to be put off until the time when it could be broken gently. Her mother had been found in a prison, having committed a terrible crime. She had been found in a brothel. She was either mad or dead. Had her grandfather raped her mother? Yes, it was clear that Helena's compassion had been awakened by something, Marina was sure. In fact, she looked as if she wanted to be alone with Marina. What to convey? Perhaps she had some dreadful hereditary disease and Maddy had taken her on in charity, hoping against hope that Marina would not find out. Perhaps Maddy had shared the secret with Arthur, and Arthur had kept it from her in full knowledge of how dire it was. She felt insecure and ashamed now of having said she hated him, of having done what she had done to his wedding ring. Maybe, on the other hand, Frances had drawn a complete blank and was simply keeping her informed. After all, she had paid the agency a whacking great sum for this.

Helena's ireful voice sailed out over the garden. She was pointedly trying to finance the expensive business of shipping a dead body. Marina felt so sorry for Paul. Helena was deliberately, she felt, speaking school-book French in order for that they might hear how difficult everything was and how hard to afford. She had almost accused him of murder last night, wilful neglect, she had called it. He had been kind enough to look after the Princess for free during his stay, and now everything he had said and done was being cast in a malign light. In one way, she longed to tell him Tanya's secret, in another way she felt as if even moving might disturb the whole balance of her universe.

Suddenly, with a sort of inner sob, she felt as if she herself were about to enter exile. Was it not knowledge that had brought about death? From all the possibilities and all the probabilities and all the permutations she had dreamed, there was only one generative act by which she had come into the world. She was filled with a nostalgia for having been without a history. She had never really lived by the metronome of birth and burial. There had been no graves to decorate. To know, now, that she was Hungarian would mean she could not be Czech; to know that she was English would mean she could not be Russian or Czech or Hungarian. To be Irish, not Hungarian, Czech, Russian or English. She believed her name had always been Marina, but secretly and equally it might have been Audrey or Hedy or Greta or Sally. To discover herself would mean to enter a particular history from which there would be no escape. She looked from Paul to Tanya. They were the sort who would want to make her find out. Was she being spared by Helena? She could choose to go on being the daughter of a king or a movie star. Was she in her silence choosing?

All at once, Helena put down the phone and came out onto the terrace. For a moment, she looked very fragile, even elderly. Marina could see what a few short years' work would do on her – her throat, her back, her breasts, her belly – all working away in a conspiracy of time, dragging the muscles down and bending the bones. It gave her a shock of pity, both for herself and Helena. Helena was dressed entirely in black now. She sat on the wrought-iron chair where only a few days ago, Marina had sat when she had met the Princess. Helena said, 'After all that work, I am afraid it looks impossible.' She said this pressing her lips against her teeth in blame. 'My aunt had no travel insurance. I can hardly believe it. I cannot meet the cost of shipping the body, and I know that Varya has less than I do . . . Oh, if only Serge would get in touch!' She actually wrung her hands.

'Helena, you have been on the phone all day,' said Paul. She looked sharply at him as if he had a nerve to speak at all. 'You know, you might try Fiona. I think it's quite extraordinary that you haven't. Fiona does have money and I am sure she would help or even insist on paying. She would do so for Serge's sake.'

'I see you are not afraid of your sins finding you out in the autopsy,' Helena said.

'I hope I should be more afraid if I had actually committed them!'

'Look, Dr Taggart,' said Tanya. Everyone turned around. 'She died of death. She was having no pains, nothing like that. I was with her.'

'Do listen to Tanya, Helena,' Marina said.

Paul looked eagerly at Marina, but then at the ground.

'What is more,' Tanya continued, 'she actively excluded him from the room on the numerous times he came to check on her. I am quite prepared to testify to all of this even if you do give me a filthy recommendation!'

'That's very good of you, Tanya,' said Paul. 'It really is.'

'No, it isn't. Anyone with half an eye could tell that you cared for Sophia Petrovna. Don't worry. If it comes to it, I can promise that I will have a lot to say.' She narrowed her eyes at Helena. 'And now, if you will excuse me, I have been invited to the wedding, and I must go to dress. It would not do to let them down.' She rose majestically and swept into the house.

'Well!' Helena exclaimed.

'I still think you ought to ring Fiona,' Paul said somehwat loftily. 'Serge actually might have rung her from Athens. And in any case, her grandchildren are adults and they ought to know.'

'Do you really *want* Fiona to know that Serge cannot be found?'

'Actually, yes. I do want her to know. She has a great deal of good sense and is quite used to this sort of thing.' Paul and Helena were staring each other down.

'She is a stupid, unimaginative little woman, and I would really rather not beg her for money!'

'Well, let me ring her then. She and I happen to be very good friends.'

'Will you both please stop it!' cried Marina. 'Stop! Oh please! Ring Serge's wife. It is the right thing to do, but I will pay.' She grappled for her handbag, her hands trembling. She fiddled and rummaged and fished out her chequebook. 'Now, how much money will it cost to have the body shipped to Paris? I, for one, would like to see Paul cleared of any accusation! I am willing to pay any amount of money at all to stop this.'

'Marina, you can't!' Helena said heavily.

'No, really, you can't!' Paul cried.

'Oh, I can. I *can*! Believe me,' Marina said, her voice almost a sob. It struck her that this might help her to buy her letter from New York. She checked herself at the unworthiness of this thought. What she could not bear was the Princess being haggled over any longer. 'I don't even know if my own mother is alive or dead,' she said, wishing she had not and not daring to look up. 'I loved your aunt, Helena. I would like to help.'

'I expect we can get it out of the estate,' Helena said. 'In fact, I don't know why I did not think of ringing her solicitor before.'

Marina looked up swiftly. Tanya had told her the truth. At the mention of her mother, Helena's inflection of voice, the shifting of her stance, her long gaze down the garden had become evasive.

Suppose, she thought, there had been a funeral with brothers and sisters gathered round when she, Marina, had been shopping, cleaning the flat, returning books to the London Library or even having her hair done. She could see the coffin sliding down on ropes with a whole, myriad family indifferent to her existence, and never likely to hear of it either. 'I can't not know,' she whispered to herself. 'I can't refuse to know.'

'I shall ring Varya now and get her to speak with them,' Helena said. 'And then, actually, I think I shall have a little rest.'

XXXI

HELENA LAY RIGID with her eyes open, on top of her bed. She did not like lying still, but she had a more profound antipathy to moving. By now it was three o'clock and all the arrangements had been made.

Word had got round that her aunt had died and since morning, a steady trickle of visitors had tried to get in to pay their last respects. Helena had refused to answer the door, and Tanya had fobbed them off. Aunt Sonya's fervent Orthodoxy was well known, her link with Father Nikon admired. Helena sensed that a general moral outrage at what she intended to do with her aunt's body was gathering almost palpably in the streets below. A locked freezer had been found in Skala and her aunt was congealing in a plastic bag. Maybe she would not be able to return to Patmos. God alone knew what Tanya had told her neighbours. She had, indeed, a formidable gift of tongues, and was even chatty now in Greek. Who knew what calumny she was spreading? She was certainly vituperative enough to Helena's face. Suddenly, Helena knew that she must not lose the house.

If only she could persuade Marina to stay! She had knocked through to a deep cave in herself where semblances and likenesses of things half seen had found their substance in Marina. Throughout the almost phantasmogorical storm of rows she had been having that day and through the night before, there had been the reality of Marina's sweetness. How gently she had behaved towards Helena! With what thoughtfulness! And Helena was sure she had begun to break the power of Paul over her. A great love for Marina strained at her chest, then filled it so it ached into her lungs and throat, emerging finally as silent tears. She made no effort to wipe them. There seemed to be no escape from this abject feeling. It was almost as if Arthur had never existed. Helena felt as if her veins, capillaries, flesh and organs were being pressed by a heavy, steady monolithic weight. She thought, I must bear this. And then, she thought, I can't. It was the revenge of time on salient things ignored. The sun came boldly through the windows and she heard the incessant whirr of the cicadas.

There was a knock at the door. At first she confused it with the tapping of the iron hand at the front, but again the rapping came. She found she could not move. 'Helena?' It was Marina's voice. 'Grave the visions Venus sends . . .' Helena felt balmed in a suffocating sweetness.

'Come in,' she said and rose to adjust the black bodice of her dress, her silver hair. The door opened a crack and Marina slipped in.

'I am sorry to wake you,' she said. She was wearing the blue dress in which she had arrived, the one with sprigged flowers, only it hung differently now on squarer shoulders. She had caught her hair up in pins, perhaps against the heat, and her face looked thinner.

'Oh, Marina, I don't mind if it's you,' she found herself saying. She ran her fingers through her hair compulsively. 'In any case, I was not asleep. I can't sleep.'

'May I sit down?'

Helena motioned to the chair by her escritoire and Marina sat in it.

'Helena, I have something to ask of you, and I do not like to do it,' Marina said and Helena saw she was shivering as if from cold. 'I believe I received a letter yesterday and I am sure you simply forgot to give it to me, quite naturally, under the circumstances.' The balance in her voice was girded by a steely undertone.

Helena put her hand across her mouth. A policeman's hand on her shoulder could not have had more weight. The letter was under the *Oxford English Dictionary* on the shelf next to the escritoire. She had forgotten to remove it and there was no way of concealing it. 'Oh, uh, yes,' she said, 'I'm sorry. I can't remember now where I put it. You know, all the confusion . . .'

'I am afraid that I think you do know where you have put it,' Marina said.

'What do you mean?' Who could have known this? How to get the letter out? It was like seeing the pram roll down the steps in *The Battleship Potempkin*. Why did punishment always seem so incommensurate with deeds?

'Helena, dear,' Marina said as if she were talking to a small child, 'I hate to tax you with this now . . .' she could not finish the sentence and broke off in a bout of trembling.

'My aunt just died. I don't know where I put it. I'll look for it, of course.'

'I have been waiting for that letter all my life,' Marina said in a small but steadier voice. 'I am afraid that I know you have it, and that you have, in fact, read it.'

'Who told you?' Before she knew what she had said, the admission had burst from her. 'It was Tanya, wasn't it? Revolting little sneak!' She broke off in horror. She had blundered into a confession.

'Does it really matter? What matters is that you did it and that you have my letter. And I shan't go away until I get it.'

'Marina, oh please, Marina . . .' Helena felt an autonomous energy in her hands. They seemed to want to reach out, beseeching. It was painful to control them, but she made them stay in her lap.

'Why did you do it? How could you do such a thing? Was it to get at me over Arthur?'

Things were going awry, astray, amiss. She made a funny little noise in her throat. In childhood, she had developed a nervous habit of clearing her throat so that she would not speak in a Russian accent like her mother. 'I wonder . . . if it is possible . . . You see, it seems likely that I have fallen . . .' Helena could not finish the sentence. She and Marina hung in silence on the unspoken words for what seemed to be quite some time. There was a terrible directness of meaning exchanged. In some detached part of her mind still left to her, Helena realized that what she now felt was what people meant when they talked about suffering.

'Oh,' Marina whispered. 'Oh dear.' She closed her eyes, then opened them. 'I'm sorry,' she said, 'I can't . . .' She extended her hands awkwardly, gesturing to show that they were empty. 'I really am sorry.'

Helena had a vague recollection that something had been said about being torn apart by lions. It had been mentioned or she had thought about it. It seemed very hard to manage stabbing, escalating pain on this order. She imagined that it would eventually stop. It was impossible to look at Marina's face. Where her brow arched and her lashes slanted were locations of sublime importance. With her eyes closed, these things were revealed to her with visionary acuteness, as if Marina's face and hair and kindness were to become instruments of a drawn-out martyrdom. She forced herself, however, into seeing. Marina sat clutching at the neckline of her dress as if to cover her exposure of her collar-bone. She looked quite miserable.

'I took the letter so that I could know you,' Helena said at last. The simplicity of this truth relieved her.

'Helena, you mustn't . . . please!'

A wild note in Marina's voice alerted one last hope in Helena. She scrutinized Marina. She inspected Marina. She probed her expression for signs of veiled love. Perhaps piety, prudery and shame inhibited her. The pain she saw, however, was that of embarrassment, the exigency she had heard in the voice had been fear of a futher declaration of love that could not be retrieved. A sharp memory of herself as a cold, cross little girl came back to Helena, the stick-thin little monster with brains and nothing else besides. How passionately she had wanted just one friend!

'We must be friends,' she said weakly, hoping to salvage something.

Marina's brow contracted with an intense sort of compassion, and it oddly moved Helena. 'I'm not so sure that would be fair on anyone, would it?' Marina reflexively put out her hand as she said this. After a moment's pause, she added, 'I think I would like my letter now.'

Helena sat with her hands on her knees, dead within herself and incapable of movement. 'It's under the dictionary there,' she said.

Marina looked at the books. 'Do you know? Do you know who my mother is?' she asked. 'Have they found out?'

Helena nodded. 'She herself has written to you.'

Marina extracted the letter. 'I don't want you to tell me,' she said. 'I have to read it for myself.' Her voice made a sharp sound, but Helena could not tell if she were angry or simply afraid.

'I shouldn't have read it, should I?' Helena said. It seemed self-evident now that one did not go around opening people's post.

'No, you really shouldn't,' Marina replied. She was hugging the letter to her chest and her face was an awful shade of grey.

'And you can't forgive me?'

'I do forgive you, Helena, but I'm not sure that is the issue.' She paused. 'Of course, I forgive you,' she repeated. In a swift movement, she turned and kissed Helena's silver head, then turned again and was gone.

Helena sat very still for quite a while. 'I should have told you that I loved you,' she said at last. 'I should have abased myself. But then, what would I have left if I had done that?' When she realized a little later that she had, indeed, told Marina and had, in fact, abased herself, there was nothing to be done with the cold, incoming tide of humiliation.

Marina fled. Where to go? What to do? She crushed the letter to her. She could not abide to read it in her room across the corridor from Helena. Where could she hide? Hysterically, she fumbled with a button on her dress and stuffed the letter in her bra where her heart beat against it and her breast touched it. The news! She bolted past the empty bedroom of the Princess. Where was Paul? No. This belonged to her.

Then downstairs into the hall she flew. She was frantic to get out. She felt as if she would have to claw the door down to do it. If she saw Paul, all she would do would be to beat her fists against him in hysterics. She knew she was hysterical and she moved jerkily, first this way and then that. Suppose Tanya saw her, Tanya with her new sang-froid? She charged the door, then stopped. Suppose Tanya were in the atrium turning away mourners? She listened, then opened. Before her was the empty atrium and beyond her, the big front door. Where to go? The thought of the Cave hit her. Of course, in the pure simplicity of the Cave she would read the letter. The Book of Revelations! Well, you had to laugh. She heard footsteps behind her and leapt forward. Gaining the front door, she unbolted it and almost slid through a crack.

A Greek woman in black with permed hair and a spreading waistline stood upon the steps. 'The Princess!' she said indignantly, but she clearly had no other words of English with which to express her feelings.

She thinks I'm Helena! Marina thought, then realized that the woman most likely knew Helena, at least by sight. She shook her head and waved her hands about. *Kah-lee-merah*! she said, remembering Paul's using this word a few days ago.

Kah-lee-sperah! said the woman.

'I'm sorry,' said Marina wildly, 'I don't know any Greek.' The woman seemed to take pity on her and she smiled. 'No problem,' she said.

With a weird jerk, Marina bounded onto the pavement and started to run . . . but which way? She turned to the woman. 'The Cave – where is it?' she cried, close to tears.

The woman frowned, puzzled.

'The Cave!' Marina said in desperation, drawing in the air with her hands. She thought, What is Greek? What is Greek? 'Apocalypse!' she cried in hope.

'*Ah, Hiero Spielo*! *Apocalypsi*!' she shed approval on Marina. '*Aristera*' She pointed to the left then downwards. '*Tha katevite efthian, ke tha stripsete deksia . . .*' She said it slowly as if it might make more sense that way, but gave up hope, and Marina ran off to the left.

Some faint memory of direction came to her as she threaded the white streets. She was panting and sweating and had to stop. She had reached a small crossroads where a man and a boy tended some mules drawing a cart. Another man was sitting in front of a taverna door, a dog asleep at his feet.

'*Apocalypsi*?' she asked, suddenly seized by the fear of having got lost.

He smiled benignly. 'If you want the Cave,' he said in good English, 'you must go down the hill, turn left at the roundabout, and then carry on downwards for quite a way until you reach a right-hand turning. It is marked.' The dog woke and thumped its tail on the ground. The mules swished away at flies. Marina's letter seemed to melt into her chest and fuse with her body. 'Are you all right?' he asked.

'Actually, I'm not,' she said suddenly. 'I'm not now, but I think I will be.'

'Let me get you a glass of water,' he said, and he went into his taverna, as clearly he was its proprietor, and quickly emerged.'There!' he said, handing her the water. She drank it greedily.

She felt extremely grateful. 'Thank you so much,' she said, a lot more steadily. 'What is that in Greek?'

'*Efharisto*,' he replied. '*Efharisto poli*.'

'Well, then, efharisto poli,' she said, and much more calmly, made her way down the hill.

She walked and as she walked she realized that she had no purse. She had forgotten money and a bag. She could see the shrine complex nestled far below her in the hills, bright in the slanting sun, and the tarmac felt good under her feet as she descended the long, winding road. The pain of her sunburn, which she had ignored all day, started to throb and cool in the gentle breeze and shade of late afternoon. Perhaps she should open the letter now, she thought, suspended as she was above the dreaming harbour, the hills dotted with pines and olive trees, but she decided not to. Some motorbikes whizzed by, roaring with strong boys. What on earth was she to do with Helena? She knew she had just enough strength to read the letter and no more, but the mechanical noise of the bikes broke in, somehow disturbing the calmed surface of her mind. She focused on her toes through the flapping sandals. It would not do to think of that unmasked face. All that had been said of Helena seemed cruel in the light of what she now knew, but how she wished her mother's secret, whatever it was, had not been violated! Her mother, her mother was alive. Marina's heart raced. She strode into a hairpin bend and quickened her pace down the road.

All at once, she heard another motorbike overtake her, but it slowed and came to a stop. A Greek woman, perhaps a little younger than herself, dismounted, turned and gestured to the saddle with her hand. '*Skala*?' she asked. Marina shook her head. 'Apocalypse!' the woman cried, triumphant with this intuition. She beckoned to Marina to share her ride. It touched her deeply that a total stranger would show her such kindness.

'*Efharisto*!' she said, awkwardly practising the new word and dumbly showing that she had no others.

'*Parakalo*!' the woman replied brightly, evidently glad of something in general. Marina clambered onto the pillion, tucked in her skirts, and they whizzed off down the hill, careening round corners with slow ease. The breeze ruffled Marina's hair and cooled her and when they reached the entrance to the shrine and she had to climb down off the bike, she almost clung to the woman's hand. She felt as though she were about to be wheeled into a major operation. She thanked the cheerful woman again and again, then left alone, made her way to the door and entered the long ambulatory filled with light.

It was empty save for some trestle tables done up with flowers and sweetmeats, lilies and little cakes. Passing these, she followed the sign that pointed to the 'Sacred Cave' and proceeded down the long stone steps. It was only when she reached the chapel itself that she saw she had made a dreadful mistake. There was a wedding in progress with incense, intoning, vestments and crowds with the bridegroom and the bride, all in white splendour.

'Oh dear!' she said softly, and fled in terrible embarrassment up the steps again. It must be Evangalia's niece. She had forgotten all about it. Tanya would be present. The thought reassured her. All at once, at the top of the flight, she saw that a little gate was open, and it led onto the roof and dome that covered the Cave. There were benches of white-washed stone set in the parapet, and it clearly seemed a suitable place to sit. 'I don't think they would mind,' she said softly. She went in, took the letter from her bodice and sat in the little enclosure. The dome arched cleanly up in brightest white. *Kyrie Eleison* rose up and filtered through the windows. '*Christe* . . .' It was no different.

The letter was damp and crumpled now and with a painful resignation, she found she had to open it. The singing from the wedding was rising. Marina had seen someone holding crowns over the bride and the bridegroom.

'Dear Marina . . .' she read, and she read the letter from Maureen, her mother, over and over again.

The ancient Byzantine intoning rose up, more and more singing. It was as if they could not ask for mercy enough. Marina did not hear it. She heard what she was reading. It seemed beyond anything wonderful. At the same time, it was the saddest thing she had ever read . . . all about the heart . . . '. . . my aching heart . . .', 'My heart was broke . . .', 'The Sacred Heart of Jesus'. Marina thought about her deb party, the dance her 'parents' had given her in the St Regis Hotel. If she had known that her mother had wanted to be standing in the lobby waiting to catch a glimpse of her, she would have torn off her white kid gloves and burnt them, trampled her flowers and rent her dress into pieces. She wondered if Maddy had been possessed.

She sat there immobile for quite a while before she really absorbed the news that her father was dead. So her maiden name would have been Grabowski if her parents had married. She felt the bones of her face. So, indeed, she was partly Slavic. She was not at all sure she liked the sound of him. So he wrote poetry, did he? Marina thought if she met another man who wrote poetry, she might well shoot him on sight, but realizing where she was she quickly repented. It seemed too final altogether to know that he was dead. She brightened, however, at the thought of her stepfather. It seemed to bode well that Maureen had told him about her, and better still that he and – Good God! – her half-brothers and sisters had sent her a message.

Marina suddenly felt a relief of such magnitude that it was hard not to close her eyes there and then and sleep like a baby. Her mother was alive and loved her. Her father had not been Arthur, nor a rapist, nor a relative. He had only been a boy with whom her mother had gone too far in the back seat of . . . behind the . . . It was an irony, she thought, that she was reading all of this while a wedding was going on. Nowadays this sort of thing did not matter, did it? It pained Marina, nonetheless, until she realized that her mother must be thinking that it would, and would be waiting on tenterhooks to hear. 'Don't worry, Marina. God forgives all.' She read it again. She had heard this sentiment all her life, and by a fine intuition, she perceived that her mother really meant it, otherwise, she could not have written the letter in the way she had. Her mother wondered if she were angry with her. Marina wept and kissed the letter over and over, pressing it to her. Marina wanted Mother's Day, Marina wanted to buy a huge, plush card. She wanted to buy a vast and gaudy bunch of flowers, no tasteful freesias. Marina wanted to send her mother a box of chocolates as big as a football pitch in the shape of a heart and wrapped with pink, satin ribbon. For Christmas she would buy her . . . what? what? She could not think of anything extreme enough to give this woman and her whole family, on Arthur's money, and Maddy's money and Daddy's money. She had found a cause. Her brother! She hugged it to herself. Her brother would go to

Harvard if he could. The sky was the limit and the only just revenge on Maddy. She could see Arthur's face! He would think Maureen 'ghastly'. She imagined that was what Helena had thought and she flushed, stung.

Well, she certainly was not the child of Audrey Hepburn (she would give her mother a trip to England and take her to tea at the Ritz), nor of Ruritanian nobility (they would try on *hats*), nor of the Kuriensky family (they would go to Ireland, stay at the Gresham Hotel and look at castles). Above the wall, she could see the sky. She stood and looked over the battlements into the harbour. She felt ashamed at wanting to offer her mother all of these material things. She would, of course, send her flowers at once, and then write, and she would return immediately to the United States. It was just that she felt she must make up for what had happened to them both.

Her 'grandmother'! She put her hand over her mouth, feeling sick. All of those happy times swanning out to the big house in the country! All the merry little birthday parties, the spotless little frocks, the Feast of the Assumption, which she had told Paul about only yesterday! The herbaceous borders, the rose garden had supplied the crown of flowers with which the peasant's child had been deceived into thinking that even the Mother of God was rich. Her real grandmother had been a servant in that house and would have brought Marina little biscuits on a tray and lemonade. She would have had to call her 'Miss'. 'I can't stand that!' she whispered. 'I can't stand it and I shall never forgive *any* of them,' she said passionately to God. 'I'm sorry. I know that bothers You. I'm sorry. I'm overwrought.' It slowly dawned on Marina that Maddy had kidnapped her. They had promised her mother one thing and then they had done quite another, and they had gulled, sugared and silenced her whenever she had asked the question they had promised her mother they would answer. The thought that Maddy had wilfully concealed her mother's whereabouts against the bargain that had been struck left Marina standing in a kind of awe. She hoped to God she had confessed it on her deathbed. Suddenly, she thought that for all the peace of mind the news had given her at first, that she would scream, wedding or no wedding, Cave or no Cave.

Paul said quietly, 'So there you are, Marina.'

She jumped and swung round. She did not know whether she was happy to see him or not.

'I have been looking for you everywhere,' he said. 'I extracted from Helena what had happened.'

She said nothing. She noticed, though, that he was not wearing his hat.

'I thought you might come here,' he continued, conversationally. 'That's the wedding of Evangalia's niece going on down there. If we look through the dome, I am sure we can see Tanya. Come on. Have a peek!'

Her hand seemed welded to the letter, but she let it drop to her side, then waved it helplessly about. There were slit windows in the dome and together they peered through. Wreaths of incense still rose, but the singing had stopped and the priest was talking. Marina could see Tanya standing in the crush. She was wearing a little suit with a smart jacket. Marina backed away. Suddenly, all the fervid intensity she had felt was eclipsed by a draining exhaustion. 'I have my letter, my letter from my mother,' she said.

'I know,' he replied. He put his head to one side. 'It must be quite a jolt.'

'You can read it if you like,' she said, feeling impelled to say this.

'It's all right,' he said, 'You don't have to show it to me.'

Suddenly, she felt she must show it to him at all costs. It seemed important to have a witness in case it was taken from her again or something happened to her before she could write to Maureen. 'Please! I do want you to see it,' she said.

They stood together on the domed platform. There was a space between them that he did not broach. The Greek singing resumed, this time unintelligible. 'Not here,' he said quietly. 'Come along, let's go.'

They left through the ambulatory and walked down the alleyway of feathery pines. 'Let's find a place to sit,' he said. 'We can sit by the mule path.' They made their way upwards until they reached the stony ascent and finding a broad, flat rock in the wall that lined the way, they sat together in the cool of early evening. Marina gave him the envelope and carefully he extracted both letters – the one from the detective and the one from Marina's mother. Checking with his eyes to make sure it really was all right, he read them.

'I think it is a very touching letter, your mother's, don't you? Or is it overwhelming? I can imagine feeling nothing at all, or too much to be able to talk about it.'

Marina was weeping. 'You must think I cry all the time,' she said.

'Oh, Marina!' he said, 'This is an extraordinary thing to have happen!'

'It's too touching to think about,' she cried. 'I can hardly bear to think about it! If only you knew the lies they told me! Indirectly, of course, but they were still lies. If only you knew the fantasies I have had!' She found a crumpled tissue in her pocket and blew her nose. 'I feel I have years to make up to her, years for what they did to her!'

'What did it do to you, Marina?'

She shook her head slowly and sadly. 'The point is they didn't think it would do anything to me but good. They ensured such a destiny for me that they assumed the history would take care of itself. I don't know what it did to me. I feel remarkably twisted up inside.'

A little evening breeze had got up. It ruffled Paul's hair slightly and in the harbour below, it corruscated the water. Marina unpinned her hair, took the combs out and shook her head, lowering it. She felt a little faint. She rubbed her eyes and then breathed out.

'What are you going to do?' he asked.

'I must go to see her! If I could fly there this minute, I would! Just, yesterday I was worrying about Arthur and Helena and her book! It is nothing next to this.'

'Marina,' he said, 'this is not going to be the easiest thing to do.'

'If I have to go back to London and that flat, I shall burn the whole building down,' she said dully.

'Look, he said, 'I'm not sure what you are going to make of this and it's only a suggestion, but you could stay with me for a few days and I could help you go through things . . . you know, get yourself together and then fly to New York.' He was prodding a weed in the mule path with his toe. 'It's meant to be a neighbourly offer,' he added defensively.

Suddenly, she felt sore and guarded, afraid of Maureen. 'That's very nice of you,' she replied, 'but would it be all right if I thought about it? I'm going to try to write her a letter first. I mean, I shall write to her or send a telegram. When I see what I'll say, then I can tell you. OK?'

'That's fine,' he said. He looked off into the middle distance. 'But I was going to say to you that it might be an idea to leave Patmos very soon. There's a boat to Athens tomorrow.'

'Paul, I am very grateful that you asked me to stay,' she said, feeling it strongly in a delayed reaction.

'The offer was not meant to evoke gratitude,' he said. 'It's a thing I want to do. It comes out of love, I suppose.' There was a lightness and a grace in his expression she had not seen. 'The idea of pinning you down to that is disagreeable.'

It struck Marina that this had been a very difficult thing for him to say. She smiled. 'Thank you,' she said.

'Marina,' he said, blurring the whole thing with a change of tone, 'I meant it when I said I thought it would be a good idea to leave the island very soon. I'm not exactly sure what went on between you and Helena earlier, but things rather came to a head after you left the house. I heard a noise, you see, after what must have been your conversation together and thinking something had happened to you, I went upstairs only to find her in a very bad way.'

'Oh, no!'

'She had been heaving things about her room. There were books and papers everywhere, and she was not at all pleased to see me.'

'Oh, it's all my fault! Poor Helena!' She remembered the look on Helena's face. In view of her mother's letter, it seemed to partake of another space and time. 'I hurt her.'

'It is most certainly not your fault!' Paul said indignantly. 'How and in what way is Helena your fault?'

The intensity of the locked gaze that had passed between her and Helena came back to Marina. It was as if Arthur had been superfluous to them both all along, and as if one woman had been the shadow of the other, united only in the poems themselves. 'It is a fault not to be conscious,' Marina found herself saying. 'I know that sounds pompous, but I was not aware of something important. I let it slip by until it expressed itself in this way.'

Paul raised an eyebrow sharply. 'She and I had a dreadful row. She hates me. She blames me for everything, not least of all, alienating you from her!'

'It has always seemed terrible to me,' Marina said, 'to refuse somone something.' She hoped she had not said too much.

Paul had a certain stiffness, and Marina realised that he knew what had occurred.

He had a different sort of mind from Arthur, Marina thought, but she admired its sharpness. She was relieved that there would never be a need to spell out what had transpired in that room. She saw it suddenly. 'The point is that I do not want *her* and for the first time in my life, it strikes me that my wishes in the matter must be considered absolutely. It is about time I reached the age of consent.'

Paul smiled, then laughed. He looked at her in expectation.

'I have to deal with this before I can be sure of anything,' she said. She waved the letter at him again. She had clutched it in her hand without knowing after he had returned it to her, and the paper was creased and damp from the palm of her hand. 'I have no idea what I shall feel after I have met my family. I honestly do not know what I shall feel at dinner time.'

He looked wistfully out at the view.

'Well, I have to come to terms with it!' she exclaimed.

'I know. I know you do.'

'Imagine having a family!'

'I do imagine it,' he said.

'But you have one!'

'Not of my own.' He picked up an ear of seeded grass and played with it.

'There is no way of my unknowing this now,' she said. 'I don't know whether I can make this one identity fit. It is a little like a death. Not knowing gave me so many possibilities.'

'I think you will find,' he said, 'that there has never been more than one identity. You were always yourself and you would have been anywhere. Isn't it possible that you might have had a good imagination coming from the home of your natural parents?'

'Look, we'd better get back to the house,' she said.

He stood, but with a show of unwillingness. 'I am not at all convinced that it is a good idea for you to see Helena at the moment,' he said. 'Wouldn't it be better to let things cool down? She is not in a rational state.'

Marina had a sudden vision of Helena on her knees amid strewn papers. After what had passed between them, it seemed horribly tactless to stay in the same house, but almost worse to go. What she could not do now was to evade a kind of responsibility for Helena. It occurred to Marina that without knowing it she had elevated constancy as a virtue beyond all others. Now in possession of her mother's letter she could see why it was that she had judged herself most harshly for being the cause of Arthur's defection from his family and, in a sense, why she had become that cause. It also seemed quite obvious to her why it had been impossible for her to abandon him. A failure to commit herself for life to Arthur would have been to repeat the whole secret history of her birth. It now struck her that it was a matter of some moral importance to behave decently to Helena. Whatever Helena had done and however little Marina was able to return her feelings, there was the certain rigour of duty to be observed.

'If she is upset, then there is all the more reason to check on her. She is all alone in the house. She might do anything.'

The house was silent when they returned. Together, they passed through the atrium with its bold, red flowers, then back into the garden. There was no one there. Everywhere, there was a peculiar, hollow resonance of emptiness. It was as if the carpets had been rolled up and the curtain taken down.

'I don't think she's suicidal,' said Paul. 'Really, I don't.'

Marina thought it ominous that he had mentioned this at all. 'I shall never forgive myself if something has happened to her,' she said.

'I want to make sure that nothing happens to you,' he retorted.

'What do you mean by that?' They had checked out the little office and now crept into the silent kitchen with its strung-out herbs and rocking chair.

'I told you. We had a very unpleasant row indeed.'

'And so, you're still angry with her? I'm not angry. At least, I don't think I am.' She flushed slightly at the thought that Paul was, in fact, Helena's successful rival. How successful he would be in the long term, she did not know. All the way up the road to Hora in the empty taxi they had found on its return journey from the port, he had tried to dissuade her from a confrontation with Helena. She did not want him managing her as Arthur had done, not even for her own good.

They returned to the hall. Marina tried the handle of the dining room door. It sprung open to reveal a heavy elegance. Paul forbore to answer her question. Instead, he said in a tight voice, 'We are simply avoiding the upstairs, you know. That is where she is bound to be. Who knows, she may be asleep after all of that emotion.'

They climbed the stairs. All the time, they had been creeping and whispering as if in acknowledgement of some inevitable catastrophe. Marina knocked on the door of Helena's room. She made herself do this. There was no reply, and so she swung the door open. It looked as if a burglar had gone berserk in the once meticulously ordered room. Ripped books lay on the floor, their jackets torn off, and pages of creamy, expensive paper filled with Helena's calligraphic handwriting lay strewn everywhere. For all that this shocked Marina, she was relieved, for she had half-imagined Helena's hanged body to be dangling from the ceiling rose. Why should she have thought that?

Surely she was exaggerating. Down the upstairs hall they went, opening all the bedroom doors, but there was no sign of her.

'Perhaps she has gone out,' said Paul.

'No,' Marina replied on an intuition, 'she will be in the drawing room. I know it.' They looked ahead of them down the corridor up the half-flight of steps that led to the drawing room.

'I think that I ought to see her alone, that is, if she is in there,' Marina said. They exchanged a fearful glance.

'If you insist,' he said. He leaned his back against the wall and closed his eyes. 'I shall not be far.'

With some difficulty, Marina left him standing there and made the short journey up the stairs.

Helena was sitting in the tasselled chair. She made no movement in response to Marina's entrance. Her body was so rigid that for a moment, Marina thought that she was, indeed, dead.

'Are you all right?' she finally asked.

Helena readjusted her neck and looked at Marina narrowly. 'What is that supposed to mean?'

Marina looked down at the Turkey carpet. 'I wanted to know if you were all right and that is all.'

'Why should you ask? Why should you care? I have been sitting here thinking about Arthur.'

Marina touched the letter in her pocket for ballast. Somehow, Helena's whole position seemed false and dangerous. She looked like someone in a film who was about to uncover the secret of Manderley or who would say 'I was expecting you' in a German accent.

'I was his goddess, you know,' Helena continued. 'Not you.'

'Yes,' said Marina, looking directly at her. 'I know.'

'In which case, a biography written by me would be irrelevant.'

'I suppose so.'

'I loved Arthur,' Helena said with mechanical stiffness. Everything in her aspect bristled with a denial of what had happened earlier between them.

There was something quite frightening about all of this to Marina. As in a certain kind of dream, it was the atmosphere and not the action that disturbed her. 'I am glad you loved him,' she replied.

'How could I have thought you could be my friend?' Helena asked. She tapped the arm of the chair over and over with her fingertips. There was a goading, bitter edge to the question.

393

'I don't know. I am sure it was very kind of you to think that I could be . . .' Marina flushed again.

'Kind?' Helena laughed. 'What has kindness to do with anything? You bowdlerize life with your little kindnesses. But then I suppose you would.'

Suddenly, Marina sensed Paul behind her and in the same moment, she knew why he had not wanted her to see Helena. Her mother! Oh surely, she would not use her newly discovered mother against her!'

Whatever she had been about to say, Helena evidently decided against it as she swerved her glance to Paul. 'I see, one's other summer guest. I wonder, as you are both here, if we could rearrange our plans somewhat, in view of my aunt's death. While you were out I spoke to Serge on the telephone and I have spoken again to my cousin Varya in Paris. It has been decided, after all that my aunt should be buried here on Patmos and my cousins are all on the way. It will be rather crowded. They are my family and this is my house. It belongs to me completely and altogether now and I have decided to stay.' Although she added this last as an apparent non sequitur, it seemed the real point of the entire speech. 'This is my house,' she repeated.

'Oh, it's much, much too much for you! I quite agree!' Marina knew she was babbling. 'One could not possibly stay under such circumstances! In fact, I was coming to say goodbye.'

'Really,' said Helena.

'How is Serge?' Paul cut in.

Perhaps it was the sound of his voice that made Helena draw herself up into an even further rigidity. She could indeed have been a goddess or a diva. It was as if she had spent her afternoon meditating on how to transcend mere being. Her eyes glittered and her back was posed in theatrical straightness. She looked as if 'Hell hath no fury . . .' had been an adage invented to describe her. She looked queenly, skilled in black arts, a Medea or a controlled Callas singing from her diaphragm, poised in robes in a spotlight. She might have killed princelings for a kingdom or eaten babies as a means to love. Her ring might have been poisoned or her stiletto heels or the tip of her umbrella. She might have possessed a poignard, slept her way through a Roman legion or torn the wings from flies. 'How dare you ask?' she said.

Marina could not bear it any longer. It seemed so pointless for Helena to behave in such an extreme manner. 'Oh please!' she cried. 'Please let's not have any more quarrelling! You've had a terrible upset, Helena. In the memory of all we have suffered, can't we have peace?'

Helena looked at Marina for a long, long time, and as she did she seemed to shrink within herself to a terrible density. 'I want you to leave me alone now,' she said, closing her eyes. Marina and Paul both turned to go.

'Isn't it ironic?' Helena continued, her words imploding, 'that there has been so much fuss about the daughter of a semi-literate servant?'

Paul put his hand to Marina's lips, then shut the door.

XXXII

IT WAS AS IN A DREAM that they had left the house and it was as in a dream that Marina envisioned Helena, sitting alone now in the gathering shadows of her drawing room. The taxi was dark and it descended into the dark, round hairpin bends in the road, its headlights flashing across guard rails and embankments. The sun had gone down, but the moon had not yet risen, and so the formidable, distant hills appeared indefinite and massed above the invisible sea below. Paul and Marina were together now, compressed into silence. They seemed to flow into a unified, but barely conscious feeling, redolent of no one thing in particular, but nonetheless profound. It was as if the darkness and silence gave Marina the power of sight, and she appraised Helena exactly, her silver head against the tasselled chair, her eyes open and impersonal, slow-blinking because now fixed into gathering the night for robes around herself.

Suddenly, it struck Marina that it was altogether possible that this was Arthur's final vengeance, that she had escaped it, and that Helena had not. She was fixed now, fixed and enthroned in a curious, loveless power, unable to control the tides of passion in herself, except by the extraordinary means of becoming immutable. She had fallen into the underhanded grip of the goddess which she had helped Arthur to discover, and it had turned her to stone.

'Are you all right?' Paul asked her softly. 'You took quite a beating back there, and I am struggling with an intense desire to avenge you.'

'There's no need,' she said simply.

'Well, I've actually tried to tell myself she's mad.'

'At least you haven't said "I told you so".'

'Well, you're right, it had to be faced out sometime.'

'I must say, I'm rather worried about leaving her,' said Marina, 'but we really had no choice.'

'No, indeed we hadn't,' said Paul. 'But I shouldn't really worry,' he added. 'She'll have Serge before long and the two of them will have to go through all of this together and then there'll be Varya. I think Helena herself is probably due for a Russian renaissance. She'll simply inherit the old lady's mantle, not that the two of them were the same at all.

396

Nonetheless, there is a power vacuum and she will ably fill it. In fact, that was what their struggle was all about, I am sure. I don't know why I didn't see that it was bound to happen.'

'Well, whatever, it is all over. I must confess, I feel rather bad about Arthur's book not getting done . . .'

'Do one yourself.'

'I don't think I could . . . but I'll have to read the journals.' She shifted in her seat. 'I mean this, will you help me? Maybe something can be arranged, another biographer found. All I know is that it actually does not matter to me so much any more. He's gone now. I feel he is gone and I have let him go.'

'So you will come back to London for a while?'

'I think you are right. I think it would be the best plan. After all, my mother will need to prepare herself for meeting me too. I was wondering if maybe I should just ring her from the hotel here. She put her number on the letter. Then I could go home in peace of mind,' Marina laughed nervously, 'and then fly to New York next week, or something like that.'

'Oh, that's much the best idea!' said Paul.

Marina looked down at her hands in the dark. 'It hurt me a good deal what Helena said about my mother.'

'I thought we'd come to that. It was appalling.'

'What did she say to you about her?'

'Marina, here we are!' They were arriving in Skala and the taxi was making its way towards the little rank in the harbour.

'What?'

'Nothing compared with what she said to me about myself, I can assure you.' The lights of the port seemed suddenly bedizening.

'She's not illiterate!' said Marina.

Near the taxi rank, there was a little square where trees were decked with fairy lights. Beneath them, there was a trestle table set up where members of the wedding party sat in a leisured, celebratory mood. Tanya was among them and she was speaking earnestly to a merry-looking Orthodox priest with a bushy beard, who nodded and smiled and encouraged her Greek, or so it seemed to Paul and Marina. Everyone looked happily dishevelled, having seen out the bride and bridegroom, it appeared, in style.

'Should we talk to Tanya about all of this?' Marina asked.

'Let's get settled first,' Paul said. 'She looks as if she is stuck in for a long evening. We can join her later.'

'She'll sort it all out,' said Marina. 'She'll even get a message to Serge.'

'I'm sure she will. She's a very capable young woman.' Paul looked relieved.

'I'm nervous about ringing Maureen,' said Marina. 'What do I call her anyway.

He gave her a swift hug.

They checked into the Patmian Hotel, where unbeknowst to them, Lipitsin had stayed only a few nights before. Marina felt relieved to be in a room of her own for which she was paying. With a sense of luxury, she opened the shutters wide and gazed into the busy harbour. She stepped out onto her little balcony and inhaled the night air, filled with the subtle scent of grilling food and herbs. The quay was full of Greeks and tourists together.

She had calculated that her mother would probably still be at work, the time difference being seven hours, but maybe she worked from home. Marina suddenly realized that her mother was not much older than herself. She must be only fifty-five, younger than Helena and Arthur. It struck her that Paul was probably just about her mother's age and this made her feel uncomfortable. She thought she had better shower and change. She went reluctantly inside, but once under the private stream of water, she bathed in its benisons. As she dressed in clean clothes, she heard Paul bumping luggage about in the next room. She slid quietly out of her room and went to await him in the lobby where they had agreed to meet.

It was quiet with cool floors, tiled and clean. Antimacassars were on the chairs and there was an engraving above the reception desk of the icon she had seen at the Monastery of St John the Theologian, author of the Book of Revelations. He seemed to be studying the profundity of his vision with abstracted eyes. In his hands, he held the manuscript and on a table behind him, there stood an inkpot with a pen in it. Her thoughts flew up to him and she felt a sudden singleness in herself that was a kind of liberation.

'*Parakalo?*' the proprietor asked. She was startled, for he had come so quietly up to the desk that she had not heard him. 'Please?'

'Oh, I was just looking at the icon,' she said.

'Have you seen it in the Monastery,' he asked with civic pride.

'Oh, yes. I lit a candle to it.' They exchanged a little smile, a greeting.

'So you have visited the Monastery!' he said. 'Have you enjoyed your stay on Patmos?'

'I shall never forget Patmos,' Marina said. She cleared her throat. 'Actually, I wonder ... could I make a telephone call to the United States from here?'

'Certainly,' he said.

'Would you mind terribly getting me the number?' she asked. 'I wish I spoke Greek, but I do not.'

'Of course, Madame,' he said.

She fished the letter out of her handbag and copied the number for him on a slip of paper.

'It is a very important call,' she said, as he dialled the operator. 'It is very private.' He gave her a kindly smile. After a brief exchange and a little wait, he handed her the telephone and retired. It was ringing. After a moment or two, someone picked up the receiver and a woman's voice answered. Marina thought she would ring off. Her mouth felt numb and she did not know what to say. 'Hello,' she said at last, 'Hello, this is Marina.'